huntress moon

by
alexandra sokoloff

· · · · ·

This is a work of fiction. Names, characters, organizations, places, events, and incidents are either products of the author's imagination or are used fictitiously.

Text copyright © 2014 Alexandra Sokoloff

Published by Thomas & Mercer, Seattle

www.apub.com

Amazon, the Amazon logo, and Thomas & Mercer are trademarks of Amazon.com, Inc., or its affiliates.

ISBN-13: 9781477822043
ISBN-10: 1477822046

Cover design by Brandi Doane
Printed in the United States of America

Huntress Moon

FBI Special Agent Matthew Roarke is closing in on a bust of a major criminal organization in San Francisco when he witnesses an undercover member of his team killed right in front of him on a busy street, an accident Roarke can't believe is coincidental. His suspicions put him on the trail of a mysterious young woman he glimpsed on the sidewalk behind his agent, who appears to have been present at each scene of a decade-long string of "accidents" and murders.

Roarke's hunt for her takes him across three states...while in a small coastal town, a young father and his five-year old son, both wounded from a recent divorce, encounter a lost and compelling young woman on the beach and strike up an unlikely friendship without realizing how deadly she may be.

As Roarke uncovers the shocking truth of her background, he realizes she is on a mission of her own, and must race to capture her before more blood is shed.

Books By Alexandra Sokoloff

The Huntress/FBI Thrillers:

HUNTRESS MOON
BLOOD MOON
COLD MOON (December 2013)

Thrillers

THE HARROWING
THE PRICE
THE UNSEEN
BOOK OF SHADOWS
THE SPACE BETWEEN

Paranormal

THE SHIFTERS (Book 2 of THE KEEPERS trilogy)
THE KEEPERS QUARTET
(with Heather Graham and Harley Jane Kozak)
THE FATES TRILOGY (2014)

Nonfiction

SCREENWRITING TRICKS FOR AUTHORS
WRITING LOVE: Screenwriting Tricks For Authors II

Short fiction

THE EDGE OF SEVENTEEN (in RAGE AGAINST THE NIGHT)
IN ATLANTIS (in THRILLER 3: LOVE IS MURDER)

Praise for the novels of Alexandra Sokoloff

The Price

"Some of the most original and freshly unnerving work in the genre."
- *The New York Times Book Review*

"A heartbreakingly eerie page-turner."
- *Library Journal*

"*The Price* is a gripping read full of questions about good, evil, and human nature... the devastating conclusion leaves the reader with an uncomfortable question to consider: 'If everyone has a price, what's yours?'"
– *Rue Morgue Magazine*

The Unseen

"A creepy haunted house, reports of a 40-year-old poltergeist investigation, and a young researcher trying to rebuild her life take the "publish or perish" initiative for college professors to a terrifying new level in this spine-tingling story that has every indication of becoming a horror classic. Based on the famous Rhine ESP experiments at the Duke University parapsychology department that collapsed in the 1960s, this is a chillingly dark look into the unknown."
- *Romantic Times Book Reviews*

"Sokoloff keeps her story enticingly ambiguous, never clarifying until the climax whether the unfolding weirdness might be the result of the investigators' psychic sensitivities or the mischievous handiwork of a human villain."
- *Publisher's Weekly*

"Alexandra Sokoloff takes the horror genre to new heights."
- *Charlotte Examiner*

"Alexandra Sokoloff's talent brings readers into the dark and encompassing world of the unknown so completely, that readers will find it difficult to go to bed until the last page has been turned. Her novels bring human frailty and the desperate desire to survive together in poignant stories of personal struggle and human triumph. But the truly fascinating element of Sokoloff's writing is her deep dig into the human psyche and the horrors that lie just beneath the surface of our carefully constructed facades."
- *Fiction Examiner*

Book of Shadows

"Compelling, frightening, and exceptionally well-written, *Book of Shadows* is destined to become another hit for acclaimed horror and suspense novelist Sokoloff. The incredibly tense plot and mysterious characters will keep readers up late at night, jumping at every sound, and turning the pages until they've devoured the book."
- Romantic Times Book Reviews

"Sokoloff successfully melds a classic murder-mystery whodunit with supernatural occult overtones."
– Library Journal

The Harrowing

"Absolutely gripping... it is easy to imagine this as a film. Once started, you won't want to stop reading."
- The London Times

"Sokoloff's debut novel is an eerie ghost story that captivates readers from page one. The author creates an element of suspense that builds until the chillingly believable conclusion."
– Romantic Times Book Reviews

"*Poltergeist* meets *The Breakfast Club* as five college students tangle with an ancient evil presence. Plenty of sexual tension, quick pace and engaging plot."
- Kirkus Reviews

Bram Stoker and Anthony Award nominee for Best First Novel

The Space Between

"Filled with vivid images, mystery, and a strong sense of danger... Sokoloff interlaces psychological elements, quantum physics, and the idea of multiple dimensions and parallel universes into her story; this definitely adds something different and original from other teen novels on the market today."
– Seattle Post Intelligencer

"Alexandra Sokoloff has created an intricate tapestry, a dark Young Adult novel with threads of horror and science fiction that make it a true original. Loaded with graphic, vivid images that place the reader in the midst of the mystery and danger, *The Space Between* takes psychological elements, quan-

tum physics and multiple dimensions with parallel universes and creates a storyline that has no equal. A must-read."
– *Suspense Magazine*

• • • • •

Chapter 1

The city teems.

A bustle of busy people on the streets under towering buildings, cars climbing the vertical hills, working people traversing the corridors, energized by the cool ocean air off the gleaming, timeless Pacific.

There is much that is beautiful about San Francisco: the sun on the Bay, the expanses of bridges over the water, the pastel-painted Victorians with their gingerbread trim, the dreamy beaming people in the parks.

But here, as everywhere, is the darkness.

While tourists swarm the markets at Fisherman's Wharf and eat chocolate at Ghirardelli Square and day trip to Alcatraz, the area formerly known as the Tenderloin swarms, too, with a different kind of activity. In the Tenderloin women and children are bought and sold, people are killed for money or drugs, the stench of urine and vomit and blood rises from the filthy sidewalks, the darkness of addiction and madness pervades.

The woman in black who walks through this flotsam is an anomaly. Too well dressed to be one of them, too clean to have business in this part of town.

She gets glances, of course, some surreptitious and curious, some longer predatory stares. Lone women don't often walk this street except for money. But something about her keeps the flies away. The men she passes shift restlessly; a few of them even flinch from her.

She is aware of every one of them as she passes. Very few of these souls are evil, but drugs and bad times have made them vulnerable. Desperation leaves their souls raw and open to attack. They are devastated creatures, furtive, pathetic... and sometimes something much worse.

The shadows of these people are stark in the light today, larger than they should be. It is always this way, close to the time.

She can see it hovering, lurking in the darker shadows, but keeping to the darkness. Watching, but not coming close.

There is no rest.

Not now, not today, not this week... this week, of all weeks...

Not ever.

Chapter 2

R oarke was worried.

Before his desk phone was back in its cradle, he was out of his seat, grabbing for the suit coat neatly hung on the real mahogany stand in the corner of his office in the Federal Building. Outside the window the view plunged precipitously, a fifteen-floor drop into the Tenderloin.

It was Special Agent Greer's third month of undercover with the criminal organization known as *Ogromni*, and in all that time under, Greer had never used the failsafe signal: a phone dialed to a dedicated number with no message left, code to request a face-to-face meeting. Greer didn't ask for meetings. He delivered his reports on time, through approved channels, and never deviated from procedure.

Until today.

Roarke shrugged his coat on over tightly muscled shoulders as he strode down gleaming hallways, walls lined with the history of the Bureau: black-and-white photographs of grim men in dark suits and blinding white dress shirts, framed original newspaper articles of famous FBI busts, glass cases displaying SWAT team weapons and equipment, diver gear, and dismantled explosive devices.

He hurried out of the elevator on the first floor and past the reception desk, framed by a wide pane of bulletproof glass. The clocks on the wall behind it each read a different time zone: Washington, Tokyo, Paris, London, Beijing. The sweep of multiple second hands started a new churning in Roarke's gut.

Something's wrong. Something's happened.

He exited the monolithic Federal Building at a clip, and braced himself against the dazzle of sunlight before starting quickly down the sidewalk of Golden Gate Avenue toward the Tenderloin. He had to force himself not to run, which would draw attention he didn't want, but he was too agitated to find a cab. He'd get to the rendezvous in plenty of time on foot, and he didn't want to wait around in the café once he got there. The walk would give him time to clear his head, burn off some of the anxiety.

He was vaguely aware that the day was gorgeous, a crisp and cooling autumn breeze after rain the night before, and for the moment the city was so clean it sparkled. None of which soothed Roarke's tension in the slightest.

His Criminal Investigations team had been investigating the Bay Area branch of *Ogromni* for four months. The name meant "enormous," and it was, a cross-national viper's nest, which first came to the San Francisco Division's attention because of a hijacked container shipment of electronics that had not been confiscated, but rather tracked.

Electronics smuggling was only the top layer of the onion. It was never just local anymore. Organized crime had blossomed into something much less tangible: Unorganized crime, Roarke thought of it, but *Transnational Crime* was the official phrase for it; no borders, and weird alliances, a hybrid of gang activity that had little to do with old-style street gangs, but rather massive criminal organizations, bad guys with no racial or national boundaries. And it always turned into the same kind of outrage: smuggling and selling drugs, guns and people.

The three evils, as far as Roarke was concerned; where there was one, there were inevitably the others, and sometimes a fourth: high tech. Sometimes it seemed as if money had only the slightest thing to do with anything; it was as if depravity spawned depravity. The longer Roarke worked, the more he felt he was wrestling with a Hydra: cut off one head and seven more grew back.

Since Agent Greer had infiltrated the San Francisco *Ogromni*, Roarke's team had been racking up the evidence to bring charges of piracy, smuggling, heroin and cocaine trafficking — and tracking the inevitable suspicious disappearances that inevitably go along with such activities. The targets were getting bolder and Greer had passed on news of a massive drug shipment imminent: perfect for a bust that could be connected to several key players in the hierarchy.

But all morning Roarke had had a bad feeling. He'd woken from an old childhood dream of a lurking monster, and it was the damn dream that had him most spooked; it always came up in times of extreme stress or anxiety and it never boded well.

He didn't think of any of this as psychic or precognitive; he'd been an investigator for far too long not to know that the human brain processes information too fast for the brain's owner to be aware of exactly where those subtle signs and warnings are coming from. Something had been off about Greer's last reports and had triggered early warning bells in Roarke's head. Cops called it "Blue Sense" or "Spider Sense—"

A horn blasted in Roarke's ear, startling him back to the present. He'd almost stepped straight into traffic on the busy street.

He lifted a hand in apology to the car that had just missed him, then breathed in and waited five more seconds for the light, and sped through the crosswalk toward the appointed meeting place.

It was a Peet's Coffee, perched halfway down the block of a steep incline, one of those streets that give San Franciscans some of the most toned asses and thighs in the continental U.S. Roarke slowed his pace slightly to cushion the shin-jarring descent.

The Peet's had a fenced-in outside seating area with wrought iron tables and chairs, set off from the curb with flowering planters. The meeting was arranged to look like a chance encounter, two random businessmen in suits, bumping elbows at the counter.

Roarke started to turn into the café, when something made him turn his head — and he saw Greer on the sidewalk across the street, about to cross mid-block. The men did not acknowledge each other in any way; that was not the plan. But Roarke felt a tidal wave of relief, seeing him.

Safe, he thought, and thanked whatever God was out there.

He would have turned away, then, to go inside as per the pre-arranged drill: get in line, order, take his coffee to the condiment station and let Greer step up to him.

But Roarke didn't turn away, because that was when he saw her, standing on the sidewalk, just a bit behind Greer.

She was medium height, tall in boots, and slim, with long, lithe muscles like a cat. This Roarke could see because her arms were bare, even in the brisk air; she wore a form-fitting black top with a turtleneck. There was something fetishy in the combination of bare arms and high neck that was arresting, but so was everything about her, her past-the-shoulder blond hair and black sunglasses, the way she stood in tight black pants and boots. The city was full of striking women, that was not what drew him. It was the stillness of her, maybe a fraction too still, and she was looking back at Roarke, looking across the street as if she knew him. And for that weird second, he felt that he knew her, too.

He would remember every detail of that moment for a long, long time. The sun on her hair. The stretch black of her turtleneck and the taut muscles of her arms. The gleam of chrome on the truck. The violent purple irises in the flower stand behind Greer. The smell of exhaust and coffee.

Roarke was still looking at the street, at her, when the truck rumbled by, a huge semi, which momentarily obscured his view of the woman in black. And then there was the screeching of worn brakes straining against the downward plunge of the hill, and Roarke turned just in time to hear a sickening thud and see blood exploding over the truck's front grille and a man's body flying, and then there was screaming, one scream on top of another, and male shouting, a building wave of panic. And then the woman was gone and the sidewalk was crowded with people turning away or shrieking in horror... and through the chaos and the screaming Roarke realized he had just watched his agent obliterated by a seventeen-ton commercial truck.

Chapter 3

Roarke didn't believe in coincidence. He never had.

His undercover man had missed a meeting, had used the default system to set up an emergency face-to-face, and less than an hour later was killed right before his eyes.

The first part was acceptable, the second was alarming. The third was a million to one, and Roarke was having none of it.

"You think they had him killed." Roarke's team member and right-hand man Damien Epps was thinking on it. Epps was straight out of Oakland, and not the gentrified part: six feet three inches and 220 ebony pounds of ex-gangbanger, although these days you couldn't tell him from a GQ model. Roarke was aware that he himself had a certain dark-haired, dark-eyed appeal: six foot even, jock's body, thick and unruly hair that women liked to get their hands into, and even more — he radiated the pure male energy of his job, which attracted some of the fairer sex like catnip. But Epps was in a different category entirely. He constantly drew pornographic looks from women — and men — of all ages and races.

They were in the café, which they had appropriated for a command post as technicians from one of the office's four investigative units processed the scene.

The SFPD was out in full force as well. The fact that Greer had been a Federal agent automatically made the investigation a Federal case, and for once there was not the slightest hesitation about deferring to Roarke and the Bureau; even City of San Francisco homicide wasn't going to argue the jurisdiction on this one. The Bureau took care of its own, and as far as the Bureau was concerned, taking out an agent was the biggest crime there was. Unforgiveable and unforgettable.

Epps glanced out at the street and the sidelined truck, where a crime tech was extracting bits of Greer from the crimson-splashed grille. On the sidewalk agents were questioning witnesses.

"Those good citizens saw an accident," Epps said neutrally.

"I saw an accident, too." Roarke felt the tightness in his own voice. "I don't like the timing."

Epps nodded. "Hard to engineer, though."

Roarke didn't bother to say that he'd seen stranger. They both had.

An agent not from Roarke's own team, Wu, hustled up. "Someone you should talk to, Roarke."

Roarke and Epps followed Wu out of the café and crossed the street. Without the traffic it felt weirdly like a film set, onlookers like actors huddled running their lines, technicians setting up equipment. Wu had the witness sitting on the stoop of a Victorian. His name was Jay Harrison: late twenties, slim and well groomed, leather jacket over immaculate jeans and T-shirt, and far too good-looking to be straight.

Epps stayed back while Wu introduced Roarke. "This is Assistant Special Agent in Charge Roarke."

Harrison gave Roarke a quick but unmistakable once-over. Par for the course in San Francisco. "What I told him—" Harrison glanced to Agent Wu, back to Roarke. "There was a woman. A blonde, in all black, this sleeveless turtleneck, jeggings, shades. Just before the guy—" the young man swallowed, "Just as the guy stepped out in the street, she said something to him, and he turned back to her. That's when he got hit."

Roarke felt a rock in his stomach. *The woman.*

He looked at Epps, back to the witness.

"Did you hear what she said?" Roarke asked, keeping his tone even.

The young man shook his head. "Too much traffic. But it must have been good. Whatever it was, the guy really whipped around to look at her."

Roarke felt a rush of adrenaline.

"And that was when..." The young man shuddered, the lingering horror of the accident plain on his face.

Only not an accident, was it?

"Ever see this woman before?" Roarke asked, over the pounding in his blood.

The young man was about to answer automatically in the negative, Roarke could see. But then he stopped, and frowned, and Roarke felt a spike of hope.

"You know, maybe. That high collar. I thought I'd seen it before." The young man shrugged. "I mean, she's hot, and not cheap about it either. She stands out."

Roarke always found it interesting how matter-of-fact gay men were about talking about women, more honestly appraising than most straight men.

"Where would this have been, that you saw her?"

Harrison thought for a moment. "Right around here, must have been. It was the last few days, day before yesterday maybe, and I've been working on a deadline at home — haven't really been out of the house except to run out for coffee."

"You live near here?"

Harrison pointed to a Victorian at the end of the block. "Two B."

"You didn't speak to her, interact with her in any way?"

The young man shook his head. "Nothing, and I wouldn't swear I'd seen her before, either. Just feels like it."

"Thanks," Roarke said. "That's a big help. If anything comes to you..." He handed the young man his card. "Agent Wu will take your contact information." He nodded to the agent who'd summoned him over, and stepped aside with Epps.

"I saw her," Roarke told his man. "Standing on the sidewalk behind Greer, just before he stepped into the street."

Epps looked at him, startled. "You see her talk to him?"

"Truck blocked my view." Roarke glanced back toward the witness. "I believe she talked to him, though. She wasn't just standing. She was there for a reason."

Epps was studying him, trying to read him. "So what are you thinking?"

"I'm thinking I want to talk to her."

The office's best sketch artist met Roarke at the café so not a moment would be wasted, and then went on to gather details from Harrison. In under an hour Epps was distributing photocopies to the agents who gathered at the back of the café.

Roarke stared down at his own copy of the sketch: the woman's lush fall of hair, her carved jaw, the fine features, rendered implacable by the sunglasses. The artist had captured her intensity, though, no doubt; her concentration burned through the page. And of course, the high collar, a memorable detail that they might just get lucky on. He looked up, around at his team and the uniformed officers the SFPD had loaned him.

He raised his voice and spoke to them. "We're going to work this block and then on out, door to door, every residence, every establishment. It's likely this woman lives or works in the neighborhood, so let's find her."

"Is she a suspect?" an agent called out from one of the coffee tables.

Roarke paused a half-second. "At the moment, a witness. I want you going wide on this first pass. Hit each building and business and talk to the manager or landlord, show the photo, then move on, until you've covered the whole block. We do four square blocks that way, then go back and start the door-to-door. I want to know immediately if you get an ID; I want to talk to her first. Let's do it."

As the others started to file out of the café, Roarke joined his own team, seated together at a corner table: tall, dark Epps; Ryan Jones, as blond, athletic and clean-cut as his name implied; and Antara Singh, a stunning Indian tech goddess who was also the best researcher Roarke had ever worked with. Roarke looked around at them gravely. "I don't have to tell you, but Greer's death takes priority from here. All our work on *Ogromni* gets directed at finding out what happened to him." Jones and Singh nodded tensely, their eyes fixed on Roarke. "Jones, I need you out there working all our CIs. Find out anything you can about this shipment that was coming in. Find out if Greer's cover was compromised."

"You got it," Jones said.

Roarke turned to Singh and indicated the sketch of the woman on the table. "Singh, for now, I need you back at the office working the databases on this woman. Get creative, see if you can find her."

"I will find her," the agent assured him in her precise Anglo-Indian accent. The two agents stood to leave, but before Jones turned away, he paused, looked back at Roarke. "What a mess," he said, bleakly.

Roarke turned back to Epps and found the agent watching him. Roarke stared back, frowning. "What?"

Epps lifted his hands. "Never heard of somebody ever killing nobody by talking to them."

Roarke said flatly, "On the day that Greer uses the emergency signal for a face-to-face, he gets crushed by a semi — just after this woman speaks to him in the street."

Epps shrugged with eloquent, silent skepticism.

He was right, of course. But then, Epps hadn't seen her.

While Greer's mangled body was transported to 850 Bryant, where the Hall of Justice housed the city morgue, Roarke stayed on the street making the rounds of the other witnesses to the accident. It was quickly apparent that no one but Harrison and Roarke himself had noticed the woman in black.

As Roarke walked the street back toward the café, his phone buzzed. He pulled it out, checked the text, and felt a jolt. He scanned for Epps on the sidewalk and gestured. Without seeming to hustle, Epps was in front of him in seconds.

"SRO on Eddy," Roarke told him. "The manager made her."

SROs, they called them, "Single Room Occupancy." The Carondolet had been a hotel at some point, and a fairly good one. Now to live there was a step away from being homeless: pay by the week for one room with a shared bathroom or half-bath, and a hotplate by the sink serving for a kitchen. The neighborhood was turning good again, surrounding streets were on the rise, but an SRO was hard to convert into something else, so while the Victorians had been gentrified and the cafés and boutiques had blossomed, the old SROs were kept afloat by government subsidies. There was a whole row of them on Eddy Street, fighting a losing battle against drug dealing and prostitution.

It was no way the kind of place Roarke would expect the woman he had seen to be staying in. No way in hell.

The manager was Armenian, Kavashian: burly and red-nosed and bushy-browed. He stood in the lobby, which was dingy and high-ceilinged, with battered Art-Deco flourishes, a cloudy mirror, a scarred wooden front counter with a rack of old fashioned mailboxes on the wall behind, a door into the manager's office. "Yes," he told Roarke and Epps, stabbing a thick forefinger on the sketch. "Her. Deposit two weeks in advance."

"When?"

Kavashian mulled it. "Friday. Five days."

Roarke's badge obtained them the room key, second floor, 208. They took the stairs.

The second floor hall was brighter than Roarke expected, with tall windows on either end streaming clear light, old-fashioned metal fire escapes outside. He felt his pulse quickening as they approached the door. Epps looked at him, and their hands hovered by their weapons. *Draw? Not draw?*

Three steps outside the door Roarke paused mid-step, alert to a familiar, strong, unpleasant smell. He saw Epps reacting to it as well, puzzlement, then recognition.

Bleach.

Both men drew their Glocks. With his left hand, Roarke pulled the key and jammed it into the lock, shoved the door open in one fluid move.

The smell hit them like a truck. The room was small, and empty. Epps sidestepped to the bathroom, kicked the door open wider to check inside, while Roarke shoved the bed across the floor with his foot to reveal anything underneath.

No one. Just the overpowering smell of bleach.

Chapter 4

She sits in the rough-riding BART train, headed to San Francisco International Airport. No need for a rental car in this city; the public transportation is faster than any other vehicle and there is no parking to be found anywhere, anyway. Parking tickets are dangerous, to be avoided at all cost; they leave a time-stamped trail. So after disposing of the bleach-soaked bedding in a restaurant dumpster she'd descended one of the escalators on Market Street to a BART stop and bought an eight-dollar ticket to SFO.

She wears a tailored charcoal overcoat, her hair is tucked up in a black, short wig, and she carries nothing but a rolling carryon bag, which gives her the appearance of dozens of others on the train, just another business traveler on her way out of town.

She feels a profound calm; there is always that feeling of respite when an encounter goes so perfectly, to its highest and best conclusion.

Only one thing mars the feeling of peace. The man she saw across the street is law enforcement. Too observant to be anything else, too vigilant; it was in his clothes, his posture, his eyes. She thinks back over every moment, fixing each second in time, examining it. Not police;

the cut of the suit said FBI. And he had seen her... but then, there had been nothing to see. The truck had been too big, too fast. Nothing too much to concern her.

Still, she will not stay another second in the city. She will find a car and take a circuitous route, go along some way where there are no people, just her and the car, no need for contact. Everything will be revealed, as it always is.

It is, after all, a whole week until *the day*.

As she sits, rocking slightly with the movement of the car, the train screeches metallically on its tracks, a surreal and disturbing sound. A weathered man is staring at her from several seats away, unkempt and on drugs at least, probably homeless, but he has the look that she knows so well.

She is more and more tense as he stares, her breath coming harsh in her throat. The sound of the train feels like screaming.

Her hand goes to her coat pocket, slips inside to finger the straight razor concealed there.

As the train slows at the next stop, the man rises clumsily, smiling vacantly, his eyes burning, and walks straight for her.

As he reaches to touch her she slashes the razor across his fingers. It happens so fast she can barely hear the shriek as he realizes his hand is dripping blood and fingers to the dirty car floor—

The man in the aisle veers away from her as if he knows what she is thinking and she rouses herself from the fantasy. Of course she has not cut him. This is a trap, part of the Game, put in front of her to taunt her, to trick her into making a mistake. There is no way to take care of him, not now, not here, there are too many people, and she must concentrate on getting clear, leaving with as few ripples as humanly possible.

He staggers off the train and her heart quiets again. Her hand stays in her pocket, loosely gripping the razor.

Chapter 5

The two Evidence Response Team techs jostled each other for working space in the small hotel room, surveying the place with UV light for traces of body fluids, vacuuming for hair or fiber, dusting with Black Dragon powder for prints. Roarke had been working with Stotlemyre and Lam for years, one an enormous German, one a reed-thin Vietnamese, and implausibly inseparable. He knew what they were going to say before they said it.

"One of the best cleanup jobs I've ever seen," Stotlemyre announced.

"Cherry." Lam nodded in agreement.

There was nothing in the chest of drawers or the medicine cabinet or small trashcans, not an object, and not a single print or fiber. The bed was stripped of blankets and linens and pillows; they were nowhere to be found. The scarred hardwood floor had been scrubbed down with bleach, the tiny bathroom had been doused with it, the windows, the doors, the walls. Most of it was dry, but some corners and cracks were still damp; she'd probably done the cleanup early in the morning, before the accident.

Lam continued cheerfully. "Could've been butchering people for sausage in here and we wouldn't be able to tell. Can't believe she didn't pass out from the fumes."

Roarke heard movement in the hall and stepped out to see Epps heading out of the stairwell.

"No bedding in the Dumpsters," he reported. "I sent a man to cover the rest of the block."

"We won't find anything," Roarke said. "She was too careful with all the rest of it to get careless about the linens."

Epps shrugged. "So we question the other residents of this fine establishment, see if they saw her coming out with a garbage bag, maybe getting into a car." He started for the door, then took another look around the room. "A pro, right?"

"Yeah," Roarke said tightly. "A pro."

Epps shook his head. "Still. A truck? Weirdest hit I ever saw."

The manager, Kavashian, had no idea where she'd come from. He shrugged eloquently. "Cash advance, no references."

And what do you think she was doing here? Roarke thought, but there was no point to the question. "She fill out a registration form?"

Kavashian brightened to the extent that Roarke expected the dour Armenian ever did. "Yes, a form." He bustled back through the open door into the inner office, and Roarke stood still, his breath suspended. Any information on the form would surely be useless, fake, and she may have worn gloves; someone this careful may even have used her non-dominant hand. But computers had made handwriting analysis very precise, and the databases were extensive.

Kavashian hadn't returned, and Roarke stepped behind the counter to the doorway to look inside. The burly manager looked up from an open file with a frown.

"Gone," he said, holding out the empty file folder.

Roarke felt his spirits sink again. *Of course. A pro.*

He shook his head, tried to contain his frustration. "Did she come and go often? Stay in her room?"

"I give her key, see nothing of her after that."

"Did she have an accent? Anything that would say where she was from?"

The manager shrugged. "American accent."

"What kind of American? Southern? New York?"

Kavashian frowned, and Roarke sighed internally. The man's own accent was thick enough that it was unlikely he'd be able to distinguish regional accents.

"She say not so much," the manager pointed out.

Roarke stepped back and surveyed the lobby, such as it was. "Do residents have to come through this way to exit?"

Kavashian shrugged again. "There are back stairs to alley. Walk to street from there."

"So it's a miracle you remember her at all," Roarke said, and waited for the answer he knew would come. But the manager surprised him.

"No. That girl, you remember." Roarke saw a flicker of lust in the portly man's eyes, and felt a twinge of revulsion. "Big coat, couldn't see much," he gestured in the direction of his chest. "But you remember."

Chapter 6

I nstead of taking the train into the airport terminal, she gets off at long-term parking. With her roller bag she looks just like any returning passenger.

She seats herself on the BART bench and waits, watching people park and remove luggage from their trunks. The optimum is a traveler with a large piece of luggage, indicating a long trip, driving a comfortable but nondescript and easily enterable vehicle: a pre-2000 Honda, Acura or GMC. She has master keys for all three makes: keys with teeth that have been filed down to fit pretty much any car of those lines. A year or so ago she'd liberated a set from a drunk tow truck driver who thought he'd gotten extraordinarily lucky. But she's always been able to make do; in a pinch, there is almost always a Toyota Camry, thirty seconds to open and start with a pair of scissors.

Another BART train slows and stops, discharging another set of travelers. As they disperse, she spots a man in a center aisle, a graying man with sunglasses getting out of a silver Honda Accord. Her interest quickens as he hefts a large suitcase out of the back seat and hustles for the BART train.

She watches and waits until the doors are safely closed behind him, then as the train departs she walks purposefully to the Accord and looks down in through the driver's window. There is a red blinking light on the dashboard, but the car is at least ten years old and she's reasonably sure it's just a decoy, a flashing LED that only simulates a car alarm.

"Locked out?" a male voice says behind her.

She turns too quickly, her hand moving to her coat pocket.

A man stands some distance away, dressed in a suit, roller bag at his side. Not airport security, just a traveler — with a hint of predator on the side.

She can feel anger rising. What man would ever think a lone woman in a deserted parking lot would want help from him? She is already fingering the razor, but is too aware that there will be security cameras.

"No, I'm fine," she says, hearing the edge in her voice, and sticks the key into the Accord's door, turning it quickly. There is no alarm.

"Thanks," she says over her shoulder to the man, as she shoves her roller bag into the passenger seat and drops into the car.

Inside, she shuts the door decisively, locking it, and waits, watching in the rear view mirror until the man turns and walks on. Now she pulls on thin cotton gloves and does a quick search. More luck, although luck rarely has anything to do with anything: the Honda's owner has left his parking ticket in the console. She'll be able to drive right off the lot without having to interact with a guard.

If the luck holds, the theft won't be discovered for days, possibly a week or more, and she and the Honda will have parted company long before then. The owner will get his car back undamaged, possibly even before he returns from his trip.

She adjusts the mirror and gives the nearly-empty lot a quick scan, then turns the master key in the ignition and drives. A few turns, a bridge, and then she is where she belongs, on the road, in the wind.

Chapter 7

Roarke sat in the contoured chair in his fifteenth floor office, facing toward the window overlooking the sex clubs of the Tenderloin and a strip of the glimmering water of the Bay. He watched the shadows from the setting sun creep across the streets and turned his mind to what he knew about professional killers.

Which was a lot.

Despite film and TV portrayals of glamorous "contract killers," in real life, professional killers were almost always plain thugs. The Mafia had its hit squads. Some outlaw motorcycle gangs had execution squads. But those killers worked only for their employers. They weren't independently contracted; they were regular members of the criminal organization who would be called on periodically to eliminate a rival or a traitor as a matter of business for the organization.

And there was nothing elaborate or exotic about the killings: the number one method of disposal was a bullet to the head.

More organized and sophisticated, if sophistication was the word, were the assassins employed by the Mexican drug cartels. Across the border from El Paso in Ciudad Juarez, the Barrio Azteca gang had evolved, or devolved, into a paramilitary team of assassins, which recently specialized in contract killing for the Juarez cartel and was possibly responsible for over one thousand killings in that city in the past year alone. And a gang known as the "Artistic Assassins" was likewise operating as contract killers for the Sinaloa cartel, which was vying for control of the billion-dollar drug trafficking routes through the Juarez-El Paso corridor.

And all of the above were men. Period.

Female hitmen, female serial killers — were figments of Hollywood's overactive imagination. The short list, and it was an extremely short list, of female assassins throughout history had been either political revolutionaries or nutcases. Not that women never kill for money, but those cases were almost always on a very personal level: the wife who does her husband — or once in a while, several husbands — in and collects the insurance, or in some cases, just gets her revenge. And a *lone* woman assassin? Aside from the political nutjobs, Roarke had never heard of such a thing in real life.

So he had no basis for comparison, no statistics with which to build a profile.

The cleaning of that SRO was a pro job for sure. But to engineer a street accident like the one that had just killed Greer was almost impossible, unless the truck driver was the woman's partner or otherwise in it with her. And the trucker had been nearly hysterical, barely able to choke out an account of what had happened, and had a clean ten-year record of driving for a legitimate company. Not exactly the profile of a killer. The chances of him having been given money for a single job like this were slim to none. And no professional would have left an accomplice like that to run the gauntlet of police interviews, it would be far too risky. If the trucker had been hired, he'd be dead already.

Which meant either that the accident was spontaneous, or the woman had orchestrated what amounted to a miracle of timing. And in Roarke's experience assassins were not inclined to count on miracles.

He considered the *Ogromni* mob. From everything they'd uncovered about the ring, they were old school: ruthless, brutal, and sexist as gangsters come. Women were a commodity to be bought and sold, like cattle. Hiring a woman from outside didn't compute in any way. Nor did the idea that there would be a woman within the organization who would ever be trusted for a job like this.

Which left an oddball possibility, but one that made marginally more sense than the hit coming from within the ring. Which was that the hit had come from outside, a rival gang, who had no idea Greer was undercover.

Implausible... and again, one hell of a coincidence.

Unless Greer had been on to some kind of takeover, or infiltration by the second gang, which made him a specific target. There was an interesting possibility.

But again, using a woman? Roarke had never once seen or heard of it happening. Using a woman as bait, usually a prostitute, to put the target in a vulnerable position, maybe. Anything else? Unlikely in the extreme.

Roarke paused to think about that, and another thought occurred to him.

Could the woman in black have been *personally* connected to Greer?

Because of the timing: the emergency contact, the coded request for the meeting, Roarke had jumped to the natural conclusion that Greer's cover had been compromised. But perhaps there was a much more mundane obvious? A love relationship gone bad, an ex out for revenge?

Roarke still didn't like the timing, the coincidence of it, but perhaps Greer's concern had been about this theoretical ex. It was not entirely outside the realm of possibility, and it made marginally more sense than any of the other possibilities.

He reached for the phone to call Epps... and then paused.

It was the scrubbed-down room that pointed away from a personal relationship gone bad. Unless this hypothetical psycho ex was in law enforcement herself.

Immediately he shook his head. *Now who's going Hollywood with this?*

It all boiled down to the same next step, though: *Find the woman.*

The glimmering ball of sun slipped into the bay, and Roarke turned his chair from the window to face his computer.

First, he set up a database search for *"professional killers: female"* with a date range of the last ten years.

Search results were zero.

"Right," he said aloud.

Then he entered the NCAVC database for a different suspect search, both more specific and more broad. He entered the physical description of the woman, being as general as possible: an age range between twenty and forty, although his best guess was thirty, height between 5'4" and 5'11", although he personally would have sworn to 5'6", Caucasian, slim. He even hesitated before adding *"blond"*; eyewitnesses seemed to see whatever they wanted to see, and a wig or a dye job was the easiest disguise on the planet. His bet was that she'd already made the obvious adjustments to her appearance.

But before he hit "Enter," he sat back and looked at his entry... and then sat forward and typed *"turtleneck"* and *"high collar."* It was the first thing he had noticed, and the first thing the witness, Harrison, had mentioned as well. Roarke couldn't say why he found it significant, but significance was the feeling. He'd play the card and take it out of the search criteria later, if nothing turned up.

Ten minutes later he was blessing the genius of computers. His odd search had landed him two hits: both unsolved murders, one in Portland, one in Salt Lake City, both within the last two years. And listed as a "Person of Interest" in both files was a slim Caucasian woman in her twenties, wearing a black sleeveless turtleneck.

Roarke felt a rush of exhilaration at his luck.

He hunched close to the computer and read quickly through the details of the cases. The Salt Lake City case was a year-and-a-half old already: a construction engineer who had fallen to his death from the twentieth floor of the unfinished building he was supervising. A woman had been seen leaving the deserted construction site minutes after his death. Her attire was described in detail: thigh-high boots and a miniskirt, a sleeveless Lycra turtleneck tank. Dark brown hair, but again, hair color was infinitely variable.

Thigh high boots, a miniskirt, Lycra. Roarke's mind was racing. *Coming on like a hooker? Luring the vic out on a floor with open walls and pushing him? That's the kind of death that would be a whole hell of a lot easier to arrange than a truck accident.*

He scrolled to the second case. Portland, nine months ago.

As he read through details, his frown creased deeper in his brow. This vic was a forty-six year old transient, alcoholic, probable schizophrenic, whose throat had been slashed while he slept under a bridge.

Now that makes no sense at all. Who'd hire a hit on a homeless guy? What would that *woman be doing messed up in that?*

In this report another street person described a blond woman in sunglasses and a turtleneck that he had seen with the vic a few hours before his death.

"Seen"? As in hooking? What the hell?

Roarke sat back and his thoughts went to Greer. *Did the blonde come on like a hooker, is that what made Greer turn?*

He thought back to the woman he'd seen on the street for that one, suspended moment, and replayed the moment in his mind, the woman standing so still on the sidewalk, locking into his gaze from across the street...

He hadn't gotten the hooker vibe. Not at all. She'd been alert, focused, no obvious signs of drug use. Her clothes: city black, but sophisticated. The high collar was edgy, but nothing unusual for San Francisco.

And she didn't hold herself like a hooker. There had been no furtiveness, none of the laxness of limb of the profession.

He skimmed through the reports again.

Both cases remained open. Neither report went so far as to say that the woman was a suspect. "Person of Interest" had no legal meaning, and was used vaguely to mean a suspect or a material witness to a crime. The phrase was in fact being challenged in court, but not every law enforcement official who filled out the database form would know that. Both reports clearly communicated an urgency in finding her.

He turned to the window to stare out at the city lights against the blue twilight.

Three men dead, and this woman had been on the scene of each death. Roarke had a trail, now. She was implicated in the death of his man, and the other deaths were interstate, making all of them FBI jurisdiction.

His case, his suspect, his responsibility.

He was jarred from his thoughts by a rap on the door, and turned in the chair to see Epps staring in at him with a suspicious expression.

"That look you got on, there? I know that look. I don't like that look."

Roarke pushed back his chair as Epps moved into the office. "Nothing, I take it."

"Right in one," Epps said. "No one in the building had anything to say about her."

Roarke swiveled the computer monitor around so Epps could read the screen. Roarke watched Epps' face move from a frown to incredulity.

"Motherfuck," he said admiringly.

"Accidents seem to happen around this lady."

Epps shook his head. "I guess they do." He looked at the screen again. "Portland, SLC, here... she gets around."

"I don't think we're looking at half of it."

Epps looked down at him sharply. Roarke gestured to the screen. "Think about it. These three incidents happened to have witnesses who saw her, and described her as wearing a turtleneck. Only reason these cases came up in my search is that I keyed in the word 'turtleneck.'

What about times they didn't see her or she was wearing something else?"

"Motherfuck," Epps said again, contemplatively. Then he shook his head. "A woman, though..."

"I know," Roarke said. "I know."

"What's the next move?"

Roarke looked at the screen with the Portland and Salt Lake City files.

"Guess I'm taking a trip."

The head of the San Francisco division was Special Agent in Charge Reynolds. When the former SAC had retired at the beginning of the year, Reynolds had been shipped in from D.C. to take over the office, and there was some very surreptitious grumbling in the office that it should have been Roarke. In fact, Roarke had turned the position down.

Now, as Reynolds skimmed through the case data Roarke had printed out, Roarke stood in the corner office that could have been his, and knew he'd made the right decision. Being even more tied to a desk than he already was... it wasn't the future he saw for himself, though sometimes he was hard-pressed to say what future he did see for himself. First, he was not an administrator and had no interest in being. But there was more to it than that. Post-9/11, even a dozen years later, the top priority of all Bureau divisions was Homeland Security and counterterrorism, which was neither Roarke's expertise nor his interest. Investigating terrorists was a criminal investigation like any other, but Roarke didn't understand and couldn't stomach people who thought they had a religious mandate to wreak havoc and kill innocent people. Ordinary evildoing was enough for him, he didn't need a religious component to fanaticism constantly in his face. And though he kept his views on the subject quiet, privately he thought there was more than enough emphasis on terrorism; it took precious resources away from other investigations.

As one of six Assistant Special Agents In Charge in the San Francisco office, Roarke headed up his own team of four and had the autonomy to pursue his own cases while avoiding the demands of bureaucracy. That suited him just fine. Reynolds had so far proven a good administrator and he understood fieldwork — and as Feds went, he was open-minded enough to take the independent San Francisco character of the office in stride.

As Roarke laid out the scenario, Reynolds looked only slightly less taken aback than Epps had.

"That is one hell of a strange lead."

Roarke made no comment; there was nothing to say. Reynolds skimmed through the case data Roarke had printed out.

Reynolds finally looked up. "Portland or Salt Lake?" he asked.

Roarke shrugged. "Chronological order. The transient vic in Portland is really off the charts. I'll start in SLC. Interview the original detectives, re-interview witnesses. I'll brief the team before I go."

"This will be interesting." Reynolds didn't add anything unnecessary like "Keep me posted;" it was one of the things Roarke appreciated about him. "Greer's family been notified?"

"Parents are deceased, no siblings."

"Never been married?" Reynolds asked.

Roarke answered in the negative and thought again of his passing psycho ex theory. The other two cases made that explanation pretty near impossible, now.

"He didn't talk much about a personal life." In fact Roarke had not known Greer long before he put him undercover. Undercovers were a breed apart; the job wasn't conducive to stable relationships.

"Hell of a life," Reynolds said, as if agreeing to Roarke's unspoken thought. "Hell of a way to end it. Let's do him justice."

Roarke met Epps in the hall before they walked into the conference room to face the team, motioned him down the hall a few steps so they could speak privately.

"I'm going to keep this short. While I'm out of town, everyone answers to you. We have only one priority now: work the CIs and sources, find out if *Ogromni* had Greer killed."

Epps nodded.

"And it means you do double duty, but I want to work directly with you on my track of investigation. Be ready to join me if I find a trail."

Epps registered his words with a slight double take.

"I know it's more work for you, but..."

Roarke didn't have to explain. Epps knew it was a promotion. "I'm right here for whatever happens, boss," he said.

Roarke looked at him. "You know I hate it when you call me boss. Makes me feel like a Southern plantation owner."

"Exactly. Keeps you humble."

Roarke shook his head. "Let's do this." And they walked in to face the team.

Chapter 8

Two hours Later Roarke was back home in his half a Victorian in the Noe Valley district. Half a Victorian and half a home, when it came down to it. His divorce had been over three years ago and there were still blank spots in the furniture arrangements, blank patches on the walls where prints and paintings used to be. Roarke's own life had not expanded to fill in the gaps that Monica had left.

He stood in the living room and looked at the bare walls in between the bay windows with their views of dark hills and jeweled city lights.

Though as a former psych intern Roarke knew the pitfalls of self-diagnosis, he was fairly confident that the divorce hadn't leveled him. In honest moments he had to admit he'd married partly because everyone around him had been marrying while he seemed to be drifting; it had seemed an island of stability in those lost first years after he'd transferred out of the Behavioral Analysis Unit and left profiling behind him. But he couldn't bring himself to share his thoughts with Monica, and she wouldn't stand for being excluded, and when she'd stood at the door with her bags, about to walk out, a voice in his head had asked him if he was losing the love of his life and another, harder voice had answered back quite clearly, *No.*

Half of him had been as devastated as a child. But the cold, hard voice had told him he'd loved her in a way, but not in the way that poets wrote about, that rock stars sang about. Not in the way that you were supposed to hold out for. He had said and done all the right things with her, but the core of him had remained untouched.

He turned from the memory and walked through the kitchen, which was the most empty room of the flat, with its granite counters and copper appliances and the breakfast alcove with another view of the city lights. The oven had not to his recollection been turned on since Monica's departure.

He wasn't home often enough for the reminders of his half-life to bother him, and with no children to keep them in contact, Monica had slipped out of his life. Marriage didn't seem to be for him.

It's not really so hard to understand, he thought. He caught bad guys. That was what drove him, that was his life. There was nothing more important, and there wasn't all that much to say about it.

He moved into the bedroom, now half-occupied by a boxing bag, weight bench and barbells, otherwise just the essentials remaining, the walnut headboard of the king bed, the brown fake suede of the coverlet.

There was no cat or dog to arrange for with the neighbors, no plants that would need watering. He opened his closet, looked in at a carry-on suitcase already packed with clothes appropriate for different regions of the country, a fully-stocked Dopp kit. He felt a rush of anticipation at the thought of being on the road again, on the trail. *Hunting,* he thought, and then deliberately blocked the memories the word conjured.

He took a look at the city lights through his bedroom window, another stunning, jeweled view... and was gone.

Chapter 9

The hotel is perfect, a lodge, really, with rustic wood paneling in the room and a deck leading out to towering trees and the deep and ancient silence of the woods. The Sequoias. She stands in the dark, looking out at the magnificent shadows.

She'd seen the road sign in the middle of the night and impulsively made the turn. She likes hotels, motels, too, the anonymity and uncomplicatedness of them.

The plan is clear. She will drive. It is a huge state, a huge country. Plenty of open areas to get lost in and reduce the chances she will be found. She always keeps moving, there is less chance of tracking her. But for the next week she must be as invisible as possible.

If she can just get through the next days...

Just seven more days.

She sinks down on the bed, turns over, and is instantly asleep.

DAY TWO

Chapter 10

The descent into Salt Lake City was surreal; there was no other way to say it.

Roarke looked down through the airplane window at the lake, huge and alien, a crater sunk into the middle of a ring of towering mountains. It was not entirely of this earth. The mountains were already snow-capped, providing a dramatic line between that dazzling white and the dark blue of the mountains below, which dwarfed the pale buildings of the city in the very bottom of the crater.

Though SLC called itself "the Crossroads of the West," the airport was tiny and nearly deserted; Roarke could imagine it bustling only in ski season. He walked past baggage claim to the car rental counters and procured a Jeep from a sleepy clerk at an otherwise empty rental booth. SLC wasn't a taxi kind of town, and Roarke wasn't sure where his bizarre trail might lead him.

Outside the day was cloudy and already felt icy; the wind needled his skin, and of course he hadn't dressed warmly enough, native Californians never do. No matter where he went, no matter how diligent he was about checking Weather.com, anything less than sixty degrees always surprised him.

But driving out of the airport he felt a surge of excitement to be on the job again, the *real* job, the field job: foraying off into some largely unknown place to search, to seek, to uncover the unknown.

Roarke loved his work, he was good at it. But it had not been enough for some time now. Some people would call it competence; he had reached a high level of it professionally and was restless, looking for a challenge. But Roarke knew that in a fundamental sense he was drifting, that he had been since leaving the BAU, that some purpose that would define his life had been lost, or had not yet presented itself.

For some reason he flashed back to a vision of himself as a child, nine-year old Matt Roarke, religiously watching news coverage of manhunts, one particular manhunt, surer that he ever had been about anything in his short life that he would become an FBI agent, would go out into the world to fight bad guys.

It was *that* feeling he was experiencing again, a pressing need to address some mysterious imbalance, something much larger than himself. And the feeling made him drive faster, into the stark, cold Utah landscape.

Roarke didn't bother finding a hotel, but followed the freeway straight downtown toward the police station. It was not a big city and the station was not far from the city center, which had a frontier flavor that was both quaint and bizarre. Going anywhere downtown meant passing the government square, a storybook castle of a complex, with turrets and a prominent clock tower; and of course Temple Square, dominated by the real epicenter of the city, the Mormon temple. At the moment the white building seemed a looming but rather plain stone canvas, existing only as a backdrop for the lone golden angel brandishing a trumpet at the top of one of the turrets.

The police station was just a few blocks from Temple Square but it felt like the outskirts of the city, lonely, somehow.

The SLC homicide squad was made up of only six detectives, which was a good thing, both for the city with so little crime that it only needed six detectives on homicide, and for Roarke, who knew that while every homicide counted for any good homicide detective, chances were in a squad of only six detectives in a Godfearing town, every homicide counted even more than most.

Roarke stopped in the doorway of the bullpen and looked over the desks in the bullpen, taking in the assorted men in shirtsleeves at their desks, the soft clicking of computer keys. He spotted Detective Coleman at once, at the same moment that Coleman spotted him. The detective stood and the two men assessed each other.

Coleman was the kind of man people used to call "salt of the earth": part farmer, part cowboy, all lawman. A big guy with weary creases in his windburned face, tough and wary without being completely closed off.

Roarke knew what the other man was seeing in him: too polished, too urban. Roarke had lived in big cities for most of his life, and San Francisco the longest: a city that prided itself on intellectual and artistic sophistication. He had fairly simple tastes but simple in San Francisco was a whole other animal than elsewhere. Even the cut of his suit was a different kind of simple.

None of this showed on Coleman's impassive face, but the sense was there. There was tension, a suspended moment when things could go either way. And then the tension shifted, and Coleman walked forward and stuck out his hand.

"Agent Roarke. I'm Detective Coleman."

"Thanks for seeing me," Roarke said at once, and returned the firm grip of Coleman's hand. He understood that he had just passed some sort of test, and was grateful for whatever it was Coleman had seen in him.

Coleman gestured to a nearby chair and Roarke swung it over to sit in front of the desk as Coleman took his own seat again. He reached for a thick notebook on top of a stack of several others in his in box, what cops called a "murder book," the investigative notebook with all the compiled police reports on the case. He handed it across to Roarke.

Roarke was surprised at its heft; this had been an extensive investigation.

Almost as if reading his mind, Coleman exhaled a breath that seemed to have been held for a long time. "I always knew I hadn't seen the end of that one."

Roarke glanced at him, opened the notebook to find the coroner's ruling on the top page: *Accidental death.*

"You're convinced it wasn't an accident," Roarke said. Not a question.

The detective reached across the desk and flipped a page of the book. Roarke looked down at a full-length photo of the dead man, Edwin Wann. Roarke blinked. Wann was enormous, doughy cheeks, quadruple chins, a massive gut spilling out over circus-sized pants.

"Four-twenty-five," Coleman said. "Tell me what a man that size is doing up on the twentieth floor of an unfinished building."

"He was the project manager," Roarke pointed out neutrally.

Coleman shook his head. "Not a hands-on kind of guy. Liked to delegate. Walking was kind of an issue."

Roarke stared down at the photo, found himself a bit repelled. "How does someone like that even get hired on construction?"

"Friends," Coleman said, and didn't elaborate.

Roarke glanced through the initial report, reading and at the same time calculating. On the phone he had told Coleman as little as he could get away with about his own interest in the case, nothing about the woman in the black turtleneck at all, just the fact that the death "might be related" to a recent incident in San Francisco. He wanted to hear Coleman's take, uninfluenced and unadulterated.

"So he was up on the twentieth floor—" Roarke started.

"At eleven forty-five at night. Want to see the site?" Coleman said abruptly.

Thought he didn't let it show, Roarke was honestly shocked. In his experience with local law enforcement, cooperation almost always involved some kind of quid pro quo. City cops had a long and deep distrust of the feds. But Coleman seemed to be bending over backward to help.

"Isn't the building finished by now?" Roarke asked, partly to give himself time to think.

"Construction got shut down a few months after—" Coleman gestured to the notebook.

"Because of the death?" Roarke asked, startled.

Coleman half-shook his head. "The credit crisis. Delusional developers."

No surprise; it had happened all over the country, was still happening. It wasn't exactly like a curse on the building, but it added a weirdness to a case that was already full of weird.

Roarke realized Coleman was looking at him, waiting.

"Yes," Roarke said. "I'd love to see the site."

It was a shell of a building, towering against the cloudy sky, almost identical to the crime scene photos in the book. As the two men left Coleman's pickup truck and walked toward it across the deserted packed earth lot, Roarke had the eerie feeling of arrested time.

The wind was up, chill and biting, and he pulled his coat closed. Coleman stopped and squinted up into the hazy light at the skeleton of the building. Roarke followed his gaze, counted off twenty levels. The building was basically an open frame; there had been a sheer drop off the side of the concrete platform that was the twentieth floor. Roarke felt his stomach hitch at the thought.

"He landed there." Coleman pointed to a spot in the flat earth. Nothing to see, of course; all blood and footprints washed away by a year and a half of rain, wind and snow. But Roarke's mind superimposed the crime scene photos from Coleman's murder book (Roarke realized he was thinking of it as a murder book despite the official ruling) that he had looked through in the car on the ride over. It was text-book thorough, just what Roarke would have expected of Coleman. From the photos Roarke knew Wann had landed face up, killed on impact. The hard ground beneath his head had been dark with blood. As with a lot of deaths from that kind of height, his insides had been crushed to jelly, but the skin had held firm, a sealed bag of broken flesh and bone.

Roarke had paid special attention to the coroner's report. There had been head, abdominal and thoracic injuries and fractures of the long bones, the pelvic girdle and the vertebral column; but given the extensive cranial injuries, the primary area of impact appeared to be the head: skull fractures and massive cranio-cerebral destruction — cranial and maxillofacial fractures and partial extrusion of the brain. In fact the injuries were macabrely similar to a number of injuries wreaked upon Greer's body by the truck, coincidental, but jarring to read.

"The pathologist found no indication of injuries sustained before the fall," Coleman said beside him. Roarke noted that the detective gave the word "fall" an ironic emphasis.

"Would that have been apparent, necessarily?"

"The medical examiner was very thorough. Some of the external injuries had the appearance of incised wounds, but the pathologist determined those cuts to be from the sharp edges of rocks in the earth where he fell."

"And you ruled out suicide?" Roarke asked. He knew that something like eighty percent of deaths by falling were eventually deemed to be intentional, the victim's own choice.

"Guy had no suicidal symptoms, according to his wife and doctor. No financial problems. Some medical issues, the obvious for someone that big: hypertension, high cholesterol, fallen arches — but nothing immediately life-threatening like cancer, and no apparent psychiatric problems."

"Nothing apparent," Roarke repeated, sensing something more.

Coleman studied the building in front of him, not looking at Roarke. "They had a daughter run away two years before. Never found."

Roarke felt a frisson of unease. "How old?"

Now Coleman glanced at him. "Fourteen."

"Jesus," Roarke muttered, remembering too late that Coleman was likely a Mormon, and might not take kindly to the "Lord's name in vain" stuff. Coleman's face didn't change one way or another.

"So that bothered you," Roarke said.

"You might say that."

Roarke looked at Coleman steadily, and felt a bond forming. "And what else bothered you?"

Coleman gestured toward the building, and started to walk. Roarke followed him.

They stepped through the open walls at the base of the building and Roarke looked around him at the pale concrete walls, the slab of flooring. The wind whistled through the concrete shafts, and somewhere in the vast empty frame there was a hollow metallic clanging, something like a chain butting up against the girders.

They ascended in an open-platformed elevator, which had Roarke holding his breath for the entire ride; he guessed the equipment probably hadn't been used in a long time. But they arrived without incident, and Roarke stepped with Coleman out onto the twentieth floor, a wide, empty space, with a hell of a draft of wind through it.

"Imagine what this looks like at night," Coleman said.

Roarke could; it would be eerie, and cold. Unforgiving.

"Why do you think someone might want to hang out here in the dark?" Coleman asked him, with studied casualness.

"Maybe he was proud of the building," Roarke answered, and then he realized the answer Coleman was going for. "You're talking about the woman."

Coleman walked toward the open wall on the front side of the building. Roarke followed.

Coleman stopped some distance from the edge, looking out at the open view of the street, the mountains, in front of them. Roarke felt his stomach flip at the height. Then Coleman pointed down at the street, a row of seedy-looking buildings.

"Pub, liquor store, pawn shop, adult bookstore... strip bar."

"So you think she was a hooker?" Roarke was being as neutral as possible. He'd already read the witness report, made by a college student who'd been out on the street when he'd seen the body falling from the building. The student had phoned 911 and had just disconnected with the operator when he saw the woman leaving the site.

Coleman looked worn out with the question. "I can't quite make that work. His wallet was on him. Couple hundred bucks in it. Even if he had brought her up here for some weird thrill, a hooker would have gotten the money up front. Sure, maybe she did, but she could've taken the rest off the body when she came back down. Dead wouldn't bother most of these girls."

Roarke nodded without saying anything.

"The witness — kid was drunk, by the way— had just left that pub down the street. Saw the woman walking off the site, through the gate. No particular hurry, just walking. Miniskirt, thigh-high boots, heels, sleeveless top with geometrical cutouts—" Coleman gestured in the direction of his chest.

"And a high neck," Roarke finished. He knew he was only here, on this trail, because Coleman was a detail man, and had included that particular detail in his VICAP entry. He wondered again how many police reports there might be that had missed that detail.

"Right. 'Kinky' is what the kid said."

Which is probably the only reason he noticed to begin with, Roarke thought. A college male, even drunk, has an infallible radar for a sex worker. And in this neighborhood, a prostitute's getup would have been a fair disguise. More than that: it may have been the woman's best approach to Wann.

"Wann have any history of buying sex?" Roarke asked, without inflection.

Coleman glanced at him, kept his own tone neutral. "Regular patron of that 'Gentleman's Club.'" He jerked his chin slightly down the street.

Roarke nodded. It was a solid approach for a female assassin, if that was really what they were talking about, and a solid track of inquiry for him. He found himself wondering if his own man, Agent Greer, had had a history with prostitutes, if that could have been part of the approach there, too. It was not a path he particularly wanted to go down, but one he knew he couldn't avoid.

"But you don't think she was a hooker," Coleman said beside him, bringing Roarke back to the moment. And Roarke understood that was the quid pro quo, here: the eternal itch of the unsolved case. Coleman needed to *know*. And it was time for Roarke to share; the lawman had been more than generous with his information.

"We think our case was a hired killing," Roarke said flatly.

Coleman's face went still.

"So I'm interested in looking at people who disliked Wann, might have wanted him killed. Badly enough to pay for it."

A wry look flickered over Coleman's face. "A whole lot of people didn't like him. All accounts he was a weird guy, didn't have a lot of friends. Held it over any fitter man who worked for him, which was all of them. They ragged him behind his back because of the weight, and he knew it. Made him prone to tirades, and he fired more people than looked warranted." He shook his head. "Not one big happy crew, s'what I'm saying."

Roarke was picturing it. "But guys like that, crew men — someone like that would be more likely to take care of someone himself than hire someone."

Coleman started to nod agreement and then stopped. "You're thinking the hooker — the woman — was hired to *hit* him?" Coleman sounded incredulous, and Roarke didn't blame him. "A woman?"

Roarke was with him on the likelihood of that, but he had a glimmer of an idea, suddenly. "Did Wann have money? Insurance?"

He sensed a spike in Coleman's interest. "Big insurance. Wife sued the company for negligence, too."

Qui bono? Who benefits? It was one of the first rules of homicide investigation.

Coleman said slowly, "So maybe the wife hires a woman..."

Roarke saw Coleman going through the same thought process he'd just been going through himself. The scenario was not likely, but possible. If the woman in the turtleneck was the doer, if she was really a pro — meaning killer, not prostitute — then the most likely person to hire her just might be another woman.

"What's the wife like?" Roarke asked, in an even tone that didn't quite cover the surge of excitement he felt.

"Piece of work," Coleman said tautly. "Nearly as big as Wann. Real control issues. Just about lost it when we brought up the hoo — the woman leaving the scene. Not what I'd call a whole lot of love, there."

Roarke briefly wondered if Coleman was married, and if he was, if it was happy. The big man wasn't wearing a ring, and he looked too sad to be in a stable relationship, but Roarke was always bringing his own baggage to an assessment like that, which was that he wasn't convinced that happy marriages existed in the human condition. He had yet to see one he wanted for himself, his own brief foray into domestic bliss very definitely included.

He wrenched his thoughts back toward the case. "This missing daughter..." he said, unaware until he heard the words that he had spoken aloud.

Coleman looked at him sharply. "You think she could be—"

"Too young," Roarke said before the detective could finish, even as he was calling the woman in black up again in his mind, examining what he remembered of her body, her skin, the way she dressed...

The wind moaned, and the metallic clanging started up again from above.

Could she be? A teenager? No, the way she held herself, her stillness and focus; she was mid-twenties at the very least. Closer to thirty.

Because he was distracted it took him another second to realize how strange the question was that Coleman was asking. "Do I think she was what?" he asked the detective, locking his eyes with the older man's.

Coleman stiffened subtly, then sagged. "I don't know. Do you think she killed him, do you think she's on the street..."

On the street?

Coleman really thinks Wann's daughter could be a prostitute? Or a killer? Or both?

Roarke stared at him. "What's the story with this girl?"

Coleman shook his head, looking bleak. "No idea. I checked back over her school records, the MP report. There'd been behavior problems in school, truancy, fights. Nothing major. No one's heard a thing about her since she disappeared."

Roarke filed that one away for later; it was the woman he needed to focus on.

Then he asked a question he knew to be unnecessary, but he couldn't help himself. "Was Wann at the strip bar that night? Could someone have seen him with the woman?"

"No one from the club saw him that night, or a woman of that description."

Roarke suppressed a sigh. "And let me guess. None of the dancers or patrons had ever seen this woman in the turtleneck."

"Not a one," Coleman said heavily. "I could see the dancers not talking, but the owner and manager — they'd turn on their own sisters. I don't think she worked there, and if she didn't work there, that's not how he met her. They wouldn't have let an outsider work their customers."

Roarke's mind was turning over the angles. *No, and she wouldn't have approached him in a bar, anyway. Too many witnesses.*

The detective continued. "We had the one witness looking through six-packs in Vice for hours. Didn't turn up anyone the kid could ID. No one else had seen her: no car, no trail. She just vanished."

Roarke nodded. "Sounds like mine," he said, and then wondered why he'd said it that way.

Coleman was shaking his head, disturbed. "I never thought of it being a hit."

"If it is, it's a freakish one," Roarke said, and he was not just placating the other man's pride. "I'm not sure what we're talking about. But I'd like to talk to the wife."

"Good luck with that," Coleman said dryly.

There was silence for a moment, with the cold wind pushing at them and the vast bowl of mountains around them. Then suddenly Coleman spoke. "Once in a while you get one that just bugs you. You know that something bigger is going on — something you can sense, but can't quite get a grasp on. You feel like you're being played, somehow. And it eats at you that it's getting away, that there's something you're never going to understand, maybe don't want to understand. And you close the book, finally, but you never really close the book."

Roarke didn't know what to say, and then he did.

"I'll keep you in the loop."

There was a moment, then the big man spoke. "I appreciate that."

Chapter 11

For someone who had made a living as a builder, the late Edwin Wann
had lived in one of the uglier houses that Roarke had ever seen.

While downtown Salt Lake City had interesting, quirky, historical design, Wann's home in a suburban subdivision was a standard,
white-paneled ranch home with fairly appalling navy blue gingerbread
shutters and flowerboxes on the windows. It was low and squat to the
ground, with well-kept but entirely unimaginative landscaping, and
very little color. Roarke's impression was that the house was trying des-
perately to look cheerfully All-American, and failing in some indefin-
able but fundamental way.

Wann's wife — that is, widow — was a nightmare.

She may have been forty-five or sixty-five, it was impossible to tell
through the rolls of flesh. She was not slovenly: her clothes were clean
and pressed and her shoes polished and her graying hair tightly curled
on her head, and she was encased in a girdle and Supporthose, and
none of any of that enclosure helped her temperament; the woman's
passive-aggressive rage rolled off her in intermittent waves. Roarke had
not called her before driving to the house; that would have defeated his

purpose. In retaliation she did not offer to take Roarke's coat, nor did she offer him coffee. Roarke knew Mormons did not indulge in caffeine, but the widow Wann's hospitality did not stretch even to water.

"What has the FBI to do with any of this *now*?" she seethed as she stomped down the dark hallway to the living room. Enraged as she was at the idea of answering questions, she was shrewd enough not to argue with an FBI shield; Roarke had seen the entire internal debate playing out behind her narrowed, piggy gaze before she opened the door to let him in. As she stepped into the living room and turned to Roarke, her voice became calculatingly plaintive. "Edwin went on to the Kingdom over a year ago. Detective Coleman assured me that the investigation was done, and that I wouldn't have to be upset again."

Roarke doubted Coleman had ever said anything remotely in the ballpark.

"There is a slight possibility that your husband's death may be tied to one of my regional office's cases," he answered, while he looked behind Mrs. Wann at the room. Overstuffed furniture in grim chintzes, doilies on the armrests and end tables. There was an acrid smell like mothballs, and it all looked as if it had been exactly that way for the last twenty years. She wasn't spending the insurance money on the house. Aloud he continued, "I'm confident we can eliminate that possibility with just a few questions. I appreciate your taking the time."

She humphed and flicked a hand to a chair in a sofa-and-armchair grouping. Roarke took the long way around so he could pass by the fireplace mantel, and let his eyes graze over the few framed photos there. A wedding photo, some matching formal oval portraits circa the 1940's: Mrs. Wann's mother and father, Roarke guessed. There were none of any girl of fourteen, or any photos of children at all.

Roarke turned and got to the point without mercy. "I'd like to know your thoughts about this woman who was seen with your husband just before he died."

Rage flared up in Mrs. Wann's face. "That boy who said that was drunk," she hissed. "No one else saw a woman."

"The boy was the only witness," Roarke pointed out.

"Exactly," the widow said triumphantly. "And he was *drunk*."

"So you think this boy was imagining the prostitute he saw with your husband?"

Roarke looked straight at her and internally braced himself for the explosion to come.

Mrs. Wann turned crimson. "My husband did not associate with prostitutes." She was shaking with indignation. "He was an elder in the Church."

Since when does that stop anyone from anything? Roarke thought wearily, but it was clear Mrs. Wann knew that, herself. She was displaying every classic sign of lying: stiff body posture with her torso turned away from him, minimal hand and arm movement, avoiding eye contact, not using contractions. The fury was real, though, certainly enough rage to want her husband dead.

The most common reason behind murder-for-hire was marital trouble or conflict in an intimate relationship. But such killings were almost always one-offs: shady people persuaded to do someone else's dirty work for money. Roarke kept coming back to the anomaly that a woman would have been hired by three separate entities to kill three apparently unconnected victims in three different states.

He pulled the police sketch of the woman in black out of his binder and held it up for Mrs. Wann, kept his eyes on her face as he asked, "Do you know this woman?"

Mrs. Wann stared daggers at the sketch. "No," she said tightly.

"Are you sure?" Roarke asked, but his chest felt heavy. For once it seemed like an honest response: no flickering of the eyes, no turning away of the body.

"I said *no*," she repeated.

It was a long shot, but Roarke took out a photo of Greer and showed it. "This man?"

"No," Mrs. Wann said. She was relaxing, another sign that she was telling the truth — and that she hadn't been, before.

And since she was coming off her guard, Roarke decided to throw a curve ball, just to see. "When was the last time you saw your daughter, Mrs. Wann?"

Instantly the woman stiffened up again, her whole posture becoming defensive.

"My daughter left home years ago."

"You've had no contact with her since then?"

"No."

Roarke waited for an explanation but there was none forthcoming; evidently Mrs. Wann considered the subject closed.

"Have you tried to find her?" he asked.

"I don't have to," Mrs. Wann said.

Roarke was unnerved. There was definitely something bizarre, here. He stared at her. The widow sniffed.

"She defied the Church. Fell in with a bad crowd. Drink. Drugs. She chose her path."

"At fourteen?" Roarke said, not bothering to keep the accusation out of his voice.

Mrs. Wann had retreated into a world of her own. She set her hands on her thighs with prim superiority. "We raised her properly. She was willful. Turn away from the Lord, and suffer the consequences."

"At fourteen," Roarke repeated, and looked at her. The widow stared back in truculent silence, and Roarke had to remind himself that antagonizing her further might be a bad idea if he ever needed to talk to her again. But suddenly he couldn't bear to be in the house a second longer, and he stood. "I'll be in touch," he said, just to get under her skin. In truth, he hoped he'd never have to have anything to do with her again.

He left the house with a literal bad taste in his mouth. He got into the rental car and then sat inside it without starting the engine for some time to needle Mrs. Wann, who he was sure would be watching through the curtains, but also because he needed time to recover.

The missing daughter bothered him. The widow Wann repelled him.

Mrs. Wann was not the type Roarke would have bet on hiring someone to kill her husband, but the capability was there. His best shot at tying her to the murder was probably in her bank records, though: a large withdrawal or several. Coleman had not been thinking of a murder for hire, so no one would have been checking financial statements. It was a long shot; if Mrs. Wann could hire a hit, she could also have been shrewd enough to cover the paper trail. Still, checking the bank and investment records was the logical next step, and one Roarke could delegate to one of his team.

But the more he turned it over, the less likely the whole scenario seemed. Roarke could not see the woman in black connecting with Mrs. Wann for any reason, no matter what kind of money was on offer. It didn't just not feel right; the idea of the two of them occupying the same universe was absurd.

And Roarke had to admit reluctantly that it could have been someone else who had wanted Wann killed. *A generally disliked man,* Coleman had made that clear.

A world of suspects, and no answers.

The college kid who witnessed Wann's fall and who had seen the woman in black at the site had graduated and moved back East. Roarke would have loved to talk with him. He might even hunt him down.

But at the moment, he had something closer in mind. Perhaps there were others who would talk.

• • • • •

The strip club, The Doll House, was a black hole: black walls, black curtains, a three-ringed setup of circular stages and poles surrounded by smudged mirrors. The music assaulted Roarke's ears as he stepped through the musty entry curtain, and he recognized the throbbing pulse of Clapton's "Cocaine." A thirty-something dancer worked the center pole in a detached haze. The patrons and the dancers, like most of Salt Lake City, were overwhelmingly white.

Roarke stopped to watch the dancer. He loved women's bodies, loved to see them in motion, loved the grace and sensuality of a woman dancing, even in a place like this… and yes, it had been too many months since he'd last been with a woman, truth be told. But he knew too much about strippers professionally and statistically to be able to enjoy himself in a strip club. He knew the dynamics of the women's childhoods and the drugs used to keep them enslaved to their jobs, and he had far too often seen their mutilated bodies in reports or in person not to feel he was part of at least a social crime just being in the place.

He stood at the entrance, looking out over the furtive working men and businessmen drinking at the round tables in front of the stages, and could feel the anger of these men who had to pay for their looks and touches. He could sense the simultaneous power and powerlessness coming off them, the rage and the shame.

Being inside, his distaste for Wann was overpowering. A man who looked like he did, with a wife like he had, coming to a place like this to leer over and grope women who would be repulsed by his very presence. A man who made a show of belonging to a church that forbade alcohol, let's not even get started on the strippers.

But the most disturbing part was the daughter. *The father of a fourteen-year old, and this is where he spends his nights? Do people think their kids don't sense what they do, who they are?*

He chose a table far back from the center ring and sat carefully. A blond, blue-eyed waitress with skin as pale as porcelain came by with a distracted and entirely false smile. "Coffee," he told her, knowing it would be bad, and then put a twenty on the table. "Were you working here a year ago?"

Her eyes flicked down to the bill, back up to his face, warily, then behind her.

"No one's in any trouble," he said softly. "I just want some information on a guy who used to come here, fell off the building across the street last year. Name of Wann."

"Fat Albert," she said immediately, and her voice dripped with contempt.

"Yeah, that one. The man didn't have a lot of fans," Roarke said.

She gave a *huh* of agreement.

He casually pushed the bill toward her. "Think someone here might want to make some money telling me why?"

The waitress bit her lip, looked back behind her again, toward what Roarke guessed was the stairwell leading up to the manager's office.

Then she pointed to a curtain, leading to the private tables. "Second booth. Fifty bucks for the champagne. I'll send a bottle over. Someone will be with you in a sec." She picked up the twenty and tucked it into her cleavage, then twitched away.

Roarke stepped through a musty curtain that smelled as if it had been soaked in cheap perfume, into a darkened space with curved booths. Each table was lit by a single fake candle, and the Naugahyde booths were angled to provide a minimum of privacy. A bare minimum.

There was already a bottle of champagne and two glasses set on the second table.

Roarke sat down in the booth, grimacing as he slid across the tacky seat. He poured champagne into two glasses and waited.

A black-haired dancer slipped through the curtain, wearing a fishnet cover-up which didn't, four-inch patent leather heels, a wide black collar on her neck and nothing else. She lowered herself to the curve of booth in front of him, and opened her knees wide, deliberately.

"I'm Jet. A hundred for five minutes, two for ten."

Twice the price of a usual "dance," so she was charging for the talk. Roarke nodded, put the bills down.

She lifted her hands to her neck and slowly ran her fingers through her silky hair. Roarke realized she was creating just enough of a show from the back to make it look like she was working.

"I understand you knew Wann," he said, watching her.

"That fat fuck." She kept her eyes focused on his face, a heavy-lidded stare as she shifted languidly in her mock-dance. As she arched her back, dropping her head against the back of the seat, Roarke saw a dark bruise on her neck that the collar had been covering. His jaw tightened.

"He abuse you, hit a friend, what?"

She shook her head, whipping her hair around her face. "He was nobody's idea of a good time. The fugly ones, they're never even half-way decent, not in here. Some of us wouldn't go near him. So he got the ones too green to say no."

Roarke felt another wave of distaste. Nothing he hadn't guessed, though. "Did you also know her?" He slid the police sketch of the blond woman out of his jacket, let it rest on his thighs, facing out toward her. Jet licked her lips and leaned forward for show, pressing her hands against his knees as she gazed down on it. Then she shook her head, shimmying her hair. It caught the blue light.

"Uh uh."

"Sure? She never worked here, never came in?"

The dancer's mouth twisted. She stretched one arm, then the other up toward the ceiling, twining her wrists: a strikingly erotic pose that made it look briefly as if she were handcuffed. "I've been here three fun-filled years. Never saw her."

"Did you know Wann had a daughter? A fourteen-year old daughter?"

A look of revulsion crossed her face. She abandoned her mock-dance, jerked forward and crossed her arms defensively. "There's a surprise."

"What does that mean?" Roarke asked tightly.

She looked away from him. "He liked the young ones. Had a radar for anyone underage."

Now it was more than distaste Roarke felt, and it wasn't surprise: it was a sick knowing. He'd felt it even in the Wann's house, a creeping malignancy.

"Well, he got his, then. Fucking bastard," Jet said softly.

"Yeah," Roarke said, and realized he meant it. "Yeah."

Chapter 12

For a time after he'd left the strip club, Roarke sat in his rental car in the parking lot, with the garish red neon of the NUDE sign pulsing on and off on the windshield.

He felt a pulsing rage, himself, and had to resist an impulse to drive straight to the Wanns' house and confront Mrs. Wann about her daughter, the one she obviously hadn't protected, a fourteen-year old abused by the grotesque parody of a human being that Wann had been. The definition of criminal negligence — and yet there was no law he could use to arrest her.

He forced himself to breathe, to calm his racing pulse. He had to believe that Mrs. Wann was living in her own private hell. For now, that would have to be enough.

It was after ten, so he circled back to the town center to check into a hotel. When he saw the turnoff for the airport he had a momentary urge just to take it, to find a flight out to Portland that night, move straight to the next crime scene, but he resisted that bit of insanity.

His thoughts were too jumbled, and he could use the quiet thinking time in an anonymous hotel room. Some piece of the puzzle might drop into place while he slept.

He chose the Marriott simply for the height of it. He wanted a view of the city; the elevation helped him think. He ordered steak and a Caesar salad from room service and then stripped for a long, hot shower, lathering his hair, letting the needles of water massage his neck and shoulders.

He was tense, and the non-encounter in the strip bar had left him with a maddening erotic charge. Before he'd left Jet had asked him if he wanted to party, and though Roarke had declined, he had been reminded that his unintended celibacy had gone on a little too long.

But it had not been a bad day, just increasingly perplexing. Coleman had been practically a saint; Roarke could not have asked for better luck, there. He'd never lost his reverence for good lawmen; they were warriors who did their best every day to keep back the dark. The detective had been thorough in the initial investigation and generous with his information; Roarke felt like shipping him a good bottle of Scotch, though he would not have been surprised to find that Coleman didn't drink.

He shook the water out of his hair, wrapped a towel around his hips and moved out of the bathroom, past the bed to the window to stand looking down at the city lights. It even *looked* cold. The blue-white peaks of the mountains and the dramatic lighting of the temple turned it into a picture of an ice castle from some other planet.

He was wide-awake, no possible way to sleep.

He turned from the window and looked at the executive desk where he'd stacked his case files. He opened the first file and removed the sketch of the woman in black, and then looked through the lower files folders for the victim photos of Edwin Wann and John Joseph "Preacherman" Milvia.

He rummaged in his suitcase until he found cellophane tape, and taped the three images up on the wall: the sketch of the woman above the two photos of the men, a triangle, killer and victims.

Then he sat in one of the high-backed chairs with his iPad to check his inboxes. Epps had sent him a file of jpegs: Greer's autopsy photos. Roarke tensed as he examined the brutal images, the mangled corpse of his agent on the coroner's slab.

"I'll get her," he promised Greer softly.

He was reaching for the phone to call Epps when it rang, with Epps' name on the caller ID.

"Enjoying yourself up there in God's country?" the deep, dark voice inquired.

Roarke smiled thinly. "Enjoying myself doesn't begin to cover it. What've you got?"

"Some labs back on Greer."

Roarke tensed just from the tone of Epps' voice. "What is it?"

"ME says he had sex before he died. Found fresh ejaculate on him." Roarke felt a chill.

Epps continued. "Doesn't think it was with himself, either. There were pubic hairs that weren't his. We're running the DNA."

Roarke's mind was racing. He knew that Greer had been unattached when he volunteered for undercover seven months ago. Greer hadn't said anything about having sex with any of his contacts in the organization, but his reports were sparse. Every manner of sex was easily available in San Francisco and no one expected undercovers to be celibate.

But what if it had been *the* woman? What if there was a very personal connection?

"What do you know about Greer's personal life?" Roarke said aloud. His voice sounded more sharp than he had intended.

There was a slight pause on the other end of the phone. "Barely anything, boss. He went under maybe two months after I transferred in. I knew him through briefings."

And undercovers made good undercovers precisely because of their rootlessness, their ability to be charming and personable without ever revealing themselves.

Roarke ran his hand through his damp hair. "Just wondering if he could have some kind of past connection with her." But how likely was that when she'd been staying in an SRO for just five days? It didn't make any kind of sense, and now that he'd said it aloud he realized it was only confusing the issue.

"Check around the office. Anyone who knows anything, has heard anything — anything at all about his personal life. And we're going to have to go over his place. You need to check his computer, phone, records — for a girlfriend, an ex. Escorts. Prostitutes."

"Sure, boss..." Epps' voice was questioning.

Roarke sighed. "The SLC vic — the only witness claimed he walked into the vacant building with a hooker."

"So she may be approaching all the vics as a hooker," Epps finished, and then Roarke could hear the frown in his voice. "But if she was with Greer alone for sex, why would she wait and kill him on the street in a freak accident?"

Why indeed. Why a lot of things.

"Not a clue," Roarke admitted. "See what you can get. I'm headed to Portland in the morning. I'll find out if there was a prostitute on scene who didn't show up in the report."

Maybe something *there will make more sense,* he thought to himself, before he continued aloud, "In the meantime, let's keep open to other angles. There's a possibility of a money motive with Wann. He was heavily insured; his wife cleaned up on the 'accidental' death. We can't rule out a hired hit. I'm putting all those factors into VICAP. Sooner or later we're going to find a pattern."

"Okay, boss."

"And Epps?"

"Yeah?"

Roarke hesitated, without knowing why. "Wann has a runaway daughter. Disappeared two years ago at fourteen, hasn't been seen or heard from since."

He heard the same silence on the other end of the line that he'd fallen into himself when he'd heard about the daughter... and he knew he had not been overreacting.

"Epps?"

The deep voice on the other end sounded troubled. "I got it. I just — don't think I like it."

Roarke stepped to the window and looked out at the city, lit up under the waxing moon. "No. Not much to like."

Chapter 13

High in the black silk sky, the moon is coming on full, bathing the gentle hills of Central California in eerie light.

She'd slept nearly twenty-four hours in the motel in the forest.

Now she is cruising 41 toward the coast, again following road signs randomly, cutting across the Cholome Hills in the middle of California, with dark looming slopes around her, dotted with twisted oaks.

Thirty hours later and she is still jumpy from the scene on the street. She wonders briefly if it has to do with the man, the agent who was looking at her.

Just six more days, now, she reminds herself. *Stay out of sight for six more days.*

She sees a sign for a rest stop up ahead, the first in nearly an hour, and unconsciously slows the car.

Rest stops are not her favorite places. Anonymous they are, but this late at night, only the lost and the guilty are on the road. She would skip it, but she is thirsty, she is always thirsty, especially this time of year when the past is so close to the surface, and she'd finished her last water bottle a half an hour ago.

She breathes and focuses her mind to cut short the sound of screams...

At the last minute she pulls off, braking on the off-ramp. A dark hill blocks the approach to the buildings, and as she rounds the tree-lined base of the slope, she sees a lone big rig parked in the truck parking area, lights and engine off. Driver probably sleeping.

Probably.

She slows and hits the button to roll down the front passenger window, looking toward the truck as she feels the air...

Nothing. Nothing apparent, anyway.

Stay? Drive on?

The thought of water draws her.

She parks properly in a slot in front of the restrooms, though she has the entire lot at her disposal. No sense in calling attention to herself in case of a random stop by CHP.

She gets out of the car and stands silently beside it for a moment, just looking, judging the shadows.

The concrete path curves up past a small brick square with vending machines encased behind wide bars, wide enough to reach in to deposit coins and retrieve soft drinks or candy, sturdy enough to keep the machines from being looted. No sight of anyone, no movement except the small stirrings of the wind.

The shadows make her uneasy. But there is no one human, no cars either, and she is so thirsty...

Finally she decides. She takes her water bottles from the back seat and up to the building to fill them from the drinking fountain, gulping down a whole one before she fills it again. The air around her pulses with crickets, and there is no sign of any human life, and she begins to relax.

Now she steps into the women's room, a dark entryway opening into a badly lit wash area: a row of sinks under a long hazy sheet metal mirror, and a turn to the right to enter the toilet area, two rows of empty stalls set across from each other.

Though she can feel there is no one in the washroom, she tilts her head to scan the floor under each row of stalls, making absolutely sure she is alone. Only then does she step to a sink, mostly avoiding looking directly at the mirror as she splashes water on her face and dries it with a rough brown paper towel.

Then quickly she chooses a stall halfway down one of the rows and locks the door to relieve herself. She stands, rearranging her clothes, but as she reaches behind her to flush, she freezes.

Presence.

Outside. Not close yet, not moving forward. The breathing is surreptitious, stealthy.

The trucker.

But so much more than the trucker.

She feels *it* there, slithering, sucking the oxygen out of the air with its vacuum of darkness.

No possible good motive for hovering in the doorway of a women's restroom. He'd seen her, and now she is trapped.

She should have known. She can never relax her guard, not for a second, especially not now, this month, this week...

She forces herself to breathe, to focus.

She feels for the razor in her pocket and holds her breath, listening with all her senses. Still no movement. He'll be waiting for the flush, expecting the sound to cover his approach.

She braces her hands against both walls of the stall and lifts her knees, placing her boots on either side of the toilet seat, crouching there as she draws the razor from her pocket.

Then she reaches out for the lock and eases it open noiselessly, so the door swings slowly open a few inches.

And listens.

She can feel him hovering, feel his building puzzlement and impatience as he listens and hears nothing.

She can sense his thoughts: *A back door? Has he lost her?* And the surge of anger that the thought is. His blood up at the thought of being outwitted, denied...

The air stirs and he moves into the T of the room... stops just before stepping into the stall area. She can sense him taking in the closed utility door at the end of the aisle.

Then the quiet, but heavy sound of boots, placed slowly, one at a time...

And the whistling, anticipatory breath, the sound she's been hearing all her life, since *the night.*

And the other sound. The sound of scratching, a thin shriek on metal. Amplified, echoing in the room, all around her now... unbearable.

She waits, visualizing with each move, each sound, as he pushes open the door of the first stall on her side. Two doors to go, and she counts each breath, each step. At the next stall she can see the top of his head, just the top, thinning greasy hair over a bald spot, and she fixes his height in her body. Another step back, his breathing just outside now...

As he takes that last step in front of her stall, she clutches the top of both side walls and kicks her whole body weight forward, slamming her boot straight into his groin. He stumbles back with a grunt and then a howling curse of pain.

She has already dropped to the floor and now thrusts another vicious kick, sending her whole weight through her heel into his balls, and he doubles over. And now she grabs the top of his head by the hair and jerks his head back to expose the neck and slashes with the razor, opening the left common carotid and internal jugular, feeling the warm blood gush over her hands as a strangled *gaah* gurgles wetly out of his throat.

Blood geysers out of his neck, spraying the bathroom in dark arcs as the trucker drops hard to his knees, clutching at the side of his throat. His hand slips away and he topples over. The knife he is carrying clatters on the floor.

She steps on his chest and slices again, the right side this time, and blood sprays again, but this time weaker, the blood loss from the first cut already catastrophic.

He is spasming now, blood still spouting, pumping from the aorta and splashing the walls, spreading in a crimson pool on the floor. He gurgles helplessly and the red fountain falters... and then stops.

She feels *it* slipping away, sullenly, thwarted.

She is shaking, shot full of adrenaline.

The bathroom is awash in blood. It drips from where it has splashed on the doors of the stalls; the floor is slick with it. The walls seem to pulse; her head is spinning.

She suddenly does not know how long she has been there. It may have been hours.

The heightenedness is slipping away, though, and she looks down with revulsion at the man at her feet. Beer gut over dirty jeans, scuffed boots, flannel shirt soaked with blood, pudgy face, eyes now bulbous with death.

And there are no thoughts in her head, just darkness, a black rage.

Out to the car, out on the road. She drives until she can't drive anymore, and that is the ocean. Some kind of parking lot, deserted, and the vast and dark and roaring Pacific in front of her. She gets out of the car and staggers, clutching the top of the car, barely able to stand. The surf is thundering, and the stars shimmer, pulsing with radiant light.

She moves blindly down a rough set of stairs and out onto the sand, out toward the water on legs shaky from the adrenaline surge and crash. The wind is up, strong and dry and warm, almost hot, those Southern California Santa Ana, but she is cold, trembling, and can barely slog through the deep, soft sand in her boots, still wet with the trucker's blood.

She reaches the water's edge and stands, swaying, and the surf foams up over her boots. Though she has thrown out all her top clothes already, and the plastic she put around her before she got into the car, there is blood on her overshirt, too, she thinks, blood everywhere, really. She strips the shirt off to fling it into the ocean. She wades in deeper and stoops to cup water in her hands and splash it on her arms and face, and then stands, with the wind buffeting her, drying the salt water on her skin.

No more, she thinks. *Too much. Too bleak, too dark, too alone.*

The sound of the surf and the wind takes the screaming out of her ears, but if she had had the razor she would have used it, right there.

But she has tossed it, too, thrown it out of the car a long way back.

She wades out into the surf, farther, farther, and stands under the light of the moon, and the ocean washes away the blood.

DAY THREE

Chapter 14

The first thing she is aware of is the rolling, thundering surf. Surging and retreating... a cleansing, healing sound. Next, the wind, soft and dry on her skin. It stirs fine particles of sand against her cheek...

She is lying in sand, curled up on her side, her cheek pillowed by a small dune. Under the continual dull roar of the ocean is a dry, whispery sound, but there is nothing menacing about the whisper; it is simply the lulling, comforting rustle of sea grass. She is cold, bone-cold and numb, her remaining clothes still damp from the sea, but the sun is warm on her back, and the smells are clean and fresh... salt tang and mollusks and the hay smell of the grassy low dune she is resting on. She breathes in deep, deeper, and feels a deep soreness throughout her body... but also she feels life.

And then another warmth comes into her awareness, a small, steady presence. Alive.

Her eyes fly open.

She sees blue sky, white sun... and a shadow. She blinks to focus.

A small boy is crouched at the top of the dune, looking down on her. His face just visible over the line of grasses and succulents, with their dots of papery yellow flowers.

He is so solemn, watching her, and so still, as only a child can be when it wants to be, a whirlwind of motion and then this stillness.

"Hello," she says.

"Are you sick?" he asks bluntly, without moving.

She looks sharply down at her clothes, but black hides a multitude of sins. Whatever blood the ocean has not washed off doesn't show.

"I don't think so," she answers and sits up slowly.

"My mommy gets sick," he tells her, and she gazes for a moment at his small, serious face.

"I'm just tired," she says, and looks around at the dune, then the beach, which is deserted except for a man far down the horizon line, fishing, maybe. The boy seems to be completely alone.

"Where's your mommy?" she asks.

"San Luis Obispo." The boy pronounces it slowly and perfectly and she feels like smiling, but she is confused. Unless she is completely and totally wrong about where she is, San Luis Obispo is close, but far too far for the boy to have walked.

"So, are you five?" she asks.

"Yeah," he says, unsurprised at the guess.

She nods. "I was five, once."

The boy looks down at her skeptically.

"I was," she insists.

The boy stands suddenly and runs, disappearing over the other side of the dune.

She pushes up from the sand, unfolding herself to standing, and stretches, feeling tender, but surprisingly good. Her pants are still slightly damp; she brushes sand from them, shakes it out of her hair, and looks around her, seeing where she has landed for the first time in daylight. The wide beach in front of her is part of a huge crescent bay, a curve of thirty or forty miles with several separate beach towns visible along the curve, and rolling green hills behind the bluffs. Half a mile down the beach, at the base of what looks like a small downtown, a long pier extends into the shimmering silver-blue ocean. She turns slowly, taking it in... And then stops, looking up at the dune.

The boy has reappeared, this time with a man behind him. The man halts at the top of the dune. He looks startled to see her. He is thirty-two or thirty-three, fit, and has the same thick tousled dark blond hair as the boy, the same chocolate brown eyes, the same smooth-cheeked seriousness. The boy points down at her.

"Told you. A lady."

"I see, Jase, don't point," the man says, a steady voice gentle with patience.

"She's not sick, tho," the boy says with authority.

"Are you all right?" the father asks her.

"Fine," she says, and brushes her hair back from her face. The sea air has curled it into a wild mane.

The man looks contrite. "I'm sorry. Jason said... I thought someone might be hurt."

"No," she says. "We were just talking."

She looks at them standing there on the rise of the dune. They are pretty people, the man and his boy, at home on the beach, not day trippers. Wealthy. The boy's clothes are fashionably battered, expensive cotton in subtle colors, not the garish dyes and cheap fabric of discount stores. J. Crew for kids, at least, and the man's are adult versions of the same, and his tan is real, not a given in California. The haircuts are professional, and the man's body professionally toned. And he wears no wedding ring.

In the split-second that she has been assessing these things, the father has been looking at her, a different kind of look. Then he seems to become aware that the moment has grown too long.

"Well. It's a beautiful morning," he says, gesturing slightly, seeming embarrassed. "Enjoy."

"We had pancakes," Jase says beside his father, looking at her.

"Did you make them?" she says to the boy.

Jason tsks at her. "Course."

She nods solemnly. "You *must* be five, then."

"We're going to town," the boy says, blithely unaware of his father's discomfort. "Dad needs coffee," he explains, rolling his eyes.

"I understand," she says, and glances briefly but deliberately at the father.

"Have you had breakfast?" the father asks, and immediately looks discomfited.

For some reason, she laughs. "No, just barely awake, yet."

A crossroads. She should leave them.

But she likes the boy, and the father likes her, and she believes in chance encounters, depends on them, actually. Moving randomly is the best way to stay hidden, under the surface, and a random roadway has presented itself.

"Let's go," Jase says authoritatively, deciding it.

They walk on the beach, near the surf, heading toward the pier and the town. She and the father move awkwardly together, too much between them already.

"Mark Sebastian," he says, and she realizes she must introduce herself as well.

"Leila French," she tells him, a name out of nowhere. She thinks it again, silently, *Leila French,* and decides she likes it.

Jason runs ahead of them, dodging through seaweed washed up along the waterline, kicking up the spindrift as he runs in and out of the shallows, stomping on the bulbs of washed-up kelp to hear the rubbery pops.

"Sugar," the father explains apologetically. "Food of the devil." She smiles at him, and can almost feel his heart start to race.

She can always tell, is always aware of this effect she has on some men. Not everyday, idle attraction, but a violent longing that has nothing to do with her age or the way she looks or the way they imagine she can fuck. It's something else entirely, something more raw, a sense of her otherness, her darkness. An unhealthy thing even in otherwise healthy men, because it is an attraction to the edge, to danger and despair; to what has happened to her, to the places she has been and the things that she has done.

But at the moment, his attraction may be useful to her.

"One of those nights, was it?" he says to her, over the low, lulling roar of the waves. She looks at him, and realizes he is thinking that she has been drunk, may still be drunk. It's not that far from the truth, except for the drinking part.

"I don't drink," she tells him. That seems to startle him.

"Really." And then after a long moment, he adds in a voice meant to be casual, but failing utterly. "Why is that?"

She considers, looking out over the rolling, translucent blue-gray waves. "It makes me feel like I'm drowning," she says finally.

He looks at her as if that is not the answer he was expecting. It all seems very important to him, something he wants to understand. She doesn't tell him what she's seen drinking do to people, what it makes them vulnerable to. But she remembers the boy's words: *"Are you sick? My mommy gets sick..."* and thinks the man might already know.

"I guess I know that feeling," he says finally, and they walk a bit, in silence, with the sun above them and the wind on their skin and the ocean shining beside them and the foam at their feet.

"Where are you staying?" he says, a slight nod to the fact that he is with a total stranger. Only a slight nod. She thinks, for the millionth time, that being a woman is the world's most perfect camouflage.

"The Dunes," she says. She can picture the cluster of cottages, the pink neon sign; she'd passed it on her wild drive in. It is just off the beach; she could easily have walked out of her room in the clothes she has on for an early morning stroll. And she likes the double entendre.

"Just getting away?" he says.

"Thinking some things through," she says truthfully, and he looks at her a beat too long.

"This is the place for it," he tells her.

As they walk on, she sees a crumpled pile of what looks momentarily like a half-buried corpse. The tide has washed up the shirt that she discarded because of the blood, now a sandy rag.

She looks away from it and smiles at Mark Sebastian.

Ahead of them, the boy suddenly reverses himself, hurtling back toward them. He grabs her hand and pulls. "Let's go in the forest!"

"There's a forest?" she says, glancing at the father. The sand stretches around them for miles. In truth she has no idea what he could be talking about.

The boy tugs at her hand, pulling her toward the pier, past the sun-bleached wooden stairs leading up to the boardwalk, and into the line of enormous posts supporting the pier, a good two stories above them. And once they are under, she understands. It is a forest of posts. The tall, weathered trunks are in rows, but not symmetrical rows. They lean at odd angles, and the silver light from the sea streams between them and the rumble of the waves creates a hollow and resonant echo.

The walkway is high above them and she can hear the faint sound of footsteps on the planks, and the sand is covered in seagull tracks and deep holes from human feet. There is a peace and a liveness about it that is deeply calming; it is like a cathedral, like being inside a Magritte painting. She breathes in deeply. "It *is* a forest," she tells the boy.

The father says nothing, but she can see he is pleased that she sees it, feels it.

She holds his eyes, and she thinks, *This could work. Six days to go, and no one will look for me here.*

She is tired, so tired. Just to rest in a quiet and bright place, with people who live in the light instead of this endless darkness...

I could be safe.

And even beyond that, there is something about the boy, something that compels her, something that must be obeyed.

The three of them move out from the forest under the pier in silence, but something has changed; the moment has bonded them.

More than that. The boy trusts her and so the man does too. That she understands.

"Up here," Jason says authoritatively, and she and the father follow him, slogging through the deep, soft sand.

To the side of the pier there is another long set of stairs leading up to the boardwalk and main drag of town. As the boy leads, she walks with the father up the stairs, the boy stomping hard enough on each step to shake the foundation of the stairs, and onto the main strip.

She stops at the top, looking out over the town for really the first time. There is the usual string of beach shops and rental booths and cafés and bars, many opening right out onto the sidewalks. The town is just waking up, store clerks setting out racks of batik purses and sparkly glass and shell jewelry and postcard stands, sleepy tourists emerging from hotels and condos and motels in search of breakfast.

The boy keeps up a steady stream of chatter, pointing out murals and surfboards and his foods of choice at each of the cafés and diners and restaurants, confirming her impression that he and his father are not tourists, but at least part-time residents.

She is pleased with the look of the town and the people. Many of the buildings are original thirties and forties architecture; the Deco and neon signs are salt-rusted and authentic. This is not the blow-dried, manicured, surgically enhanced crowd of Orange County or Los Angeles; there are bikers and blue-collar families, retired professors and gaggles of teenagers, a mix of Latino and white, and an overall scruffiness that appeals to her. The town has an edge that makes her own edge less conspicuous. And though it is past summer, it is warm, still beach weather; the town is full of tourists, a high turnover, easy to get lost in.

This could work, she thinks again.

A decrepitly elegant old hotel has a vertical sign on top with the word PISMO. So that's where she is, Pismo Beach. She has passed it in her travels.

She stops on the sidewalk, looking up at the sign, and the father and son stop with her, looking at her. She can feel the power she has over them already, it is massive.

"What are your plans for the day?" the father asks.

She lets him twist in the wind with that for a moment before she says vaguely, using the name of the town the boy had referenced earlier, "I have friends in San Luis Obispo." Can't be too fast about these things.

"Of course," he mumbles awkwardly, in an agony of embarrassment.

She waits a beat before she asks, "How long are you here for?" And she sees the quick rush of hope in his eyes.

"Six more days," he says, and that seals it for her. Her time frame exactly. It is meant.

"So am I," she says, and sees that the moment is significant for him, too. "Then maybe I'll see you again."

"Promise," the boy says beside his father, darkly, on the verge of sulky.

"Well. If you can find me," she says to the boy, Jason, a challenge which makes him light up with confidence. And then she slides her eyes to the father, in a second challenge. She feels the heat rise in him, and holds his gaze.

"He's very good at finding people," the man says.

"We'll see," she says lightly.

She turns from them and walks up the street, knowing that the father is watching her.

Chapter 15

Roarke's plane descended into an ocean of velvet green, threaded with silver ribbons of river. The city center clustered on both sides of the biggest ribbon, with the odd conical peaks of three dormant volcanoes and active Mount St. Helens in the distance.

Portland was located at the junction of two rivers; Roarke vaguely remembered an early American history of sawmills, fur trappers and river traders. Now it was known for being one of the most "green" cities in the U.S., not just literally, but in the environmentally friendly sense. It was lesser-known as a radical center, a haven for anarchists, crust punks, DIYs, and other activist subcultures.

Despite the airport's omnipresent billboard invitations to use the light rail system, Roarke headed for the car rental counters, feeling slightly like a capitalist running dog, but a running dog who would fight to the death for the inalienable right to his own vehicle. While he waited at the counter, he studied the VICAP file again.

The Portland victim was John Joseph Milvia, a forty-six year old Caucasian homeless man known on the street as Preacherman, a likely schizophrenic, who regularly spouted his own version of Biblical anarchism in the public arenas of Portland's downtown.

The Preacherman glared up at Roarke out of a mug shot, taken during one of his many minor arrests for disturbing the peace, loitering, and trespassing. He could have been any one of a hundred transients Roarke encountered on the sidewalks of his own city every day: bushy hair and long beard, sun-and-wind-burned skin made more leathery by alcohol abuse, burning, unfocused eyes. His body was found in a sleeping bag under a culvert near the Willamette River, his throat cut in two deep clean slashes to his left and right carotid artery and jugular vein, most likely with an old-fashioned straight razor. The killer had taken him by surprise; there were no signs of a struggle of any kind. Preacherman's meager belongings had been tossed, as if the killer had searched for anything of relative value, and perhaps had taken things; it was impossible to say. The murder weapon had not been recovered.

Roarke brooded over the whole scenario as he found his rental car — a Prius, of course — in the lot and drove out of the airport facility, following the directions of the silky-voiced GPS toward the downtown police bureau.

He knew Portland from a stretch of three months he'd done almost six years ago now, back during his stint with the BAU, the elite "profiler" unit of the FBI, which focused exclusively on serial killers, serial rapists and child killings. His team had provided investigative support to local law enforcement tracking a killer hunting street kids working the Northwestern prostitution circuit of Seattle, Portland and San Francisco. It was a time of Roarke's life he didn't care to think much about; it had cost him his idealism and his marriage, even if truthfully the marriage would not have lasted, and the ideals — probably not either.

From the time he'd spent in the city he knew that Portland had the largest homeless population in the U.S., topping San Francisco's just a few years ago, and consequently, like San Francisco, the city supported a large number of homeless shelters in the downtown area. Or there was a huge number of homeless because of the large number of homeless shelters, a chicken or the egg kind of effect.

In fact, Portland was home to a whole semi-permanent tent city, Dignity Village, a self-regulating, government-recognized encampment that had operated with its own elected community officials for the past ten years.

Roarke knew this because the witness he was hoping to see, Elias Marias, the homeless man who claimed to have seen Roarke's mystery woman with the Preacherman, had lived in that village at the time of the murder.

In the witness report Marias claimed a woman in a black turtleneck had sat in downtown's Pioneer Courthouse Square watching the Preacherman ramble and rant for more than two hours on the day that he was killed.

A bizarre story in every way, and it threw a huge wrench into the "hired hit" theory.

Why a homeless man? Why this *homeless man?*

Greer's death and Edwin Wann's looked on the surface like accidents. Preacherman was a cold-blooded killing. Physically it would not be so difficult to slash the throat of a sleeping — and according to the autopsy, drunk — man who was encased up to his neck in a sleeping bag.

What kind of mentality that would take was another story.

And *why*? Why would someone want this man dead?

Roarke was itching to head straight for the square, to walk the same places that the woman had been, to get more of a sense of the scene. But protocol won out and he continued to the downtown police bureau.

The street Roarke drove in on skirted the river and was typical of the downtown homeless scene; shaggy men with brimming shopping carts and panhandling signs, some passed out in shapeless bundles on the sidewalk.

The police bureau was a bland cube two blocks from the river.

Unfortunately the detective he was going to interview had been the junior detective on the case; his partner had died of a heart attack just a few months before. And as Roarke stood in the bullpen shaking hands with Detective Wayne Alder, he could tell Alder was no Coleman. Alder was young, with farmboy good looks, just two years with a shield, still proving himself, which meant arrogant, and skeptical as hell that the Preacherman murder could have anything to do with anything else, anywhere. Roarke didn't entirely blame him.

"It's this woman in black that the witness, Marias, talked about," Roarke explained, as neutrally as he could manage. "She's the possible link."

Alder tipped back in his chair, a casual move designed to disguise his immediate defensiveness. "Marias," he snorted. "Gotta tell you, *Agent* Roarke. Marias ain't much of what you'd call a solid witness."

Roarke understood the defensiveness. From the file, it was clear that both detectives on the case had dismissed Marias's account. It was always an uncomfortable feeling to have to consider that you'd been wrong.

"It's not like it was even much of a description," Alder continued, picking up the report and reading from it with a more than a tinge of sarcasm. "'Blond, slim, legs, sunglasses, dark clothes?'"

Go ahead, tell him it's the turtleneck, Roarke thought to himself. *Guy looks like he could use a laugh.*

"I'm just investigating all avenues," he said aloud. He removed the police sketch of the woman from his file packet, slid it across Alder's desk.

Alder took a decent amount of time studying the sketch before he said, "Never seen her." But when he looked back up at Roarke, he had a look on his face that Roarke understood too well: flat-out disbelief. The detective drummed a finger on the sketch.

"You want to tell me *this* woman cut a homeless guy's throat in a culvert?" He snorted. "Tellin' you, the Preacherman geysered out like

Old Faithful. You ever see a woman do something like that? Homeless man. In a culvert. Makes no sense."

No, it doesn't. That's my problem, Detective Alder, right there in a nutshell.

"I agree, it's a stretch," Roarke said. "You never found any other suspects, though."

Now Alder looked well on the way to pissed. "Far as I'm concerned this woman was never a suspect, if she ever existed at all. I don't have to tell you the stats, Agent Roarke. Eighty-five percent of homeless have drug and psych issues. The only witness who claimed to see the woman, Marias, has a criminal record and a psych record—"

"But not recent." Roarke had pulled Marias's sheet himself.

Alder all but rolled his eyes. "He's cleaned himself up some, but you know that never lasts. He coulda been seeing angels that day, for all we know." Then Alder sighed and leaned forward in a show of good will. "Preacherman pissed a lot of people off, it was his nature. On top of being mental, he was a mean drunk. He got in people's faces and told them they were going to hell, and he liked to get real specific about what was gonna happen to them there. Guy like that is going to come to bad ends one way or another." He flicked the police sketch back toward Roarke. "But I can't see *her* being at the top of the list of people to do it."

On the street outside the police station, Roarke leaned against his rented Prius and looked up at the building. Maybe Alder was no Coleman, but Roarke couldn't find a single argument with his assessment. Practically, it would make sense to get back on a plane to San Francisco and work the case around ground zero: Greer.

But there was one thin thread connecting the two other dead men, Wann and Preacherman. The conclusion of both investigating detectives involved in their cases was that they were abrasive men with multiple enemies. Neither detective had felt surprise at the deaths.

Roarke felt an uneasy twinge.

So if we're talking victimology, what does that say about Greer?

The thought made him — uncomfortable didn't even begin to describe it. It meant that he could have read his own man wrong, and he didn't like that idea at all.

He pushed suddenly off the side of the car and zapped open the door to get in. Marias was the key. He'd either seen the woman or he hadn't. Roarke needed to meet him to know.

Dignity Village was located about seven miles from downtown, on a paved city lot called Sunderland Yard.

Roarke parked on the street outside the compound and walked toward the crude but distinct front gate cut into the fencing. Just outside the entrance was a bulletin board, its wooden frame proudly hand-carved with the words DIGNITY VILLAGE. Beneath the sign was an elaborate collage of photos and newspaper articles with graphics detailing the history of the village.

Roarke stopped to read, and what he learned took him by surprise. San Francisco had more than its share of programs for the homeless, and Roarke was familiar with the concept of "supportive housing": shelters that offered services and counseling along with the beds. But Dignity Village was more than that: a village built by squatters led by homeless activists who had taken their housing situation into their own hands, and agitated through well-organized public protests and appeals to the city government for a permanent, city-subsidized location of their own.

DV called itself an "intentional community." What that meant, practically, was that it was a drug and alcohol and violence-free zone, and residents were required to contribute to the community by working set schedules on kitchen, garden, building or cleaning details. The village was governed by bylaws and an elected Board of Directors.

The presentation was impressive and inspiring; any law enforcement officer was too well aware of the burden that chronic homelessness puts on a city, and Roarke's hat was off to anyone who was even attempting a solution. But he was also as always reading between the lines for the darker implications: he noted that children were not allowed in the village because residents were not screened out for past criminal convictions, including sex crimes.

He stepped into the small, open shack that served as a gatehouse. A street-wizened man of sixty, or maybe fifty, looked up from an industrial-looking metal table, where he was printing out some kind of sign in careful block lettering. The wall behind him was papered with announcements for the community, cooking schedules and work assignments.

"I'm here to see Elias Marias," Roarke told the sentry.

The man's eyes narrowed. "Government," he said flatly, not a question.

"Federal agent." Roarke showed his credentials. "He's not in any trouble. I'm following up on a case he filed a witness report on."

The guard nodded sagely. "Preacherman."

"That's right," Roarke said. "Did you know him?"

"Everybody knew Preacherman."

The man's tone of voice was impossible to read.

"Any thoughts on who killed him?" Roarke asked, carefully casual.

The sentry stared at him without expression. "Government got him."

Roarke looked back at him. "Thanks," he said dryly.

"Marias. D Street, Number Four," the sentry said, and dropped his head back to his lettering.

Roarke stepped out of the shack, shaking his head as he walked across the concrete lot toward the neat rows of small, square dwellings.

Everyone's a comedian. Or maybe he really believes it. With these guys, who knows?

On the other hand, Dignity Village was already a much more interesting place than he had expected. A much more political place than he had expected. And politics could make someone some interesting enemies.

Was it possible that Preacherman had not been just a random homeless man, but a radical activist? In which case, could his politics have provoked someone enough to want him dead? Someone powerful enough to *pay* to have him dead?

A wild theory. But no stranger than the idea that the Preacherman would have ended up on a hit list that included Agent Greer and Edwin Wann.

Roarke had reached the structures and turned down the first "street" between tidy rows of Not to Code buildings. On either side of him were solid wood platforms on which stood 10x10 and 10x15 structures, mostly shacks consisting of a wooden frame draped with plastic sheeting or tarps. He nodded to a grizzled man sitting on his steps who watched him warily; otherwise he was the only one on the street. As he walked slowly on the packed dirt, Roarke could see that some of the dwellings had tents pitched inside the draped tarps for an extra layer of warmth. But there were a few straw-and-clay houses with adobe veneer, and some of the houses had neat white-painted wooden stairs with handrails leading up to the front door of the dwelling. Not exactly the American dream of a house, but still a far cry from sleeping in a cardboard box in an alley. Roarke was impressed and even touched by the obvious signs of pride in ownership.

As he reached the end of the first street and turned left onto the cross-street, Roarke passed a school bus serving as a library and a windmill which seemed to be providing electricity. Then came a row of portable toilets, a wooden building of shower facilities, a communal kitchen, and a farm plot where several villagers were weeding and watering, apparently growing their own vegetables. Each street was marked by a carefully fashioned street sign: A, B, C.

Roarke turned again on D Street.

The witness, Elias Marias, lived in Number 4, one of the more finished buildings, with a set of stairs to his door and a solid roof above the dwelling, including a narrow and sharp-pitched roof over the stairs. A mansion, by Dignity Village standards. Roarke noted the well-maintained bicycle chained to the stair railing.

He climbed the stairs, feeling the solid carpentry under his feet, and stopped on the tiny landing. Despite the solid walls, there was no actual door to the house, just a draped canvas painting tarp, fastened closed with a bike chain laced through several holes in the tarp. Roarke glanced around him and then reached to knock loudly on the wooden door frame.

"Elias Marias?"

There was no response. Roarke waited, considering his options. He had no idea if Marias was inside or not, but his feeling was always that truth was the best approach, so he spoke aloud. "Mr. Marias, I'm Special Agent Roarke, of the San Francisco Office of the FBI. I've read your witness report on the death of John "Preacherman" Milvia, and I would like to speak with you about the woman you saw watching him the day he died."

Roarke stepped back on the small landing and waited again. A breeze swept through the street, rippling the tarps on other dwellings, an eerie flapping sound that for no good reason made Roarke want to draw his weapon. His right hand went to his shoulder holster.

"Mr. Marias," he began, and then suddenly there was a slick sliding sound, whip fast, behind him and he spun around toward the door, in time to see the bike chain sliding through the holes in the tarp door and disappearing. A second later the tarp was roughly pulled aside, and a short dark man stood in the shadowed entrance, glaring out at him.

"Bout a year late, aintchu, G-Man?" he said softly.

Marias did not invite Roarke in. They sat on the steps, Marias on the landing, Roarke below, Marias compulsively jiggling his foot on his knee, an unconscious and constant twitch.

The man was a mix of races that Roarke didn't even dare to guess, and his age, as with most street dwellers, was equally mysterious —

though if someone had put a gun to Roarke's head he would have said Marias was still in his thirties. His accent sounded vaguely East L.A., but with the drawl filtered through an unmedicated hyperactivity. His long black hair was smoothed into an oily or pomaded ponytail, it was hard to tell which.

"The Preacherman was a friend of yours?" Roarke began.

"Preacherman wasn't nobody's friend. Preach walk alone. But he a street brother. Don't nobody be messin' with the family. Don't matter who. They be coming after us when we sleep, that needs justice, yo."

Marias's face was dark, and Roarke had the sense of absolute conviction radiating from the man. At the same time, he was pretty sure there was no love lost between him and the dead man; Marias was not trying to claim any intimate bond.

"Did he live here, in the Village?" Roarke asked.

Marias laughed without much humor. "No, man. Not his thing. Preach don't play well with others, dig? He have his own place."

"His own place. Under the bridge, you mean? Where he was killed?"

"Yeah, he camp under the bridge. An he say he have some place in the hills."

Roarke raised an eyebrow. "A house? A cabin?"

Marias shrugged. "No idea, yo. He disappear sometimes, a week, two weeks, turn up again and say he be at his place."

"But you have no idea where he meant."

"I get the feeling toward Hood, maybe."

Mount Hood. Roarke wrote it down. *Interesting.* He'd have to ask Detective Alder.

"Did you see him often? Before he was killed?"

"We cross paths. Used to be he at the Living Room most every day."

Roarke actually understood the reference, but only because of his short stint in Portland. Marias was talking about Pioneer Courthouse Square, a planned public space affectionately known as "Portland's Living Room," used for everything from art fairs to large concerts, and a popular hangout for the homeless.

"Where else did he hang?"

"Took some of his meals at Our Lady."

The church sounded vaguely familiar. "That's a soup kitchen, right? Downtown?"

"Ninth Street," Marias nodded.

Roarke knew he had to step very, very carefully, and he made his next question general instead of honing in on what he really wanted to ask.

"You think someone would want him killed?"

Marias hesitated, considering.

Don't speak ill of the dead, right, yo? Roarke thought.

Finally the smaller man answered neutrally. "Preacherman had enemies, no doubt. But — *want* him killed?"

It was an astute question. Roarke asked more bluntly, "Do you think someone would have hired someone to kill him?"

Marias studied Roarke obliquely. Roarke could feel his suddenly heightened interest.

"Maybe the G."

Roarke stared at Marias. *The G as in the government? Seriously? That's two for two. Maybe these guys know something I don't.*

Marias suddenly looked defensive, as if he knew what Roarke was thinking. "Preach, he be smart, science and shit. Could be he know something he not sposed to know an' the Man put him down."

"The Man," Roarke repeated, thoughtfully. "But you described a woman."

Marias gave him a sly look. "Wan get close to someone, wan catch a brother unawares, you send a shorty, no? And this blondie, no one gon say no to her, you compehend?"

"I do," Roarke said, and was uncomfortably aware that he meant it. "I'd like to hear more about her. Maybe you could start from the beginning — everything that happened that day?"

Marias looked Roarke over, as if he were deciding, and then he nodded. "We was chillin in the Living Room, feel? Preach up on the stage, doin his thing. Speakin his word. And this blondie, she in the seats."

Roarke thought back, and vaguely remembered the setup of the Living Room. A part of the Square had a coliseum-like design, with a semicircle of huge temple pillars, and arena seating where tourists and locals would sprawl, sunning themselves, eating lunch on work breaks, and watching the parade of humanity. The circular seating plan created a natural stage space, and the more eccentric and extroverted homeless often took the stage in search of attention.

"So Preacherman was preaching, and she was watching."

"Not just watching. She be fixated, yo, you know? Leaning forward, watching nonstop." Marias demonstrated with his own body, and Roarke was unnerved. The homeless man was perfectly mimicking the stillness that had made Roarke notice the woman to begin with, that intent, watching look.

"Were there other people in the stands that day?" He asked.

"Tons," Marias said. "Nice sunny day."

"So by tons, do you mean dozens? Hundreds?" Roarke asked casually, trying to get Marias to set the scene, describe the big picture.

Milvia frowned, looking into the distance. "Dozens, yeah, mos def. A hundred, maybe."

"So out of all those people, what made you notice this woman?"

Marias gave him a scathing look. "This girl you notice. She never move. Two, three hours, just watchin. Preach just keep doin his shit, and she just keep watchin."

Roarke found the image unnerving; there was an oddly predatory feel to what Marias was describing.

"Did Preacherman notice her, too?"

"Oh, yeah. After a while he be talking right to her."

"Do you remember what he said?" Roarke asked, trying not to telegraph his excitement.

Marias shook his head. "Same shit he always sayin. Bible shit. Plague and death and war. The Beast walking."

Revelation. All-time favorite of unmedicated street evangelists everywhere.

"But he was sayin it to her, after a while," Marias added.

"Saying what to her?"

"Talkin about the Beast. Saying it *about* her. Like the Beast was her."

Inexplicably, Roarke felt a chill start in the base of his spine and start its way up his back. *The Beast.* Why did that bother him? He shook his head to clear it.

"What did she look like? I'd appreciate it if you'd tell me everything you remember."

"All black. Pants, black turtleneck — only no arms." Marias made a slashing motion at his shoulder.

"No sleeves," Roarke corrected automatically, but the description was another ripple for him. All kinds of women wore turtlenecks, all the time, but a turtleneck with no sleeves, you noticed.

Marias was continuing. "She thin, but strong, too, like a acrobat, know what I'm sayin? She didn't move much, but there was this power. Never took those big dark glasses off, but her face was all sharp, like a fox." Marias paused, and then said almost ruefully. "I won't lie. She fine. But you don't notice so much 'count of the strange."

It was her. Roarke felt not the slightest doubt. *The strange...* Marias was describing all the things that Roarke had noticed himself. He felt almost lightheaded. It was incomprehensible, but it was a link.

Marias nodded. "Telling you, something not right about that chica. She be looking good, but she fucked up inside."

Roarke said nothing, but didn't entirely discount the assessment. People who lived on the streets sometimes had a heightened awareness: of danger, of crazy, of all kinds of things. Living outdoors brought out animal instincts, it was a survival mechanism.

"So you were there in the square for two, three hours? Were you just watching all this time?"

"Nah, no man," Marias said. "I be signing."

"Signing" was the street word for panhandling with a sign. "So you were set up someplace that you could see the stage?"

"Close enough. Work the sign, get some coin, go get some food, come back." Marias didn't look at Roarke when he said the last.

Roarke didn't think it was useful to press the issue, but knew it was far more likely that Marias had left his post every time he'd gotten enough spare change to score a nickel bag or a Colt 45. Which Detective Alder would have known just as well, and it would have been a big reason to discount anything Marias said about the mysterious woman. That coupled with the statistical improbability, to put it mildly, of a woman cutting a homeless man's throat while he slept, would have made Marias's story a non-starter to pretty much any cop.

"You ever see this woman before that day? Or after?"

Marias frowned. "No man. First, last, and only. But when Preach turn up dead? I knew. She done him."

"Why?" Roarke said, so intensely that Marias flinched beside him. Roarke amended, "I mean, how did you know?"

Marias was silent, for a long moment staring off, as if remembering. "They got somepin between them. You could see it. Somepin live."

Chapter 16

The beach lot has filled up and it takes her a few passes through the columns of parked cars to be sure, since she can only vaguely remember what the car looks like to begin with. But finally it is clear that the Honda is gone.

She stands in the rows of vehicles, the ocean gleaming beyond the asphalt and sand, and considers this.

She had left nothing in it; all trash and water bottles pitched out onto the interstate, there is no problem there. The roller bag she had discarded after the night in the Sequoias; she prefers to buy new clothes when she leaves a city instead of risking carrying any trace evidence with her from whatever tasks she has performed. All she really needs is what she carries in a money belt around her waist: the cash, the cards, the various identities. And she had somehow summoned enough presence of mind to wrap herself in a plastic garbage bag from one of the rest stop's bins before she got back in the car. There might be minute traces of the trucker's blood in the car — if that — but someone would have to be looking for it to find it.

If the car has been stolen, that can actually be good, it will put another layer between her and San Francisco.

What would be bad was if it has been impounded; sooner or later they will contact the registered owner. And not that it is likely, but if they do a thorough workup of the car, for whatever reason, it could turn up things she doesn't want to turn up. So again, it comes down to how long the owner will be out of town.

She has an urge to flee right now, to find the next car and go.

Instead she looks out at the ocean, the reflecting light. She moves toward the strip of boardwalk between the parking lot and the sea, and walks down the stairs, onto the sand and out toward the sea until she finds a dune where she can sit. When she is settled, soft sand under her hands and the sun on her face and the wind in her hair, she forces herself to think through the night before, the trucker and the mistakes.

The trucker presents a problem.

Not that he himself can be a problem to anyone, anymore, and that is a good thing. But she'd been taken by surprise, and now there could be repercussions.

It isn't irrevocable, nothing is going to stop because of a mistake. What is worrisome to her is *why*. Why she was caught so completely off guard. Why she overreacted, comparatively speaking. Why she had left the scene without any attempt to clean up or redirect attention.

It had been a messy kill, a bloodbath, bloody and ugly and startling, unignorable.

It all amounts to a breakdown, there is no other way to say it.

Breakdowns she has had before, ever since the night. Periodically but never predictably. A part of her life *After*.

It does seem, though, that the breakdowns are more frequent.

She feels another strong wave, an urge to flee.

But the rest stop is more than a half hour away, near an intersection of several major highways and any number of densely populated cities and towns. There is no reason in the world for anyone to trace her to Pismo, or the trucker to the car, or the car to her. And she knows enough about the central coast to realize there is a good chance the killing of the trucker will be attributed to the massive meth traffic in the region.

And then there is the boy.

She thinks of him, small and serious and confident.

And there is the answer. That is the sign. Whatever has led her, has led her to the boy. It is meant. She is on the path.

And now it seems that the father and son are on the path, too. They are part of something, certainly, there is too much of a pull here, too much of an indicator for it not to have been meant.

The thought is calming; it is all calming, the air, the sun, the rumble of the surf, the vast, sparkling water.

Decided, now, she stands and walks back up the stairs into town, and finds a phone booth where she calls The Dunes motel and reserves a room for a week over the phone under the name she gave the father. If he calls there, and he might, it will look as if she is there; the clerk might say she hadn't checked in yet, but that could easily be dismissed later as the clerk's mistake.

Then she walks up the main street, Peabody Avenue, past the salt water taffy stores and the beach rental shops and tattoo parlors and the Bar-B-Q pits, past the giant concrete clam in the middle of the street, surrounded by tourists with cameras out, clicking photos of themselves beside it. She enjoys the retro feel of the buildings and signage and colorful murals on the sides of buildings, the sense of different eras layered on top of each other. It makes her feel even farther from the reality she has just left.

Off the main street, her first stop is a large drug store. She chooses shorts, flip-flops, sunglasses, beach hat, a beach towel, and a big straw beach bag, all the most generic looking she can find, and a T-shirt with a high-enough collar. She adds a miniature can of shaving cream and a pack of disposable shavers to the basket. Then as she stands in the cosmetics aisle, trying on a jasmine-scented skin lotion, she hears a strange scuffling one aisle over and feels herself tensing in response. She puts her basket silently on the floor, and moves to the end of the aisle, edging around the corner to look down the next.

What she sees is a lean, hard older man, later sixties but ropy with muscle, and dark flat eyes, with the twitchiness of a meth addict; she has seen more than a few on her walk. He towers over a little girl of maybe six, who shrinks back from him against the lower shelving of the aisle. "Mama," she whispers, barely audible.

The man jerks the little girl's hand and growls in a tobacco-roughened voice, "Stop your whining or I'll give you something to cry about."

She is up beside him, stepping between him and the little girl, before he can react. "You're scaring her," she says softly, too low for the girl to hear.

He looks up and around as if he can't believe anyone would have the audacity to speak to him. Then his eyes narrow, and he looks her over. He decides instantly she is not a threat. His mistake.

"Mind your business, girlie," he says loudly.

Faster that he could ever think possible, she reaches for his arm and grabs it at the wrist, twisting it away from his body sharp and hard so the humerus rotates dangerously against the scapula, a fraction of an inch from complete dislocation.

The whole rest of his body goes limp in pain and shock. She leans close to his ear so the little one can't hear. "If you touch her again, I'll give you something to cry about," she says, her voice almost inaudible.

His eyes go wide and he almost tries to pull away, but she applies more pressure and he freezes again.

"I wouldn't," she says. "Your arm will break in two seconds." He stays still. "What are you doing with her?"

"Babysitting. Granddaughter..." he gasps out, a shallow wheeze.

"Where are her parents?"

"Mother — at work."

"Where?" she says, keeping up the pressure. His eyes burn at her, a deep-banked rage. It is only because of the child that she does not take care of him right then.

"Restaurant across the way."

"You're going to take her right back there now and you're going to tell her mama you won't be able to babysit any more."

He grits his teeth and she turns his wrist slightly, maximum pain for minimal effort. "Say it."

"I can't babysit no more."

She keeps the pressure on and shoves her other hand into his pants pocket, pulls out his wallet.

Then she shoves him away from her. As he cradles his arm at the elbow in dazed disbelief, she flips open the wallet and reads his name and address off his driver's license. "Thomas Munroe, 383 Acacia, Pismo Park." She looks up from the license. "Well, Thomas Munroe, now I know where to find you. And you better know I'll be watching you."

She steps back, pocketing his wallet. He stares at her in sullen fury. She settles on her stance, prepared to kick his knee out if he makes one wrong move, and she sees him realize she can do it, will be happy to do it. He turns, slowly, stiffly, and heads for the front doors, with the little girl trailing behind.

She watches them, following at a distance to see them leave the store, and stepping outside to watch them cross the parking lot to the coffee shop he'd referred to.

He opens the door of the restaurant and follows the little girl in.

Only then does she exhale, and go back into the drugstore to find her abandoned basket.

It is a reckless thing for her to have done, but bullies rarely cop to being assaulted by a woman, so chances are fairly good he'll never report it.

Even if he does, what can he say?

She is probably safe enough.

She makes her purchases at the drug store, and then heads out to the street to find a pawn shop.

She will be needing another razor.

Chapter 17

R oarke stood in front of the elaborate historic courthouse, looking out over Pioneer Courthouse Square.

The day was overcast and windy, with a dampness to the air, and the Square was lightly trafficked, compared to what Roarke recalled from sunnier days. But it was an even more striking space than Roarke had remembered. Although at first he had been put off by the sheer concreteness of the plaza (which was absurdly called a park, though there was not a blade of grass or an unpotted tree to be seen), it had grown on him, until he could acknowledge it as an amazing modern playground, a combination of theater, sculpture garden and street fair, that somehow encouraged interactivity. There was the historic courthouse for which the Square was named on one side, a modern visitors' center on the other, and a vast open brick space in between the two, all surrounded by towering office buildings.

Roarke started down the wide, long brick levels — too big really to call steps — in front of the courthouse onto the plaza.

On this blustery day there were more transients than locals or tourists, including the usual slew of body-pierced punkers and anarchists, and one street performer Roarke actually recognized from five years ago: The Card Trick Guy.

It hadn't changed much. Only now Roarke knew that the woman in black had been there. And late as he was, he was on her trail. Elusive and inexplicable as she was, she was revealing herself. He felt the thrill of the hunt in his veins. He would find her, he was certain. And he would understand her.

He walked deliberately through the flotsam of humanity, across the expansive plaza, over bricks engraved with the names of hundreds of the Square's sponsors, toward the amphitheater ringed with the Romanesque columns. At the end of the ring the columns were artfully collapsed to form long tables where gamers gathered to play chess.

He passed rectangular fountains with unnervingly realistic metal sculptures of otters, bears and ducks playing in and out of the water... then a bizarre "weather machine," then the famous "Umbrella Man," a cast-iron businessman caught mid-stride in the open plaza, hefting a wide-open umbrella. Roarke thought to himself, not for the first time, that street art was nothing more than a diabolical haze designed to mess with the minds of the chemically altered.

As he moved across the plaza, his eyes scanned the tourists taking cute photos of their kids posing with the animals and the Umbrella Man, the usual handful of Greenpeace activists, the shirtless hacky sack players, the tripping punkers, the hyperactive meth heads, a businessman striding in circles, barking orders into his Bluetooth. And of course, flocks of pigeons, strutting around the never-ending banquet.

On the bricks outside the inevitable Starbucks was a large seated grouping of panhandling homeless teens, a sight that always made Roarke wince and feel somehow he had failed, that he was in the wrong profession entirely.

He turned from them and scanned past the various food carts, doing only a slow business today, and let his eyes rest briefly on everyone he saw.

He realized he was in some way looking at the crowd as if he would see *her*, which made no sense at all. She'd been in Portland over nine months ago, and was clearly a traveler. No telling how many cities she'd been in in the last two or three years, and no telling where she might be headed next.

They actually did call them "Travelers" in the BAU, meaning killers who were constantly on the move, crossing state lines, staying under law enforcement radar by making sure that each kill was in a separate jurisdiction.

But she's not a serial killer, Roarke reminded himself.

Or is she?

He was so struck by the thought that he stopped dead in the middle of the plaza, in the sheer disbelief that he had never considered the possibility before.

Profiling used to be his *job*, damn it. A part of his FBI career he would rather forget, had done his best to forget, except when absolutely necessary to evaluate an ongoing case. But *actually* forgetting — meant he was not doing his present job.

He had to stay still for a moment in the brisk breeze to regroup, and in that moment he realized that of course it was precisely because of his profiling experience and training that he had not considered the possibility that the woman was a serial killer, that he had immediately gone to the unlikely, but still much more plausible theory that she was a paid assassin.

Serial killing was in Roarke's mind the definition of evil, and an appallingly misunderstood and misreported phenomenon. Roarke knew more about it than anyone would ever want to know. And the number one characteristic of serial killers is that they are men.

Psychologists and law enforcement officials and sociologists could argue and produce examples until the end of time about women who killed, and who killed in numbers. But Roarke knew that female multiple murderers fell overwhelmingly into two types: the "Angel of Death," almost always a medical or health care professional who killed patients as the ultimate control, or even in some twisted desire to end their misery, or the "Black Widow," a woman who married or mated with the intention of killing her spouse or lover for his or her savings or insurance money.

Serial killing was a completely separate psychology, more accurately known as sexual homicide. As with rape, the motive was sexual gratification by violence, often accompanied by sadism. And women didn't do it. The women who killed in tandem with a male partner were sexually and physically dominated by that partner. Even Aileen Wuornos, infamous as the only identified female serial killer, was actually considered by the best profilers Roarke knew to be a vigilante killer, not a sexual predator.

So statistically, the chances of the woman he had seen being a sexual predator — especially considering the physical appearances of at least two of the two murdered men — were less than zero.

A female vigilante, *though?*

Roarke felt cold and hot, a combined rush of sensations that he was accustomed to, always a clear signal that he was onto something important.

He thought of Coleman's words about Wann: "*A whole hell of a lot of people didn't like him.*" And Alder's words about Milvia: "*Preacherman pissed a lot of people off, it was his nature. Guy like that is going to come to bad ends one way or another.*"

It was a link, a shared characteristic: These had not been good guys.

So, a non-*professional killer? A vigilante?*

He had a sudden image of the single, bare room in the Tenderloin, scrubbed down with bleach.

If that's a non-*professional, we're in trouble, here,* he thought uneasily.

But he was getting ahead of himself. Right now, he could file the idea as possible, but only possible, not anything near probable.

He walked slowly across the bricks of the plaza toward the arena seating, feeling the wind ruffle his hair and push into his overcoat. The fast-moving clouds above cast moving shadows on the plaza, turning the whole space into an impressionistic blur of movement.

As he reached the graduated curves of seating, a couple of transients with signs stared toward him balefully. He knew they recognized him as law enforcement. He met each man's gaze, one, then the other, sending out a clear message: *Don't make trouble and I won't make it for you* — as he moved past them to take a place in the seats. He was not alone; there were perhaps two dozen scattered random citizens: a young Asian female wearing earbuds, textbooks spread out around her; a tired-looking later-in-life Caucasian mother walking a toddler along the circular rim of seats, with an infant nestled against her chest in a sling; another mixed-race male student type dozing flat on his back; a cowled nun knitting something elaborate and unrecognizable out of fuzzy multicolored yarn; an older European-looking man just slumped, lost in thought. All completely innocuous.

Roarke settled himself facing straight toward the "stage," the half-circle of brick pavement below, and let his mind drift, picturing Milvia's face from the mug shot and conjuring the Preacherman walking the bricks: sunburned, hungover, his burning bloodshot eyes crackling as he ranted about the Apocalypse.

The Beast.

And she had watched him, watched him intently, for hours.

Roarke concentrated, saw her sitting before him, blond and lithe in a long coat, sunglasses hiding her face, leaning forward on her thighs, focused straight ahead.

Did you have the razor in your pocket then? Were you fingering it as you watched him circle and rant?

What were you looking for? What did he say that caught your attention? What did you see, that would make you kill him? Were you looking for anyone, *and he was there, or was it something about* him? *Did he accost you earlier, "get in your face," as Detective Alder said was his habit?*

What were you looking at for two to three solid hours?

He looked toward the bricks again, imagining Milvia pacing below him. The more vividly he pictured the Preacherman, the more troubled Roarke felt. Wann hadn't been a choirboy, but his extreme obesity made him an easier person to outmaneuver. Preacherman, by contrast, had been lean, hyped up, and out of his mind, in Roarke's experience a lethal combination. The idea of a woman approaching him late at night, even asleep, even drunk, even though she had a razor...

It was off the charts.

And then there was that question hovering at the back of his mind.

Why Greer? What did she see in Greer? Where does Greer fit in on that spectrum, her spectrum?

He didn't know Greer well, personally, though he knew him to be a damn fine undercover. But undercover was a different world, with a different set of rules. Thrown into the temptations of the criminal underworld, cops and agents went bad more often than anyone on the job wanted to admit.

Roarke pulled his mind away from that line of thought. Right now, he needed to focus on *her*.

He stood from his brick seat, filled with a raw impatience to be doing something, anything, to get to the next level, and started walking back across the plaza, just to move.

He was at a crossroads, the next step maddeningly unclear.

If what he was thinking was on the right track, then there were other victims. He didn't even want to think about how many other victims, about how long she could have been trolling, killing and remaining completely under the radar because no one would have thought to look.

How do you pick them? he thought at her.

For that matter, how are you picking your cities? Salt Lake, Portland, San Francisco... are you only working in the West, or do you roam the entire country? Is it only cities?

Should he go back to San Francisco and try to pick up her trail there?

You left the SRO, does that mean you left the Bay Area?
Where are you going next?

He looked up just at that moment and was startled to find himself staring up at a towering signpost, with a thicket of arrows pointing all directions not just to Portland attractions like WATERFRONT and MT. ST. HELENS, but world cities and famous attractions: TIMES SQUARE, 2400 mi.; WALDEN POND, 2500 mi.; CASABLANCA, 5637 mi.

He had see it before, of course, it was one of the Square's public sculptures. But at the moment it seemed surreally ripped directly from inside his own head. He had an urge to laugh, and had to fight it down.

She really could be anywhere, by now.

All right, then, start on the computer? Get plugging other possible search criteria into the databases?

He reached for his phone even as he thought it. Singh was brilliant at the kind of wide-net brainstorming required to manipulate the crime databases into coughing up suspects.

And while Singh got to work on that, he saw two avenues for himself. He could work the past cases in order to find some link between the victims, or he could return to San Francisco and try to pick up her trail.

He thought briefly of driving to the airport and catching the first flight back to the city, of getting back to the freshest trail.

Then he realized that there *was* someone in Portland who might be able to help him.

Who might be able to tell him he wasn't crazy.

Who might be his best lead to her.

Chapter 18

She sits in a café on the boardwalk, now comfortably disguised in her drugstore purchases, her hair tucked up in the cap. Her legs are folded up under her on the low couch and she sips from a giant latte as she browses the discarded newspapers scattered on the wide coffee tables.

There is a good selection: the L.A. *Times*, the San Luis Obispo *Tribune*, the Santa Barbara *News-Press*, and several smaller local papers. As is to be expected, the murder is front and center:

Brutal Slaying of Trucker at Central Coast Rest Stop.

All the articles showcase two points: the savagery of the slaying and the fact that the police have no idea as to motive. The fact that the trucker was killed in the women's restroom does not appear in any article; apparently the investigators are withholding that detail.

If they'd printed it, the motive would be a little more clear, she thinks, but it is her lifetime experience that people have an infinite capacity for ignoring the obvious. Of course it would be even clearer if she'd left the trucker's knife where he'd dropped it, but she hadn't known at the time if he'd scratched her, if there might be trace evidence on the blade. No matter; the trucker is taken care of, whether people understand what he was or not.

At the end of most of the articles there is a tip number given to report "any information," and she memorizes it, in case she needs at some point to create a diversion. But is no mention of a woman, the car, or anything else incriminating and it is likely there never will be. She will simply have to monitor the situation and remain alert, her perpetual state of being in any and all events.

She puts aside the newspapers and turns her thoughts to more pleasant and pressing matters. The new clothes she is wearing are good camouflage for the beach, but for the man, she will need something different.

She finishes her latte, savoring the perfect creaminess, and then leaves the café.

She walks along the main street with the sun on her skin. Most of the young women walking the sidewalks are in bikini tops and micro-shorts. Her own oversized T-shirt serves her well as protective covering; she gets barely a glance from most of the men she passes. The beach is seeming like a better hiding place every minute.

The little beach shops have halter dresses, both cheap and pretty, batiks in tropical colors. She browses in no great hurry, matching her pace to the rhythm of the sea and the slowly shifting clouds, and finds a sea-green dress printed with abstract fish and starfish. The boy will like the creatures and the man will like the dress. She tries it on with a fringed silver and green pareo, a length of batik material that female bathers wrap around their waists like sarongs. For her it makes a striking scarf, and covers what it needs to cover.

She puts her shorts and T-shirt into her beach bag, and leaves the dressing room to buy the dress. And then in a flash of inspiration, she stops by the Dunes, the beach hotel where she has told the father she is staying. The attached café sells pink T-shirts and beach bags with the hotel logo; she buys one of them and a pink signature visor as well, subliminal back up for her story.

She isn't worried about finding them again. She walks unhurriedly out onto the pier, where she sits on a bench in the sun, with the surf crashing right under the rough planks beneath her feet, and smooths herself all over with lotion. The jasmine fragrance is light and soothing and a million light years away from the scene at the rest stop, and she takes a deep breath of the light and teasing sea air.

When she is ready, she stands, and walks barefoot down the stairs, out over the warm sand to the water's edge, and drifts along the foamy water line, not thinking of anything but the light, the warmth, the feel of the sand and the water. She sees the shapes of them first, one tall and one very small, shadows against the silver sunlight. The small shape breaks free and barrels forward, little running feet that make barely a ripple of vibration in the earth or air, until he is right upon her, grabbing her hand as he races by.

And immediately the father's voice, pleased and embarrassed. "Jase, come on, you don't just—"

Before he can finish his sentence she spins around like a top, pretending to have been set in motion by the strength of the boy's blow, and takes him down with her as she tumbles to the sand in a heap. The boy dissolves in delighted giggles. She feels his sweet little boy weight on top of her, the aliveness of him, a whole human being in just fifty pounds.

She remains sprawled in the sand until the father catches up with them, and looks up at him from her prone position as he pulls Jason up off of her. When she sits up, she takes her time.

"Dangerous sea monsters on this beach," she mock-complains. "Very fast sea monsters."

"They really should post signs," Mark Sebastian says.

"Except it might scare away the tourists." She is still sitting, bare legs stretched out in the sand. Jason drops to his knees in front of her.

"We're going to the butterflies," the boy informs her excitedly. She knows about this, vaguely, one of the attractions of the area, the migrating Monarch butterflies. There are colonies of them scattered up and down the coast.

Sebastian reaches down to her. She puts her hand in his and lets him pull her up to standing. The electric charge is unmistakable, undeniable, and it is a moment before he releases her hand.

"He said you were out here," the man says, looking at her. "He wanted to find you." He pauses, and adds, "So did I."

"Well, good," she says. "I wouldn't want to miss the butterflies."

Chapter 19

It was tucked into a cul-de-sac in a forested neighborhood. The beamed house with glass walls and an arched red door like the entrance to a Hobbit house, in the middle of a clutch of pine trees, presently drifting with mist under ominously darkening skies.

Roarke hadn't set foot in it since his BAU days.

At the time the legendary Chuck Snyder had been the Supervisory Special Agent of the BAU 3, which provided investigative support in solving serial or mass murders and other violent crimes to local law enforcement throughout the country, and Roarke was part of Snyder's team on the Street Hunter killings, a series of murder/mutilations of street youth in their late teens and twenties that had ended up teaming agents from the Seattle, San Francisco and Portland offices.

Now semi-retired from the field, Snyder traveled all over the world instructing law enforcement agencies in the psychology of the most violent offenders. But his home base was Portland, and Roarke was pumped to find that he was in town and willing to meet with him.

The threatening skies finally opened and rain poured down as the older man opened the door. Roarke looked in on the Snyder he remembered: slightly Nordic looks, a little taller than average, the face of a battlefield surgeon or a priest. Lighting cracked across the sky, like an ominous omen from a movie, and both men laughed.

"I knew one day you'd come back through that dark door," Snyder told him, as he gestured him in.

"Looks red to me," Roarke deadpanned, and walked into a house that he used to know well; he'd learned much of what he knew about the darkest side of humanity in these rooms.

Snyder closed the door behind him, and the men clasped hands warmly; then the older man stepped back to study Roarke in a manner that was pure Snyder, unapologetically assessing, yet pensive in a way that made it hard for people to take offense.

"Matthew, you look good. Intent, but good."

"So do you," Roarke returned.

Actually Snyder showed the last five years of age, but he retained a gentle calm, an equanimity that belied the horrors he still faced every day. Roarke had not been able to maintain the same balance himself. It was a part of his life he hadn't examined lately, and he found himself more uncomfortable than he had expected to be, face to face with his past.

Rather than think about it, Roarke moved without invitation toward the study, as if no time had passed at all. He stepped into the room and looked out through a wall of windows at the green forest beyond the redwood deck. The rain was already coming down in sheets, gray and ominous. Then he turned to survey the room. It was much as he remembered: a comfortable sitting area, a huge desk under a window, and on the wall-to-wall bookshelves, Snyder's terrible library of the worst crimes ever perpetrated against human beings. Snyder was an academic not unlike Roarke's own father, but he was also a lawman, a hunter who was uncomfortable behind a desk, only truly himself in the field.

Snyder moved to the comfortable leather armchairs by the window, and lowered himself into one of them, just a tad slowly. Roarke pretended not to notice. "A sufficiently gloomy day for a dark visit, I wager," Snyder said, with a glance toward the windows. Then he turned that laser focus on Roarke. "What's troubling you, Matthew?"

Roarke sat in the opposite chair, although what he really wanted to do was pace. "I've got a strange one for you."

"A strange one," Snyder said. Of course "strange" didn't begin to cover what constituted his daily work. "How thoughtful of you."

"Well, I missed your birthday," Roarke said with a straight face.

Snyder lifted a hand. "Then, by all means."

Roarke looked at his old mentor head-on. "I think I have a female hunter."

This got no more than a raised eyebrow from Snyder, but Roarke knew he'd gotten the profiler's attention; he could feel a heightened stillness in the air between them as he continued.

"I lost an undercover agent right in front of me, hit by a truck on a busy city street. Timing too convenient to be a coincidence. I thought it might have been a hit, and that's still my best guess. The woman was on the sidewalk behind him. A witness saw her say something to my man just before he stepped out into the street, and that's how he died. I only wanted to talk to her as a witness, but when we tracked her down, she'd been staying in an SRO, left that day, and had scrubbed the whole place down with bleach."

It was always enormously focusing just to talk to Snyder, to put the facts and his own thoughts in order with someone who would understand every implication. The agent was nodding, probably not even aware that he was doing so; Roarke could sense his brain clicking.

"So yeah, I know the stats on female assassins. Aside from a few political revolutionaries — zero. And the chances of the crime ring my man was investigating sending a woman to off him? Unlikely in the extreme."

Then Roarke found himself saying something he hadn't said to anyone before, even himself. "But I saw her. She was..." he didn't have a word for it at first. "She was *there*. She was focused. She had intent. I didn't know what it was at the time, but she was—"

"Hunting," Snyder said.

Roarke met his gaze, and nodded. "Hunting."

Snyder raised his hand again, inviting him to continue.

"I don't have a clear physical description of her. She's late twenties, slim but healthy, intense. Attractive. She was wearing sunglasses and possibly a wig. But she wore a sleeveless turtleneck, and that's how I got two more hits out of VICAP. A woman of that description wanted for questioning in the deaths of two men, one in Salt Lake City last year, one here in Portland in April, the first a suspicious accident, a fall from a building under construction, and the other the murder of a transient. The killer slashed his throat while he was sleeping under a bridge."

Roarke went on to detail his interviews with Detective Coleman and Detective Alder about Wann and Preacherman. Throughout the account, Snyder never broke his intent focus and attention on Roarke, though sometimes his eyes were far away, visualizing.

"So?" Snyder waited.

Roarke looked at him. "So I'd like to hear your analysis."

"I'd like to hear yours," Snyder said calmly.

Roarke felt a rush of irritation — that he immediately realized was something more than irritation, it was anger rising from somewhere deep inside him. Roarke didn't want to go back into the mindset. He'd walked away from this part of the job years ago. Snyder knew about his choice, knew why, as much as Roarke had been able to explain. He had been expecting — hoping — Snyder would do the analysis for him.

Instead, Snyder was looking at him, waiting, and Roarke knew there was no way out.

So he stood from his chair, and when he spoke, his voice grated. "Working on the proposition that she killed these three victims... This is not a spree killer. The three deaths occurred over a time period of more than a year and a half, and it's reasonable to assume a cooling-off period. She's a traveler, with no apparent pattern to her choices. So far the killings are only on the West Coast, but the geographic radius is huge, three states so far. And chances are high that there are other murders; the *only* reason I was able to connect the three deaths was because of the high collar she was wearing, and it's fairly certain that there could be reports of other deaths in which that detail does not appear."

Snyder was nodding slightly, following.

"The victims are adult white men, age range from thirty-three to fifty-two. So far she's hunting within her own ethnic group." It was rare for serial killers to cross ethnic lines. "One vic was married, two were not. Two appeared to be accidents, only one was an obvious murder. There was no ritualistic behavior that I can see, no trophies taken, no staging of the bodies or the scenes, except for the basic attempt to make the transient's murder look like a robbery. All three killings took place outdoors, never in the men's homes. They lived in and were killed in different states; they had different professions and were from different socioeconomic levels. I have agents following up with the victims' families and acquaintances, but they do not appear to have known each other."

"Random targets?" Snyder murmured.

Roarke shook his head tightly. "I don't think so. Agent Greer may have been randomly targeted, chosen because of opportunity, but she would have had to follow the Portland victim back to the culvert where he was killed, and the Salt Lake City victim was up on the twentieth floor of an unfinished building. She would have had to meet him or lure him up there. And in the SLC case she was described as being dressed as a prostitute. That shows planning."

"So the victims appear to have been specifically chosen," Snyder said.

"Yes."

"What's the overlap?"

Again, inevitably, the subject had turned to the one Roarke did not like to think about.

"The detectives on both the Wann case and the Preacherman case said something similar about each man. Something to the effect of: 'This was not a good guy.'"

Snyder looked across at Roarke, and of course, asked quietly, "And your man Greer?"

Roarke shifted uncomfortably. "He was a good agent. He was undercover, doing some significant drug buys from this crime ring. I'm sure he wasn't coming off like an angel. He could have rubbed any number of people the wrong way."

Snyder looked out the window at the rain, and didn't say anything for a long time. "You're right. It's a strange one."

Roarke started to sit on the arm of the couch, but instantly stood again. "I wanted to see you to see if — I don't even know. See if it's possible. To see what kind of psychology it would take for a young woman to be hunting adult men, if it turns out it's *not* for money."

Snyder looked maddeningly neutral. "I don't have to tell you the basis for profiling. We work with statistics and patterns to predict probable behavior. So what do you see, based on the statistics?"

Roarke suppressed another wave of anger, then forced himself to access the mindset. It was a moment before he could answer, but when he did, it was calmly and evenly. "There's no medical setting, so I'm not looking at an Angel of Death; and the woman has no marital or otherwise intimate relationship with the victims that we know of; she didn't inherit because of the deaths, so she's not a Black Widow. There are a few high profile cases of women who have helped a male partner kill multiple victims, or lured them for her partner to kill. But a lone woman committing serial stranger murder like this? The only previous example we've got to go on is Aileen Wuornos, a mentally unstable prostitute who was acting out rage built up over a lifetime of sexual abuse, by killing johns whom she claimed had raped or attempted to rape her."

Roarke finally stopped. He felt lightheaded, and slightly nauseous. Snyder looked at him with a look that was both approving and sad. "Just so. You have a gift for this, you always have."

Roarke felt his defenses rising, and then forced himself to stay calm; there was no point in rehashing old arguments. He'd made his choices and Snyder knew it.

"I must have been channeling you," he said.

"Hardly," Snyder said.

Roarke forced himself to breathe. "You interviewed Wuornos. I didn't. I would really like to know what you think."

Apparently Snyder had been satisfied with Roarke's account, because he finally started to speak.

"Yes, Wuornos. An extraordinary case, a masculine-identified bisexual. And very possibly born with a Y chromosome. It's to my eternal regret that she did not undergo karyotype testing before her execution."

Roarke couldn't speculate as to what his mystery woman's sexuality was, but he knew she didn't present as aggressively butch. Not even close.

Snyder continued after a slow, thoughtful pause. "Wuornos never knew her father; he committed suicide while in prison for the rape and attempted murder of an eight-year old boy. Wuornos was raised by her grandparents and claimed childhood sexual abuse by her grandfather, which I have no reason to doubt. Possibly there was an incestuous relationship with her brother as well."

Snyder had not consulted any notes; he was recounting all this from memory; Roarke knew he could have been equally detailed about any serial killer anyone might name.

"She suffered stranger rape at fourteen, from which she became pregnant. She gave birth in a home for unwed mothers and gave the child up for adoption, shortly after which her grandmother died of liver failure, and her grandfather threw Wuornos out of the house. So at age fifteen she was living in the woods and supporting herself as a prostitute — a life of constant sexual exploitation."

Roarke felt himself roiling with unwanted feelings: tired rage at the state of humanity, reluctant sympathy for Wuornos, a desire to turn away from all of the implications for his own case.

Snyder rolled on relentlessly.

"Wuornos lived a marginal existence; along with the prostitution and various convictions for assault she was a convicted armed robber and forger, and was diagnosed with Borderline Personality Disorder. Then in a single year between November 1989 and November 1990 she shot and killed seven men. Five of those men were killed within a two-and-one-half month period, an extremely compressed time frame much more typical of spree killers than serial murderers. There was not the cooling-off period we find almost universally in the sexual homicide model, and while Wuornos may have been experiencing sexual gratification from her murders, in the interviews I did with her all I sensed from her was rage."

Roarke remembered some of the information from his training; it was all coming back.

"As to her motivation: she initially entered a plea of self-defense, claiming that all seven of her victims had raped her or attempted to rape her, but she later recanted, saying that her first victim Richard Mallory was the only one of her victims who had raped her, and that the others 'only began to start to.' Mallory had in fact been incarcerated for attempted rape and during that time was evaluated as having 'sociopathic tendencies'. Personally I believe Wuornos *was* raped by Mallory and that was her trigger incident, the stressor that began the series of killings, which she acted out in a spree."

Roarke paced beside the window, looking out at the volcanoes in the storm. "So my killer could be coming from a sexually abusive background, possibly presents with Borderline Personality Disorder, and could have experienced a violent trigger incident."

Snyder spread his hands. "Based on what little we have to compare the case to, it's an obvious potential scenario."

"Or it's none of the above."

Snyder gave him a rueful look. "Exactly. The trouble is, there is no established psychology to look to, here. In other words, a live one. You have your work cut out for you. I will be fascinated to see how it all unfolds."

"Actually I was going to send you out into the field after her," Roarke said.

Snyder half-smiled. "I wouldn't want to get in your way. But thank you for the interesting birthday present. You know me too well." He rose. "You're staying for dinner, of course, and staying the night."

Roarke was set to automatically demur, and then he realized that would be crazy. For one thing, it was pouring; outside the window the rain was thundering down in what looked like a solid wall of water. For another, if he stayed, he could take the rest of the night to pick Snyder's brain. "Thank you. I will." He stood, and then he looked at Snyder. "But you do think it's possible."

Snyder looked back. "I have no doubt." He paused, and met Roarke's eyes. "As you know, we haven't seen anyone like Wuornos before or since. But to be perfectly blunt, I've never understood why we *don't* see more women acting out in a similar way. God knows enough of them have reason."

Chapter 20

The butterfly grove is in the state park south of the main beach, too long a trek for the boy, so the three walk back to the beach house for Sebastian's car.

The house is exactly as she envisioned, a two million dollar slice of heaven at the edge of the bluffs at the more private end of the beach, where the hotels and condos give way to private homes, from newer McMansions to 1940's bungalows and villas. It is not a rental, but the father's own, a comfortable little gem: two stories, a large white and yellow square with a smaller square on top, both with wraparound decks, walls of windows with breathtaking views of the ocean and the entire crescent of the bay, and even a lovely drought-resistant garden of lilies, statice, succulents and sweet alyssum.

They do not go into the house and the father does not claim it as his, but she has noticed unmistakable signs of ownership: the boy pats each inset light on the stairs on the way up the cliff, counting under his breath, and at the top of the stairs he runs to the mailbox in front of the house to check for mail.

The car parked in the driveway is a late-model hybrid SUV. Luxury and social responsibility, a winning combination for those who can afford it. And this beautiful piece of property is a second home only; the man has said they are there for six days.

She waits, looking up into the sun, as the man straps the boy into the car seat in the back, something the boy endures with practiced resignation. Then the man opens the passenger door for her, making an effort not to stand as close as he wants to. She can feel the warmth of his body, and smell him, a clean, expensive soap and his own male scent underneath. It is an odd thing that they are doing together; they both know it, and it is bonding them.

She sits in the passenger seat. The car is clean, well cared for, like the man and the boy. It still has a new car smell, a fragrance of safety and comfort. She turns around in the seat and smiles at the boy. She has not shared a car like this in she can't even think how many years; she has not been so close to normal people in quite some time. When the man gets into the car and starts the engine, they look like a family. It is a great irony, and a great cover.

The butterfly grove has a big public parking lot and wide circles of paths through the enormous trees, set off by wood post fencing. She and the man and the boy get out of the car and walk on the gray-green gravel path past the docent trailer decorated with paintings of the delicate orange and black Monarchs. The boy is tugging at her dress, the dress, which the man has also noticed. The boy points out the display boards picturing the life cycle of the butterflies, and the maps of the migration. The boards tell them that in the late fall through winter, the Monarchs sleep in the eucalyptus groves of the central coast. She understands perfectly; there is something ancient and calming about the massive, smooth-trunked trees, and the spicy fragrance of the dry olive-colored leaves is warm and peaceful. If she could sleep in a grove like this for four months, she would, herself.

They walk down the path, with pines and eucalyptus towering above them breathing oxygen and chlorophyll into the air. Their feet crunch on strips of papery bark and eucalyptus buds. She can see the man looking at her bare legs and sandaled feet. They walk close, but he does not touch her, yet. The boy takes his father's hand and then takes her hand with his other, so the three of them are linked, with the boy in the middle. Just exactly like a family.

The path opens onto a wide circle in the heart of the grove. There are already dozens of people gathered, faces turned up to the trees, where there are basketball-sized clusters of what look like brown leaves.

The man lifts the boy up to his chest and the boy comfortably settles on his arm, hooks his legs around his father's waist, so the three of them are the same height. "Those are them," the boy informs her, pointing. "The brown baskets. They're asleep."

"Lazy things." She smiles at him.

"They're tired," he says earnestly. "They fly a long, long way. And they have to sleep to fly again. They sleep together to keep warm."

The man's eyes touch hers, then he quickly looks away. She keeps her focus on the boy. "You know a lot about them," she says.

"We're big butterfly fans, aren't we, Jase?" The man looks at her again. "He's a walking encyclopedia of wildlife."

"I can see that," she says, not smiling.

One restless sleeper emerges from the brown ball and flutters by them, landing for a poised, breathing moment on one of the wooden rails of the fence, wings slowly pulsing, and the three of them gaze down at it. Orange wings outlined with black, and delicate black veins on the orange, with white spots like stars in the black outlining.

"They're bugs, you know," the boy says loftily.

"Insects," his father says, trying not to smile.

"No," she says to the boy, in mock shock. "They're way too pretty to be bugs."

"Uh huh," the boy insists. "Bugs."

"I can never think of them as bugs," the father says. "They're not like — other bugs."

"They're bugs," the boy says imperiously, then concedes, "Pretty bugs."

A group of tourists with cameras ambles down the path, following an elderly but spry docent in brown khaki shorts and white T-shirt, expounding for his group. "Pismo Beach is home to the largest over-wintering colony of Monarchs in the US. Every fall, the Monarch begins a long journey. First they fly inland, to the foothills of the Sierra Nevada mountains. They lay their eggs there on milkweed plants, and then the butterflies die."

"The caterpillars eat poison!" the boy tells her in a loud whisper. "So no one will eat them!"

The docent overhears, and nods vigorously. "Right you are, young man. The eggs hatch and the larvae eat the poisonous milk-weed leaves, incorporating the toxins into their bodies to poison predators. The caterpillars molt four times before they form a chrysalis, a protective shell in which the entire body of the caterpil-lar is transformed into a butterfly. The butterflies emerge from the chrysalis and this second generation flies across the Sierra Nevada mountains, to feast on the nectar of flowers in Oregon, Nevada, or Arizona. It will take them eighteen hundred miles and four genera-tions before their descendants return to where their great-grand-parents started."

Beside her, the father stirs, looking up toward the clustered sleep-ing butterflies. "Eighteen hundred miles. Practically half the country," he marvels. "Those tiny things. I don't know how they do it."

"But why do they leave?" the boy asks loudly. His face is cloudy and his small body is tense, leaned away from his father, and there is the distinct sense that he is asking about more than the butterflies.

"No one knows," his father says softly.

"It's nice here," the boy says darkly. "They shouldn't leave." He looks ominously on the verge of tears.

She speaks without thinking. "Nature tells them to," she says. The boy looks at her.

"How?"

"The wind talks to them. The ocean talks to them. The stars move in the sky, and the seasons change, and the butterflies listen, and something in them says, 'Go.'"

"But *why*?" the boy asks. Fate rests in the question, and she takes her time before she answers.

"Because Nature has plans. It all fits together, and we don't see it most of the time, but there is a plan."

The boy frowns, but this time it is concentration, not a tantrum. "Does Nature talk to us?"

She can feel the father's intense focus on her, although she does not look at him.

"All the time. If you listen."

"How?" asks the boy.

"How did you find me on the beach?" she counters.

The boy pauses, thinking. "I just knew. And you were there."

"Well, maybe the sun said, 'Who wouldn't be on the beach on such a beautiful day? I, Sun, am on the beach. The wind is on the beach. The beach is on the beach.'"

The boy giggles at this, and keeps giggling, in that infectious way that children have.

"Anyone with a brain in their head is on the beach," she continues. "Everyone who is anyone is on the beach. So I was on the beach and the wind and the waves and the sun told you, and you found me."

As the boy is silent, considering, a wind ruffles through the trees, and above them, the brown basketballs start to rustle and stir... and then break apart in a flurry of color, hundreds and thousands of delicate, winged creatures. The crowd around them breathes in, a sound of pure pleasure.

"The wind told them to wake up," the boy says excitedly.

"It did," she says back. Around them are fluttering spots of orange. The whole sky is full of them now, and the whispery beat of their wings.

"Do the butterflies talk, too?" the boy asks, eyes fixed on the tiny bright shapes.

"Let's listen and see," she says.

The butterfly cloud envelops them; there are spots of orange everywhere. And the man looks only at her.

On the path back, the docent strikes up a conversation with the boy, who is happy to demonstrate his superior knowledge of the Monarchs. She walks a little more slowly, deliberately, and the father falls back as well, drifting closer to her under the whispering eucalyptus, and the barely audible beating of wings. "Thanks," he says softly.

She lifts her shoulders, but she knows what he is saying. There is something fragile about the boy. She has picked up on it from the start. But it is a growing awareness, now. For all the boy's precocity, the father worries. Nothing specific, it is a free-floating anxiety that occasionally spikes in intensity with no clear reason that she can see. She can sense it all, and more.

She does not judge this, nor does she seek answers, she merely observes. What she is to know will be revealed. It is the way.

"That wasn't about butterflies, obviously," the man continues.

"No," she says.

"I'm divorced," he says, and she senses a huge release in him. "In case you were wondering."

She glances at him. He is joking, the pain making it sound self-deprecatory. "I wasn't really," she says.

"That obvious," he says. She doesn't answer, doesn't need to.

Before he can say more, Jason is racing back. He grabs both their hands again, pulling them forward.

"I hope you didn't have other plans for dinner," the father says to her, over Jason's head. "I don't think he's going to let you go."

She smiles at the father. "I've been kidnapped, huh?"

"Kidnapped!" the boy says joyfully.

"Then I guess I surrender," she says.

Chapter 21

The beach house is as perfectly lovely inside as it is out.

As the man and the boy walk her in, her eyes go quickly to the exits; as always in an enclosed space, she is planning escape routes. There is the front door they have just come through. A back kitchen door leading to the garage. A hallway to a bedroom and bath, a stairway up to the top cube, what is obviously the master suite. The sunny living room has French doors leading out to the deck, which access the stairs down to the beach, and at this she relaxes, for the moment. As she exclaims over the view and compliments the coziness of the house, she is looking closely at the contents, assessing.

The living room has a fireplace, and above the fireplace mantel are framed photos of the boy and his father and older people who must be grandparents. There is also an actual oil painting of the boy, a little younger.

There are other obvious indicators of wealth; the latest flat screen TV, the high-end kitchen appliances. She revises her estimate of the man's income up another zero, and is glad that the slightly worse-for-wear clothes he first saw her in were designer items; even under the circumstances he had been able to see what he wanted to see. The alcoholic wife, or ex-wife, obviously clouds his judgment of women; it makes him vulnerable to damaged types. Whether or not he understands that about himself, it is useful for her purposes.

But she has no illusions; ultimately, she is here because of the boy. The father doesn't trust his own judgment, but he trusts his son's.

The tour does not include the master suite, but she has gotten a glimpse from the outside: three almost solid walls of windows, and a massive brass bed taking up nearly the entire room. It would be like floating on top of the world, in the middle of the sky with the whole of the ocean spread out beneath.

Once she has had the tour, she sits on a barstool at the breakfast bar and watches as the boy orders his father around the kitchen, deciding on fish for the adults and hot dogs for himself, choosing the oils and condiments and plates. All of the supervising is done entirely without brattiness, but rather in a way that makes her think the divorce is very fresh; it is the boy who is holding his father together.

They take all the assembled foodstuffs outside to the deck to cook on the grill, with the ocean a vast sparkling canvas in front of them. The man cannot stop stealing looks at her.

They have managed to go much longer than grown people usually do without disclosing professions, backgrounds. He likes not having to say, of course, he's wealthy, and doesn't want to think that is his primary attraction. But as he expertly prepares the meal, combining oils and spices and basting with a pleasing masculine economy of motion, he brings it up anyway.

"You haven't asked me what I do."

She half-shrugs. "We're at the beach."

He laughs, a surprised sound. "So, don't ask, don't tell?"

"Or don't ask, and tell what you want to."

"Well, if you're going to wheedle it out of me," he says in mock-irritation, and she smiles. "We have an olive ranch."

"An olive ranch?" she repeats, looking at him.

"What, I don't look like a rancher?"

She smiles again, finding that uncharacteristically comfortable to do. "I wasn't aware that olives needed ranching."

"Oh, but they do," he says with a perfectly straight face. "Constant need of ranching. You'd be surprised what they get up to, unsupervised."

She reaches and picks up the bottle of green-gold oil he has been using to cook with. "So you made this." The label reads *Artemis*.

"My father, actually. The ranch is his. It was his father's. They're growers. I'm more of a manager."

"A dynasty," she says, without inflection.

He looks at her. "A family business. Some of our trees were brought over by Spanish missionaries. These days it's more of an agribusiness, high-density orchards. But I love those old trees."

He does not add that he wants to show her the ranch, it is too much, too soon. But it is implicit in everything he says.

It is easier to talk to him than she thought. In truth it is a relief to be with someone who is so simply earnest. The darkness in him comes only from a wound from a dark person. The rest of him is light, a pocket of innocence. But now it is her turn to talk, she knows; there will have to be a story, a façade of a normal life. She has many. For the man, something creative, and quirky. She tells him she is a researcher.

He pauses in the midst of drizzling more of the oil over a salad of dark greens and looks at her, intrigued. "For who?"

"Anyone. Writers. Producers."

"Hollywood," he says, already creating the details for her. It is always amazing to her how quick men are to guess, to fill in, doing all the work for you. And how much they enjoy being right. "Interesting work," he says. "There's always something new."

"And people send me on trips," she agrees.

"Is this a research trip, then?"

"No, this is for me."

He glances at her from the grill. "And how's it working out for you?"

She holds his eyes. "So far, everything is fine."

He smiles and turns the fish.

"Just fine," she repeats to herself.

Chapter 22

Snyder's guest bedroom had dark hardwood floors covered with a thick Middle Eastern carpet, and a wall of windows looking out in the misty trees and drenched undergrowth.

Roarke showered in the skylit bathroom, with his past washing over him as well, as hot needles of water worked themselves into his subconscious, bringing the memories to the surface.

The BAU was once the hottest division of the Bureau, the plum assignment that agents from all over the country fought to get. *Hell, yeah, I want to go toe-to-toe with the baddest of the bad, evil incarnate, the lowest life forms that walk the earth.*

Put just one of these monsters out of commission — the child sellers, the serial rapists, the mutilators, the torturers — lock just one of the breathing, crawling scum away for the rest of their miserable lives, and the entire balance of the world shifts. Who wouldn't want a license to do it?

It had been Roarke's dream since he was a kid. Not many trainees coming through Quantico had started reading criminal forensics textbooks at age nine. In fact, on his tenth birthday Matt Roarke had written a letter to the then-Director of the FBI stating his intention to come to Washington and be an FBI agent.

Roarke's father was a physics professor who disdained sports and all non-intellectual professions and had his generation's distrust of the government. Roarke's older brother was a math whiz who was deconstructing COBOL on the science lab computers before personal computers even appeared on the market. Consequently Roarke Senior had been — "bemused" hardly began to cover it — by his younger son's non-negotiable, no-holds-barred career choice.

Roarke grimly ignored all opposition, took his BA at Cal Poly with a double major in psychology and criminal justice, and met the Bureau's work requirement by doing two years as a clinical psych intern. He got in just before 9/11 radically changed the Bureau's focus to counter-terrorism.

And Roarke had been good. He had a retentive memory for character patterns — or you could say he just had a knack, that extra something that put him on alert in the presence of a suspect or a lead. Even more than that, he was relentless in his desire to understand something incomprehensible, or failing understanding, to stop it cold.

He also had a knack for being noticed, and Snyder had seen something in him, had pulled him out of the pool, young. Roarke was one of the only recruits accepted for Behavioral Sciences training.

But working with killers in custody was different from hunting them in the field.

Roarke had never been able to adequately describe what had happened to him on the last profiling assignment he had performed for the BAU team. Snyder had accepted his transfer request with regret, but without protest.

But it was as Snyder had said on the stoop of his house. Roarke had known it wasn't over. He'd had his reprieve, his rest, and this time there would be no escaping what had been his path since that fatal year of his life, twenty-five years ago now but still haunting his dreams.

He reached to turn off the shower, and left the warmth to face it.

Dinner was served in the dining room by an obviously doting housekeeper who treated Snyder with irreverent reverence. Good wine, good food, and less dark conversation, several years of catching up. Snyder tactfully avoided the obvious question until the first bottle of Pinot was empty.

"And Monica?" he finally asked.

Roarke shook his head, and Snyder looked rueful, but not surprised. Snyder had never married, a fact that had not escaped Roarke's attention. Roarke had always suspected that the older man had seen too much to want to foist it on a loved one, which didn't bode well for Roarke's future.

Snyder pushed back his chair. "I imagine you'll want to check in with your team. The library is yours, of course, whatever you need."

"Access to your databases would be good."

"By the way, is she on a moon cycle?"

Roarke looked across the table at him, stupefied. Serial killers sometimes had a pattern of killing at the full moon. But he hadn't been looking for a serial killer, so he had never thought to check.

Snyder reached for an iPad, which Roarke hadn't noticed until that second, but which sat on the side serving table, so close Snyder didn't even have to get up. He punched up a lunar chart. "What are your murder dates?"

Roarke rattled them off as Snyder checked the charts.

"Edwin Wann: October seven, 2010."

"October seven was a full moon."

"John Joseph 'Preacherman' Milvia, April fourteen, 2012."

"Full moon."

The men looked at each other across the table. Roarke's mouth was dry as he spoke the last date. "Agent Kevin Greer, the twenty-first of this month." He held his breath as Snyder consulted the calendar.

"Ah. Not a full moon," Snyder said. "That was on the first of the month."

Roarke stood still, wondering what that meant. Then Snyder looked at the chart again, and something changed in his face.

"What?" Roarke asked, tense.

"There's a second full moon this month. A blue moon."

"When is the second?" Roarke demanded.

"Sunday. Five days from now," Snyder said.

Roarke stood silent, feeling a rollercoaster of adrenaline. He didn't know what it meant, but it sure as hell didn't sound good.

Snyder looked pensive. "The native Americans call the October full moon Hunter's Moon." His mouth quirked in an expression that was not quite a smile. "Perhaps the blue moon is the Huntress Moon."

Roarke had an uneasy feeling that he was right.

Roarke had called Epps earlier to let him know where he was, and to schedule a conference call. Now in Snyder's library, Roarke quickly set up the videoconferencing equipment, and connected with Epps. Antara Singh was at the conference table with him, carved gold bands glinting on her wrists as she arranged several stacks of files in front of her.

"Nice crib," Epps said, looking past Roarke to the bookcases and the wide windows.

Roarke forced himself to sit down at the desk so his agents wouldn't have to suffer his pacing on screen. On the screen behind Epps was the case board, a six-foot wide standing corkboard pinned with all the relevant details and photos pertaining to the case. The police sketch of the woman centered on the top of the board, and Roarke had to force his eyes from her image to begin.

"I've been consulting with Chuck Snyder of the BAU, and we're changing directions, here; we're going to add an entirely different psychology into the mix."

He could see the instant ripple of excitement in their faces.

"Entirely different?" Epps repeated.

"There are other murders. She's done this before. And possibly for a long time. We're looking at a profile that might be closer to an Aileen Wuornos than a paid assassin."

Roarke filled them in on his discussion with Snyder, the profile of Wuornos, the possible points of intersection with their killer.

Epps stared out at him from the screen. "You mean she's offing these guys for kicks?"

"Not for kicks. But something personal."

Roarke could see Epps processing this, his eyes narrowing.

"Wann frequented a strip bar. And Milvia, the Preacherman, was just an abrasive character in general."

"And Greer?" Epps pointed out.

"I know," Roarke said. "It's a theory. I'm not saying it adds up. But let's follow the track that she is preying on men in some way. And we need to investigate this prostitute connection."

Prostitutes, with their ever-changing names and a.k.a.s, their penchant for wigs and other identity-disguising accessories, and their transient lifestyles were hard enough to track in the databases even if you had a name. And Roarke wasn't in any way convinced she was a prostitute, but maybe there were other places besides Salt Lake City where she might have been mistaken for one.

He looked toward the dark-haired researcher on screen. "Singh, I need you to hit the databases tonight and do a comprehensive search for prostitutes fitting our suspect's description."

"Righto," she said.

"I want the police sketch going out to all law enforcement agencies in California, Oregon and Utah, and Arizona and Nevada for good measure. And Singh, I need you to search for murders of adult white men that occurred during full moons, as well as slashed throats, razor attacks, falls, and unusual accidents."

He paused. "And this is not for public consumption, but we need to look hard at Greer, see if there was some connection to prostitutes there."

Epps spoke up. "Boss, about that. Jones has been working our CIs, and one of them told him the shipment that Greer was monitoring, the one coming in on the day that he died, wasn't heroin." He paused before he finished, "It was women."

Roarke felt a white-hot tingling at the back of his ears. He had no idea what it meant, but it was too eerie a parallel for his liking. Greer had never said anything about a lead on human trafficking. Maybe he hadn't known. But what if he had?

What *if* he had?

Roarke found himself unable to answer his own mental question.

"Tell Jones to dig deeper," he said tightly.

After Singh had left the conference room, and before Epps signed off, he hesitated and looked into the screen, directly at Roarke. "This isn't new territory for you, is it?"

Roarke paused; he knew Epps didn't mean Portland. "Not entirely." His eyes went to the sketch of the woman on the case board. "But she... she may be something we've never seen before."

"Huntress Moon," Epps said, thoughtfully. And something deep inside Roarke shivered.

Chapter 23

When dinner is done, and the dishes are washed, she tells the father she should go, and though clearly he wants her to stay, he doesn't press it, it would be too odd.

He walks her not just to the door, but all the way down those long stairs on the cliff, back down to the beach.

"You know I can drop you off," he says for the third time.

She smiles without looking at him. "I'm here to walk on the beach."

And they stand for a moment in the dark, with the wind in their hair and the stars above them and the ocean gently rumbling in front of them. He looks down at the sand, then at her.

She lifts her eyebrows.

"I'm not used to this, 'Don't ask, don't tell' thing," he confesses.

"What would you like me to ask?" She lets her eyes hold his, and feels the heat from him instantly; there is more fire in him than he has been letting on.

He answers slowly. "Am I ready, maybe."

She lets that have the beat of meaning it deserves, then asks, "Are you?"

"We'll see," he says, in a way that makes her think there may be more to him than she is acknowledging.

She leaves him, then, feeling his wanting in her wake. She does not look back, but she lets her movements be easy and languid, knowing that he is watching her until she is an unrecognizable dark mark against the white glow of the surf.

The boy and the father are no longer merely on the path. They have, for the time being, become the path.

Chapter 24

The house lies on the outskirts of the desert community, lone and isolated. A strong wind blows over the surrounding land, swirling dust demons across the fields. The front gate in the split rail fence surrounding the large wooded yard stands open; the wind moves it and the wood seems to be alive, shivering. In the black of sky, a million stars tremble around the full moon.

He passes through the opening and moves up the dirt road, through the small grove of Eucalyptus and olive trees. The spicy scent surrounds him, the dry leaves whisper above. The house comes into sight through the trees, and he sees the front door is standing open as well.

The wind gusts around him and the feeling of doom closes in as he walks up the pavers toward the triangular arched front entrance... and stops just outside the open door.

Nothing but silence from the darkness within.

He steps through the open doorway, past the carved wooden door, into the entry hall with its white painted brick walls and tiled floor.

And then he sees the blood.

The horror comes rushing back over him. He has been here a hundred times before. Every detail is as it always is, the tiled floor, the white stucco walls, cold moonlight through the tall arched windows... and the harsh breath of the thing that is waiting for him at the end of the hallway.

He is no longer a man, but a boy, just a boy, no match for whatever lies behind that door. The terror has turned every cell in his body to ice; his feet can barely move him forward. On the floor around him is a pool of dark, he is up to his ankles in it, and it is not cold, like water, but warm, like...

Smells like....

Copper. Stink. Death.

And those crumpled shapes, on the floor around him, sleeping mounds... but not sleeping, no, the eyes are open, staring... an entire family, slaughtered.

But the horror of this bloodbath is nothing compared to the horror that lies behind the door, the thing that killed these people, that spilled their blood. A shadow looms that has been waiting for him since his birth, since the beginning of time. He can feel it reaching for him... feel the scream rising in his throat—

Roarke sat straight up in bed, grasping for the Glock under his pillow before he was even completely sure where he was, only knowing that the presence in the room is not a dream, it is real —

Then Snyder's voice cut through the dark, low and clear.

"Matthew, it's me. I'm sorry. I heard you..."

Roarke realized he must have shouted or cried out. He lowered his weapon and swiped at his face with a hand.

When he spoke, he was careful not to let his voice shake.

"Sorry. I'm... it's doing all this again. It's bringing it back."

"Forbes?" Snyder asked, a name Roarke hadn't heard or thought of in years.

"No," Roarke said. "Just a dream."

Snyder stood, a shadow in the dark, then nodded, knowing there was nothing to say. "Try to sleep," he said gently, and silently closed the door behind him.

DAY FOUR

Chapter 25

Roarke woke before dawn and could feel no other movement in the house.

He was still tense from the dream. It was the old dream, the dream he had been having since he was nine years old. It was everything he knew about evil, what people could do to each other; it was everything that had pulled him into law enforcement to begin with, and everything he feared.

But emotion was not helpful. The only solution was to keep moving.

He packed his few things, took the sketch of the woman and the photos of her three victims down from where he had taped them on the wall, and left Snyder a note on his desk.

Gone hunting. I'll be in touch.

He closed the red door behind him, and headed through the misty trees for his rental car with an odd sense of unease and anticipation. He'd given up profiling cold turkey. Now he really was back on the hunt. It was a weird curve in the road, and he wasn't sure how he felt about it.

Except urgency. Urgency that raced through his blood in an insistent pulse. Wherever she was, he was certain he had to find her soon.

It might already be too late.

· · · · ·

She sits on a dune, feeling the wind on her skin and inside her clothes, watching the sun rising, pouring waves of light out onto the sea.

And listening.

After a time she hears the light pounding of small feet, and then the boy flings himself down on the sand beside her. She strokes his hair as she looks up at the man.

The moon had been bright in the sky last night, almost full, climbing, seeking.

Today will show her the way.

Chapter 26

Our Lady of Mercy was a late eighteenth century neo-Gothic church, nestled between skyscrapers in downtown Portland.

The rain had cleared and the soup kitchen line was already around the block as Roarke made his way past ragged patrons down the side steps to the basement entrance.

Roarke had an uneasy relationship with churches, having grown up with a father who scorned all religion and a mother who dragged Matt and his brother to Mass every Sunday until the boys pointed to their non-attending father and flatly refused to go. The work churches did for the homeless was one of the only aspects Roarke was truly unambivalent about; he wished the church would stick to that kind of mission.

A few of the in-line homeless looked him over balefully as he moved past them down the line, but most merely stepped aside and looked elsewhere. Street people could generally spot law enforcement from two blocks away.

Roarke stepped through the open metal door at the bottom of the stairs and was assailed by a wave of heat and smells, a generic aroma of institutional food and the more overpowering scents of some of the patrons.

There were greeters at a table just inside the door. A severely dressed woman in her late fifties with a don't-fuck-with-me look was deep in an escalating conversation with an elderly man in a wheelchair. The other greeter, a heavyset young Latino man, was nodding and smiling beatifically to the line as the homeless shuffled past, addressing many people by name.

Roarke looked over both greeters and decided the woman was the one in charge. A nun, no doubt; despite the civilian clothes there was no mistaking that edge of authority. She had already had a sobering effect on the scruffy gentleman in the wheelchair.

Roarke decided to wait for her, and hung back, taking a look around him.

Through the kitchen door, he could see a cafeteria-style counter line of heating stations where steaming food bins were heaped with scrambled eggs, pancakes and hash browns. Aproned, hairnetted workers at each station ladled food onto the trays, and a server at the end of the counter handed out the filled trays to the line of patrons as they filed past, carrying their food into a long dining hall set up with lines of folding tables. Close to a hundred guests already sat eating.

"May I help you?" A dry female voice spoke behind him.

Roarke turned to see the nun standing, feet planted, looking at him assessingly. He showed his credentials wallet. "I'm Agent Roarke, FBI, San Francisco Bureau. I'm looking for information on a man who used to take meals here. People called him the Preacherman."

"John Milvia," the nun said, with an expression Roarke couldn't immediately interpret. "We stop serving in twenty minutes, if you can wait."

When the front doors were closed and the diners all seated with their meals, the nun introduced herself as Sister Frances and motioned Roarke toward a closed door in an inside wall. She unlocked it to reveal a small business office, barely big enough for a desk, a file cabinet and two battered office chairs on wheels.

She indicated one of the chairs, and began to sit with him, then said, "I'm sorry, I didn't ask you if you wanted to partake."

It took Roarke a split second to realize she was offering him a meal. "No, thank you," he managed, but apparently the look on his face amused her.

"It's better than it smells," she said with a straight face, and sat, smoothing her gray wool skirt.

From hookers to nuns, Roarke thought. *No one can accuse me of not covering my bases.* Aloud, he said, "Do you have a title, here, Sister, if you don't mind my asking?"

"I'm the Director of Counseling Services."

Even better, Roarke thought, and asked, "Masters in Social Work?"

"From the University of Chicago."

And I bet you have one hell of a story, Roarke thought to himself.

"So, Milvia," the nun said.

Right down to business. Roarke was fine with that. "You know he was murdered in April," he began.

"Oh, yes," she said. Again, that uninterpretable look.

"I think I have a related case."

She tensed. "Another homeless victim?"

"No. But there seems to be a connection, and I'm trying to understand what kind of person Milvia was. I noticed you don't call him 'Preacherman,' by the way."

She sniffed. "I don't, and I didn't. His kind of 'preaching' gives religion a bad name."

Roarke sat forward. It was always gold to have a witness with opinions. "What kind of preaching was that?"

"His so-called religion, which wasn't religion at all but Milvia's special brand of hate. A thoroughly detestable character."

So much for turning the other cheek, Roarke thought. He'd had too much exposure to nuns to believe they were universally charitable and forgiving. But Sister Frances struck him as fair, if blunt. She was also absolutely convinced of what she was saying.

"This 'brand of hate'... was there anything political about it?"

She frowned. "A dash, I suppose. He called himself an eco-anarchist."

Only in Portland, Roarke thought. He raised an eyebrow and Sister Frances gave him the Cliff's Notes version without his having to ask. "Eco-anarchism, also known as green anarchism, anarcho-primitivism, anarcho-naturism, anti-civilization anarchism... I could go on."

Roarke matched her dry tone. "I think I'm getting the picture."

"Basically these philosophies espouse rejection of modern technology, radical ecology, ethical consumerism. Some propose eco-villages, the more radical preach 'rewilding': a return to hunter-gathering." She snorted. "Good luck with that."

"Thanks, that was very—"

"But all that was a sham, really," she interrupted him. "I don't for a minute think Milvia believed a word of it."

Roarke studied her, intrigued. "Why do you say that?"

"He was just having people on. He was a panhandler; he'd rattle off the party line to get money from the true believers. Quote Thoreau for the college types. He was pulling in quite a bit of money with that hogwash."

"What about the preaching?"

She waved a hand. "More sham. He used Bible quotations as a weapon, and he'd misquote in subtle ways that were really quite cruel."

"Cruel how?"

The nun's face grew distant as she remembered.

"He *judged*. He was a sham, but—" she glanced at Roarke. "You're familiar with con artists, I'm sure. He had a conviction about him that was almost hypnotic. He would look at people as if he could see the worst thing they had ever done, and took pleasure in speaking it aloud. He especially liked targeting the vulnerable; I once saw him reduce a mentally challenged man to tears. The man attempted suicide that night."

Roarke was staring at her, fascinated. And he thought about the huntress, watching Milvia for hours in Pioneer Courthouse Square, fixated on him. *What had he said to her? What had she heard?*

The nun was speaking again, still with that distant look on her face. "*Revelation* was his favorite. I think he loved talking about the Beast. He had a sly way; made it sound as if he'd had personal acquaintance with the Adversary."

"Did Milvia..." Roarke suddenly felt like the ex-altar boy he was, unsure of how to broach the topic with a nun. "Was he particularly harassing toward women?"

She looked him straight in the face. "Sexually harassing, you mean?"

"Yes." Roarke said, and managed not to redden.

Her eyes clouded, and she didn't answer for a long moment. But then she shook her head slowly. "I never saw that in him. He was contemptuous of women, but no more so than he was of men. He was harassing, he was predatory, but asexually so."

Roarke looked at her, considering this. *Well, that's not exactly ringing support for my theory that she's killing predatory men.*

"There was something not right, though," the nun said abruptly. "He wasn't anywhere near as disordered as he put on. I never believed he was clinically schizophrenic at all. Now ask yourself. Why would someone want to *fake* that?"

Roarke looked at her. But before he could speak, his phone vibrated. He glanced down at the caller ID. Epps.

He looked up. "Excuse me, Sister—" The nun flicked a hand at him to take it.

"Epps," he said into the phone.

"You're gonna want to get right back here, boss."

Roarke tensed at the tone of his voice. "What've you got?"

"White male trucker, found in the bathroom of a rest stop at the junction of the 101 and the 41. Throat slashed, bled out. First officer on the scene said it looked like a pig slaughter."

Central California, Roarke had time to think. But not just Central California. He knew that junction well. Before he could consider further, Epps continued.

"It was Wednesday night, boss. Thirty-eight hours after Greer."

Roarke felt adrenaline spike like an electric current through his body. He was on his feet without realizing he'd stood. "Get yourself down there with a team. I'll fly into SLO and meet you. On my way to the airport now."

"Boss—" Epps said urgently, before Roarke could disconnect.

"Yeah."

"It was the women's bathroom."

Roarke clicked off, standing still as he tried to process that last. He was aware that Sister Frances was bent over the desk writing something on a notepad.

"I'm so sorry—" he began, and she waved a hand.

"Your work, obviously."

The woman was a gem. Roarke smiled at her. "You've been incredibly helpful. May I call you to follow up?"

She tore the page he had seen her writing on off the pad: it had her name, the church name, a phone number and email address.

He looked up at her in surprise. "Thank you." He started toward the door.

"Agent Roarke," she said behind him.

He turned. She looked at him, and her voice was quiet. "What is it you think Milvia did?"

He stared at her, startled. Then he said slowly, "I'm not sure." He glanced down at the number she had given him. "I'll be in touch."

Chapter 27

The weather forecast had said rain, but it is a warm day, a beach day. The father has come loaded down with beach implements, pails and shovels and plastic sandcastle molds, which is a new concept to her. She thinks possibly it defeats the purpose of sandcastle building, but does not say this aloud, and simply joins in, scooping out moats and building up fortresses.

The fact that the father and son have walked this far down the beach with all their sandcastle accessories is a good sign; it would have made much more sense to do the building in front of their own house, so she knows that they have gone out of their way to find her.

After the sandcastle there is lunch, at a local eatery called the Splash Café, which serves the best clam chowder she has ever tasted and keeps the boy entertained with its murals of animated clams on the walls, happy, smiling clams on the beach, surfing, parasailing, recumbent biking, playing beach volleyball, all apparently oblivious to the fate that awaits them in the kettles and pots behind the kitchen doors.

And then they go back out on the beach where they should have been all along, the strip of beach in front of the bluff where the house is.

As the boy is digging in the sand, the father gets a call on his cell phone and whoever it is instantly darkens the sunny day for him. Not just the father, but also the boy tenses up. As soon as the father has glanced at the number he stands and walks away, back toward the stairs, far out of earshot. As he speaks his voice rises and his body becomes even more stiff, and he starts up the stairs.

The boy goes silent. He turns away from his father and stares out at the sea. And then as she watches, he begins a new sand construction.

Not a castle this time, there are no neat ridges, no towers, no moats. Instead he is building conical hills of sand, heaps of piled rocks. He flattens out a space and lines up trucks from his toy box. Instead of helping, she watches; the boy is building something in particular, something specific. He is very focused, and his face is taut.

He leaves the construction site and goes down by the water to look for items: pebbles to build into a pyramid of rocks to match the sand piles, driftwood sticks that he arranges like chutes between the piles of rock and sand, long diagonals like ladders connecting the conical heaps. There is something familiar about the look of all this to her, but she says nothing, just watches.

And then he makes another trip to the water's edge with his pail, and this time he brings what she is startled to see are the carcasses of sea creatures: crabs, half of a bait fish.

He piles them up, too, and the smell is strong and unpleasant.

She wrinkles her nose, frowning, and says, "Yuck."

The boy glances at her, and says nothing.

"What is this place?" she asks him.

The boy's face grows darker, but he continues his building of the scene. Finally he says something, so softly she almost doesn't hear. "The bad place."

She considers this without reacting, then takes a stick and tentatively pokes at a mound of carcasses. "I don't like those. What are those?"

He does not look at her, and again he does not answer for a long time. Then finally he speaks.

"Monsters," he says.

Chapter 28

B ehind the wheel of yet another rental car, Roarke drove through the winding road through the green hills of the Central Coast, toward the junction of the 101 and the 41.

California's freeways and interstates have pretty names, some of them even immortalized in song: the Golden State Freeway, the Foothill Freeway, Ventura Highway, El Camino Real. But no real Californian ever used those names, it was always the numbers. Car-dependent natives spoke them casually, but with a hint of the reverence other states accorded their legendary mountains and rivers.

Roarke knew these highways and this particular junction intimately.

It was located in some of the most beautiful, gently rounded hills of Central California, a breath away from wine country, a stone's throw from some of the calmest ocean on the notoriously tumultuous California coast, and just twenty minutes away from San Luis Obispo, where Roarke had attended college.

And the town closest to the rest stop itself was Atascadero, home of Atascadero State Mental Hospital, where Roarke had spent his last days as a criminal profiler.

It was more than a little unnerving, how the investigation was taking Roarke back into his past in some way he couldn't quite fathom.

But he had no time to think about it, because up ahead an official sign at the turn off marked the rest stop CLOSED: which meant Epps was already on the job.

Roarke pulled in slowly past an emerald green hill, noting the split in the road, which diverted trucks to a parking area separate from the cars.

Several Crown Vics, a black-and-white, and one Cavalier were parked in the spaces outside the restrooms and vending machine area, an unmistakable fleet of law enforcement.

He felt a rush of anticipation as he got out of the rental car and just stood for a minute in the sun, with a light breeze ruffling his hair.

The scene before him was tranquil and pleasant: soft curves of green hills dotted with small twisted oak trees, and winding paths with flowerbeds between the buildings. But there was always a dangerous edge to these rest stops. It was possibly the lurking presence of the massive trucks that were almost always parked behind the family pic-nicking areas, felt even without the actual trucks, today.

Roarke looked around, letting his mind see the place at night, feel-ing the dry wind, hearing the crickets and the rustle of leaves... and seeing the woman getting out of her car, alone, standing and looking through the dark at the cluster of buildings.

The murder had taken place at 1:30 in the morning; a desolate time of night at a rest stop.

Were you here? he asked her silently. *One-thirty a.m.? Why?*

He moved slowly up the neatly landscaped, curving path toward the restroom building, passing the vending machine area with their caged-in snack machines.

There was movement in the shadows ahead... and then Epps stepped out of the restroom area and walked down the path to meet him.

"Made good time, boss," Epps greeted him. "The CHP officer who called in the body and the Sheriff's detectives just got here. Lam and Stotlemyre are with me. Officer Moreno was just taking us through it. Everyone's playing nice."

Roarke asked without much hope, "The place been cleaned?"

Epps grimaced. "Yesterday. But the photos are good." He lifted the thick file he was carrying. "Want to go through it before you go in?"

Roarke didn't reach for the file. "No, I want it in order."

He followed Epps to the covered patio between the restrooms, where he nodded to Lam and Stotlemyre and shook hands all around with Officer Moreno of the CHP and Detectives Solis and Voelker of the San Luis Obispo County Sheriff's Department.

Roarke was always alert to possible tension between local authorities and the Bureau, but he didn't feel any hostility from the detectives or the officers. Epps had obviously done a good job putting the men at their ease. It was a way he had.

Now Epps started everything off. "First of all, gentleman, again, we deeply appreciate that you entered the report in the VICAP database right away."

The detectives exchanged a glance, and the big blond one, Voelker, replied, "We've been getting the bulletins for the Highway Killings Initiative."

Voelker was referring to a recently initiated FBI program, the Highway Serial Killings Initiative, designed to target the troubling number of predators trolling the nation's highways. The program encouraged law enforcement agencies across the country to report murder victims dumped along highways or at truck stops or rest stops. There were more than five hundred murder victims in the database, mostly prostitutes and runaways, women living high-risk, transient lifestyles. The two hundred suspects were predominantly long-haul truck drivers, and of course, men.

Which was exactly what Detective Solis said next. "All kinds of overlap with this one, 'cept the trucker's the victim, not the suspect."

Exactly, Roarke thought. He looked at the young CHP officer. "Officer Moreno, you were first on the scene?"

"Yes, sir."

"Take us through it."

Moreno straightened his shoulders with the eagerness of a new recruit. "911 got a call at oh-five-seventeen Tuesday morning, from a trucker, Harold Lamar Otis of Temecula, DOB twelve-twenty seventy-one, reporting a body in the restroom. Said he'd pulled into the truck lot at approximately oh-three-thirty, and noted another truck that was dark, engine off. Otis turned off his rig and slept for approximately two hours. When he woke up, the other truck was still there, hadn't moved. Otis walked down to the buildings to use the restroom and noticed dark stains leading out of the women's bathroom."

Roarke nodded to Epps, who was ready with the file, open to crime scene photos of the concrete where they now stood, showing dark smears, partial footprints from a boot-like shoe.

Moreno continued, his voice a hollow echo in the tiled space. "Otis stepped into the doorway and called out, asking if there was anyone inside. There was no response. He walked partway into the restroom, saw the blood and the body — then he says he came right out and called 911 immediately."

Roarke nodded to Epps again, who extended the file again. This time Roarke took it and looked down—

At a bloodbath. The photos showed the floor of the restroom as a vast pool of blood, with a large male body collapsed in the center. The walls and stalls dripped with crimson spray.

Holy shit, Roarke thought numbly, as he paged through images of the carnage. *She did* this?

Finally he looked up. His mouth was dry as he spoke. "Otis didn't touch the victim?"

Moreno shook his head. "Said from what he saw, no way the guy wasn't dead. I can tell you that's right."

Roarke knew it too, from the photos. "So Otis phoned 911."

The young officer nodded in the affirmative. "I was on duty and just fifteen minutes from the scene. Otis locked himself in his truck to wait." The young officer hesitated, looking troubled at the memory. "Can't blame him, seeing — what he saw. He told me he watched the buildings and the other truck the whole time he was waiting for police and didn't observe anything moving."

Roarke nodded. She'd have been gone, long gone.

"I left him at the truck and drove down to the car parking lot. I drew my weapon and walked up the path to the restroom — that's when I saw it was the women's restroom."

Yes, the women's restroom, Roarke thought. *How about that?* Aloud he said, "Take us inside."

Roarke, Epps, the two detectives and the crime scene techs followed Moreno as he stepped through the restroom door. Roarke could see that the rectangular building was built in a T-shape: the sink area formed the top and the stall area was the longer base of the T. The aisle leading into the stalls was in the center of a dividing wall; there was no way to see into the stall area from the doorway.

Moreno put his back to the inside wall and moved along it.

"I stayed to the wall, away from any blood. When I looked around the corner, I saw the body in the middle of the floor."

Roarke stepped around Moreno to stand in the opening of the wall, and looked into the stall area. When he looked at the floor, he could see the spreading pool of red, the collapsed body, the gore-splashed walls.

In reality, the stall area was clean, no sign of the mayhem from the photos. There was a stench of bleach that made him tense up, though of course from the photos it was clear that she had not cleaned up after herself this time.

Moreno echoed his thoughts. "There was blood everywhere, like someone had used a hose to spread it around."

A razor, Roarke thought. *Like Preacherman.*

"Two slashes to the throat. Cut right through the carotid and jugular on both sides of the neck," Detective Voelker supplied.

"Geysered out like Old Faithful," Roarke said under his breath, and didn't realize he'd said it aloud until the other men looked at him.

"Yeah," said Voelker. "Like that."

The CHP continued. "And at that point I knew he was dead. I could see his eyes: open, fixed, dilated. But everything about it, I mean, just no way was he alive. So I backed out, didn't touch anything, and called for backup. Then I stood guard for anyone inside the bathroom or on the premises while I waited for the detectives."

"That was good work, there," Epps said, and Roarke nodded his agreement at the young officer. Countless patrolmen contaminated scenes by ignoring the obvious.

Solis took over from there. "Detective Voelker and I arrived at the scene at oh-five fifty-five, followed shortly by three other CHP. The officers secured the area and searched the rest stop while we worked the scene. No weapon found on the premises, no witnesses. No sign of a struggle anywhere except inside the bathroom. And the victim was robbed: no wallet anywhere."

Staging, Roarke thought. *Making it look like a robbery. Or maybe she needed the money.*

Solis was still talking. "Coroner ruled the time of death as somewhere between midnight and three a.m."

As Solis paused, Voelker added, "Victim's name was Brent Martin Hartley, DOB four twelve sixty-seven, last known address 419 H Street, Victorville, California. But that was eight months ago. Looks like he was living out of his truck."

Roarke looked to his own crime scene techs. "How did it happen?"

Stotlemyre stepped forward. "The blood arcs in these photos indicate the killer initially came at him from this direction." The crime scene tech moved into the aisle between the stalls and faced Roarke.

Roarke stared at him. "So you're saying the killer was already inside the restroom when Hartley entered."

"Correct," Lam agreed. "Hartley also had bruises to his scrotum, premortem. The bruising was severe. The injuries occurred no more than one or two minutes before death; it was probably the first blow, a kick. And the positioning of the bruises in the groin area makes me think that the strike angle of the kick was from above."

Roarke stared at the criminalist. "How tall was Hartley?"

"Five-eleven," said Epps, behind him.

"And the kick was from *above*?" Roarke was about to add, *"How does that even happen?"* Then he suddenly turned to the stalls.

"Right, boss," Lam said placidly. "We think the unsub was standing on a toilet. Probably the middle stall; there's this one weird thing." The tech stepped to the first stall, and pointed to the door with a gloved finger. Roarke stepped closer and saw what the tech was looking at: a ragged scratch in the paint at about chest height. There was something about it of an animal scratch, but not, and the look of it made Roarke uneasy.

"Knife?" he asked.

"Maybe," Lam said dubiously. "They didn't find one at the scene. Something sharp. It's here, too." He showed Roarke and Epps the door of the second stall: the same long ragged scratch mark in the paint, at chest height.

Roarke looked to the third stall. No scratch.

"Right," Stotlemyre said. "We think maybe the unsub was standing in the third stall, heard Hartley scraping that — whatever — across the first and second stalls, and was ready for him by the time he got to the third." Stotlemyre moved into the stall, and stepped up onto the toilet, to demonstrate.

"Prints?" Roarke asked.

"Nothing usable on the walls here. The rest stop gets hundreds of visitors a day, it's a mess."

Roarke nodded, and Stotlemyre continued. "So the unsub waits for Hartley to move in front of the third stall, grabs the tops of the dividers to brace, swings out and kicks him." Lam and Stotlemyre went into a dance Roarke had seen them do many times before, a reenactment of the action. Lam approached the open door of the stall, Stotlemyre mimed a kick and Lam staggered back, doubled over as if in pain. Stotlemyre dropped to the floor in front of Lam, raised an imaginary knife, grabbed a fistful of Lam's luxuriant black hair and slashed down at his neck.

"Two slashes, direct slices to the carotid and jugular on the left and right. No hesitation marks whatsoever. A perfect kill."

Lam collapsed to his knees, limp. "It didn't take long," he said cheerfully, from his position on his knees. "The vic is bleeding out already, blood gushing." He wiggled his fingers at his neck to illustrate. "The floor was drenched — there are boot smears in the photos."

"We got those in plaster," Solis spoke up.

"Good work," Roarke nodded to him.

"Hartley's already on the ground by now," Stotlemyre continued.

At this, Lam obediently went limp, folding himself down onto the floor, neck up and exposed.

"But the unsub is careful," Stotlemyre said, as he stepped over Lam's body and looked down. "There's a boot print in blood on Hartley's chest." Stotlemyre placed his foot lightly on Lam's chest. "The unsub steps on him, reaches down, and slashes him again, just to be sure." He demonstrated, again gently, grasping Lam's hair and drawing his empty hand across the other tech's throat. "At that point, death would have been almost instantaneous."

Lam lay still for a second, then popped up, gesturing toward Stotlemyre. "And with the arterial spray, the unsub would have been *covered* in blood at this point. Just dripping."

Stotlemyre offered Lam a hand up and the wiry crime tech bounced to his feet, brushing off his pants.

"And the unsub walks out at that point," Stotlemyre continued. "There are footprints, smears, all going in one direction: toward the parking area."

The men followed Stotlemyre out of the bathroom, blinking at the sudden sunlight.

"The killer wipes most of the blood off his boots on the grass right off the path," Lam adds, miming it. Roarke looked to where he was pointing: the grass had been cut away in a square piece of sod, taken as evidence. "And then stops again, here," Lam halted before the trash can, standing right up against it. "Clever bit, this: I think he took the plastic trash liner out to put over his clothes. The trail gets cleaner after that. But still, we can follow smears of footprints all the way down to the parking lot. He was parked where you are, boss," he noted, and Roarke felt — odd.

"And there we lose him," Solis concludes. "Obviously, no witnesses. Whatever happened, it was just between them."

Roarke took a minute to process. *Just between them...* He looked across the concrete path to the men's room. "The men's restroom was open and in service Tuesday night?"

"That's right," Solis confirmed.

Roarke stated the obvious flatly. "So Hartley enters the women's restroom for reasons unknown and is attacked and killed."

The two sheriff's detectives exchanged a glance. "We keep going back to that," Solis acknowledged. "This setting, the first thing you think is a drug deal. But the perp attacking from the stall, that doesn't fit. More like the perp is a man lying in wait for a woman or kid to walk into the restroom... who gets the surprise of his life when Hartley walks in instead..."

Voelker continued. "Or this is a homosexual encounter gone wrong. The two truckers see each other... Hartley follows the perp into the women's bathroom, thinking he's going to get lucky. Instead he gets dead..."

"Or it's a woman," Epps said quietly, looking at Roarke.

The two sheriff's detectives and the CHP looked at Epps.

"We were talking about that," Solis said, a strange note in his voice. "Only..."

"Only it's not exactly textbook," Roarke said.

"Right," Voelker said tightly. "If this was self-defense it was the best job of self-defense I've ever seen."

It was Epps who spoke now. "Hartley did two years in Folsom for aggravated sexual assault." He looked at Roarke as he said it.

Roarke felt a shiver through his entire body. *That's it, then.*

"He was driving a truck with a felony conviction?" Officer Moreno asked.

Solis and Voelker were shaking their heads. "That Folsom conviction was a misdemeanor," Solis argued.

"He pled it down." Epps shrugged, cynical. "Some companies aren't too particular."

Detective Voelker thought it out. "So maybe Hartley was up to his old tricks, coming into the restroom after our unsub with the intent of sexual assault, and got more than he bargained for."

The men's silent thoughts coalesced, echoed.

Finally Solis said it. "Are we really saying that a woman kicked this guy's balls halfway up his intestines and slashed his throat like a pig?"

Epps said neutrally. "I think that may be what we're saying."

"Holy fucking shit," said Voelker.

"Madre," Solis agreed, crossing himself.

Chapter 29

Epps and Roarke left Lam and Stotlemyre to re-process the scene and walked out to their cars, through the idyllic setting that had played host to such madness.

The weather was coming up as they drove the winding road into town; gusty wind and ominous clouds rolling in over the hills.

Roarke stared out the window as they passed one of California's ubiquitous cement and gravel plants, silent heaps of rock and sand connected by long diagonal conveyor belts, rusty ladders and chutes and tanks. Abandoned, as so many were these days, stripped of equipment to use in more viable plants. *Like dinosaur graveyards.*

Roarke watched the dust devils spiraling between the conical piles in the rising wind.

Epps was increasingly restless in the driver's seat.

"I got all kinds of problems with this, boss."

Roarke tried to be neutral. "I know you do. So do I."

"First off, you're the one who doesn't like coincidence. Let's just say Hartley is a rapist, going into that bathroom with bad intentions. What are the chances that he comes in on a vigilante, gets his due?"

"I know. Poetic justice, maybe, but on the whole, not too fucking likely."

"Got that right," Epps muttered ominously.

Roarke looked off through the window, past the plant, into the hills.

"We don't even know this is our girl, or any girl at all." Epps said.

"No. We don't."

"It's a women's *restroom*, that's it. Could be a drug deal. Could be truckers on the down low with each other..." Epps trailed off.

"Yes, and we need to check if Hartley has any history of homosexual activity. He could have picked it up in prison." But they both knew it was unlikely. The sexual assault conviction had been for an assault on a woman. And it was true that the Central Valley had a raging meth problem, and truckers were often addicts, but as Solis had said, Lam's scenario of the unsub lying in wait in the stall wasn't consistent with a drug exchange.

"Bottom line, you think she was trolling."

"I think it's possible."

"Or lured him."

"Possible."

Epps shook his head, tightened his hands on the steering wheel. "What next?"

Roarke paused. He hated like hell to put the sketch of her out into the general public, hated to tip their hand, alert her to the fact that there was a manhunt out for her. But he thought of the scene at that rest stop and knew he couldn't delay it any longer.

"She left a very messy scene this time," he said aloud. "Partial boot prints, possible fingerprints. And two kills in two days..."

"Not a good sign, no matter how you look at it," Epps finished for him.

"Right. We need to get that sketch out, start circulating that to local law enforcement, local papers, see if we can pick up her trail here, where it's most fresh. We take a look at Hartley's rig, maybe find out what he was up to, or a connection to her, or a connection to Wann and Milvia."

"And Greer," Epps said grimly.

"And Greer," Roarke agreed, his voice hollow. "Where's Hartley's truck?"

"Atascadero impound."

"Let's get the sketch on the wire and go take a look."

Atascadero was a small town, with a historic downtown geared toward wine-tasting tourists. The lot the police used for impound was just two blocks from the station, and was obviously barely used, which turned out to be convenient since the dead trucker's semi took up half the parking spaces.

The attendant pointed and Roarke and Epps approached the monster truck. Hartley's rig was a freight liner, Century class. It wasn't one of the cushiest cabs, Roarke and Epps had to sidestep each other for position once they were inside, but it wasn't bad. Truckers spent so many days, weeks, in a row out on the road, the cab amenities had improved over the years. Roarke looked over a sleeping area with a narrow bed in a cubbyhole, a heater and fan attached to the wall inside the cubby. There were draw curtains that could be pulled over the windshield, and the driver and passenger seats swiveled toward the back to create a small living room space. Storage areas above the seats contained owners' manuals, paper towels and other sundries; plastic storage bins with netting held food supplies.

Roarke's eyes settled on a pullout desk with a rat's nest of computer cords. "There's a laptop?"

Epps consulted a list. "It's already in evidence."

"I want to see his Internet use. And email, too. He may have been lured."

At the same time he was saying it, Roarke doubted it. If she'd contacted him via the Internet, it wasn't likely she'd have set up a rendezvous at a truck stop. It looked to him like a chance encounter that was the ultimate bad luck for Hartley.

The question is, did he—

Roarke's mind balked at finishing the thought, but then he plunged ahead. *Did he deserve it, that's what you want to know. Was he a bad guy just getting what was coming to him? Did he deserve being slashed like that?*

If it was self-defense?

He felt himself on a dangerous precipice and reminded himself of the other murders. *They're not all self-defense.*

He stepped behind the driver's seat to examine a triple stack of plastic bins, a compartment to hang clothes, a compartment for food. On the other side of the cab another bin had a TV strapped into it. The one underneath that one was almost entirely filled with porn: magazines and DVDs.

Roarke glanced up from the stash at Epps. "Yeah," Epps said. "Long drives, long nights. Man was entertaining himself. What are we saying, boss?"

"We're saying Hartley is looking like the kind of guy who would follow a woman into a rest stop bathroom in the middle of the night in the middle of nowhere."

He looked toward the narrow bed. "Need to have it checked for body fluids. And blood."

As soon as he'd said it, the cab felt unhealthily claustrophobic, and Roarke turned to the driver's door and climbed out. Epps followed, and once on the ground they blinked at each other in the setting sun, a dramatic study in red and gold through the wash of massing clouds.

"So after she gets Greer killed, she ends up killing Hartley a day later in *self-defense?*" Epps shook his head, and Roarke shook his head, too.

"Maybe not self-defense. With Wann, the witness described her as dressed like a prostitute. So maybe she *was* trolling. Maybe that's what she does. She's looking for them."

Epps looked grim, and conflicted. "What you're thinking is she could have worked the streets or the highways, like Wuornos, and at some point she turns on the johns. Turns the tables."

"Not like Wuornos," Roarke said automatically. *Not her.* "Not that kind of desperate. But I don't like Hartley's rape conviction."

Epps looked at him, frowning.

"Could be random. *Could* be. But what if she's picking them?"

"How?"

Roarke stared off into the sky, the fast-gathering clouds. "Exactly. *How?*"

Chapter 30

Back at the beach house, they are all sleepy from the long day at the beach. An amazingly *normal* day, aside from the monsters.

As the sun begins to set, she could leave them, but she doesn't, and now they are grilling swordfish on the deck, with the wind coming up and the clouds racing past the sinking red-gold sun.

In the middle of dinner the father's cell phone rings again and his face darkens to match the sky. He steps into the house to take it but this time that fails to mask the escalation of his voice, the argument that ratchets up louder and louder.

His voice drops to almost nothing, but she focuses through the sound of the wind and the waves and hears the words from inside the living room. "You're *on* something. As if I can't tell by now."

At the table across from her, the boy hunches further in his seat, not eating at all, and there is darkness coming off him, too. He is uneasy, more than uneasy; the unease is masking terror. He stares out at the gathering clouds.

"It's bad."

She looks at him. He points to the sky. It is a moment before she answers.

"There is bad out there. But not the rain and lightning and wind and water. Rain and lightning and wind and water aren't good, aren't bad. They're power."

She senses the father behind them and turns. He steps forward and crouches in front of the boy.

"We're completely safe, homes. This house doesn't mind a storm. There's nothing out there that's going to hurt you."

The boy looks to her for confirmation, but she is silent. She can feel the father's surprise, and then disapproval rolling off him in waves.

"I'll read to you, how's that?" the father says to his son. The cheeriness is a little forced. The boy looks to her and she nods to him, just the barest movement, hoping the father will not take the exchange hard. Then the boy turns to his father and his father swings him up and takes him down the hall.

As she is left alone, her face tightens and she becomes very focused. She moves to the mantle and studies the photos arranged there. All recent, and there is a conspicuous absence. So she turns to the bookshelves, scanning until she finds an oversized album, which she pulls out and opens. Here are the missing older photos, family photos with the mother, a young, pretty person with a self-centered wildness to her, a wounded combination of fragility and narcissism.

A weak person, she thinks coldly, as she flips through the photos, assessing. *Weak enough to be dangerous to anyone who loves her.*

Behind her, the curtains billow at the windows in a gust, and she turns to look. The wind draws her, and she steps out on the deck, into the dark, and stands looking out at the sea. The lights of downtown seem far away, and most of the surrounding houses are dark. She turns off the deck lights to see more clearly, and it feels suddenly as if the house is alone in the sweep of black. The waves below are a constant roar, now, the churning white water lashed by wind that sends sand spinning down the flat of beach.

She lifts her face to it, leans into it, listening. The voices are layered, turbulent. There is always disturbance this close to the day. But before she can focus on what she hears, the curtains part behind her and she can feel the man standing in the doorway. She lets him look at her for a long moment before she turns.

She meets his eyes, but he looks away, not at her, but the sea. Finally he speaks. "He goes to his mother in three days. She's with someone else already. And it's not her first. She gets drunk, and — whoever's around." His jaw flexes as he says it. The tone is self-deprecating, not bitter, but there are waves of pain coming off him, and anger, too.

"It went on for years. She waited until I was out of the house and drank herself into unconsciousness. The house could have burned down around them. And still, *she's* the one who left. How pathetic is that?" The self-deprecation is back, full force.

She keeps her voice even. "You have joint custody?"

"Three quarters, one quarter. Her father's lawyers were as good as mine." He stares down at the waves. "And then sometimes I think I'm making up danger because I still can't believe — any of it." He shakes his head, and the self-deprecation is now self-loathing. "I was in some kind of dream world for so long. He's seen way too much. Some of it from me, I'm afraid."

"What does *he* say?"

He glances at her. "He's too young to understand most of it."

She feels a flash of anger. What is there that children don't understand? It's only later that it gets clouded, adults guessing at what is normal or rational.

"I feel guilty every day that I subjected him to — all of it. And I feel guilty every day that we broke up the only home he had."

"You did what you had to do," she says without inflection. *But not enough,* she thinks to herself.

He stands for a moment, silent, and then moves as if he's remembered something.

"He's asking for a story."

When she doesn't answer right away, he adds quickly, "You don't have to."

She steps forward, close enough to him that she hears him catch his breath. Then she steps past, through the curtains, through the door.

Inside the house, she moves down the dark hall, and steps into the rectangle of light.

The boy's room is half little boy chaos, half designer chic. The blues and greens are sea-colored, artfully mixed. One wall is all wildlife, including a spray of butterflies, but not girly butterflies; they are almost photographically perfect.

She has not been in a room like this in a long, long time, and it is a vertiginous feeling.

There is a play area with bins of toys, and a low table for art projects and writing. A kid-sized desk holds a computer, and there is a television as well. The light is low and warm and cheery, the comforters soft and heaped high on the bed. It should be safe, but the boy is so small in the bed, and she is suddenly frightened for him.

Monsters, he had said on the beach.

"I heard someone wanted a story," she says lightly.

"A good story," he says, lounging against plumped-up pillows like a small prince.

"Of course a good story," she says, and moves closer, pulling a footstool up beside the bed, so she is as small as he is when she sits.

He looks up at her seriously, and says, "About the monsters."

"Oh, the monsters," she says, and what she feels is rage. The boy should be spared, it isn't right.

She breathes in deeply, composing herself, and puts herself back in a time of her life when someone told her something that made sense for once, and when she speaks she is not entirely herself; she is simply the story.

"There once was a boy who lived in a tribe out on the plains with the sun and the moon and the wind and the rain. And all day long he played with the other children of the tribe, played in the grass and the sun and the wind, and he knew that he was safe because all the grown-ups of the tribe, the warriors and the wisewomen, all of them were looking after him. And he was happy.

"Then one night there came a big storm, with lightning cracking and clouds racing across the sky and all the elements stirred up. And as the boy shivered in his bed, listening to the thunder and the wind and the rain, big shadows appeared on the curved walls, big scary shadows of monsters. And before he could call for his parents, the shadows grabbed him and took him."

The boy doesn't gasp, but his eyes are big and he is very still.

"They took him into the dark, far, far away from the village, into the dark woods that his father had warned him never to go into. And deep, deep in the woods, the shadows left him, alone, all alone.

"He was so scared he couldn't move. And then it was even worse, because he was not alone. There were spirits all around him, dead things that were alive, and live things that were dead. Things with bone faces and fire eyes."

The boy in the bed is completely fixed on her.

"And the boy couldn't move, and he knew he would be eaten by the horrible things in the forest. And then... he started to run. He ran in the woods and he ran through the wind and he was lighter and faster than he had ever been. He was running with the wind and then he was the wind. No boy had ever been as fast, or as strong."

The boy's eyes are big, still, but now shining.

"He ran and ran and ran, out of the woods, across the wide plain, all the way back to his village. And when he got back all the elders were waiting for him. And they praised him for his bravery and cleverness, and told him the spirits had given him a power, and they asked him to speak and tell them all what it was. And the boy realized it was true, and he told his tribe, 'I run like the wind.'

"And everyone in the tribe nodded and exclaimed, 'Runs Like Wind.'

"And they fed him and they heaped him with strings of shells and beads and gave him a spear. Because now he was a man, and he had found his power, which forevermore would help the tribe, in the hunt and in battle."

She looks steadily at the boy in the bed, with the comforters drawn around him.

"Do you understand?" she asks him.

The boy nods, and breathes out, a long breath, and she knows he does. She leans forward, and says, very low.

"Do you remember your dreams?"

He looks up at her with clear eyes. "Uh huh, some dreams."

"Can you remember your dreams tonight?"

"I will remember them," he says.

"Good. You'll tell me tomorrow, then, what you dream?"

He nods, very seriously.

Then slowly, slowly, she leans forward, and kisses him on the forehead.

When she rises from the small stool, the father is in the doorway. He looks at her from the shadows. She stands for a moment facing him, looking at him, then she walks by him, into the hall, and out.

Chapter 31

oarke and Epps drove through town under ominously black clouds. The wind flattened the grass and blew swirls of sand across the road in the headlights. Roarke thought that the bad weather seemed to be following him, but he welcomed the idea of a storm; it might dissipate his own raging feelings.

At the local police station in Atascadero the local detectives had put the police sketch of the woman in black on the wire, describing her as a "Person of Interest" in the rest stop slaying.

Epps went about sending out an APB and distributing the police sketch and contacting gas stations and motels along the 101; it was extremely likely that she had stopped at least once on the road from San Francisco. And Roarke parked himself at one of the police station's computers. Combing through computer records was mindbendingly tedious work, not something that Roarke would generally have handled on his own. He could have left it to Singh; he could feel himself micromanaging in a way he knew was inefficient, an old, bad habit that he'd worked years to break. But just this once he would let himself indulge. He wanted to get a sense of Hartley.

As it turned out, it didn't take long. When he pushed back his chair an hour and a half later, he knew more than he ever wanted to know about the trucker.

And he didn't like the guy. At all.

Epps had booked rooms in a renovated historic hotel downtown. The agent was as discriminating about accommodations as he was about his clothes; he'd grown up on the streets of Oakland but had taken to the elegance of San Francisco like a deposed archduke finally coming home. The other agents ragged him but secretly enjoyed the bargain luxuries Epps was always able to find on the road. When Roarke inserted the key into his door, he walked into a room that was not a suite, but worlds above the generic chains: European-style, Old World, with high ceilings and intricate moldings, gilt mirrors and a small wrought-iron balcony.

Roarke showered and went downstairs to meet Epps in the bar; a dark space with thick drapes and antique moldings and a carved fireplace. The tall windows provided a sweeping view of the main street under the gathering storm, and the dark cones of hills beyond.

"Lovely. Nice historic touch," Roarke told Epps dryly as he dropped into the leather booth opposite. There was already a bottle of wine on the table; Roarke had no doubt it would be excellent.

"I know The Madonna Inn is more your style, but it was full up," Epps deadpanned back, referring to Central California's notoriously campy theme hotel, with its red velvet cocktail bar and rooms with rock waterfall showers, hunting lodge rooms, suites with Tiki motifs, with names like The Caveman and the Daisy Mae. To say it was antithetical to the Bureau image was putting it mildly. Roarke had to suppress a smile, thinking about it.

"Tragic," Roarke told him. "I've dreamed of getting you alone at the Madonna Inn."

The agents caught each other up over decent London broils, and the Cabernet was excellent. One advantage of off-season was that they were nearly alone in the bar and didn't have to keep their voices down.

"Couldn't find much family for Hartley," Epps said as he sawed into steak and speared a bloody piece. "Mom's a drunk, no known whereabouts for the father. A sister who hasn't seen him since his first lockup. Told her he was dead and she said, and I quote, 'Good.'"

Roarke felt himself tensing up. Not surprising, but not good.

"He was total scum," he said flatly. "Downloading from every rape porn site he could find. Nothing with boys, but everything else. Anal rape, schoolgirl rape, Asian rape, gang rape."

"Another bad guy, that's a fact," Epps agreed.

"So what we have is Wann: a bad guy. Hartley: a bad guy. Preacherman: a bad guy."

"And Greer," Epps said.

"Greer. Unknown." Roarke pushed his plate aside. "Looking at this from the angle that she's the doer in all four crimes," he began. "There's a whole slew of problems with this last one. It looks like a disorganized crime."

Epps shook his head. "But the others... pretty efficient for disorganized. Two years minimum she's been out there and no one makes her as a suspect until you."

"Exactly. But this time she leaves the scene of the crime, leaves an incredibly messy crime scene, could be evidence all over it. Why wouldn't she clean up? We saw what she did in that SRO."

In profiling it was called decompensating. With most serial killers you saw a fairly long period between murders; the killer would "cool off," and content himself with fantasizing about the latest kill, reliving it in memory, until the urge began to build again. A cooling-off period could be months, or a year or more. But sometimes killers began to unravel, in a syndrome called decompensation: the deterioration of a previously functional system from stress. At this phase they might go on a killing spree with no cooling off period whatsoever; obviously a very dangerous situation; it made Roarke tense to think about it.

"Unless she just walked away cause she figured no one would ever make her for this one," Epps said. "Thing is, she doesn't know we're tracking her. She has no way of knowing that anyone could connect the vic in Portland to this one. She doesn't know she's been tied to Portland or Salt Lake. She's got no connection to the guy at all so from her point of view the truck stop killing should look completely random."

Roarke thought about it. Logically Epps was right; it just didn't *feel* right. It felt like she'd had a meltdown. "Yeah. Let's hope."

"She will know now, though, with the BOLO."

"Which means chances are she goes out of state," Roarke said, and thought, *Fuck. We shouldn't have put out the BOLO. But what else could we do? This is like chasing the wind.*

Epps was looking at him. "So the plan is—"

"Find her."

"If she's still in the state at all. This girl moves."

"Yeah." Roarke said. It worried him, too. Especially after a bloody scene like the one in the rest stop, she may well have left the state entirely. But that, they had no control over. They had no choice but to look for her in California; it was the hottest trail.

Epps was watching him. "So we're giving up on the idea that she's a pro."

"What do you think?" Roarke asked him, neutrally.

"A vigilante or a hunter?" Epps sat back, rubbed his neck with a huge hand. "I just don't know bout that. Question is, why? I mean, this is some dedicated shit. I found *nothing* connecting the vics. Zero. No crossover between cities, states, job histories."

"That means no connection to each other," Roarke pointed out. "They could still all be connected to *her*."

"There's nothing evident. That's the problem. We know next to nothing about her. No way to tell, yet."

"Right," Roarke sighed. "Right." He sat, thinking, then straightened again. "Let's go back to this. Hartley took her by surprise, but he was after the wrong victim, and got what he had coming to him."

"Coincidence," Epps said flatly.

"Yeah, but let's go with it. She's taken by surprise, too, but takes care of him, and leaves him because she's shaken up."

To his credit, Epps sat with the thought for a decent interval before he answered. "What do you like about that, boss?"

Roarke scrubbed his face with a hand while he contemplated the question. Outside the windows, the wind gusted against the building, swirled sand down the sidewalks, flapped the canvas awnings. A wild night.

"I just keep thinking this last one's an anomaly. Sure, same murder weapon as with Preacherman, but Preacherman was killed with two slashes to the throat while he was virtually restrained in a sleeping bag. That bathroom was a slaughterhouse."

"Every vic was different. The pattern is there's no pattern."

"Right," Roarke said, not meaning it.

Epps leaned back. "So you tell me."

"I don't know. She flipped. I don't know." He fell silent.

Across the table, Epps studied him. "So, you being your profiler self when you say she's a vigilante?"

Roarke stared back. "My what?"

"This is what you did, back in the day, right? BAU, BSU. The whole mindhunter trip."

Roarke stared at him. *Am I? Being my profiler self? On the mindhunter trip?*

"She's not like anything I ever saw in the BAU," he said, finally. He picked up his glass, drank it off.

"Roarke in among the crazy men," Epps said admiringly. "Don't know how you did that."

"Oh, I was hungry. I wanted to know all about it. What makes people..."

He paused, because he'd never known how to say it. *What makes people into monsters. What makes them do horrific, hurtful things to people they don't even know.*

He didn't have to say it aloud. Epps knew.

"So what does?"

What does? Nature, nurture — a fucked up childhood, drugs, alco-hol, something missing in the brain, good old-fashioned lack of con-science. And maybe, just maybe, something else, too.

Wind suddenly blew through the restaurant as the door slammed open and a man stumbled in from the street, off-balanced by the gust. "Jesus Christ," he gasped as he steadied himself, then looked around the dining room apologetically. "Bad out there," he muttered, and hur-ried toward the hotel lobby.

Epps looked back across the table at Roarke. "I sure don't know how you worked with those guys day after day."

"It wasn't the guys," Roarke found himself saying. He felt slightly dissociated from his body, the kind of tired and wired that often came after a long day, exacerbated by the combination of adrenaline crash and alcohol buzz. He knew he probably shouldn't be talking, that his filters were down. He had never talked about this, even to Snyder, though he had his suspicions that Snyder knew, in his way.

Epps took a drink, not quite looking at him. So casual. "So what was it?"

Roarke looked at him.

"I knew that's where you came from," Epps said. "What I don't know is why you left. I mean, except for the fact that — who wouldn't?"

Right, who wouldn't? Roarke didn't want to keep talking about it, and yet he did.

He'd spent his whole life running toward a thing and once he got it, he'd turned right around and run away from it.

"It wasn't just one thing. It was a gradual build up of the same thing. These men we studied, hunted, chased — sometimes there was mental illness, a mind so chaotic it was a miracle they were able to function at all. Sometimes there was sociopathy, a complete lack of recognition of the humanity of the victims. But sometimes there was just something — else."

Epps was watching him in the dark of the bar. "Something else like what?"

And then Roarke had to go to the place in his mind that he'd been carefully avoiding since he'd gotten off the plane in San Jose. The thing he always came back to.

"I was able to interview Carl Eugene Forbes before he died."

He could see from the jolt in Epps' eyes that he knew exactly who Roarke was talking about.

Forbes was a serial rapist who was caught after he'd graduated to killing his first victim, as so many rapists did. The dehumanization that is rape is only a breath away from murder, and statistically a large number of rapists who weren't caught and incarcerated eventually crossed that line. Forbes was fatally wounded while attempting to escape arrest, but lingered on for weeks as his internal organs shut down.

"He was going to die. No question. So my boss sends me in to talk to him, to get as much information on other victims as we could."

Roarke reached for the wine bottle and filled his glass, again. "It was just down the road. Atascadero State Hospital." It was the worst assignment Roarke had ever had. Forbes gleefully related tales of days-long torture which were elaborate constructions of lies, truth, and fantasy. *Getting off on reliving pain.* And Roarke was forced to play along, digging into the man's twisted psyche to get corroborating details. He'd spent day after day with a man who was physically and mentally deteriorating into something less than human; even now Roarke could see the ghastly color of his skin as his organs failed, the smell of him. Hair greasy and soaked with sweat, his physical condition matching his mental corruption.

As the days spun out, Roarke found himself sinking into a state of depression that felt almost suicidal in its nihilism; every day he was less sure that he wanted to live on the same earth as a creature like Forbes.

And then something else crept in. Roarke felt his own mind unhinging; there seemed at times another presence in the hospital room with them, a stifling, dark pressure. It wasn't the first time

Roarke had experienced it; sometimes among the criminals at Atascadero and in the criminals he hunted and studied as a BAU agent he would encounter that same sense of presence: an aura of evil, was the best way he knew to describe it.

The presence was especially heavy on the last day Roarke visited Forbes; the air felt so thick in the hospital room Roarke was having trouble breathing. He felt nauseous and hopeless, as if his life force was being sucked into a black hole of nothingness.

"And then..."

Epps looked at him, waiting.

"Forbes died," Roarke finished quietly. "Death rattle and all. He was there — and then he wasn't. Eyes fixed and dilated. No chest movement... just the flatline sound of the machine. But whatever that thing in the room was... *it* was still there."

The air had changed. There was something present, sucking all the life out of the room. Roarke had suddenly felt all his convictions that the world was a solid, real place draining out of his body, and for a moment he thought he would lose his mind entirely.

"It was aware... watching. It... I could feel it smile at me."

Epps was staring at him. Roarke's arms were covered with the same gooseflesh he'd experienced that day in the prison hospital. A feeling that evil was a *thing*. A separate, live, sentient thing, all on its own.

"Shit," Epps said, a strangled sound. "Motherfu — what happened, then?"

"Then the doctors rushed in from Forbes flatlining. They started CPR and there was a lot of commotion and — whatever it was was gone."

The two men sat in the dark bar, with Roarke's story hanging in the air between them.

Roarke drank to the bottom of his glass, set it carefully down. "So at that point I realized I was coming apart and better get the hell out of there before they shipped me out. And I transferred out of the BAU to Criminal Organizations."

Epps was silent for what seemed like forever, and Roarke felt the heaviness of the dark. He massively regretted saying anything; it was a terrible breach. He was the supervisory agent, not a pal. The kind of thing he was talking about had nothing to do with—

"I know what you mean," Epps said softly, and there was a tone in his voice that made Roarke go still. He looked at him across the table.

"When I first signed on to the Bureau I worked undercover in L.A. Man of my *qualifications*—" Epps indicated his face, his skin color — "Got sent in to about a million buys. Ended up in a shooting gallery once or twice. Kids, fourteen, fifteen, sixteen years old sitting in a circle, cooking up. And when that needle went in and those kids went limp..." His eyes were clouded. "You said it. Sometimes there was something *else* there with them in that room."

The agents looked at each other. In the moment Roarke didn't know if he felt relieved or disturbed that Epps understood.

"I don't talk about it because... " He shrugged.

"You can't," Roarke said.

"You don't hear it in class. You don't get it in training. But I don't think we're the only ones who've been in a room with it, boss. I just can't see that."

As the silence went on, they were both uncomfortable. And what either one of them would have said next was dissipated when the waitress stepped up to the table. Roarke was aware that Epps flinched, just as he did.

"You guys okay?" she asked, and the double meaning was not lost on either agent.

"Fine," Roarke said. "Thanks," Epps echoed him, and the waitress moved on.

"So, tomorrow," Epps said, and the subtext was gone. And both of them were glad.

"Tomorrow," Roarke exhaled, thinking of the bloody restroom. The question was time. How much time they had before she came across the wrong person again. "I hope to God the APB turns up a lead. We need to get her off the street." He thought again of decompensation, and what it could mean to any innocent person she happened to run into at this point.

Epps nodded, then hesitated. "We're going to find her, boss. You can't do something like she did at that rest stop and not get noticed by someone."

"I know," Roarke said. But there was only unease in the thought.

Chapter 32

She and the man are perfectly silent in the hall, facing each other. Then she moves past him, down the dark corridor, into the living room.

There is just one low lamp on in the room; he must have turned off the lights when he came in to listen to the bedtime story. But she can see that the wind has whipped the curtains through the doors and knocked over a wood sculpture; the boy's coloring pages are scattered all over the room.

She moves out the doors onto the deck again, where the wind is so strong she has to grasp on to the deck railing; the power in it could blow her off the cliff. She braces herself and leans into the force. She feels, rather than hears, the step behind her.

She faces him full on, without speaking. If he wants to talk, he will have to do it himself.

His face is conflicted; he is struggling, but determined to speak. "I try not to scare him, when he's obviously anxious."

She is overcome by a hot wave of fury. *And yet you leave him alone, over and over, with a mother who has neglected him, abandoned him, who has left herself open to darkness.*

She sees him flinch, as if he has heard every word of her thought.

"It's not the storm he's afraid of," she says evenly. "I'll go if you want."

There is a hot, thick silence.

"You know I don't want that," he says.

At least he is honest.

"I'll go anyway."

Lightning cracks through the sky. The man glances behind her, at the sky and sea. "You can't go out in this."

She almost laughs. It's nothing, the storm, compared to what she has seen.

She says nothing, just tries to sidestep him. He blocks her. The lightning cracks again, accompanied by a boom of thunder almost immediately, making them both turn toward it.

"There's — a guest room."

"You want me to stay in the guest room," she says, without inflection; the only mockery is in the thought.

"No, I don't want you to stay in the guest room," he says quietly, and with admirable dignity.

"What do you want?" she challenges him. The air is electric between them.

"I want... to be sure what you want."

She steps sharply toward him and he flinches; she doesn't blame him, since she herself has no idea what she is going to do next. She reaches her hand around to the back of his neck and laces her fingers through his hair, pulling hard enough that his neck is exposed.

He closes his eyes, and she brings her lips to his throat, kissing and then biting, and kissing.

His arms go around her and he bends his head forward to her, and his mouth is on hers. She is a live thing in his arms, fighting as much as yielding, and she can feel her writhing electrifying him, feel the heat in the response of his body, feel the blood racing under his skin and his heart pounding against hers as they kiss.

She pulls back from him, pushing him away hard, and he stands against the light of the doors with the wind billowing the curtains behind him. Then she turns and walks by him, into the house, into the hall, up the stairs.

She walks straight into the master suite, past the huge brass bed, and stands in the middle of the sky and the wind and the dark. When he steps in after her, she is pacing beside the window.

He closes the door behind him, and she goes still.

She turns abruptly to the doors and pulls them open. Wind rushes into the room and she closes her eyes, feeling the current on her face. Her hands are gripping the doorframe.

He steps behind her and she stiffens, her nails digging into the wood of the frame. Then he puts his hands on her waist and kisses her neck and she twists to face him, and her hands are under his clothes, her nails tracing his stomach, digging into his back, and he is hot and hard against her, and as the rain crashes down outside, he is inside her.

Chapter 33

Roarke snapped awake with his heart pounding and gooseflesh raised all over his body. For a disoriented second he did not know where he was or how old he was; he was still in the dream's grip, with the monster's hot breath on his neck...

Then the dream slid away like a shadow and he remembered the hotel room, and why he was there, and then his name.

He sat up and threw back the blankets to stand and collect himself.

Two nights in a row, he thought. *Third time this week. What's three times bad news? Nothing good, is what I think.*

He forced down an apprehension bordering on superstition. The only solution was to do what he did best: hunt.

He turned to the wall, where he'd taped up his triangle: the sketch of the woman and her known victims below, four now: Roarke had added the photo of the trucker, Hartley, to the pyramid.

Portland? Salt Lake? Here?

He wanted to be everywhere at once.

The storm raged outside. Roarke knew he wouldn't sleep. He stood and crossed the room.

He could hear the wind whistling against the side of the building even before he opened the French doors to the balcony. The curtains whipped and billowed inward as he stepped out through them.

The elements were not merely moving, but battling, a symphony of violence.

And Roarke had a sudden feeling that he needed to be out, to be battling whatever was out there. A feeling like falling from a great height, that something inevitable was happening that night, something he was powerless to stop even if he knew where, when, why?

He looked out over the city; toward the ocean... at the clouds veiling the moon in dark, and shuddered.

• • • • •

Twenty minutes away, in Pismo Beach, the electrical storm lights up the entire ocean.

She listens to the boom and crack of thunder while the man sleeps beside her, a warm, solid, live presence. The bed seems to float in the dark of the sky, with the lightning branching around it through the blackness. After a time she eases herself up out of the bed, slips silently across the floor toward the door, and down the stairs.

In the living room, she steps out on the deck, into the rain.

The storm has come up hard, with the whistling wind and flying debris and gusts of rain. Every living and inanimate thing outside is moving; even the lightning between the racing clouds seems to be shaking in the wind.

The weather is angry. She is not allowed to rest, not allowed such normal things as she is finding in this house, with these people. There will be a reckoning, and she is not the only one at risk.

And yet the wind, the lightning, the ocean... this is tremendous power, and it is not the power of *It*, it is power only, and power that she might take for herself, to do as she would do, not out of weakness or fear, but out of choice.

She stands and feels the rain washing over her, and the tide pounding in her blood, and she listens.

DAY FIVE

Chapter 34

She wakes to sun shining in through the windows, bright white light, and the heat of the man's body beside her in the huge brass bed. Her own body is all awake, alive. The sun reflects off the ocean like a mirror.

And her dreams have been clear.

As she moves to get out of bed, his fingers close around her wrist, lightly.

"Don't go," he murmurs, half-awake.

"I need clothes," she whispers back.

"No you don't."

"I do," she says, and bends to kiss the pulse at his throat. He groans in longing and is starting to turn over when she says, "Sleep." And then, "I'll be here."

In the hall, she pauses at the next door and looks in on the boy as he sleeps.

Then she takes the man's keys, takes his car, and drives.

Chapter 35

Just before dawn, Roarke gave up on sleep. He showered, dressed, took his roller bag and went downstairs and got into his rental car and drove the fifteen miles to the tiny, scenic SLO airport to board the next plane to Portland, via San Francisco. He gripped the steering wheel and watched the sun coming up over the vineyards, knowing that he was very possibly making the worst mistake of his life, going in the wrong direction, getting colder instead of warmer, as the old kids' game went.

But he was feeling a sense of urgency he couldn't shake, and he needed to do something, and he still had the strong feeling there was more to learn from the Preacherman. They had sex abuse with Wann, a rape conviction for Hartley, and semen on Greer before he died. It was turning into a pattern of sexual predators, and Preacherman was the anomaly.

And Roarke had learned to follow the anomaly; the exception often did prove the rule.

He called Epps as he was boarding the small express plane. Epps' voice was gravelly from sleep. "What's up, boss?"

"I'm at the airport. I'm going back to Portland."

Roarke could hear the adrenaline spike in Epps' voice. "What happened?"

"Nothing like that. It's just a—" Roarke didn't want to say hunch. "I couldn't sleep."

"So you're going to Portland."

"To follow up on Preacherman. I want to dig deeper, see what this guy was about." *See what* she *saw*, is what he meant, but he didn't say it aloud. "Maybe the nun was just wrong. And if Preacherman had a history of sex abuse, then we've got a solid victimology."

"Anything I can do?" Epps said.

"Get me some prints," Roarke said, not kidding. "Tell me who she is."

As the flight attendants started their safety demonstration Roarke was so on edge he almost got up and walked off the plane.

But in the end, he didn't.

As they lifted off, he watched the rising sun turn the ocean into a vast mirror of light.

Sometimes, you roll the dice.

Chapter 36

It is an address in San Luis Obispo, one she copied from the man's iPhone while he was sleeping, and she finds the place easily, driving through the historic downtown with its mission and museums and arty boutiques and vegan cafés into a neat residential neighborhood nestled against the striking green mounds of volcanic hills. She parks across the street to survey the small bungalow, which, having seen the beach house, she knows is a greatly reduced circumstance for Sebastian's ex-wife.

On this brilliantly jewel-toned morning, all the shades at the windows are drawn, making the house look furtive, and there is a motorcycle, a big, bad one, parked in the drive.

She watches the house for some time, until the door opens and a man comes out, young and lean and wolfish, with greasy black hair and the sallow skin of an addict. He walks, loose-limbed with sex, and mounts the Harley aggressively.

Now the wife comes out, the ex, the boy's mother. She is wrapped in a thin short robe and she is thin, far too thin, and as stupidly languid as the man.

The wife moves toward the Harley and twines herself around him like a vine, clinging, dazed with desire, begging him not to go.

All this she watches coldly. Everything is perfectly apparent. Alcohol is the least of this woman's problems.

A weak person, an unworthy person.

She watches as the wife's lover revs the motorcycle engine and rides away, leaving the wife stumbling in the drive, screaming after him.

And she knows what she has to do.

Chapter 37

It was another overcast day in Portland, and the line at the church was around the block again.

Roarke found Sister Frances at her post in the soup kitchen.

The dour nun looked almost happy to see him, and this time she led him straight out of the dining hall toward the miniscule office.

"Sorry to bother you again, Sister," Roarke told her as he followed her inside.

She waved a hand airily. "Knew you'd be back."

I bet you did, Roarke thought, and sat himself awkwardly down in one of the battered chairs, then cut to the chase. "I learned from a witness that the Preacherman — Milvia — had a cabin up in the mountains somewhere. I've come back to try to find it."

"Somewhere?" she repeated dryly. "That narrows it down."

Roarke fought a smile. "It could have been in the Mount Hood area. You never heard anything about that?"

She looked sour. "I didn't make a point of talking to the man. And he certainly made a point of avoiding me."

Roarke remembered that the sister had been slow to warm to conversation, and tried another prompt. "He would go up to this cabin, wherever it was, every other week or so."

She thought about this, and nodded slowly. "Makes sense. His attendance here was irregular, but it was irregular in a regular way. One week on, one week off..."

Good girl, Roarke thought silently. *I know you can help me, here.* He spoke contemplatively, as if he were working things out in his own mind, aloud. "He didn't have a car, and he's not exactly a likely person to be picked up as a hitchhiker. I figure the only way realistically he would've been able to get himself out there is by bus."

The nun brightened. "There's a transit subsidy program. I can check the records for you."

Yes. Roarke thought. "This would have been outside the city, though, not inside it," he said, and held his breath.

The nun waved a hand imperiously. "Doesn't matter. It's a voucher program — he could have used it on Greyhound as well as Tri-Met."

It was always a plus to have a personal in with God. One phone call to the transit subsidy program and Sister Frances was able to inform Roarke that before his death the Preacherman had been receiving a monthly transit voucher.

And the next phone call, to Greyhound, was even more auspicious: there were only two drivers who regularly drove 84, the main route up toward Mount Hood, and one was actually in the station that day. The driver remembered Preacherman well, and not especially fondly.

"You could smell him coming," he told Roarke dryly when Sister Frances passed him the phone. "But in the People's Republic of Portland... you have to let them on as long as they're not eating other passengers or tearing up the bus."

"Can you tell me where he got off?" Roarke asked, and found he was holding his breath again.

"I don't think anyone knows where that guy got off." Another comedian. Roarke waited patiently until he continued. "His stop was Mount Hood Village."

"And how often would you say he made that trip?"

"I saw him maybe twice a month. Once or sometimes twice outgoing, once or twice incoming."

When Roarke hung up, Sister Frances was watching him. She looked almost smug.

"I can't begin to thank you," Roarke said, and meant it. "I'd have been nowhere without you."

The nun leaned back. Her eyes were shrewd. "Then tell me what this is about."

Roarke hesitated.

"Agent Roarke, we're the same," Sister Frances said bluntly. "We deal with good people, and we deal with evil people. We hone our skills so we can separate the evil from the good, see what's coming before it has a chance to do damage. I always knew there was something off about Milvia and I want to be able to name it for the next time I see it. It's my work, every bit as much as it is yours. We need to be able to name it to fight it."

It made more sense than anything Roarke had heard in a long, long time, and he felt himself compelled to answer.

"Sister, I don't know what Milvia did. I don't know that he did anything. But I believe he was killed by someone who was killing bad—" he was about to say *people*, but he reconsidered and said, more slowly, "Men."

The sister registered this with a subtle jolt in her eyes. "I see. And that's why you asked about sexual predation."

"It's a theory," Roarke said.

She nodded, and Roarke could see she was thinking it through. Then she shook her head. "I'm sorry. I just don't know. I never saw it. Not that. And I've seen..." her eyes clouded. "A lot."

Roarke had no doubt.

"I'm going up to Mount Hood to look for his cabin." He leaned forward. "And I promise you, if — *when* I find out what he was doing, I will tell you."

They sat there in the closet-sized office for a suspended moment, and finally, finally, she nodded. "Thank you, Agent Roarke."

He left her, feeling better that they were on the same side.

Chapter 38

She comes back to the beach house with pastries, and having changed into clothes she bought at a Wal-Mart, along with expected cosmetics, an overnight bag; a carefully calculated number of things: as if she'd stopped at her motel, but not checked out, as if she is not assuming anything.

The boy is already up and coloring at his small table in the living room, but happily stops to help her make coffee and arrange the pastries and muffins on a plate. She is cutting up fruit when the man comes down.

When Jason is turned away, the father comes up behind her and buries his face in her neck, breathing her in. She forces herself not to stiffen at the surprise of it, then slowly relaxes into his touch.

"I wasn't sure you'd come back," he murmurs.

"I wanted to," is all she has to say. It is enough.

And she turns to him, putting her mind off what she's just done.

Chapter 39

There is an uncanny shape about volcanoes, not in any way like other mountains. They are a pressure cooker for molten lava, not just an imposing presence, but an active and lethal force that can explode and wreak havoc at any moment.

An apt enough metaphor for the huntress, Roarke thought, as he drove up the curves of the mountain road toward Mount Hood, and realized that he had unconsciously adopted Snyder's term. What had created her volcanic anger? What set her off?

Mount Hood Village was about two hours from Portland by car, so it would have taken Preacherman three at least by bus. Roarke had his windows down and the air was crisp and fresh, laced with pine smells and the stone scent of granite baking in the sun, but he felt increasingly foolish as he wound the car up through the green hills, further and further into wild and scenic forest. Here he was, driving off the map, with only the vaguest idea where he was going and what he was looking for to begin with.

He knew there were always miles and miles of unincorporated forest around national parks. And national forests were prime hideouts for all kinds of outlaws; it was easy to get lost in them. In the last two decades several serial killers had operated for years, undetected, dumping bodies that would never be found in the endless woods between Oregon and Washington. Not to mention the meth labs and marijuana fields that tended to get hidden in National Forests and their surrounding areas.

It was bad guy territory for sure, but there was so *much* of it. The chances of picking up Preacherman's trail were... well, Roarke didn't want to think about it. He was too close now to stop, but he was also increasingly antsy as he studied the GPS on the dash.

There were two of the huge parks on either side of the town: Mount Hood on the Oregon side, Gifford Pinchot on the Washington side. The Columbia River ran along the border; he was driving alongside the Columbia River Gorge now, with the sparkling rush of water below him and the strange peak of the volcano on the horizon. He had no idea even what side of the border this possibly mythical cabin was on, except that the homeless witness, Elias Marias, had mentioned Hood, not Gifford Pinchot.

Preacherman being as paranoid as he was, Roarke could imagine he would have employed all kinds of misdirection to keep his hideout a secret. He might regularly have gotten off at a stop that was far from his final destination. On the other hand, as Roarke had told Sister Frances, Preacherman was not a good candidate for hitchhiking; his general dishevelment and the extra special something that people seemed to notice in his aura would have made catching rides a dicey proposition. So Roarke was gambling on Preacherman being lazy, riding the bus close to wherever his cabin was and then packing in the rest of the way.

And then... people in mountain towns know everything about everyone. And Preacherman stuck out. Maybe someone had noticed him. Maybe, just maybe, it was a matter of finding the right person.

It was the most tenuous of threads. But Roarke couldn't shake the feeling that Preacherman held some sort of key. If he could find out for sure about Preacherman, he might learn something about the huntress. She had *chosen* Preacherman, it wasn't random.

As Roarke pushed his foot down on the accelerator, his phone buzzed on the seat beside him. He picked up and could instantly tell by the lilt in Epps' voice that there had been a breakthrough of some kind.

"Think we might have something, boss. Car stolen from SFO long term parking on Monday, a couple hours after Greer bought it. There's a woman on the parking security tape — the hair is black and short, but I think it's a wig. Sure looks like your girl to me."

Roarke felt a spike of hope. To have actual tape was a huge step forward.

"The tape shows her breaking in?"

"Negative. She walks right up to the driver's side and sticks a key in. But the owner has his keys on him, says no one has a set but him and his wife."

Roarke stared out at the road in front of him, thinking fast. "She uses a key but she doesn't disengage security. So she has a master key."

"Looks like. And there's more," Epps said. "The reason we have the tape is the car got abandoned. It got ticketed and towed. Owner is still out of town, would never have known the car was gone, but the wife opened the mail and found the ticket and impound notice."

Roarke's mouth was dry. "Where'd she leave it?"

"Pismo Beach. Traffic cop found it in one of the beach lots early Tuesday morning. No overnight parking allowed, so it was ticketed and towed."

"Pismo." The beach town was less than an hour from the rest stop where the trucker had been killed.

Epps was already answering Roarke's next question. "Lam and Stotlemyre are on the car, combing for trace evidence. Condition of that rest stop scene — there's gonna be blood in that car, boss." Epps sounded downright exhilarated. "Could be prints, too."

Roarke's mind was racing. If there were prints, those would take the least time to run. Blood typing was fast, DNA was slow. It would be faster to determine that it wasn't the trucker's blood in the car than to say for certain it was. But prints, if she'd ever been arrested — that could change everything.

"We've got her tied to the trucker, I can feel it," Epps exulted.

But where was she?

"I'm coming down to Pismo," Roarke said.

There was a slight hesitation on the other end. "She's probably long gone, boss, don't you think? If I'd dumped a car after a murder like that, I'd be as far the hell away from it as I could get."

If *she dumped it,* is what Roarke's mind answered back, surprising even him.

If?

Okay, why did I just think that?

Because if she's organized enough to steal a car out of airport long-term, where the chances are good it won't be reported for days, even weeks, then why is she leaving it illegally parked where it's going to set off red flags almost immediately? It makes no sense.

Which means she wasn't thinking, that night. Not after the murder, she wasn't. She's making mistakes. She might even be injured. That was a hell of a fight in that restroom.

He felt a surge of adrenaline... and then the rush was undercut.

Or it's a red herring. Epps is probably right, she's long gone.

He spoke aloud. "Did Lam confirm it was *only* the trucker's blood in the bathroom?"

"He's checking," Epps said. "You really think she might still be hanging around?" He couldn't keep the skepticism out of his voice and Roarke didn't blame him.

"Unlikely," Roarke admitted. "But try the hospitals, see if they got a woman of her description in that night."

It was a long shot that she would have gone to a hospital. *But she might be injured, and she might be falling apart, and she might just be smart enough not to leave the vicinity because she's thinking that no one in their right mind is going to be thinking she'd stay in the vicinity after a murder like that.*

And that's the kind of second-guessing that can make you crazy, he chided himself.

He suddenly had the strongest urge to just turn the car around and get to the airport, get on the next plane. He fought the impulse down. He was less than an hour from Preacherman's hideout, if it actually existed, and it made no sense not to keep going.

He spoke aloud, into his Bluetooth. "I'm almost to Mount Hood Village. Keep me posted."

"And you, boss," Epps agreed.

Then Roarke punched off the phone and drove on, toward the volcano.

Chapter 40

The sheriff's station was a log building right outside of Mount Hood Village, and Roarke's first stop.

He parked his rental car and stood for a minute in the gravel lot. It was cooler here than in Portland; a brisk wind rustled through the long-needled pines above him. Squirrels and birds chased each other through the foliage.

The sheriff was not much past his own age, clean-cut, competent and alert as Roarke explained the situation briefly, that he was looking for information on a murder victim who might be tied to another case.

The sheriff glanced at the Preacherman's mug shot and nodded immediately. "Oh, yeah. Not a local, but he came around."

"You have any trouble from him?"

"Nothing anyone ever reported. He'd breeze through pretty fast, didn't stay in town. Mental issues, obviously, but I never got any complaints."

"I'm looking for a cabin he might have had up here."

The sheriff shook his head. "Always thought he had a place, but I couldn't tell you where it is. Definitely not one of the RV parks. If he had one, it's probably illegal, but there are lots of places to hide out up here."

Roarke knew very well.

"Mind if I ask around town?" It was a courtesy question only, but Roarke was a big believer in courtesy.

"Help yourself," the sheriff said pleasantly. "Good people."

The main street of the town was rustic: Old West-style board store-fronts, most with wide plank porches equipped with rockers and even a battered couch or two. A gas station, a diner, an outdoor supply shop, an auto parts store, a donut shop, a ski shop, a barbershop — and, Roarke was happy to see, a general store.

He was glad he had dressed down, khakis and long-sleeved shirt and boots, the casual/hiking outfit he always packed when he was on the road. If he had any luck he would be out in the woods sooner rather than later, and the non-city clothes might go over better in a tiny town like this.

Armed with a mug shot of Preacherman, he stepped through the screen door of the store.

Bells jangled at his entrance and a man in his sixties looked up from the counter, someone who looked like he'd been right where he was for just about forever, and moreover, was happy about it. This might not be a wasted trip after all. Roarke mentally crossed his fingers as he moved up to the counter.

"A man on a mission," the man observed, already sizing him up. Roarke half-expected him to pull out a pipe.

"I am," he said, and showed his credentials, and then the mug shot. "Looking for someone you may have seen around here."

The man harrumphed at the image of the transient. "You don't forget that one. Haven't seen him in a long time, though."

'No one has. He's dead."

The man looked unsurprised.

"So, he shopped here?" Roarke asked.

"Canned stuff, mostly," the shopkeeper agreed. "Tuna, sardines. Bread. Soup. Lantern oil."

"He come in with a pack?" Roarke asked. "Did it look like he was pitching a tent?"

The shopkeeper cocked his head, thinking back. "Don't think I ever saw him with more than a backpack," he said finally.

Roarke felt a surge of hope. If Preacherman wasn't packing a bedroll or a tent, he likely did have a cabin or some shelter. "How often did you see him?"

"One or two days in a week, then not for a couple of weeks. He came up on the bus from Portland, would stay for a while, disappear."

Roarke silently blessed the scrupulous nosiness of small towns. "Word is, he had a cabin up near here. Probably not legally."

"I think that's right," the man said neutrally. "Don't know where, but I know someone who might."

The "someone who might," turned out to be "Ed at the coffee shop," a big trucker type in his late forties. Ed didn't own the coffee shop, or even work there; apparently he just never left it. He was seated at what was surely his regular booth, a deeply scratched pine table at a front window looking out on Main Street.

Ed put down his coffee, took a look at the mug shot Roarke offered, and nodded vigorously. "Yup. Seen him packing off-trail down near Five Mile Hollow."

"You ever see a cabin that way?"

Ed hesitated just a beat too long. "Thought I did," he admitted. He didn't meet Roarke's eyes and Roarke instantly got the impression he'd done more than *see* the cabin. "It was a while ago, maybe even two years now—"

Roarke interrupted him pleasantly. "The man's dead. I'm just looking for his place. Appreciate it if you could steer me that way."

"Sure, sure." And miracle of miracles, Ed proceeded to draw a map.

The area Ed directed him to was thick forest, and not part of the park; it was in the miles and miles of no-man's land on the outskirts of the official lines of the National Forest. Preacherman may have been an outlaw and a drunk, but he was a canny one. No one official was likely to have bothered him here. It was a two-mile hike in from a distinctive curve in the road, but there was no other marker, no clear trail, and no reason for anyone to decide to go exploring in the area. Ed had been able to give clear directions because of a volcanic rock outcropping he'd described as looking like an upright iron. Roarke found the rock mass, and there was a dry creek bed to follow from there.

Sunlight slanted through glistening pine needles and the layered silence surrounded him; the call of blue jays, the crunch of pine needles under his feet, the soft thud of acorns falling onto the forest loam. A rabbit bounded across his path and Roarke started back, then shook his head, amused at himself.

He hiked on, gauging the distance and direction with his iPhone, and just about two miles in he found it: a sudden sinking of the land into a small clearing in the woods. And in the middle of trees, he spotted a small cabin, no bigger than the fifteen-by-fifteen- foot dwellings Roarke had seen in Dignity Village. In fact the cabin was so similar to those structures it might have been airlifted straight from the village, a carbon copy of Elias Marias's place, front stairs, narrow porch and all. The similarity gave Roarke a shiver of anticipation.

The clearing was scrub brush and small trees and stony ground, surrounded by maple and towering pine. A footbridge led across a small depression to the cabin itself. Roarke could see a closed padlock on the door.

Tiny birds cheeped in the trees around him, and the wind whispered silkily through pine needles. Somewhere nearby water rushed in a stream. Roarke breathed in, surrounded by green.

He took a step forward toward the bridge... and then stopped in his tracks.

The hair was standing up on the back of his neck, and his breathing had become deep and labored. *Something wrong, here.*

He had an overwhelming instinct to bolt. A rush of adrenaline, that fight-or-flight panic. The feeling was so strong he couldn't breathe.

Danger.

The whole clearing vibrated with it.

Even more than danger. There was a creeping sense of evil. A sense of presence, of being watched, even stalked.

Spider-sense. The subconscious registering details that the conscious mind takes longer to process.

His head was pounding, all of his training screaming at him to run.

He reached into his jacket and drew his weapon, but slowly, not moving anything but his hand and arm, while he stayed very still, staring toward the house. There was no movement of any kind, no signs of life. He forced himself to survey the area, eyes sweeping in front of him just inches at a time, trying to take in what he was seeing, what was lurking in the ocean of green surrounding him that was giving him this fight-or-flight reaction. He saw the silver threads of a spider's web... sunlight on the leaves...

His eyes kept returning to the tree closest to the footbridge. There was something about it... but there was no one behind it or near it. He frowned and looked again, toward the ground.

There was a mud-streaked shirt at the base of some scrub, carelessly discarded and looking a little like a collapsed scarecrow. And a little further, an odd depression in the ground at the side of the footbridge; a little crater that looked disturbingly familiar, but wildly out of context.

Then it came to him like a thunderclap.

His eyes moved up, to the tree that had kept drawing his eyes, forcing himself to look harder.

And he saw it. Among the brown twigs and green needles, a flash of white, a too familiar shape. What was left of a human skull.

Chapter 41

The bomb squad of the Portland Bureau office arrived just short of two hours later, spilling out of a pair of vans dressed in bomb suits, hauling out tools for subsurface exploration, including a Wheelbarrow: a remote-controlled device outfitted with cameras, microphones and sensors for chemical, biological and nuclear agents.

Roarke had phoned the squad from where he stood, and then waited, not moving an inch from his spot, for the entire two hours. He had had plenty of time to see that the "discarded" shirt he'd seen half-buried in the dirt actually contained human remains, whatever the forest animals had left, and the streaks of mud were actually dried blood and decomposition fluids. The crater Roarke had seen, if only subliminally, was a detonated mine. Some distance away from the crater there was also a half-buried pair of shorts and a hiking boot. The victim's head had been blown off his body and caught in the tree, and thus the skull had not been carried away by wildlife. Roarke was fairly certain he'd registered the white of the bone first without realizing what he was seeing; that was what had triggered his sense of imminent danger. He'd had time to scan the ground of the clearing many times over, and identify depressions he thought could be additional landmines; he'd made a careful grid and sketch on the back of the map that Ed had drawn him. On his approach he had walked right by two of them that he could now see; it was only blind chance that he had not set one off himself.

He'd had plenty of time to realize how easily he could have died.

The bomb squad unloaded their equipment and cleared a trail to him first, moving him back to a van for safety. Even after two solid hours on his feet, Roarke was too tense even to sit while they began to sweep the clearing.

There was a lot to sweep.

The footbridge was rigged. The second step of the porch was rigged. The front door was rigged. And the bomb squad quickly corroborated Roarke's guess that the whole perimeter of the cabin was planted with homemade landmines.

As the bomb squad began the painstaking process of sweeping, clearing and rendering harmless, Roarke reached for his phone to call Epps and fill him in.

"Turn any open operations over to Jones. I need you up here. I want someone else to see this."

A bomb tech brought one of the dismantled mines over to Roarke to show him: a simple wooden box, less than six inches wide and only a few inches tall with a hinged lid that acted as the trigger mechanism. "It's a homemade form of a Schu-mine 42 anti-personnel device, a wooden landmine developed by the Germans in WWII. They used them in Angola and Namibia in the 1970's and 1980's."

Roarke examined it gingerly. A slot was cut into the side of the lid that rested on the striker-retaining pin. Inside was a block of cast TNT with a variety of fuses.

"The wooden composition makes the mines invisible to metal detectors," the tech explained. "We're having to use Ground Penetrating Radar to locate the bombs."

Preacherman had buried the mines shallowly so that they would be triggered by a step onto the lid, forcing the retaining pin out of the striker, which then hit the detonator. Some of the boxes had rotted in the ground. Others were still fully operational. There were three dozen of them.

The bomb tech explained grimly. "They're designed to destroy the legs and drive dirt and bone into the upper regions of the body. What happened to your vic was a really unlucky step. You rarely see someone's head blown clean off."

A wallet found in the victim's shorts identified him as a Canadian tourist gone missing four months before, but who had been traveling alone on a road trip and had not been known to have been in the Mount Hood area, consequently the region had never been searched. He had walked through the clearing, stepped on one of Preacherman's Schu-mines, and had been blown to bits.

The Preacherman had killed him six months after he himself had been killed.

Sweeping the clearing and exterior of the house took most of the rest of the day, enough time for Roarke to check into a hotel off Main Street in the village and for Epps to make it up on the next flight.

Epps remained silent through most of the tour of the site, but he had been stiff with tension since entering the clearing, when Roarke had shown him where he had stopped and spotted the landmine crater and the hand. Risk of life and limb was a constant awareness in their work, but there was something about the unexpectedness of this brush with death that was more than usually disturbing. It was the timed-release malice that was getting to Roarke.

By then the squad had gone through the cabin itself, which was also a ticking time bomb.

The ceiling was barely seven feet high, and if a man spread his arms wide he could almost touch both walls. A potbellied stove served for heat. Pull-down stairs led to an attic. Crude but bizarrely neat shelves were built against one wall, stocked with canned goods, dry goods and hunting gear. There was a table made of a board atop a steel storage drum, a propane fridge, solar panels on the roof. The bed was a wooden platform with a thin, dirty sleeping pad and an even dirtier sleeping bag. The space reeked of smoke and sweat.

And it was full of booby traps: some just sadistic false scares, like the mousetrap rigged with caps nailed above the front door that had sounded like a gun going off when the first squad member came through the door. Others were real. A flashlight set on a crate beside the door was rigged with explosives, a detonator, and batteries inside the casing. Dynamite was rigged to the attic door, enough to blow the whole cabin sky-high.

Besides the horrific, there was also the simply stomach-turning: plastic Coke bottles filled with stale urine, improvised chamber pots that had never been emptied.

"Charming," Epps muttered, revolted. "This was one classy dude."

Preacherman had been practicing making bombs for a long time. He had a whole stock of materials: soldering equipment, sulfuric acid, sugar, cotton, potassium chlorate, various electric saws. There were notebooks and notebooks full of diagrams, materials lists, test reports, scribbled records of calculated madness. There were homemade hand-grenades made from condensed milk cans, pipe bombs packed with dynamite, a whole set of used law books hollowed out, pages glued together, then sawed out to accommodate explosives.

But those were just baby bombs. Sketches and raw materials proved that Preacherman had much, much bigger plans in mind.

The base of the crude table, a fifty-five gallon standard steel shipping drum of the kind often used as trash cans, turned out to be filled with ammonium nitrate fertilizer mixed with liquid nitromethane and Tovex, a water gel explosive used by oil companies for blasting, tunneling and seismic exploration. And Preacherman's last notebook, entitled **Armageddon,** diagrammed the bomb he had been in the process of making.

"Same composition as the Oklahoma City bomb," the bomb squad chief told Roarke and Epps. It was clear from Preacherman's sketches and notes that he had intended to detonate the bomb in Pioneer Court-house Square during a popular international street fair, World On The Street, featuring foods and crafts and dances from many countries. It was an annual event that drew thousands of people.

"What kind of damage are we looking at?" Roarke asked the squad chief.

"McVeigh used sixteen of those things packed together in a truck. That killed 168 people, injured more than 680, and destroyed or damaged 324 buildings in the immediate vicinity. But even one this size... the effect of the blast would have been equal to over 300 pounds of TNT."

Roarke and Epps listened with increasing horror.

The explosive shock wave would have caused bodies anywhere near the bomb to be thrown through the air, with effects anywhere from instant death to dismemberment, internal bleeding, severe burns, bone fractures, ruptured eardrums.

"It would have killed or grievously injured anyone within two dozen yards of the blast seat. Fatalities in the dozens, injuries in the hundreds," the chief summed up.

All the ingredients had already been purchased, or more likely stolen, and were stored in the cabin: ten fifty-pound bags of fertilizer, eighteen-inch long sausages of Tovex, electric blasting caps, spools of shock tube, cannon fuse.

The drum had already been outfitted with a stenciled sign saying RECYLING ONLY. According to his notes, Preacherman had planned to wheel the drum into the square on a cart (*So easily looking like a garbage man*, Roarke thought to himself) and leave it with the other trashcans, detonating it from a distance with a remote detonator.

Milvia's notes and diagrams indicated that optimum placement would be in front of the plate glass of the visitor's center, where the shattered glass would turn into deadly projectiles. He had scribbled the words MAXIMUM KILL and underlined them several times.

Roarke was just contemplating that when Epps said, "Look here, boss." He pointed to a sentence scrawled in pencil across one of the wall planks:

Isn't it scary that one man could wreak this kind of hell?

"Tim McVeigh said that," the bomb squad chief said, and everyone in the cabin went silent.

The fact was, if Preacherman had carried through with his plans, it could well have been the third deadliest act of terror ever committed on U.S. soil, surpassed only by 9/11 and the Oklahoma City bombing.

"When was this street fair?" Epps asked tensely.

"Three days after he died," Roarke said. "I looked it up. Nine thousand seven hundred attended. No injuries."

Chapter 42

The little inn off Main Street of Mount Hood Village was a former family home that had quaint but fairly large guest rooms. Epps' assessment was "doesn't suck," but in a town the size of the village, Roarke didn't think he'd done too badly. It was worth the price of admission for the stunning views of the snow-topped volcano.

The agents climbed the stairs together and stopped at the landing between their rooms. Roarke felt his leg muscles trembling under him.

"Fried," he said.

"Almost being blown to bits will do that to you," Epps told him.

They were both slow to speak, still reeling at the level of rage and evil intent contained in that tiny cabin.

But that was no longer Roarke's concern.

The FBI would do what it did. The Portland office would launch a full-scale investigation into Preacherman, his possible connection to hate groups, possible co-conspirators, any still-extant threats. But for Roarke, the question was settled with that one quote on the bomb diagram: *Isn't it scary that one man can wreak this kind of hell?*

He could get caught up in the months of investigation that would now go on into Preacherman, but that was a cold trail, and he had a hot one in Pismo.

And there was something else Roarke couldn't get his mind off of.

The murder of Preacherman had quite possibly saved dozens, even hundreds of lives.

Apart from his extremely conflicted feelings on that subject, Roarke couldn't get the question out of his head: *How did she know?*

The nun had said, "There were no politics involved," and in Preacherman's extensive notes there was no indication of vengeance against the government or any other entity. It was pure, unfocused hate.

So when the huntress sat in Pioneer Courthouse Square, listening to Preacherman rant, had he said something that made her understand what he was planning?

Was she killing not only sexual predators, but predators, period?

They had reached the landing, and Epps turned to Roarke. "You think she knew?" Epps asked, as if he'd read Roarke's thought.

Roarke kept his voice neutral. "Good reason to kill someone, isn't it?"

"Who the hell says she had a reason?"

Epps didn't usually explode and Roarke was taken aback, but he waited patiently to see what this particular explosion was about.

Epps finally shook his head. "We got something on Greer," he said, and Roarke could hear reluctance in his voice. "You know the shipment that was coming in the day Greer died was live cargo."

"Women," Roarke said flatly.

"Right. Well, Jones found a CI who said there was some talk in *Ogromni* that Greer was sampling the merchandise."

For a moment Roarke felt completely off-balance as his mind raced through the implications. So did the organization have Greer hit after all? Were they back to a paid assassin? Or if the huntress had *not* been informed about Greer by the organization, how did she know?

Roarke suddenly understood why Epps had exploded. He was back to total confusion.

"He was sampling the merchandise as in the trafficked women?"

"I don't know, boss. That's all Jones could get."

Roarke scrubbed his face with a hand. He looked out the window beside them at the moon over the volcano. *Just two days to full,* he thought uneasily. *Two days.*

Then he turned back to Epps. "Get some sleep. We're going down to Pismo tomorrow."

Roarke shut the door of his room behind him, kicked off his shoes and dropped onto the bed, needing to be horizontal. His legs were shaky from the stress and adrenaline overload of the day, and the question pounded in his head.

How does she know?

He got immediately up again, rummaged in his case to find the sketch, and taped it to the wall.

Then he stood, staring at her image.

How do you do it? How do you know?

Chapter 43

Late, late at night, after the boy has been put to bed and they have made love again, she lies awake in the man's bed, feeling his rhythmic breathing through her skin. She is very still, listening to the wind and sea.

The voices are stronger, insistent. All of nature seems as agitated as she feels.

After a time, she wriggles carefully from under the sheets, silently stands.

She walks down the hall in the dark and stops in the next doorway, watching the boy as he sleeps, with the moonlight a pale veil on his face.

After a time, she moves on, out onto the deck. It is two days away, two days until the day, and she can barely hear her own thoughts over the screams. The wind surrounds her, pushing at her, knocking her breath from her. The violent force crashes into the waves, stirs the stars above her, and the gusts and the sea are overwhelming, she is drowning in the sound. She turns in a circle, pressing her hands to her ears to shut out the screaming.

"What's wrong?"

She whips around toward the small voice. The boy stands in the doorway, looking at her, his eyes big.

She takes a careful breath, forces her mind away from the blood. "Too much noise," she tells him shakily.

The boy glances out toward the ocean. "They're talking?" he asks.

She nods, and sits hard on the stairs, puts her head on her knees.

The boy moves closer, and puts his hands on her head. "It's okay," he says. "It's okay."

They sit together in the wind.

DAY SIX

Chapter 44

Roarke had blacked into unconsciousness the second he hit the bed. Now he jolted awake, bolting up from a dream-memory of fire and annihilation, so disoriented it took him a second to register where he was and what he was hearing: a fast pounding on the door.

"What?" he said loudly, his voice gravelly.

The pounding stopped. "Me, boss," Epps' voice came from behind the door. His tone was urgent.

Roarke felt around for the light, then abandoned it and walked to the door in the dark in his bare feet. He was still fully dressed; he'd never made it out of his clothes.

He pulled open the hotel door and blinked at Epps' giant silhouette, backlit by the hall light.

"We got the prints back," Epps said, and walked past Roarke into the room.

Roarke felt a surge of adrenaline. He closed the door behind him, turned on the light, and turned to Epps.

Epps had stopped still and was staring at Roarke's wall, where he had taped up his pyramid: the sketch of the woman, with her four victims below. This time Roarke had written across the men's faces: *Child molester. Bomber. Rapist. Rapist.*

Epps turned away from the pyramid, and his face was strange.

Roarke ignored it. "So she has a record?"

"Not exactly."

Roarke could almost always read Epps, it was why they worked well together. From the beginning they had fallen into an intuitive groove, finishing each other's sentences, picking up on each other's thoughts. Until now. For the first time since Roarke knew him, Epps was totally unreadable. There was nothing but strangeness in his face.

"What?" Roarke said, hearing the tension in his own voice. "She's *not* in the system?"

Epps shook his head slowly. "She's in the system. But not as a perp. Look, boss, I think you should read for yourself. I uploaded some of this shit to your email. Just — take a look."

Roarke looked at Epps for a long moment, then went to his laptop and hit a few keys to call up the screen and click on the downloads.

A scanned newspaper article filled the screen... and hit him like a truck. It was from 1987, and he knew the headline as well as other people could remember the collapse of the Twin Towers, the Challenger explosion, the assassinations of the Kennedys and King:

Massacre In Sleepy California Town

As he scrolled down, the scanned headlines screamed at him.

Five-Year Old Survives Family Slaughter

Fate Spares Youngest Of Murdered Family

Miracle Girl Recovering From Fatal Attack

"I'll be next door," Epps said quietly. Roarke didn't even hear the door shut behind him; he was a million miles away, and twenty-five years in the past.

• • • • •

228

The sun was just coming up over the Saw Tooth Mountains, and the Santa Ana wind gusted across the road, swirling sand and tumble-weeds. Shannon Pizer was still half asleep as she turned off the River-side highway into the long drive that led to the Lindstrom's sprawling ranch-style home. In the back seat of the Land Rover, Pizer's eight-year old daughter Emily was uncharacteristically silent, still sleepy herself, but she perked up as the Lindstrom house came into view. They were picking her friend Amber Lindstrom up for a birthday skating party, and Shannon Pizer was gearing herself up for a very noisy morning, charged with little-girl excitement.

But Pizer could feel something was wrong the moment she turned the Land Rover on to the property. The first sign was that the front gate in the split rail fence surrounding the large wooded yard stood open. That in itself wasn't unusual, the Lindstroms would be expecting them. But as she motored through the small grove of eucalyptus and olive trees and the house came into sight, she saw the front door was standing open as well.

In the back seat, Emily was already reaching for the door handle.

"Stay in the car, Em," Pizer told her sharply.

She got out of the car. The wind was still strong, not anything like the gale-force gusts of the night before, but the dry flat leaves of the trees swirled above her and the front door was banging slightly in the moving air, and she couldn't shake the bad feeling as she walked up the pavers toward the trian-gular arched front entrance and stopped just outside the open door.

"Gillian?" she called into the house.

There was no answer.

She stepped through the open carved wooden door into the entry hall with its white-painted brick walls and tiled floor, and felt the eerie, heavy silence of the house around her.

And then she saw the blood.

Officers Martinez and Compton were first on the scene. Their journey into the house started with the smears of blood on the white walls of the front hall. They followed the smeared red footprints on the tiles into the terrible stillness.

Two wings of the house fanned out from the great room and family room in the center.

The officers steadied their weapons in front of them as they eased into the right wing. The master bedroom door stood open at the end of the hall, and the policemen heard their own breath breaking harsh in the air as they crept the endless distance to the door.

Inside was total carnage.

The bed was drenched in red; crimson splashes painted the walls. The bodies of Wallace and Gillian Lindstrom were still half under the blankets; they had been attacked in a frenzy, stabbed over and over again, slaughtered before they'd even made it off the bed.

The officers rushed back through the great room and into the next wing, where an identical hall led to the children's rooms.

The walls told the grim story: blood smeared on both sides of the corridor, staining the carpet. The killer had tracked it into each room he'd hit.

The first room was a teenage boy's, with heavy metal posters on the wall, the usual teenage chaos. The bed was unmade and the boy's body was half-in, half out of it; stabbed so many times that at first the officers were unable to process that the boy's torso was bare, covered not in a red shirt, but in blood.

A younger boy's body lay in the doorway of the next room. And in the pink and purple room at the end of the hall, the bodies of two young girls lay on the floor like dolls tossed to the ground. The smaller one was curled tightly around a child-sized stuffed animal that was as drenched in crimson as the girl was.

Officer Compton dropped to the floor beside the child; Officer Martinez, who had a seven-year old daughter of his own, couldn't bear to look.

"Oh my God," said Compton. "This one's alive."

She had curled herself into her stuffed tiger, and her hooded pajamas had twisted around her neck. The pressure had nearly strangled her — but it had saved her from bleeding to death.

• • • • •

Reaper Strikes Again

Evil stalked the sleepy town of Blythe, California on the night of October 29, claiming the lives of all but one of the Lindstrom family.

Sometime between midnight and three a.m., while the Lindstroms lay sleeping, an unknown assailant entered the house through a bathroom window, armed with what investigators say was a butcher knife. The intruder sliced open the screen to gain entry to the house, and entered the master bedroom where realtor Wallace Lindstrom and his wife Gillian slept. The killer attacked in a frenzy, stabbing and slashing dozens of times until husband and wife were dead. Police are withholding exact details of the slayings, but have confirmed that "various other implements were employed."

Probably awakened by their mother's screams, Joe (15) and Donny (13) were halfway out of their beds when the killer accosted them, again attacking in a frenzy and leaving them to bleed to death in their rooms.

The killer then entered the bedroom shared by Amber (8) and Cara (5), cruelly attacking both girls. Then, taking nothing but the family's lives, the killer disappeared into the night, leaving behind an orgy of blood.

When police officers arrived at the scene, they determined that miraculously, five-year old Cara had survived the attack. She was rushed to Palo Verde Hospital where doctors performed emergency surgery to repair a near fatal wound to the neck. She remains at the hospital in critical condition.

As of this morning, the police have no witnesses and no suspects.

• • • • •

Roarke looked up from the article. There were more, but he didn't need to read further. He knew the details of the case as if it had been one of his own.

He had been just nine years old the year of the attack. His family was living in Palo Alto, halfway up the state, but all of California had been riveted by the story; the brutal massacre, the miracle survival of a five-year old who had witnessed the slaughter of her entire family.

Third-grade Matt had watched the news coverage of the event obsessively, and read the newspaper every day, mystifying his parents, who previously had only ever seen him reach for the comics.

No killer was ever arrested, or even suspected. There were no leads whatsoever. The entire family had been killed; there were no immediate living relatives save an aunt with no history of trouble with the law and an airtight alibi, no neighbors or co-workers with grudges. It had been the most terrifying of all crimes, a random attack of inconceivable savagery.

And it wasn't the first.

Three families were massacred in a year and a half, all in small to medium-sized towns in different parts of the state; the Lindstroms were the third. The girl Cara was the only survivor of any of them.

Epps had uploaded original police reports and files; Roarke started from the beginning now and read every word of the reports, looking for the basics.

The locations were small cities, all in California: Blythe, population 12,155. Arcata, population 17,204. Bishop, population 3575. The kinds of towns that no one had ever heard of, eclipsed as they were by California's hundreds of more mediagenic locations; they were places where ordinary people lived and worked and managed never to be noticed by the world at large.

Until they were brutally thrust into the headlines, one after another, by the killer's work.

The first, in Arcata, California, was the Granger family: an economics professor at Humboldt State, married to an RNP, with two children: a ten-year old girl and thirteen-year old boy. The killer put them down with a stun gun and then went to work with a knife, slashing throats, stabbing, a frenzy of bloodletting.

Almost unbelievably, the massacre was not initially investigated as a serial killing. Arcata was located in Humboldt County, on the far north coast of California, two hundred miles north of San Francisco; a former timber town turned college town that was now famous for its green politics, redwoods, Victorians — and as the marijuana capital of the U.S. Though Donald and Lisa Granger were never proven to have any drug connections whatsoever, their farm was located close to major crops, and the theory they'd had a run-in with a local dealer that turned to lethal retribution was not off-the-wall. When people went dead in Humboldt, drug money was almost certainly the cause. Maybe the professor had smoked a little on the side, what Nor Cal professor didn't? and had had a delivery gone bad.

The massacre, being the first, and at the time an isolated incident, became a political football. Home invasion robberies to get at pot growing inside private homes were an escalating problem, and politicos on the marijuana eradication front were eager to use the massacre of the Granger family as a dire warning of the dangers of the crop. Looking at the crime scene photos now Roarke knew that anyone with the slightest exposure to sexual homicide would recognize the excitement of the killings themselves as the motive, rather than anything extraneous such as money or drugs. The political debate had completely obscured the real motivation of the killer. But hindsight is always 20/20.

The second family was seven months later, in Bishop, California, a gateway town to the Sierra Nevada mountains, a must-stop on the summer hiking and camping route because of the famous Schat's Bakery. The Merrills were another *nice* family: forest service dad, kindergarten teacher mom, three boys of 14, 11 and 8, massacred in the middle of the night, but this time the bodies were all over the house. At the bottom of the stairs the killer took away the axe that the father had tried to use on him and felled both parents with it before reverting to the knife for the children.

A second family massacre in seven months, and this time no one in California needed a VICAP analysis to understand that the killings were done by the same perp. The use of the axe and the brutality of the crimes prompted the media to christen the unknown killer "The Reaper."

The FBI's Behavioral Science Unit, as it had been called at the time, had first come into prominence after solving the Atlanta Child Murders in 1981, and now the western regional team went to work on the Family Massacres.

No DNA was found at either scene. There was no evidence of sexual assault but assault by knife was often sexual in motivation, a substitute for penetration, and clearly the killer reveled in the blood. The frenziedness of the attack pointed to a disorganized attacker, possibly overtly psychotic. He didn't seem to care about leaving traces, and yet the crime scenes were maddeningly clean of trace evidence.

And then six months after the Merrills, the Lindstroms, in Blythe.

The killings stopped after the girl survived. That was one of the vast mysteries of the entire story. The state, and surrounding states, continued to live in fear for the next year and the next while the media milked the terror of the story. Families throughout California were frantic with it. While realistically the chances of being attacked were one in ten million, the barrage of news coverage on "The Family Massacres" made it seem a real possibility twenty-four hours a day.

The FBI and local law enforcement ran down every bizarre lead and tip, to no avail. There were never any substantive leads. There were never any plausible suspects to compare the profile to. No one ever knew who, or why. But there were no more attacks after the Lindstroms.

Nine-year old Matt had wondered in his own mind if the girl had somehow killed the monster. She was the last one to ever see him. Perhaps she'd done more than survive him, but had actually banished him to whatever depths of hell he had come from.

But Matt could not get the situation out of his head. For months, he played out scenarios: how he would react if he woke to the presence of creeping evil inside his own house. How he would save his parents, his brother, confront the killer... mow him down.

In his dreams, the Reaper was more than a killer. It was a shadow as big as a room, as big as a house, many-headed, inexplicable, invincible.

And the girl. Cara. Matt Roarke had dreamed of the girl, over and over. Sometimes he was with her in the dark, sometimes it seemed he *was* her, hearing the screams of her family, the insane rasping of the Reaper's breath, the obscene words he gibbered as he killed one after the other, and then turned to her... seizing her hair, lifting her like a doll, slashing her neck with his blade.

Roarke stood from the desk and pulled himself back to the present, out of the multiple layers of memory, reality and dream. He forced himself to focus on the hotel room, the bed, the windows, the trees and volcanic peak outside.

And then on the impossible situation he now found himself in.

It can't be her. How can it be her?

It was too surreal, too beyond coincidence... like being in a dream that he couldn't quite wake up from.

But he had seen her on the street and *known* her, somehow. Not knowing, but knowing, some inexplicable mix of the two.

How?

Roarke finally felt together enough to go next door, where Epps was awake, dressed, waiting.

Roarke said the first thing that came into his head.

"Does she have a record?"

"A sealed juvie record. That's not unusual for kids in the foster system, which she was. My feeling is if it had been anything big, it would have been reported; she was a celebrity in her way. But I woke Singh up and got her on this double full-time: drivers' license, credit checks, residency. And we can get a look at the juvie record, of course—"

"No criminal record, though," Roarke said over him.

"No, but that's the odd thing. I just tried to get current info on AutoTrack." AutoTrack was a searchable extended database that checked public records nationwide; the Bureau had an account. It provided current and past addresses, phone numbers, Social Security numbers, neighbors and friends, sometimes bankruptcy listings, liens, and real estate records.

Epps paused and Roarke jumped in. "And?"

"There wasn't anything."

Roarke stared at him. Epps lifted his hands.

"I mean, nothing. So maybe she's living under an alias, something..." He trailed off.

Roarke was pacing the room, trying to get his jumbled thoughts to behave in some rational order.

It can't be, it can't be.

He fought against the spiraling feeling of losing all sense and control.

Epps was looking concerned. "What the hell, boss? What's going on?"

Roarke leaned his hands on the frame of the window, looking out at the bluish light on the snow of Mount Hood.

"This girl. This story. I know all about it."

"I'd heard of it, too," Epps said behind him. "Killer never caught, right?"

Roarke shook his head. "You don't understand, I—" He turned from the window, paced, not sure how to explain. "That case. I was nine and I got — obsessed with it. I wanted to do something. Be a lawman, fight monsters, make it stop..."

I wanted to save her, is what he didn't say.

"It's what made me want to be an agent. *This case.*" He trailed off, looked up at Epps. "So you tell me how that same girl could show up on the street, twenty-five years later — that I would see her kill Greer, end up on her trail..." he stopped, tried to speak. "How does that happen?"

The big man radiated calm. "Maybe somehow you had a sense — you're used to seeing age progressions... could probably do them yourself in your sleep by now. Hell, *I* probably could. So you see her on the street, and you look harder cause something in you knows."

It was the most rational thing anyone could have said at the time, but Roarke knew that it wasn't enough. He looked across the room, but he wasn't seeing Epps. He saw *her* again, standing on the street, looking at him. So still. Like a ghost. Face so pale above the turtleneck...

The turtleneck. Her neck. Her neck was slashed.

It had been thought she would never talk again... her first words got more publicity than the President's speeches, that month.

Her neck.

"She killed Greer," Roarke said. The words sounded hollow in the room.

"It's freaky, boss," Epps said slowly. "But freaky things happen. You know that. Whatever you want to call it, sometimes there just ain't no solid explanation for what happens in this life."

Both men were silent. Epps moved to the desk, and looked down at the screen of his laptop, at an array of crime scene photos from the family slaying.

"That's one hell of a trigger incident," Epps said softly. "Way to fuck you up for life."

Roarke fought through the storm of his thoughts. Epps was right. That part was completely logical. *A childhood imprint like that...*

It still felt that a ghost had walked out of his past and come straight to him.

And there was something so strange about the timing, so ominous...

He suddenly bent over the computer and clicked back to one of the articles reporting the massacre, scanning...

And finding the date of the Lindstrom family slaying, feeling a cold stab in his gut as he stared down. "October twenty-ninth," he said aloud.

Epps stared at him. "What?"

"The date her family died."

Epps frowned, then his eyes went still. "You're not saying..."

"It's October twenty-sixth today," Roarke said, then looked at the clock on the bed table. "October twenty-seventh, now. Two days to the twenty-ninth."

Finally Roarke had a name for the formless anxiety that had surrounded him since the beginning of this case, the urgency, the sense of time racing by, the feeling that the killer was escalating, decompensating.

There was no reason to think that there was a significance to the date. Nothing tangible.

But then again, there was. Anniversaries of traumatic events could be triggers. Early events were psychological wounds that killers played out subconsciously, sometimes to the very time and place. If the Huntress was decompensating, it might be because of this upcoming anniversary, the psychic weight of the massacre of her family.

It made her much more dangerous, just when he didn't think things could possibly be more dangerous.

"What are you thinking?" Epps asked.

Another coincidence? Is there any such thing?

"Two days," Roarke said. "I'm thinking I don't like it."

Two days.

I don't like it at all.

Chapter 45

As the sun came up over Mount Hood, Roarke and Epps sat in Roarke's hotel room on a conference call with Antara Singh. That is, Epps sat in the window seat while Roarke paced and Singh talked them through what she'd been able to gather. Roarke was trying to maintain a professional demeanor while inwardly his whole world view was rippling like water.

There had been no official record of Cara Lindstrom for years. No driver's license, no credit record, no employment history, no known places of residence.

At the age of eighteen she had simply disappeared.

Singh took them through it in her painstaking way. "I put together as much of a timeline as I could. After the deaths of her family, Cara Lindstrom lived first with her aunt, Joan Trent, née Lindstrom, and the aunt's second husband, Timothy Trent. The aunt was made guardian by the court and the general hope was that she and her then-husband would adopt Cara, but Cara remained with the family for only six months and then the aunt returned her to Family Services, claiming inability to deal with Cara's behavioral problems."

"At age five?" Roarke said. He could hear the outrage in his own voice.

"I know," Singh said with profound calm. "But Joan Trent's own children were just six months and eighteen months when she took Cara in. That would have been enough to slay me, just the two babies, without taking in a severely traumatized five-year-old. The aunt cited a slew of emotional problems..." Singh paused. "No surprise there—"

"Diagnosis?" Roarke said, more harshly than he intended.

"There are conflicting reports over the next few years. Early onset schizophrenia was one. Childhood bipolar disorder is in there, because the symptoms seemed seasonal."

"What season was that?" Roarke asked, and then answered himself before Singh did. "Fall?"

"Yes, fall," the researcher concurred. "And later there are a number of reports that diagnose borderline personality disorder."

Right, Roarke thought, with an inward sigh. *Borderline, of course, what problematic younger female isn't?* It had seemed to him for some time that BPD was mostly a catchall diagnosis for all the intangible ways people could be fucked up by abuse, usually sexual abuse. It was a kind of post-traumatic stress disorder.

Which you would expect of anyone who had been through what Cara Lindstrom had been through.

"I want to read those," Roarke said aloud. "Please," he added, having no idea how he was coming off.

"I am sending them through," Singh said serenely.

"Where did she go next?"

"The state calls it OPPLA: Other Planned Permanent Living Arrangements, only in Cara's case it turned out to be nothing resembling permanent. She had a string of foster care placements, none of which lasted more than six months, and most, less. None of the foster parents petitioned for adoption. Unfortunately, Cara was classified as "special needs adoption" because of the psychological and behavioral problems. And she had a particular history of running away. Children found to be unable to function in a foster home are placed in residential treatment centers, which is what happened when Cara was ten."

Singh paused. "I have to say that psychologically she is an odd mix, Cara. Until the violent trauma at age five, she was raised in an excellently supportive and educated family, which means that in the critical developmental years between age three and four she was nurtured in the most stable and stimulus-rich environment imaginable. The processes that govern the development of personality traits, stress response and cognitive skills are formed during this period, and Cara had a situation that was optimum for neurodevelopment. She was also unusually precocious, with an IQ tested in the 140s. At the age of five, just before the attack on her family, she was already reading at a fourth-grade level."

Roarke was listening numbly. But he was not surprised.

"Her grades at each subsequent school varied wildly with each foster placement, from top of her class to failure across the board. She certainly suffered from PTSD, as well as eating disorders and a stint of self-mutilation. And like most wards of the court she was over-prescribed medication: antidepressants, attention-deficit/hyperactivity disorder drugs, and antipsychotic agents. But she has no drug-related offenses or incidents on her record, which under the circumstances is rather astonishing.

"At age twelve, though, she was arrested for a brutal attack on a boy in her group home, hence the sealed juvie record. She nearly killed him. He was fifteen years old at the time, three years older than she was," Singh paused. "And according to the record, he had seventy pounds and seven inches on her. Also for the record, sexual abuse of children in group homes is twenty-eight percent more prevalent than in the general population—"

Roarke interrupted. "Are you saying this boy sexually assaulted her, or attempted to?"

"I am giving you statistics, sir," Singh answered. "The record holds no mention of sexual assault." Roarke was silent and she continued with her rundown. "Cara was remanded to the California Youth Authority and served two years in detention, after which time she was returned to OPPLA, and lived in three more group homes until she reached the age of emancipation at eighteen.

"There was a pile of insurance money from her family's death; her parents had policies totaling over one million. As the only surviving child it all went to her. It was held in trust for her and administered by a business associate of her father's, a realtor at the father's firm. The money came to her at age eighteen, with substantial accrued interest, and at that time Cara Lindstrom changed her name to Eden Ballard."

A name change. Also not unexpected.

"Then she turned twenty-one and completely disappeared. She moved the money out of the bank where it had always been held, and there is no record of where she put it. We can assume she changed her name again. The 'Eden Ballard' identity still exists but with no credit, employment or address history past 2004."

"Pretty easy to start over with a million dollars cash," Epps said dryly from the corner where he had been quietly sitting, scribbling notes.

Nothing truer. Cash made identity papers irrelevant. Cash created no paper trail. She could have bought a house or condo with cash, anywhere in the US or outside of it. She could be anywhere. Roarke fought a too-familiar sinking feeling.

"But why the delay?" Epps asked.

Roarke spoke without thinking. "It gave her time to set up a solid fake identity. She took her time, did it right." That in itself was worrisome.

"It looks that way," Singh agreed from the phone. "And that is a rather amazing feat. Nearly half of all children in the foster care system become homeless when they turn eighteen. But in Cara's case, despite eleven years in the Social Services system, she was obviously high-functioning enough to create a complete new identity and disappear off the map. Also, she has no prison record under the name she held for three years: Eden Ballard. Her only criminal conviction on record is the one at the age of twelve, the attack on the boy in the group home."

Roarke stood still, trying to wrap his mind around everything Singh had just enumerated. "So we have no idea of her location, her name, or any activities whatsoever for the last eight years."

This hung in the silence for a moment. *Could she have been hunting for eight years?*

"We cannot assume a criminal history," Singh finally said. "After living under a microscope for her entire life, having to relive that tragedy over and over again, it is no surprise that she would want to change her identity, drop off the map."

"I want to talk to the aunt," Roarke said.

"The aunt is dead."

"How?" Roarke said, with a bad feeling.

"By all accounts, natural causes, a heart attack at age fifty-four."

That at least was a relief. Roarke had seen far too many cases of killers who started with their own relatives.

"Who else who would have known her? What about the aunt's children?

"Remember, they were just babies at the time the aunt took her in: six months and a year and a half. I can run them down, but the chances that they would remember anything..."

"And the aunt's husband?" Roarke interrupted.

"Second husband. He left Joan Trent just months after she'd placed Cara with the state."

"Track him down anyway," Roarke snapped. "What else?"

"That is all of it," Singh said. "From there, nothing."

It was astonishing, really, that a twenty-one year old would have been able to disappear so effectively. Of course, young people fairly often didn't begin to accrue a credit history until they were in their twenties. On the other hand, money always leaves a trail, unless you actually know how to hide it. It spoke of planning, and intent.

Singh was speaking. "I will keep looking, it just may take a while. And some creativity. This woman definitely does not want to be found."

"Good. And Singh, I want you to search for unsolved homicides in the towns she was living at the times she was living there."

"Starting when?"

Roarke hesitated. "From the beginning," he said slowly. "1987."

Epps looked up from his notes, startled. "Since she was *five*?"

"Just humor me. Anything unusual that comes up."

"Will do, chief," Singh said.

Roarke punched off the speaker phone and looked toward Epps at the window, with the peak of Mount Hood behind him. For a moment the men were silent.

"We go to Pismo," Roarke finally said, answering the unspoken question. "The trail is in Pismo." And then he glanced at the computer.

Epps unfolded his tall self from the window seat. "I'll go book us some flights. You've got reading to do."

Roarke looked first at her juvie record, the juvenile conviction for assault at age twelve, but it was clear to him, reading the sealed record, that the fight, with a boy at the group home, had been mutual. She'd just come out of it better than the other kid, the boy three years older than she was. Roarke thought of the rest stop bathroom, the possibility that — at least in that case — she'd been surprised and fought back.

Fought back hard enough to kill and leave the bathroom looking like an abattoir.

Roarke sighed and reached for the psychiatric record. It was all over the map.

In one report it was schizophrenia. Another: "psychotic disorder not otherwise specified." Paranoia. Hallucinations. Drug-induced psychosis.

After some skimming, he counted how many evaluations she'd been through and tallied the bottom line diagnoses:

Nine evaluations, three for bipolar disorder, two for early-onset schizophrenia, four for borderline personality disorder, one for borderline personality disorder with bipolar symptoms.

Enough to shake anyone's faith in the efficacy of psychiatric evaluation.

In other words, fucked up. A highly disturbed individual with a traumatic past who might be slaughtering men in a way that would be a first for the books, in terms of female killers.

And I've got her, Roarke thought, with what felt like a touch of hysteria.

Karma, clearly.

But that thought was just too weird.

He reached for the phone and called Snyder.

Out on the deck of the hotel, with the cone of Mount Hood rising against the sky in the distance, Roarke watched Snyder as he sat in an Adirondack chair, paging carefully through the case files, the news articles, the police reports.

"So?" Roarke finally said impatiently.

Snyder looked up at him. "So?"

"Does that—" Roarke pointed to the case file on the Lindstrom family massacre, "Lead to *that*?" He pointed to the stack of files on the huntress's four male victims in the present.

Snyder swiveled in his chair and looked at him sharply. "You know the answer to that. Possibly. Maybe. What do you want me to tell you, Matthew?"

Roarke was brought up short by the question. He had to focus himself through the chaos and frustration in his mind to answer it properly.

"Why. I want to know why."

Snyder looked out the window, nodded. "That, only *she* can tell you, and maybe she can't, either. I hope you find her so that we can ask." He looked out over the forest, frowning. "There is one thing you need to remember. A trauma like this shatters a child and fixes her in the age at which the trauma occurred."

Roarke felt a shiver. It was true. The syndrome was often seen in child molesters, who fixated on children the age that the molester was victimized.

Snyder was continuing. "Five years old is before the age of reason: it means as an adult she will be prone to magical thinking that could very well present as some of the diagnoses in those files: hallucinations, schizophrenia, delusions."

Roarke was intent. "She thinks like a five-year-old."

"In some ways, yes. Her reality may look more like a dream state or a metaphor to us. A more fantastical than concrete existence."

"What kind of fantasy are we talking about?"

"Who knows?" Snyder shrugged. "But whatever it is, she acts it out... like this." He put his hand on the stacks of the files of murdered men.

Roarke stepped to the wood railing and looked out at the volcano.

"So now, are you going to tell me what's really bothering you?" Snyder said from behind him.

Roarke went still, then turned to face him.

"This is *the* case. This was the case that set me off on the law enforcement path, twenty-five years ago. Twenty-five years later that girl in those reports stands in front of me on a San Francisco street and kills my agent in front of me."

The older man just looked at him. Roarke spread his hands. "How does that happen?"

Snyder sighed. "Things happen. Life happens. Sometimes we draw things to us. Maybe it's fate. I can't tell you, Matthew. But it seems that for whatever reason, this one's yours."

Roarke was still. And then Snyder's face clouded. "This alignment of the moon cycle and the anniversary of her trauma — those are two extremely volatile influences. The confluence will undoubtedly intensify whatever delusion she's operating under." He met Roarke's eyes. "Do not let your guard down. Not for an instant."

Before Roarke could speak, Epps banged through the door out onto the porch. The tension of excitement was in his face and body.

"We've got a witness who says he saw her in a drug store in Pismo Beach, Tuesday morning around nine."

The agents looked at each other.

"She's still there," Roarke said.

Chapter 46

The ocean was vast, rolling and sparkling beyond the sun-swept beach. As Epps drove the highway from the SLO airport to Pismo Beach, Roarke looked out over that blue-gray infinity and the gently winding coast road, thinking of Cara Lindstrom, the scarred child, the traveler, the huntress.

Is your life on the road? Do you have a home at all?

Maybe she just drove. It was a characteristic of serial killers; they put thousands of miles on their cars as they roamed restlessly, ceaselessly trolling for victims.

Or maybe she lived in Pismo.

Pismo Beach was a tourist town, not nearly as famous as other California beaches, but a popular beach vacation destination, with about 8500 permanent residents, overwhelmingly white, well educated and well off. The population doubled in summer months, bringing a much more diverse mix of beachgoers. The town was known for its clams; a reputation the town playfully commemorated with a giant concrete clam in the middle of Peabody Avenue, downtown.

As Epps drove past the clam, Roarke stared out the window at the scruffy, retro downtown.

Was this a safe place to stop? Did you want to rest? Are you here? Eden? Cara? What are you doing?

The witness who claimed to have seen Cara, Thomas Munroe, lived in a trailer park off the coast highway, a few miles from downtown. Of course, a trailer park at the beach in California could be a lot better living than a single family home in a lot of other places, and many of the homes in the park had gardens, freshly painted lawn furniture, birdbaths, even an impressive multi-basined fountain in one yard.

But Munroe, who pronounced his own name *Mun*-roe, wasn't making much of his castle. The siding was stained and there was no attempt at a garden; in fact the strip of land surrounding his trailer seemed shriveled, somehow, leached of life compared to the carefully tended dwellings around his.

Munroe himself was hardnosed and blue collar; tall and slightly stooped, with ropy musculature and a smoker's rasp to his voice. Roarke could smell the cigarettes on him from a good six feet away.

He balked before he let them inside his trailer, but clearly didn't want to have the conversation in the open. The dim interior smelled of sweat and old alcohol and more smoke.

"We want to thank you for coming forward, Mr. Munroe," Roarke said, as he and Epps shuffled for position in the cramped space.

Munroe gestured to a local newspaper laid out on the built-in kitchen table: in the center of the front page was the sketch.

"Knew it as soon as I saw the picture. She was in the Rite Aid, up on Five Cities, couple days ago. I was with my granddaughter and I saw her bein' real interested in the girl."

There was a tone in his voice that Roarke found odd, a kind of sly satisfaction, a self-righteousness that had nothing to do with being helpful.

"How do you mean, 'interested'?" he asked neutrally.

Munroe gave him a small, mean smile. "She was followin' us. Whatever aisle we was in, she was there, hanging around. Staring at my girl. Didn't have no shopping basket or nothing. Thought she was some kinda transient at first but the way she kept looking at my girl, I knew sumpin was up."

Roarke found it odd that Munroe was not using his granddaughter's name. "Your granddaughter's name is?"

"Bailey. Bailey Scott. She lives with her mama. I was just sitting for her."

"How old is Bailey?"

It took Munroe a minute to answer, as if he had to think to remember. "Six."

Roarke felt a prickling down his spine. So close to the age Cara Ballard had been when her family was attacked.

Fixation at the age of trauma...

Was it significant?

How could it not be significant?

Roarke saw Epps looking at him tensely, apparently aware of Roarke's raging internal dialogue. He forced himself to focus, to bring himself back to the present. He didn't know what the age parallel meant, but it made him reluctantly take Munroe more seriously.

"Did this woman speak to your granddaughter?" he asked, keeping his tone as neutral as possible.

The older man's face darkened. "Didn't have no chance. Wasn't gonna let her near the girl. I told her to get lost."

"How did she respond?"

Munroe's eyes took on a faraway, mean look. "Oh, she was mad, all right. Let off a string of curse words like you wouldn't believe."

Roarke would bet money that Munroe was a pretty good curser himself. The whole interview was making him uneasy. Not only did he have a strong sense of dislike for the man, he had the absolute sense that he was lying. Shifty was the old-fashioned word.

He cleared his throat; the sour smell of the trailer was getting to him. "And then?"

Munroe spit toward the sink. "I took my girl and got her out of that place. Then I seen that drawing in the papers and I knew that was the same one. Looks just like her."

That was a plus, anyway: they had an accurate sketch.

"Can you give me other details about how she looked? Clothing, appearance?"

"Black pants, boots... this dark high-collar thing."

Roarke felt a chill. *That high collar. To cover her throat?*

"And she was a mess. Like she been sleeping on the street."

Roarke frowned at that. "What makes you say that?"

"Everything looked wrinkled. Sandy."

Disheveled. Interesting. If she killed the trucker this would have been seven or eight hours later. Did she kill the trucker and just lose it?

"Did you see any blood on her?" he asked aloud.

That seemed to take Munroe back a pace. "Blood?" He scratched at his face. "Don't think so. Didn't get that good a look, though."

"Did you see her get into a car or some other vehicle?"

"She was still in the store when I took my girl out. I made sure she didn't follow us out."

"Did you report the incident?" Roarke asked.

Munroe looked blank. "Why?"

"If you were concerned for your granddaughter's safety..." Roarke suggested dryly.

Munroe's face closed. "I took care of her. No beach tramp's gonna get through me."

And other children don't count, Roarke thought silently.

Munroe may have picked up on his disapproval; his gaze narrowed. "Tell who, the hippies posed as cops who work here? Like they would be good for anything."

"You do a lot of babysitting?" Roarke asked abruptly.

A strange, sullen look crossed Munroe's face. "Not much," he said.

Glad to hear it, Roarke thought. *I wouldn't want you near my kid.*

Roarke and Epps walked down the sandy path of the trailer park toward the parking lot. Thigh-high sea grass rippled beside them in the breeze.

Roarke could feel himself brooding, and Epps picked up on it.

"Piece of work," Epps said.

"Yeah," Roarke answered.

"Lying," Epps added.

"Oh yeah." Roarke was silent for a moment; grains of fine sand rushed by them on the path like streams of water. "The girl, though..."

"Six years old," Epps said.

"Right," Roarke said. "Not good."`

Epps had rented a Tahoe; it was up ahead. Next stop was the Rite Aid, to see if there were any store staff who had seen Cara Lindstrom, or who could corroborate Munroe's story.

"Drop me at the Rite Aid, would you, and check up on whether Munroe has a sheet."

Epps took a long look at him. "Hmm," he said.

"I know, but — check," Roarke said.

The Rite Aid was just a block off Main Street. Roarke talked to the manager on duty, a round-faced young woman in her thirties, and showed her the sketch of the woman in black. She shook her head at the sketch, hadn't ever seen her. But she knew Munroe as a regular.

"Pack of Marlboros and a case of Bud," she said dryly.

Roarke nodded. He had no doubt. "That would be the one."

He showed the sketch around to the clerks, and hit the jackpot with a skinny twenty-something stoner who remembered ringing Cara up.

"Remember what she bought?" Roarke held his breath.

The kid thought. "Same as most tourists. Beach stuff. Flip flops, beach bag, T-shirt I think, maybe shorts. Towel."

Beach stuff. Roarke felt a thrill. *So maybe you didn't just pass through. Sounds like you intended to stick around.*

He left the Rite Aid and called Epps to order an immediate cancellation of the media distribution of the sketch. Even if it might be too late. He didn't want the risk of causing her to bolt.

"Will do. Oh, and — Munroe has no criminal record."

Roarke felt what might have been a stab of disappointment. "Okay, thanks. I'm on my way over to the station."

"Want me to—"

"I'll walk." It was a whole two blocks to the station, and Roarke needed the air and space to think.

As he punched off, he was asking himself, *What did you expect to find, anyway?* And the answer came back immediately.

Child molestation, that's what I was looking for. Not her. Him.

He was looking for a reason Cara would have engaged with Munroe. A reason he might have caught her eye.

But then again, she didn't kill him, he reminded himself.

And the very train of thought unnerved him. Because it meant what he was thinking was, *If she didn't kill him, he couldn't have been that bad.*

He shook his head to shake off the thought.

Focus. Just find her.

He started off across the parking lot, under a perfect blue sky. There was a gnawing feeling in the pit of his stomach. He knew that releasing the sketch had led to the report of her sighting in Pismo Beach. It was the right thing to have done, only now his problem was, if she had seen the sketch herself she may already have fled miles or even states away.

But if she had not seen the sketch, she might — *might* — still be in town. Roarke thought again, with hope, of the beach clothes she had bought.

He stopped on the sidewalk and just stood for a moment, feeling the wind and sun on his face.

Are you here? he asked her. *Are you?*

The Pismo police station was a small triangular brick building sandwiched in between a tiny firehouse and a primary school on a tidy residential street. Roarke stood in the clean and skylit lobby, reading the department's framed mission statement on the wall as he waited for Chief of Police Wilson.

The Pismo Beach Police's unique form of "Tourism-oriented policing" enhances our community's reputation as a fun, family-oriented vacation destination, enjoyed in a safe and peaceful environment.

His eyes lingered on the phrase: **Family-oriented vacation destination.**

If she's a traveler, and this is the place she's chosen to stay, why? *What would attract her about a family-oriented destination?*

Before he could explore that troubling thought, Chief Wilson stepped out of his office. It was Brian Wilson, like the Beach Boy, and he looked the part: a former surfer for sure, with sun-streaked hair and a laid-back easiness to his professionalism. *"Those hippies in the police department,"* Munroe had scoffed.

"Agent Roarke," Wilson said, and stepped forward, extending a hand. Roarke moved to meet him.

In his office, Wilson studied the sketch Roarke handed him. "Yeah, I saw this on the wire. Looks like about a million pretty girls. California," he added wryly.

It's true, being blond on the beach is good camouflage, Roarke realized. *Is that the way you saw it?* he asked in his head, and realized with a start that he was talking to Cara again.

Wilson was looking at him quizzically.

Roarke forced himself back into focus. "My team is going to need to canvas the town. We think she might be staying here."

An odd look crossed the chief's face.

"Is there a problem with that?" Roarke asked.

"No, absolutely fine by me. You just picked the wrong weekend to try to find someone. The good news is that we have extra security all weekend. The bad news is we're going to have thousands of people downtown. Two festivals, concurrently: 'Pumpkins On The Pier' for the kids and our October Jazz Festival, 'Jubilee By The Sea.' We're expecting upwards of twelve thousand people."

Roarke stared at him in dismay. And he found himself talking to Cara Lindstrom in his head again:

Perfect camouflage. Did you know that, too?

Chapter 47

"**B**atman," the boy says decisively.

She and the boy are draped over the kitchen island, studying the newspaper, which is open to the Pumpkins on the Pier costume contest. The boy had been serenely untroubled to find her in the kitchen in the morning, a good sign.

"Batman. Of course," she says. And it does make sense, the Caped Crusader. "Do we need to get your costume together?"

"Oh, no," the father says, from behind his coffee at the other end of the counter. "The costume he has."

They were being casual with each other but there was an electricity between them; when he thought she was not looking he could not stop looking at her.

"I guess that makes me Catwoman, doesn't it?" It is an easy costume, a staple in adult stores, and one she won't mind wearing at all. She has been feeling a need to take extra care, so to be practically obligated to go out masked and hooded is a boon.

And she can see the father doesn't object. Men never object to Catwoman.

"Yay, Catwoman! Prepare to die!" The boy races around with his arms extended behind him in a fair approximation of a cape.

"No cat-killing," the father says mildly.

"A Bat's got to do what a Bat's got to do," she tells him.

"And that leaves the Joker for me." The father's eyes go to her, questioningly, and she pretends to consider it before she nods. She can see the scene: she will put the makeup on his face and feel him tremble under her hands.

She is excited about going out. She has been restless, and the wind is making her more so. There is something out there for her, she can feel it.

She has been careful to wear her sunglasses any time she steps outside, and to tuck her hair under a hat or scarf. She wears a beach cover-up out in public and leaves the dresses and tank tops and bathing suit and shorts for when she is alone with the father. But the real disguise is that she is never alone. She is one of three; looking at them, no one sees anything but a family. Even if she is to some men a MILF, Mom I'd Like to Fuck, the overwhelming factor is Mom.

The amazing, miraculous thing is that while she has been with them, she has been left alone. No one has approached, there has been no compulsion, no need to do battle. She can hardly believe it, but the world has been light. As if her new identity has kept away the shadows as well. She wants to hold on to that, for whatever time she has left. They can have this little indulgence, a pretend Normal.

It will all be over soon enough.

DAY SEVEN

Chapter 48

In the early hours of the morning Chief Wilson called an emergency meeting to coordinate the extra hired security. Roarke and Epps had briefed the town cops the night before and all were armed with copies of the sketch. A deputy had been calling hotels, motels and B&Bs all night, looking for lone women guests. There were blond women of the right approximate age being checked out. The entire contingent of coastal law enforcement was on the lookout for Cara Lindstrom.

Roarke was pleased as he and Epps left the police station to drive through town to the pier. But his heart sank when he saw the downtown.

Chief Wilson had not exaggerated about the influx of people; it was already a mob. The streets were blocked off to traffic and Epps was diverted to a city lot to park. Free shuttle buses were lined up to take loads of people to the pier.

Roarke had dressed for the occasion. Even the jeans and casual shirt he always had packed in his carry-on were not casual enough for a day at the beach, so he'd found some khaki shorts and a T-shirt at a beach store around the corner from the motel they'd stayed in last night, and had donned sunglasses for his surveillance of the pier. Epps was in similar camouflage. But even casually dressed as they were, together they were unmistakably law enforcement.

"Split up," Roarke said softly to Epps.

"You leaving me alone with all these white people, boss?" Epps straight-faced him. "White" was not entirely accurate; there were many Latino families in the throng. But African Americans were underrepresented, to say the least.

"Just try not to make any sudden moves," Roarke told him.

Epps squared his shoulders and headed for a shuttle.

Roarke opted to walk, since there was no particular place he was more or less likely to see her. If she was here at all.

"Crap shoot," he muttered to himself, drawing looks from two colorfully beach-garbed older ladies.

At any rate, it's a day at the beach, he told himself, and strolled with the families through the funky downtown shops toward the boardwalk.

The sun was bright and the wind was warm and the Halloween theme was everywhere. Kids and whole families were dressed in costumes, including person-sized Monarch butterflies and every version of every superhero and Harry Potter character imaginable. The advertised cash prizes didn't hurt, he imagined. Tiny children in costume with trick-or-treat bags were marching in and out of the rows of shops on both sides of the street, whose proprietors were equally costumed, handing out goodies. As he looked down the sloping street out onto the pier, he could see hundreds of orange spots, apparently where the pumpkin-carving contest was going on. Rows of green cornstalks fenced in an artificial pumpkin patch, complete with hay bales and scarecrows. Colorful tents lined the wide pier on both sides, with a thick crowd of people milling in between the rows.

He stopped for a moment and gazed down the boardwalk. So many hundreds of people, and there was no reason to think she was here at all. At such a family event? The kind of person that she seemed to be? It didn't make any sense.

And yet, he had no impulse to leave. Rather, he was feeling an ever-greater urgency to move forward.

As he hit the pier, parallel to the beach, he had a choice. Ahead of him was the pier; on the boardwalk to the right, balloon-sized tents and slides were set up for the kids. The pier was where the pumpkin carving was going on at long tables with boxes of decorations for the carving and tents with other carnival-style activities: face-painting, fortune-telling, henna tattooing.

To the left of the pier in the expansive parking lot was an array of blinding white marquis tents, a wine tent, a food tent, one with a jazz band, where couples swing danced on a portable hardwood floor in front of the platform stage. It was shaping up to be a lively party, and certainly was more of an adult venue.

But for her? Unlikely in the extreme.

Something made him turn toward the right instead. There were children everywhere, most streaming toward the pumpkin carving. And that got him thinking about Munroe's story.

The man had said Cara was following them. *"Looking at my girl."*

Were you really scoping out a six-year old? Roarke asked Cara in his head. *Why?*

The thought made him start watching the kids.

The kids.

He moved toward the pumpkin patch.

• • • • •

The costuming is a smashing success. She helps the boy dress in a rocking Batman costume, several cuts above the drugstore variety, obviously procured from an upscale shop. The boy takes flight, dashing around the house in his cape while she paints the father's face with clown white and draws Heath Ledger slashes in lipstick on his face. The air becomes thick between them and he puts his hands on her hips and kisses her neck, breathing her in... before

Jason zooms in again, nearly crashing into them, oblivious to the sex in the air.

Of course, the Catwoman suit is a big hit. She had borrowed the car, driven far enough out of town to feel anonymous, and found the catsuit just as she'd predicted: in an adult store, which also took care of the whip and boots. Now she paints her face carefully, changing her skin tone, making herself look slightly Asian, altering the shape of her eyes and mouth. There is not a trace of blond showing under the hood with its kitty ears.

No one could know her.

• • • • •

The ocean stretched out on both sides as Roarke walked across the wide rough planks of the pier, weaving through clusters of families, past a fake graveyard with amusing inscriptions on the tombstones, a pirate cave bedecked with jewels. He honed in on the five-year-olds, or what looked to him like five-year-olds.

He reached for his phone and called Epps, never taking his eyes away from the passing people. "What are the dimensions of a five-year-old?"

There was a pause on the phone while Epps calculated. "Fifty pounds, about knee-high? Maybe a little higher?"

"You're no help," Roarke told him.

"That's what Google is for."

"Well, Google it and be on the lookout for five-year-olds." Roarke thumbed off his phone.

Google confirmed the fifty pounds, and gave a height range of 39 to 48 inches. Tiny.

And that's the size Cara Lindstrom was when some maniac slashed her throat.

Inconceivable.

Roarke focused on the crowd, on the tiny ones, and started looking for lone women who might be watching them as he drifted past the craft tables with children crowded around them, creating their pumpkin masterpieces.

But the flaw in that strategy soon became evident. He was the only solitary man out on the pier, among all these children, and not a few parents were looking at him warily. Without a child of his own he looked like stranger danger.

He stopped at the pier railing and took as broad and long a look as he could manage down the expanse of pier, looking for a lone, slim, intense, possibly blond woman. And saw no one who fit the bill.

He casually turned around and headed back toward the boardwalk, where he would not be so conspicuous.

• • • • •

They walk, a trio, on the beach toward the pier, past the huge rainbow-colored inflatable moon bouncers and jump castles and balloon slides set up in the sand. The pier and boardwalk are swarming, and she exults in her anonymity as they climb the stairs to join the fray, a festive, carnival atmosphere. The boy's excitement is infectious; he zooms like the Caped Crusader he is, ahead of them, around them, expertly dodging anyone in his path.

It is as they hit the boardwalk, going shop to shop trick-or-treating amongst all the other costumed locals and tourists that she sees him coming off the pier: the man from the street in San Francisco. The hunter.

He is alone, and also costumed, in his way; he wears what look like new canvas shorts and a T-shirt instead of the tailored city suit. But he is too full of purpose to be anything other than what he is: law enforcement on a mission.

She is startled to see him, and then not. Something in her has known from the time she first saw him that he would be looking, even that he would find her. It is no accident, any more than the father and the boy are accidental. It is part of the path now; meant, as is everything else, just as it has happened.

But he is not meant to see her yet, she thinks, she is too perfectly disguised. Just one of hundreds of costumed tourists, no one would know her; in fact she has seen others of her species as they walk in the throngs. And she has her ultimate camouflage: her matching Caped Crusader and Joker.

She squeezes both their hands now as she walks hand in hand with her superhero family, subtly guiding them with her so that she can watch the lawman from a safe distance.

He strolls the outdoor craft fair, a gauntlet of vendors behind their tables full of beach jewelry, the ankle bracelets and toe rings and psychedelic glass; the watercolors that look so enticing all in a rush of color, but one at a time are nothing but mediocre. He looks toward the stalls, but he watches the people around him, not the art.

How does he know? What does he know? she wonders, as she and the father wait to the side, watching Jason run up to the next costumed shopkeeper, holding his trick-or-treat bag open wide.

She has a sudden memory of the dried-out man with the little girl in the aisle of the drug store, his quick, hot hatred, her own reckless response.

Yes, he would have made a call. Something had made him do it, despite any potential humiliation. But why not to local law enforcement? Why would he have called a San Francisco agent unless...

She grows still inside even as she stoops to exclaim over the boy's latest treat: a chocolate jack o' lantern sucker from a candy shop. Even as she lets the boy lead her onto the pier, pulling her toward the pumpkin patch.

Unless her photo is being circulated.

She did not see the agent, the man, take a photo. But somehow it may have been done. Or there may have been a sketch.

The boy is weaving ahead of them, now, dodging between pumpkins, hundreds of huge orange globes arrayed on the pier among bunches of cornstalks and hay bales and amusing scarecrows that seem to have no effect on the seagulls picking at the hay. On the outside she watches the boy, laughing at his antics with the father. Inside the thought grows in her.

It has been years, *years* since she's attracted the slightest attention from the police or law enforcement of any kind. And now this one, following her from San Francisco, all from just a few moments on the street.

And likely not alone.

She is suddenly rabid to know more.

She steps close to the father, and says softly, "I need to run across the street." She nods toward the public restrooms. Then louder, "Anyone want drinks? Ice cream, maybe?"

The boy shouts, "Ice cream!" as the father says, "Maybe not a great idea to start on that yet," and then circumvents protest by telling the boy, "After we carve the pumpkin, eh, sport?"

She presses her fingers lightly into the father's arm, smiling, and then steps away from them, weaving gracefully through the crowd, feeling him watch her. She has not much time left, that is clear now — less time than before. Her feelings about that are unreadable, even to herself.

She moves through families and couples, through the happy din, off the pier and onto the boardwalk, the strip of shops where she had seen the lawman strolling and watching. After all, he will not likely be casing the pumpkin patch and all its families. She forces herself to move casually. She is taking a chance, leaving the protective camouflage of the father and boy. She may be costumed and masked, but she knows too well that now that she is alone, the costume makes her more conspicuous, not less. She is already tense with adrenaline, the alertness of the hunt.

She feels an excitement about that. For years she has moved invisibly, unseen by the normal world. And now it seems finally someone has seen. This one is actually on her trail. He must be.

She glides through the half-costumed, half-beach-garbed crowd, and casually browses the jewelry and craft stalls, the straw hats and watercolors and batik purses, as she studies the passersby.

She spots the lawman again easily: he is the lone soldier in a crowd of civilians, a hunter among farmers. His body has a coiled tension and the beach sun and air is not relaxing him in the slightest; he is as focused as she remembers him being from San Francisco. Watching, looking, seeking.

Her own body coils in response as she strolls on in her costume, watching him.

• • • • •

Roarke was increasingly antsy, and he didn't know why. He looked back and around him through the bright ocean air, wondering. Hundreds of people, thousands. Happy families. Teenage lovers. The idea that he could spot her in a costumed crowd like this was absurd, he knew it. And yet his inner radar, that spider-sense, was on high alert.

He stopped and forced himself to be still. And then he started to his left and let his eyes pass over the crowd one fraction of an inch at a time, letting himself register everything he saw, not even looking for faces now, but just letting himself feel.

• • • • •

She has seen him go still, and now she watches as he systematically, with excruciating slowness and care, scans the crowd.

He knows. He knows I'm here, she thinks to herself, and there is a kind of excitement in the thought.

You're playing with fire, now, she tells herself. *You think he won't know when he sees you? He is hunting, and the costume won't shield you from him any more than that T-shirt shields him from you.*

As she watches, he stops, moving out of the flow of traffic, and pulls a phone from a cargo pocket. He speaks into it, listening and offering short, terse sentences back. Instead of looking out to the ocean, he constantly watches the crowd.

And then suddenly she sees a tall, lithely muscled black man talking into his phone as he leans back on the railing of the pier, the sand and the ocean behind him. Another fit, intense man looking at the crowd instead of at the sea, his eyes always roaming, stopping, evaluating, even as he talks into the phone. Another lawman. They are together, speaking together, she is sure.

• • • • •

"A lot of pretty people, boss," Epps said into his ear. Roarke smiled tightly.

"Don't ever let anyone tell you you're not pretty, Epps."

"Not the same thing."

"You do stick out a bit."

"And she doesn't. It's these costumes that are killing us."

"She's here," Roarke said, and was not aware that he had said it aloud until Epps' voice came back at him, sharp and hard.

"You saw her?"

Roarke was disoriented, and had to regroup. "No. But she's here."

There is a loaded and awkward pause on the other end. "So keep looking, is what you're saying," Epps said warily.

"She's here," Roarke said.

• • • • •

She sees the tall black man speak into his phone, and the hunter speak into his own phone as soon as the black man has stopped talking, and she is sure that they are not only talking to each other, but talking about her.

And then she realizes she is indulging herself. She knows who he is, and she knows what it means, and she needs no more than that for the moment. She is too far from her protective camouflage and he has somehow tracked her this far.

She steps back, fading in, letting the crowd conceal her.

· · · · ·

Roarke spoke abruptly into the phone. "Epps, I'm moving." He disconnected without explanation and started moving ahead in the crowd. It was a blind thought, he had no idea where he was going, only the sense that he had to move.

· · · · ·

She sees him put the phone back in his pocket and move, and she draws further back into the crowd, drifting slowly, matching her pace to those around her so as not to draw attention as she makes her way back toward the pier and the pumpkin patch.

She stops at a shaved ice truck and smiles at the vendor as she buys three of the rainbow treats — temporary camouflage: the cones make it abundantly clear she is not alone.

She turns away from the counter, balancing the cardboard tray of cones... and then he is running to meet her, the boy, so very obviously hers, and the disguise slips around her again. Mother with child, unimpeachable, invisible.

· · · · ·

Roarke moved faster through the crowd, almost running, now, dodging couples and families, skidding around them in impatience. He nearly collided with a drunk and over-steroided young body-builder. "Watch where the fuck you're—" the body builder started, but then caught a closer look at Roarke and backed down.

Roarke held up his hands, and turned from the chastened body-builder to scan ahead of him, right, left, around. Costumed people milled around him on all sides, laughing kids, chatting families. He felt his pulse start to slow, and he realized that whatever it had been, the sensation was passing. And he felt loss, and frustration, and a certainty that she was close, so close. And a resolve that however it happened, he would find her.

O

Chapter 49

I t is easy to lure them back to the privacy of the beach in front of the house with the suggestion of a picnic and slight hints about discomfort in the restricting black costume.

Back in the beach house she disappears into the guest bathroom with her clothes. She slips off the Catwoman suit and changes into shorts and a high-necked top, then turns the shower on for cover and looks through the papers she has bought on the sink.

She finds it immediately. The sketch of her stares out at her from the newsprint, unmistakable.

Her own looks are inexplicable to her, but there is no doubt that the sketch conveys what men respond to or against in her. It conveys her essence. And that means her time is up; she must move.

She feels an odd pang at this, although she has known from the start that the beach, the father and the boy were a way station only.

It is a fleeting thought; there are more practical considerations.

She rolls up her cat costume in a bundle, carefully opens the door an inch to listen. She hears the man and the boy in the kitchen, dishes being banged about.

She slips out through the hall to the back door and goes down into the garage, where the laundry facilities are. She puts the costume into the dryer to tumble, then silently opens the door out to the side drive, where she finds and cuts the wires to the Internet and cable. She needs the man and boy isolated for what she is about to do next.

When she lets herself back into the laundry room, the father is waiting.

Her pulse spikes, and her hand closes around the razor in her pocket.

The father steps toward her, into the laundry room.

Then she draws in a breath, half-laughs. "You scared me!" she chides, like any normal person, as she eases the razor into the back of her waistband.

He looks at her, obviously wanting an explanation but not quite able to ask her. She moves into the laundry room and steps to the dryer to take her cat suit out.

"You washed it already?" He looks quizzical.

"Just tumbling out the sand. We didn't even sit but..." she rolls her eyes. "Sand everywhere."

He smiles, but there is something behind his eyes.

"What's wrong?" she asks bluntly.

He smiles again and there is a definite shadow. "You seem so — distracted, today. I wondered if it was something I did. Something I could fix."

Always the caretaker; always taking responsibility. She wavers, feeling the pull to be taken care of. Then she closes that impulse off inside, while outside she shakes her head to reassure him. "It's been a beautiful day. I just wanted to be home."

She uses the word deliberately and can feel his energy lift. For a moment she feels something like guilt. Her feelings about the man are complicated, unlike her feelings about the boy. And then she hardens herself. There is work to do.

· · · · ·

She has been on the father's iPhone while he and the boy make dinner and now knows who the hunter is: Matthew Roarke, Assistant Special Agent in Charge, San Francisco Office of the FBI. Criminal Organizations is his division, so his interest in her is entirely because of that moment on the street. Somehow he knew, and he has tracked her thus far. She is not, after all, invisible. Someone has found her.

Now she looks down again at his face on the screen. The formality of the pose does not disguise the watching restlessness in his eyes.

She knows she has to go, and there is no time to waste. He is good, very good.

But the boy. There is more to be done there, that *must* be done.

She feels her heart starting to race, and becomes aware that she has not taken a breath for some time. She breathes in, and stills herself, and realizes that it is meant. It is all meant.

Perhaps it is even what she has longed for.

They eat on the deck, where the wind is light and enticing, and she pours glass after glass of wine for the man, and she keeps stifling yawns, which encourages him to give in to his own drowsiness.

"I'll do the dishes. You go take a nap before you pass out," she says softly to him.

"I'm fine," he starts, and she shakes her head.

"You are so *not* fine. And I want you awake, later."

He smiles in a daze and goes in to collapse on the sofa. He is out within minutes, thanks to the Ambien prescription she'd found in his medicine cabinet the first night.

She leaves the dishes and goes out to the deck, where the boy is staring out over the ocean. She holds out her hand to him. After a moment he puts his small one in hers and together they walk down the stairs to the beach.

The boy is subdued, increasingly dark.

They drift across the wide expanse of sand toward the water's edge and look out at the rising moon, full tomorrow, the ripples of blue-white light on the water. She feels it like touch on her skin.

"Why are you dark and sad?" she says to the boy directly.

He stares down at the sand, kicking at the water, and she waits, watching the water, and him out of the corner of her eye. Time is different with children.

"You're going away," he says finally.

"Hush," she says. "Let's listen to the sea."

He shivers, and she draws him against her, feeling his small, live presence. She folds herself down to sit in the sand, and he sits with her, draped over her thigh. She puts her arm around him and puts her chin on his head and looks out into the waves, and finally she speaks.

"We need to talk about the monsters, now."

• • • • •

Roarke and Epps stayed to the bitter end, as the festivities went on through the night; children and families starting to disappear around sunset as the wine tasting stepped up in the marquis tents and the bands got raunchier. The music was distracting; it was hard for Roarke to focus. Not that he expected to find her; he had not felt anything since that one moment at the pier, near the pumpkin patch.

And you're a psychic, now? he mocked himself. But the feeling remained that he had had his chance, and missed it, and that he would regret it for longer than he wanted to contemplate.

He looked out on the dark ocean, the pale strip of beach where lovers walked in the surf. The lights of beach houses up on the bluffs glowed in a row.

Where are you? he asked the tide. *What next?*

DAY EIGHT

Chapter 50

The light was gray and gentle, but Mark Sebastian's first moments of consciousness were groggy and disoriented. First, there was only pain in his back and an unaccustomed feeling, like cotton in his head. Which when he sat up — slowly — made more sense. He was on the couch, and the soft light coming in through the living room windows was dawn, not sunset. And that was when the anxiety kicked in.

He stood, and had to fight a wave of dizziness. Then he strode toward Jason's bedroom, calling, "Jase?"

He stopped in the doorway, and every parent's worst dread hit him like a speeding train. The bed was empty, made, unslept in.

"Leila?" he managed through a dry mouth. He lunged for the stairs, bolted clumsily upward toward his own bedroom and pulled open the door.

Bed made. Empty. Silent. Through the windows, the ocean stretched out around him, infinite, implacable.

They were gone.

Chapter 51

Roarke's phone vibrated on the night table, and he squinted at the time before he punched on. Barely 6:00 a.m. It was an operator on the tip line, patching through a caller. Before Roarke could even ask the caller's name, a man's voice cut in, wired with a kind of agony Roarke had heard too many times before.

"This woman you're looking for — is she dangerous?"

Roarke took a beat before he answered.

"I believe so."

There was a long and awful silence.

"She has my son."

• • • • •

Roarke stood in the beach house, right on the bluff he had been looking at the night before. Just hours before.

A ten-minute walk from the pier, he was thinking. *She was right here all along.*

He walked the living room slowly, past the wall-to-wall windows with the best view of the ocean he could ever remember seeing. Framed photos on the wall and above the fireplace showed a towheaded and serious upper-middle class child, Jason Sebastian. Epps was busy taking photos of the photos and uploading them to the Bureau's Child Abduction Rapid Deployment team.

Police Chief Wilson was already on the scene. After receiving Sebastian's 911 call, the Chief's first call had been to the CHP to activate an Amber Alert; his second call had been to Roarke. He'd promised all the help the Pismo Beach department could give and at the same time made it clear he was entirely ready to hand over control of the manhunt to the Bureau.

"All that matters is that that boy gets back safe," he'd told Roarke, out of earshot of the father.

Jason had been gone a little over four hours, if the father was to be believed; he recalled awakening and seeing Cara Lindstrom in the room with him just after 3:00 a.m. It appeared she had drugged him with his own Ambien prescription.

Alerts were already being issued through the Emergency Alert System, which pre-empted radio and TV broadcasts to get information to the public immediately. Caltrans would be flashing the alerts on the state highways' electronic message boards, and photos of the boy and the police sketch of "Leila French" were being disseminated through Critical Reach, an image-based system linking state, county and local law enforcement.

The Bureau's Crimes Against Children Unit had established a nationwide child abduction team to provide on-the-ground investigative, technical and resource assistance to local departments, and the Western region team was being dispatched to Pismo. Roarke welcomed the extra hands. He would be able to leave the CARD team in Pismo with Chief Wilson, and concentrate on finding Cara Lindstrom himself.

He was not sure how grave a danger the boy might be in, although of course it was imperative to act as if the danger was imminent and dire. But given Cara's previous victims, it didn't follow that she would harm a child. Necessarily. It was a strange situation.

He looked toward the father on the couch, where he had been sitting quietly, watching every move the agents made, and started with the question he had to ask first.

"You're divorced," he said. "Shared custody?"

Sebastian hesitated. "She has a week per month. I was supposed to drop him off at his mother's today; it was her weekend."

"Why the uneven split?"

There was definitely something loaded in the look on Sebastian's face. "My wife — my ex-wife — is an alcoholic. Her visitation is contingent on mandatory counseling and AA meetings. She is not allowed to drink within eight hours of contact with Jason."

Roarke knew too well that all the court-ordered counseling and meetings in the world had no influence over whether an alcoholic was going to drink or not. He looked to Chief Wilson. "Has the mother been interviewed?"

"One of my first calls was to the SLO police. They've interviewed her. She was at home and sober, and there was no sign of the boy."

Roarke nodded. Under the circumstances it was unlikely that the mother had anything to do with the boy's disappearance, but it was the first avenue of inquiry. And there was one more thing that he had to focus on right away.

"Jason is five, Mr. Sebastian?" he asked.

"Yes."

Five. And tomorrow is the anniversary of the massacre of Cara's family and her near-death at five years old. This is so not good.

Roarke kept all of those thoughts off his face as he told the father, "You're going to have to tell us everything, from the beginning. Please leave nothing out. How and when did you first encounter 'Leila French'?"

Sebastian had to swallow through a dry mouth. "It was on the beach, on Tuesday morning. She was up from L.A., staying at the Dunes."

Chief Wilson cut in. "I went over there on the way here. A clerk remembered a Leila French calling in, but no one by that name ever showed up to check in. No one at the motel ID'd the sketch."

Sebastian looked as if someone had punched him in the gut.

"You've tried to reach her cell phone?" Roarke prompted him.

The man looked angry, helpless. "I don't know her number."

Epps turned from the fireplace, and exchanged a glance with Roarke. "You didn't ask for her number?"

"I..." the man looked confused, and then defensive. "She said she was staying at the Dunes, and then — we just kept running into her."

I doubt there was any "just" about it.

Sebastian stiffened at the agents' silent appraisal. He spoke quietly. "I'm not an imbecile, Agent Roarke. She had a joke about being on the beach, and she just never carried a phone. People these days are so plugged in, and — it seemed so different."

Different is what she is, Roarke thought grimly, but he squelched his inner commentary and tried to be neutral and gentle. "Did she say where she lived in L.A.? Where she worked?" Whatever she had told Sebastian was almost certainly false, but there were clues in every lie.

"She said Los Feliz, and that she worked at home. A researcher for the film studios." Roarke could see Sebastian was only half-present, now reevaluating everything that had occurred under the lens of the current circumstances.

"So she said she was up for vacation."

"Not exactly. She said..." Sebastian stopped, and looked out the wide windows at the sea. Roarke could see him thinking, examining his recollections for hidden meaning. "She said she was here to think some things out."

"What kind of things?"

"Life things, I assumed."

"You said you met her on Wednesday morning. What time was this?"

Sebastian breathed in. "Early. Jason is always up at the crack of dawn; we were walking on the beach and he — he's the one who found her."

"*Found* her?" Roarke tried to keep the sharpness out of his voice, but the time frame meant that the father and the boy had seen her just hours after she killed the trucker.

Sebastian didn't answer. Roarke had to rein in his raw impatience.

"Mr. Sebastian, whatever it is you're thinking, you cannot hold anything back. For your son's sake, it's vital that you tell us everything."

Sebastian looked away. "I think she may have been sleeping on the beach. I thought at first — I assumed she was drunk, or sick."

No, just fresh from a killing, Roarke thought grimly.

Aloud he asked, "Why? Was she disheveled, incoherent?" The question he really wanted to ask was is if she had blood on her, but he'd hold off for a second.

"No," Sebastian said loudly, defensively. "It was more that she seemed — not even sick, but very distant. I never saw her drink, the whole time."

The whole time. Meaning there was a whole lot more contact that you've been letting on.

Aloud Roarke asked, "But nothing alarming."

"Alarming like?"

"Bruises, blood."

Sebastian looked shocked, and then disturbed. "No. No, nothing. Of course not. I wouldn't have..."

Roarke waited.

"She was so good with Jason," Sebastian said miserably. "She knew just how to talk to him. He's been very subdued since — my divorce."

To his credit, Sebastian was now not trying to hold back, though it was clearly painful to him to have to open his life like this, under such circumstances. But he had held back at first, Roarke knew now.

"Mr. Sebastian, you told Chief Wilson that 'Leila French' went for a walk with your son and never came back. But she was here in the house overnight, wasn't she."

The man turned even more pale under his tan. "Yes," he said, a strangled sound.

And then Roarke knew. Sebastian had slept with her. Whatever Cara Lindstrom was, this very straight and civilized father had taken her into his house, with his five-year old son, and begun a sexual relationship with her in the space of mere days.

Aside from an obvious wound from his divorce, Sebastian seemed a paragon of responsibility and concern. Which meant she had fooled this citizen on every level.

And what she would want with the boy... a five-year-old boy...

Roarke tried to keep his face and voice neutral. "She's been staying with you?"

Sebastian's face crumpled. "I know how that sounds now. My God." He stood, and moved without focus around the room. Roarke knew what that was, had seen it before, the jolt of an adrenaline rush, an abduction victim's relative's sudden remembrance of the absolute terror of his circumstances, the violence of the situation in this sunny sanctuary of a home.

"But Jason adored her—" he stopped, a sick beat. "*Adores* her."

Roarke could feel the horror in the pause. He looked to Epps. "Where are Lam and Stotlemyre? They need to go over the whole house."

"Flying into SLO. Be here within the hour."

Sebastian turned on Roarke, suddenly. "Who is she? Why is she doing this?"

Roarke reached for calm. "Mr. Sebastian, we have no evidence at the moment that she's a specific danger to children." *Only the report of a man with his own agenda,* he thought, mentally crossing his fingers that he was right about Munroe. "She may have taken your son as security, if she realized that we were in pursuit."

Or it may have some bizarre connection to the fact that her whole family was massacred in front of her and she was nearly killed herself at the exact same age your son is, exactly twenty-five years ago tomorrow.

Sebastian was staring at him. "You do know," he said hoarsely. "Who is she?"

Roarke took a deep breath, and told him.

Chapter 52

They drive on Highway 227, the boy firmly strapped into his car seat in the back. She'd taken it from the father's SUV.

The car she has stolen from a beach house on the block. She has been watching it for the last four days, the empty house and the car sitting silently in the under-house garage. She will only need it for a day; chances are good the owner won't return until the weekend, at least. At any rate she doesn't intend to be conspicuous. And there is nothing to tie her to the car; it is a good camouflage, which she needs right now.

There is an Amber Alert out for the boy already; she has not been playing the radio for just that reason, so that he does not pick up his own name on the broadcast. But she had seen the alert flashed on one of the LED traffic condition signs on the 101, and subsequently has pulled off onto the 227 toward San Luis Obispo. Hills with endless rows of carefully trained grape vines flash by outside.

The boy had objected. Now he says it again, darkly: "This is the long way."

She smiles at him in the rear-view mirror. "Are you in a hurry?"

He frowns. "When is Daddy coming?"

"Soon," she says, her face clouding slightly. It is a great risk she is taking, but there is no choice. There are the monsters to consider.

She focuses on the road ahead, and drives.

Chapter 53

Sebastian had gotten progressively more still as Roarke spoke about Cara Lindstrom.

"I remember this," he said suddenly. "Of course I do. I was seven, eight... it was all over the news. The Reaper. Kids talking about it, those families. My mother wouldn't let me go anywhere for a year. Horrible year."

Sebastian was a native Californian, then, like Roarke. It had been an indelible part of childhood, a legend, like the Zodiac Killer: the unknown killer, the families slaughtered en masse.

Sebastian was frowning. "But the girl. Wasn't she..." He was very focused, frowning. "She was almost killed, too." He went off someplace uninterpretable, his face as gray as the ocean behind him.

"What are you thinking?" Roarke said sharply.

"Her neck," Sebastian said.

Roarke and Epps looked at each other. "What about her neck?"

"She has a scar," Sebastian said. He drew his finger across his neck, an uneven line.

"The turtleneck," Epps said, looking at Roarke.

"The scar is very prominent, then," Roarke said to Sebastian, his pulse racing.

"Not anything like you would expect," Sebastian said. "But she thinks it is, I think. She always covers it."

She always covers it. Even in bed, you mean…

At the moment Roarke was having trouble focusing. He was having feelings he had no business having. Feelings that would make him question his own mental state. Jealousy, possessiveness — and it may have had something to do with the possessiveness any lawman feels about his quarry, but Roarke had to be honest with himself that there was something purely male about his response.

"Did she explain the scar in any way?" Epps was asking, filling the silence.

Sebastian stepped to the glass doors and looked out over the ocean. "She said her parents died when she was five. She said a car accident." Then he stopped, and finished flatly. "But it wasn't."

"No, it wasn't," Roarke said.

Sebastian was frowning, something obviously bothering him. He finally said it aloud. "Jason is five."

It was exactly Roarke's own unease. Inexplicable, yet it felt so unignorable, relevant in some maddening way. *Fixated at the age of the trauma.*

What does she want with the boy?

Sebastian suddenly moved, a jerky, wild movement that resolved into pacing. Another rush of fear.

"Why would she take him? What does she want?" The anguish in Sebastian's voice was nearly unbearable.

Roarke summoned as much calm as he could muster. "We don't have any evidence that she's endangered children before. He may just have been a convenient hostage."

Sebastian stared at him. "But there's something else, isn't there."

Roarke paused. There was no easy way to say it. "Tonight — tomorrow morning — is the anniversary of the massacre of her family."

Sebastian didn't move for long seconds, then began shaking his head. "I don't understand." But Roarke could see his breathing was escalating, a tension spiked by the adrenaline stiffening his muscles.

He might not understand, but he knows it's not good, Roarke thought. *Just like I do.* "Mr. Sebastian, I don't know what it means, or if it means anything. It could be significant to her, or it may not. You said she has a warm and caring relationship with your son."

"Yes," Sebastian said, clutching for that hope. "Very."

"That's positive," Epps said firmly.

"But you need to go through everything that she ever said and did. We need to know where she might be going—"

But even as he said it aloud, Roarke knew.

She'd be going home.

He looked at Epps, who was equally frozen in realization.

The Pismo police chief looked from one agent to the other. "Where?" he said tersely. Epps was already pulling out his cell phone.

Roarke felt a superstitious reluctance to say it, as if he would jinx it. Then he just did.

"She'll go back to Blythe. To the house where it happened. Her childhood home."

Epps snapped into the phone. "City of Blythe Police Department."

"Why?" Sebastian turned to Roarke. "Why would she take him there?"

Epps said into the phone. "This is Special Agent Epps of the San Francisco FBI. We're coordinating a child abduction response." He began flipping quickly through a paper file as he spoke into the phone.

Roarke turned on Sebastian. "Did she have a car?"

"Not that I ever saw."

"And yours is here, she didn't take it?"

"It's here. She took the car seat, though."

Roarke looked at him. *Well, it's good news. The boy isn't in the trunk,* he thought, but didn't say aloud.

Epps glanced over from the phone. "She's got a master key; a car's not going to be a problem," he said. "So another Honda, is what we're saying."

"Probably," Roarke agreed.

Epps relayed that information to whoever in the PD he was speaking with, and then looked back to Roarke. "The house is bank-owned. Went into foreclosure last year and has been standing empty ever since."

Roarke checked the time on his own phone. Blythe was a six-and-a-half-hour drive from Pismo Beach. It was now 8:00 a.m. And Sebastian had seen her in the house at approximately 3:10 a.m., the one time during the night he'd awakened.

"She wouldn't have made it to Blythe by car, not yet." He turned to Epps. "Get a patrol car over there. They're to check for any persons inside the house but not disturb the scene. Then have them stake out the house. We can get a chopper from the L.A. field office." With the Child Abduction Response in effect, the Los Angeles field office, which had jurisdiction in Blythe, was already on alert and had a helicopter reserved at Roarke's disposal.

Epps put down his phone. "Closest airfield to us is SLO. Chopper can be there in just over an hour."

Roarke turned to Chief Wilson. "My evidence response team will be here any minute. They'll go over this whole house and be in constant contact with us."

Sebastian moved forward, his face set. "I'm going with you."

Roarke put out a hand, blocking him. "I can't let you do that."

Sebastian looked quietly murderous. "This is my son."

Roarke heroically refrained from pointing out the obvious: that he should have been thinking of that sooner. "You're going to have to let us handle that."

"But you haven't finished interviewing me."

Epps glanced at Roarke, and his silent message was clear. Sebastian had a point.

Sebastian pressed his advantage. "And I know her. You might need me. It might help."

That thought was a spike of rage for Roarke, but he suppressed it. It was true; he needed to know what Sebastian knew about her.

"You can come along to the airport and we'll continue the interview," Roarke said. His tone of voice made it clear that there would be no arguing beyond that.

Epps drove, Roarke riding shotgun, with Sebastian in the back. There was no rush to the airport; it was fifteen minutes away and they would beat the helicopter by an hour, but Epps drove tensely and fast nonetheless. They sped on the coast highway, with the silver-gray ocean on their left.

Roarke stared out through the windshield, thinking. The Blythe police department had already called back; the house was empty, no one there. Roarke was almost sure that was where she would be going, though.

"What's a master key?" Sebastian suddenly asked from the back seat.

The agents looked at him as if they'd forgotten he was there. "A filed key, so she can get into any car of that make," Epps said.

The look on Sebastian's face was pure disorientation. Roarke knew that on top of everything else this civilian was now trying to get his mind around the idea that the woman was a seasoned con artist, a car thief, among many other more questionable activities. The father looked dashed into a million pieces. Roarke felt contempt, then despised himself for feeling it. *Blaming the victim. A normal person shouldn't have to be looking over his shoulder every second, watching out for these things.*

But the stark truth of it was, normal people *did* have to worry about these things. If they didn't, all was lost.

"I guess you're thinking I'm about the most irresponsible parent you've ever met," Sebastian said to Roarke directly, then looked away briefly. "I know that's what I'm thinking."

"Not by a long shot," Roarke said, and actually meant it. In his book stupidity didn't hold a candle to deliberate malevolence, and never would.

"If you'd met her you'd know—" Sebastian stopped, and looked out at the vast blue-gray ocean spread out to the side of them. "I would never have believed she would hurt Jase. Never. She seemed lost, and maybe damaged. But who isn't?" He looked up defensively. "She's a good person. I know that."

That would be a whole new definition of good, Roarke thought. *But I hope you're right, for your son's sake.*

"She was so gentle with him. He just attached himself to her."

Maybe she reminded him of his mother. You're a stellar judge of character, aren't you, pal? But Roarke refrained from saying it. Barely.

Roarke had filled Sebastian in on Cara's childhood, but the father hadn't asked what she was wanted for as an adult. Maybe a subconscious oversight, but it meant he either didn't want to know or he already knew. Roarke had not yet told him because he was unsure of his own motives. He didn't want to add to Sebastian's agony for no reason; on the other hand a jolt of realistic terror might shake loose information that they needed to find Cara and the boy. But Roarke didn't want to make any moves out of anger or retribution. He was having trouble identifying his own emotions, and thought it best to stick to the med school rule: *First, do no harm.*

In the back seat, Sebastian's face was hollow, his eyes distant; he was thinking about something specific. "Why do you think she would want to take him back to that house? Where it happened?"

That's the million dollar question, isn't it? I haven't got a clue, just this sick feeling in my stomach.

Roarke turned in his seat so he could look at Sebastian head on. "Tell us more about her interaction with the boy," he said.

He found it interesting that Sebastian's face relaxed, the tension lines smoothing as he considered the question. "She was wonderful with him. From the beginning, she talked to him like an equal."

Roarke wasn't entirely surprised. *Fixated at the age of the trauma,* Snyder had said.

"I'm sorry to have to ask this, Mr. Sebastian. Did Lindstrom — Leila — seem to have a sexual interest in your son?"

Sebastian recoiled. "No," he said immediately, revolted. "Not in any way. They were physical together—"

"How do you mean, physical?"

"They raced and wrestled, she picked him up, swung him, carried him. Nothing sexual at all. She seemed very accustomed to children."

That doesn't compute. Or does it?

"She never mentioned having children, or working with them?"

Sebastian thought before he shook his head. "No. She was just a natural."

He fell silent again, looking lost.

Roarke considered this quickly. None of Cara's suspected victims had young children; Wann was the only one who had a child at all, the missing fourteen-year old, who had been gone months before her father's death.

But there was the incident in the Rite Aid store, Munroe and his granddaughter. *Is she changing her M.O.? Looking for children for some reason? But what? For that matter, why would she sleep with Sebastian?*

He finally asked the question he had been putting off. "The two of you were sexually involved."

Sebastian's face went through a dozen different changes in seconds.

"Yes," he said bleakly.

"You met her on Wednesday, and she moved into the beach house with you when?" Roarke asked, his voice inexorable.

Now Sebastian actually reddened. "She wasn't — she didn't move in."

"Last night was the only night she spent in the house?"

"Last night, and the night before," Sebastian said tightly.

"And the other nights? Wednesday? Thursday?"

"She left."

"What does that mean? She was with you but didn't spend the night?"

Sebastian was holding back anger, now. "She had dinner with us on Wednesday, and left after dinner."

"And what happened on Thursday?"

"There was a storm, a bad one. I didn't want her to go out in it, and..."

Sebastian looked away, and there was no doubt what "and" meant. Roarke suppressed a wave of some emotion he didn't want to look at. He remembered the storm. He had been just thirty miles away, on the balcony of the Atascadero hotel.

"And then?" he asked evenly.

"Then we spent the day together..."

"And she stayed the night."

"Yes."

"And she stayed the next day," Roarke pressed on inexorably.

"Yes."

"And night."

Roarke felt Epps shift uncomfortably in the driver's seat, a sign that Roarke might be going too far. Roarke shot him a look. *Yeah, it's uncomfortable. The man was sleeping with a killer, with his five-year old son in the same house. There's nothing that's not uncomfortable about that.*

"So you could say that you had a high level of trust with this woman, 'Leila French.'" Roarke could hear the sarcasm in his own voice and regretted the words as soon as they were out of his mouth.

Sebastian breathed in, out, gathering himself. Then he met Roarke's gaze and spoke quietly. "You could say that I felt we had a connection that I haven't felt with anyone in a long time. You could say that my judgment was impaired by unresolved feelings over my recent divorce. You could say my judgment was impaired, period. Or all of the above. I trusted her with Jason and I was wrong, and I'll regret that for the rest of my life."

Roarke felt small, and sorry.

"We are going to get your son back, Mr. Sebastian," he said. And again, Epps tensed. *Never make promises, it tempts fate.*

Roarke fell silent, then, and looked out at the sea.

SLO was a tiny airport in the rolling hills, with only three regularly scheduled commercial flights out.

There was a black-and-white waiting for them at the airport gate. Lam and Stotlemyre piled out of the back, with luggage, and a Pismo police officer got out of the driver's seat.

Roarke stood from the car as the officer approached Roarke. "Agent Roarke? I'm Officer Cleary. Chief Wilson sent me to pick up your men and deliver them to you. Then we got the message you were en route."

"Right, thank you." Roarke turned to his evidence response team. "Stotlemyre, you'll go back with Officer Cleary; I need you to process the beach house. Lam, you're coming with us."

The two techs nodded and immediately dived into their kits to divide up their equipment.

Roarke glanced toward Sebastian, who had emerged from the car as Epps did, and spoke to the officer. "And you'll take Mr. Sebastian back home."

Sebastian turned on Roarke. "You said I was coming with you."

"No, *you* said that," Roarke said mercilessly.

"We can't take along a civilian," Epps stepped in, with his best smoothing-things-over voice. "We're going to do our jobs, Mr. Sebastian."

Roarke relented slightly. "You have my cell number if you can think of anything else that will help us. Any information we get about your son, you will know instantly."

Sebastian wasn't happy, but he was also resigned. "Thank you," he said. There was no color in his face or voice.

He started to turn away and then stopped, looked at Roarke. "Don't—"

And he stopped. Roarke looked at him, waiting. Sebastian shook his head and turned away.

Roarke and Epps and Lam checked in at the counter and then hustled out to the field to wait for the chopper. Epps looked at Roarke sideways.

"Harsh on the man," he said quietly, so Lam couldn't hear.

"If you think so," Roarke said.

"She's a con artist. She's a good one. The man got conned. People do."

"So I'm blaming the victim?" Roarke said.

Epps stared off at the hills beyond the airstrip, where the chopper was cresting the range, approaching the field. "She's fooled a whole lot of people for a whole long time. He's not the first. S'all I'm saying." He looked to Roarke. "Is he supposed to know more because he has a kid?"

Roarke stared back. "Yeah. Yeah, he is."

"Well I say — easy to say when you don't have one. Which neither of us do. The man is still a man."

Roarke was spared any further talk... as all words were blown away by the backwash of the chopper.

As the agents watched it descend and settle, Roarke went still, thinking.

Suddenly he pulled Epps away from the others and shouted over the engine noise.

"I need you to stay."

Epps looked at him, startled.

"I'm sorry," Roarke shouted through the chopper's wind. "But we might be wrong about Blythe, the house. She may not be going anywhere near there. I need you to be close to the father, close by here, in case there's something Stotlemyre finds in the beach house, something that gives us a clue."

There had been a flash of disappointment on Epps' face, but he'd hidden it almost immediately. He was already nodding. "I get you, boss."

"And there's one more thing," Roarke said, and glanced toward the gate where the black-and-white still stood, parked. "The mother. Sebastian's ex-wife. I don't know, but... it couldn't hurt to go interview her."

"You got it," Epps said.

"I'll be in touch. You be in touch." Roarke said, nodding his thanks. Then he motioned to Lam and hustled for the chopper.

Chapter 54

Blythe straddled the Sonoran and Mojave deserts, right where the mountains started to get strange along the California/Arizona border, a stopover city on Interstate 10 as it crossed the Colorado River between Phoenix and L.A.

Roarke stared down over the vast sweep of desert from the helicopter. There were jagged rock formations, flat housing developments, an uncanny number of palm trees, and a number of golf courses, but his overwhelming impression of the town, even from the air, was that the whole place was a natural breeding ground for meth labs.

The local police had already been by the house to check for inhabitants, even though it was pretty nearly impossible for Cara Lindstrom to have gotten there with the boy in the time frame. They'd found it empty.

The chopper pilot shouted back over the grinding of the blades. "I'm coming in over 95. If you look to the left you can see the Intaglios."

Intalyos, was what Roarke heard; a term that was very vaguely familiar but he couldn't recall from where.

And then he saw Lam staring down toward the freeway, mesmerized. Roarke looked down, and was equally riveted. Next to the river, carved into the desert floor, there was an uneven pentagonal shape, and within it, a giant stick figure of a man, like something out of *The X Files.* "Geoglyphics," the pilot shouted. "Native Americans did them, thousands of years ago. No one knows what tribe or what for."

"How big is that thing?" Roarke shouted back.

"Hundred and sixty-five feet. They call that one The Hunter."

Roarke felt a jolt at the name, but he remembered now, the giant figures that UFO conspiracy nuts claimed proved the existence of extra-terrestrials who apparently had given aboriginal tribes directions for carving the shapes into the rock.

No stranger than anything else at this point, he thought.

"Coming over Riverside Drive, now," the pilot shouted.

The agents looked down on a lot of several acres with a house fanning out in four sections like an accordion, bordered by thick patches of old-growth trees. The property was surrounded by agricultural fields on three sides, the other side of the lot butted up against a road. There was no other house adjacent at all. The closest residence was across that highway.

Roarke felt a frisson of déjà vu; he had seen this aerial view on the TV reports countless times as a child, during news reports on the massacre.

There was no sign of a car on the property, but there was a large garage and also some kind of shed. There was no sign of any people moving below, either.

"Isolated. Very isolated," Lam said, softly, not trying to shout over the chopper noise. But Roarke heard him. Isolated it was. *Perfect,* was the word that floated through his mind. But perfect for what?

The pilot landed the chopper at Gary Field, a wide, flat stretch of desert, ringed by mountains in the far distance.

Two of the Blythe PD's three criminal investigators, Sergeants Danner and Saenz, were waiting for Roarke and Lam just off the runway in a Crown Vic.

They were doing their level best to conceal it, but it was hard not to notice the locals' excitement as the men shook hands all around. This was clearly the biggest crime in Blythe since...

Probably since Cara Lindstrom had been the victim, not the abductor.

The agents strapped on Kevlar vests before they got into the car, the Blythe PD investigators did the same.

"To our knowledge the suspect has not used a firearm before, but we can't take that chance," Roarke told them.

In the car, he stared out the windows at sand and palm trees and barrel cactus as they drove and Sergeant Danner filled them in.

"The house on Riverside Drive is for sale. Bank-owned. It was a foreclosure, no surprise these days, but it's got a history of high turnover, defaulted mortgages."

Like a curse. Bad energy.

The house had already been checked out; they knew Cara was not inside. The police department had her sketch and Jason Sebastian's photos, and had been staking out the house since Roarke had called that morning; no one had come near it.

But she could have been living there, Roarke thought. *It's been empty for all that time. If I were going to hide out, that's a pretty damn good place to do it.*

Roarke was also not sure that she would show up before Sunday, if she showed up at all. It was the flimsiest of hunches; he had no idea what he expected her to do with the boy in the house. Satanic ritual? A reenactment of her own attack? There was no logical sense to it.

The plan was to check the house for recent habitation, in case she had been squatting, there, in case there was any indication of what she was planning.

And then wait.

Roarke came back to the present as Sergeant Danner asked a question.

"So you really think this is the Lindstrom girl?"

Roarke paused. "We know she is."

With the sprawling fields around it, the house had more of the feel of a ranch, but the realtor packet indicated the fields were not part of the property itself. There was a packed dirt road leading from the highway to the house, which was surrounded by a split-rail fence. The lawn beyond was dry and brown, but the eucalyptus and olive trees were huge and healthy, cooling the air with their spicy sage green leaves.

As the Crown Vic turned into the drive, Roarke stared out the windows with a powerful feeling of déjà vu. He knew the place: he'd seen it, studied it, dreamed it. He felt a sense of reality wobbling to encounter it in waking life.

"Four bedrooms, four baths, three thousand nine hundred eighty-four square feet, four point four seven acres, mountain view." Lam read from the realtor sheets. "Built 1967, asking price $250,000!" He whistled in city-bred disbelief.

Sergeant Saenz drove up the driveway and parked in front. The men got out of the car, drawing their weapons, and moved up the pavers toward the front entrance. There was a dry breeze, nothing like the wind that had been reported on the night of the massacre, but enough to create a dry whispering in the trees around them that made the air seem alive. Roarke's twinge of déjà vu had blossomed into a full-on feeling of walking into a dream.

The recessed porch had a high triangular arched entrance and a wide door with ornate carved wooden panels. There was a lock box on the door handle. Danner used the key.

The door swung open into the silent house.

The entry hall was ornate wood beams and white-painted brick walls, with tiled floors. Roarke went in first and motioned the others back, and just stood for a moment, listening, *feeling*.

The great room was huge and gorgeous: more ceramic-tiled floors, cathedral ceilings of beamed dark wood and antique ceiling fans, two huge arched windows framing a double-size fireplace. Afternoon light spilled through the windows but the house was glacial, even with no AC running.

According to the floor plan, the great room, family room and kitchen were all in the center of the house; the master bedroom and a study fanned out in one wing to the right, and three smaller bedrooms fanned out in a left wing.

Roarke signaled for the Blythe investigators to go left, as he and Lam moved right. The men eased forward, weapons drawn.

They walked through the house, checking for evidence that anyone had stayed there. The whole house echoed under the vaulted ceilings... it seemed to have been deserted for years. "Last occupancy 2010," Lam confirmed under his breath.

The family room had a sprawling brick fireplace along one whole wall, a built-in bar, beamed wood ceilings, all very dark and cool. Sliding glass doors led out to a tiled patio with the same high vaulted wood ceilings and ceiling fans, a brick barbeque, a dry pool with dry spa.

Room after room was completely empty; the men's footsteps echoed off the ubiquitous tiles. There were no windows open or broken. There were no smells of food or perfume or sweat, no evidence that any of the sinks had been used, no piles of blankets, no candles, no writing on the walls.

More mirrored emptiness in the master suite. More tile and a spa tub in the master bathroom. No sign, of course, of the bloodbath that the room had been.

Roarke kept his ears open for sounds from the other wing, but there was nothing.

"All clear!" he heard echoing from the next hall, and he and Lam lowered their weapons.

The four men reconvened in the great room.

"No sign of anyone," Sergeant Danner reported. "And it just doesn't feel like anyone's been here."

Roarke felt the same. If she had been using the house, or had been there at all, there was no trace of her.

There was a trace of something else, though. He had the same eerie feeling of arrested time that he'd experienced at the construction site in Salt Lake City — and truth be told, at the rest stop in Atascadero. *She strikes and leaves the place hollow, empty.*

Only here in this house, it had not been her that had struck.

Chapter 55

As it turned out, Epps didn't exactly interview Sebastian's ex-wife. He drove the rental SUV through the charming historical downtown to the small bungalow where she lived in San Luis Obispo and when he turned down the block toward the house, she was just leaving.

Epps hung back in the rental car and got himself a good look at her as she hustled herself into the little Mazda she was driving. Pretty, if you liked that doe-eyed anorexic type, but there was something too familiar about her. He knew the desperate look an addict got when those feel-good chemicals started drying out of the blood.

"That woman looks *furtive*, to me," Epps said to himself.

So he followed her.

He stayed well back on the quiet streets, not that she would have noticed, as she drove out of the pleasant enough residential neighborhood into a not-so-pleasant one that had all the telltale signs of badness: graffiti, trash, tires, weeds, all the sorry ass signs that people were too doped up to be taking pride in their surroundings, or even attempting some basic dignity.

Then she turned onto a street that changed. The houses on either side of the street were not rundown apartment complexes but larger private residences, or they had been at one time. Now half of them looked foreclosed on and half of them looked like rentals, with wash hanging on once-respectable porches and flowerbeds long gone to seed.

The wife pulled into the drive of one of the ghost manors, and drove straight back. Epps cruised slowly past the drive, staring down it, and saw there was a guest cottage in the back. The wife parked in front of it and scrambled out of her car, bumping into her own door with the clumsiness of an addict.

"Well, now, who might we be going to see?" Epps muttered. "I just wonder."

He stopped the car at the curb down the street and checked his weapon before he reached for the door, because in Epps' experience drugs and guns went together like peas and carrots.

He got out of the car and hovered beside the hedge lining the driveway to look down toward the back house.

The wife used a key to get in to the cottage, which was interesting because Sebastian hadn't said anything about his ex-wife having a second residence and as far as Epps could tell, Sebastian looked like a man who kept up with these things.

Epps began the long walk down the drive, staying in the shadows of the tall and ancient hedge on the left hand side of the property, moving past the falling-apart main house. It was a shame, really, all that beautiful California architecture going to seed—

A scream came from inside the cottage.

Epps bolted forward down the drive, running full-tilt toward the cottage, and just as he hit the porch the wife barreled out of the door, slamming the screen open, and ran right into him.

She screamed again while Epps held her arms and said into her face, "I'm a Federal Agent," and then she started babbling, everything incoherent except two words she said over and over and over. "He's dead, he's dead, he's dead," the babble rising up to a shriek.

Epps felt a jolt of dread. He kept his Glock trained on the door with one hand as he dug the fingers of his left into the woman's shoulder, gripping her.

"The boy? Is it your son?"

The woman was only wailing now, hysterical and useless.

Epps pushed her aside and grabbed the edge of the screen door, shouting inside, "FBI! Drop your weapons and hit the floor!"

And then he was in, and hit by a wall of black. The contrast between the brilliant fall sun outside and the complete darkness of the cottage was disorienting, dangerous. As Epps stared hard through the dark, willing his eyes to adjust, he realized there were blackout shades on the windows, favorite of drug dealers everywhere. The AC was on high, and the room was freezing.

But there was a smell.

Oh, Jesus, Epps thought. *Please not the kid.*

He could see shapes now, in the dimness and stink, and his heart gave a lurch. There was a body on the couch, half on the floor. He felt a rush of relief that it was an adult figure, male, with an impressive head of long black hair. The smell was of death, of voided body fluids, but Epps stepped to the body and checked for a pulse anyway. Nothing. He turned from the dead man and quickly moved through the rest of the small house, calling the boy's name.

There was only silence.

In the living room again, Epps jerked down on one of the curtains and it flew up, rolling itself into that spring-tight coil. Sunlight flooded the room.

In the now-dazzling light, Epps looked over the body: a mixed-race man in his early thirties, Latino and white, addict-thin.

There was drug paraphernalia on the coffee table and around him, baggies of crank, yellowish chunks the size of puffed rice, a glass pipe, a set of scales — and the corpse showed classic signs of a overdose: bluish lips, skin and nails, though the dead man had no obvious signs of the lesions Epps associated with meth use.

He went out onto the porch, where Sebastian's ex-wife was collapsed on the stairs, sobbing. "Ma'am. *Ma'am*," he said sharply. "Did you see your son anywhere in the house?

"N-no," she shook her head, and kept shaking it, as if to keep thoughts and words at bay.

"Who is that man?"

Her face crumpled, but Epps could see that she was stalling to lie about it.

"Your son is missing, ma'am, and you've been holding out on us. If you care anything about him at all, I suggest you start talking."

"S-Steven. Steven Torres."

"How did you know Mr. Torres?"

"I don't," she started.

"You entered this house with a key, ma'am," Epps said dryly.

"He was a friend," she mumbled.

"What were you doing in his house?"

She was silent.

"A little stressed, maybe? Needed a little something to relax you?"

"I just wanted to see a friend," she said stubbornly.

"Do you shoot up with your friend? Smoke a little something?"

This got him only a stony look. Epps fought down distaste. "Do you know where your son is, Miz Sebastian?

"No. No. I don't."

"Because you'd tell me if you knew anything, wouldn't you?"

She looked at him with wet, uncomprehending eyes, and he shook his head.

"Yeah. Sure you would."

Epps reached for his phone to call Chief Wilson.

Chapter 56

The Blythe detectives fanned out outside the ranch house to check the grounds and outbuildings: a two-car garage, and since it was a horse property, a long horse barn of corrugated aluminum painted white.

Inside, Lam got to work processing the house.

Roarke stood in the room that had been Cara Lindstrom's, the room where her sister had been killed in front of her, the room where a monster had picked Cara up like a doll and slashed her throat open and left her to die. Roarke's own life had changed as irrevocably as hers had that night—

He started as his phone buzzed in his pocket. He glanced at the screen, then answered. "Singh. I need good news."

"And I have it," the agent answered in her serene voice. "I have found you one of the original detectives on Cara Lindstrom's case. He is nearby, too, and willing to speak with you about Cara and the family."

Not the news he was hoping for, that the boy had been found, but that wasn't Singh's department. "Excellent," he said.

"He can see you today. Do you want me to set that up?"

"How far away?"

"Forty-five minutes, by Google."

Roarke thought fast. He hated to leave the house, but hated to be idle. "Yes, any time this afternoon that he can do it, I'll be there. Thank you, Singh."

"I will call you right back," she said, a pillar of calm.

Roarke disconnected. The phone rang again almost immediately and he answered, expecting Singh. Instead it was Epps' tense voice on the other end.

"Something major here, boss."

"The boy?" Roarke mentally crossed his fingers.

"No sign of him yet, sorry. But the mother is a piece of work."

"You interviewed her?"

"I followed her. She went straight to her boyfriend's house, only when I say boyfriend, I really mean dealer. Steven Torres. Has a record for cooking, dealing, trafficking. The mother was here in for ten seconds and ran out screaming. Torres is dead, a day or two. It looks like an O.D., but I think this was staged."

Roarke understood what he was implying, and his pulse jumped. "How would Cara Lindstrom even know where the guy lived?" he demanded.

"Not sayin' it was your girl. Not sayin' it was anyone. Just telling you what I see. Stotlemyre's coming over from the beach house to process the scene. Chief Wilson already picked up the mother, took her down to the station for questioning. But it's not just drugs here, boss," Epps said, and there was a peculiar tightness in his voice. "This guy Torres was seriously up to no good. I'm sending photos through."

Roarke found his bag and grabbed his iPad. When he signed on to his account, the email was already there, with attached jpgs.

Roarke clicked through photos with increasing disbelief. They were all of the boy: five-year-old Jason in the bath, in his bathing suit on the beach, being undressed in a bedroom, showing just a glimpse of the hands of whoever was undressing him, presumably the mother. Sneaked photos; Jason seemed unaware he was being photographed.

Roarke felt cold rage, looking at them.

"These were on Torres's computer," Epps said, startling Roarke, who'd forgotten he was still connected. "He hasn't just been taking them — he's been emailing them somewhere. I've got a trace going."

"Jesus Christ," Roarke said.

Drugs, guns and people. Once the bad guys started selling one, they seemed to move on to the others.

"She took him to protect him," Roarke said aloud. "She was keeping him away from the mother."

The silence on Epps' end was deafening. "She's killed five people that we know of. I wouldn't be handing out any medals."

Roarke didn't give a fat rat's ass how it sounded. It was the only thing that made sense. Another bad man was gone, and he was supposed to give a good goddamn?

"Try telling that to the boy's father," Epps said, and Roarke was startled to realize he'd been speaking aloud.

And then suddenly there was background noise, and though Epps' voice was muffled, Roarke could hear the adrenaline spike in his voice as he said, "Hold on, what are you—"

And then the phone went dead.

Chapter 57

E pps was as still as he'd ever been in his life. It was the woman, the woman in Roarke's sketch, and she was standing above him, holding a gun to his head.

"Easy," he said softly, putting all the gravity of his whole life and his love of it into the word. His entire body was on alert and he could *feel* her: the gun, her laser focus, his mortality in her hands, everything. He could see out of the corner of his eye, and her grip was very steady. He had been sitting at Torres' desk in front of his computer as he talked to Roarke on the phone, so she had the advantage of height on him. And surprise. And what looked from this angle like a Ruger.

That's a new wrinkle for her, he thought, a rational thought through the heart-pounding certainty that he could die at any second. At the same time he instantly knew where she'd gotten the weapon, and possibly any number of others. Torres had quite a stash; Epps had already come across several handguns hidden in random but easily accessible places around the house. Drug paranoia.

"Keep your hands flat on the desk," she said calmly.

"I will," he assured her. "Right here on the desk." Inside his mind was racing. The woman had killed five men, at the barest minimum. He was so fucked.

Aloud he said, "Where's the boy?" And hoped Roarke was still listening.

"You have to keep him away from the mother," she said.

"I agree with you there," Epps said, very seriously. "Bad news."

"Check on Torres. You'll see," she said. "There are more. In the desert. A whole nest. You'll know it when you find it. Be sure you check everything."

"I will do that," Epps said. He felt a surreal rush of lightness as it occurred to him that she was speaking as if he had some kind of future.

"Put your head down on the desk," she said. "Slowly."

That rush of hope plummeted as fast as it had risen.

His gut tightened as his heart hammered in his chest and he slowly, slowly lay his head down.

"I have something for you," she said, a voice in the absolute blackness of terror.

And then there was silence behind him that seemed to go on for eternity and then some brief kind of scuffle. Epps braced himself to die... and then a soft, young voice spoke into his darkness.

"Are you the policeman?"

Epps' head shot up from the desk and he whipped toward the voice.

He saw a small silhouette in the half-light behind the door: a boy standing in the doorway of the dark study. God, he was tiny.

"Jason?" Epps said in disbelief.

"She said I'm 'sposed to go with the policeman," the boy said. His voice sounded irritated but the kind of irritation that in kids is a second away from tears.

Somewhere outside, Epps heard the sound of an engine. He leapt up from the chair, and the boy shrunk back at the sudden movement and also probably from the size of him.

Epps dropped into a crouch beside him, quickly looking him over without touching him. "Are you hurt, son?"

The boy shook his head, a little wide-eyed.

"I am the policeman. You're good, big guy. You're so good. Stay right here a minute," Epps told him, and then bolted for the door.

Outside the sun was nearly blinding, and the sheer surprise and relief of being alive with a live, recovered, and apparently unharmed victim made him lightheaded. But the long driveway was empty. Whatever she had been driving and wherever it had been parked, she was gone.

Chapter 58

Roarke was shouting into the phone, shouting for Lam, and trying to see across time and space to figure out what was happening to his agent, when the phone buzzed in his hand and Epps was suddenly back on the line.

"I'm here, boss."

Roarke had never been so happy to hear a voice in his life. "Jesus Christ, Epps, what the hell?"

"It's the boy."

Epps was speaking low and Roarke had a split second of complete terror until Epps finished quickly, "He's fine. He's right here. I'm keeping it down, don't want to scare him. He seems all right — not hurt, not scared, not traumatized."

Roarke automatically lowered his voice, too. He was reeling. "But how—"

"She walked him right in," Epps said. "I think she was watching the house."

Roarke felt chilled, exhilarated, relieved — and frustrated in the extreme that he was not there, that he had missed her, missed everything.

"She held a gun on me and left the boy. She got away, boss, I'm sorry."

Roarke said the only thing he could say. "Are you all right?"

"Not a scratch. Weirded out, hell yeah, but okay. I've already alerted SLO PD and the CHP. They've got an APB out. The father's on his way here."

Why, though? Why take the boy from his father only to leave him thirty miles away? Where did she get the car? And what was she doing with the boy for six hours?

Roarke spoke loudly. "The boy described the car?"

"Not a good description. He said blue, but 'not like the sky, like the sea,' which sounds more like gray to me. But probably a mid-sized four-door. There was a door beside him in the back."

Vague, too vague. Roarke fought impatience. "It's something, any-way. And we know where she is, now. Can you ask the boy if they were driving for a long time, if they made any stops?"

There was a long pause, as Epps spoke and a small, light voice answered. Then Epps was back on the phone.

"He says they were driving for a long time and they went to McDonald's and to a gas station and to this house." Epps' voice dropped to nearly nothing. "She was watching it. The kid said they were parked in the car outside for a while, and then she took him inside just a few minutes ago."

"How did she get him in the car to begin with? Did they walk to it, did she leave the beach house and pick him up later?"

He found himself holding his breath as Epps relayed the question, even as he reminded himself that this was a five-year-old.

"He woke up in it, he says. She must have carried him out of the house early in the morning."

While Sebastian had been drugged with his own Ambien.

Roarke focused on a game plan.

"You're going to need to question the boy about the photos. It doesn't look to me as if he knew he was being photographed, but who knows what he knows? And everything he can tell you about her. He could be a gold mine, and I think the father will cooperate."

"I think so, too."

Roarke finally got to the questions he had been holding back.

"Did she say anything to you?"

"Yeah. She said to check into everything about Torres. Everything." He paused, and then his voice was odd. "She said there was a nest."

What the hell?

"And she said to keep the boy away from the mother. And I am telling you what I told her: I couldn't agree more."

"What did she look like?" Roarke asked. He had not seen her since that moment on the street in San Francisco.

There was silence for a moment.

"I mean, how did she seem?"

Epps said, "Hold on a minute," and Roarke waited, hearing the sound of Epps moving, a door closing. From the ambient sounds Roarke figured he'd moved outside the house. Then Epps came back on the line. His voice was tense.

"Just had to say, boss. That girl is stone crazy."

Roarke said nothing, and for a moment it didn't seem like Epps was inclined to, either. Then Roarke could feel the hairs on the back of his neck stand up as he spoke again.

"As crazy as they come," Epps said softly.

Roarke's mouth was dry. "All right. All right. Stay with the boy and the father. I'll check in."

As he disconnected, Roarke was roiling, torn between two courses of action. His nerves screamed with frustration that he was off in the desert instead of in SLO. *Wrong call, wrong call.*

But was it?

She could still be headed this way, to Blythe, to the house where it had all happened. Tomorrow was the anniversary. It was a gamble for him to stay, but what could he really do in SLO? Cruise around looking for a blonde in a gray or blue car? She could be and probably was miles in any direction by now.

It made more sense, as far as sense had anything to do with anything in this case, to sit tight and see if she came to him.

Roarke suddenly found he did have to sit, and he did, on a windowsill of one of the arched recessed windows. He was beyond relieved that the boy was safe. Relieved for the boy, relieved for the father — and apart from the obvious reasons, relieved for himself, that Cara Lindstrom was not a monster, not a child-killer. He realized with no small discomfort that he could bear to arrest her; he could not face having to despise her.

He reached for the phone and called Epps back. "When you talk to the father, see if there's any chance he and the boy will come here to talk to us."

"Will do, boss."

A five-year-old might just be the best information they could get on Cara Lindstrom.

Chapter 59

Blythe PD officer drove Roarke out into the desert, past more palm trees and rocky hills, toward Indio. Singh had called back with the appointment and directions, and Roarke was far too agitated to stay put.

The lead detective from the Lindstrom massacre, who'd made police chief in Blythe before his retirement, was living in a golf community on what must have been a comfortable pension.

Former Chief Jeffries was tanned and, though thick through the middle, fit and healthy; he obviously made good use of the golf course Roarke could see from his back patio. He offered Roarke iced tea and they sat on deck chairs in the strong afternoon sun. Jeffries looked relaxed and comfortable, as if retirement suited him. But the mention of the Lindstrom case darkened his features, an old wound.

"You've been over to the house?" Jeffries asked.

"Just came from there," Roarke told him.

"No owner or renter has stayed in it more'n a year. Bad blood. Bad vibes. Ought to just burn the thing." He studied Roarke. "You one of the fellas do that profiling crap?"

There was no malice in the question and Roarke took no offense. "I have, yes."

Jeffries shook his head. "Didn't do the Lindstroms much good."

Roarke had to agree.

"Feds opening up the case again?"

It was a logical assumption; Roarke hadn't told Jeffries that Cara was his suspect on a new case and didn't plan to. He started to answer, and then stopped.

Am I opening up the Lindstrom case again?

There's a fresh case I should be concentrating on.

But the answer to now is in the past.

He wrenched himself away from the voices in his head and focused on the older man. "I have a case that's directly relevant. I'm trying to talk to anyone who knew Cara Lindstrom, find out as much background as I can from people who were there."

Jeffries took a long swallow of tea. "Well sir, you know the girl was just five years old. Her aunt took her after what happened."

After what happened. Roarke had heard the phrase throughout his entire career. It encompassed every kind of tragedy: war, rape, suicide, miscarriage, abduction, the massacre of an entire family.

"And the aunt is dead?" he asked.

"Oh, Joan, yes, she passed five, six years ago."

"And according to the records I've seen, she didn't have Cara for very long."

"Not for very long," the older lawman agreed. "She did her best, I know that for a fact. But something died in that child that night. It was hell on Joan — she had two of her own, and she was raising them by herself after the first year. Their stepfather left when the kid — Cara, I mean — moved in."

Roarke frowned and held up a hand. "He left — you mean, immediately?"

"Month or two."

"Was Trent ever looked at?"

"For the murders? Oh hell yeah. First thing. But he alibied out, for all three families."

Roarke nodded. Of course, there were three massacres to think about.

Jeffries kept talking. "He wasn't the father of Joan's kids to begin with. Then Cara came and he was out of there."

"Any idea why?"

A shrug. "Didn't sign up for it, is what I think. Three kids, now, and the one was just strange."

Since the older man seemed so willing to speak, Roarke decided to press the advantage. "Can you be more specific?"

"Family didn't live in Blythe. Temecula is 'bout three hours away. But we heard things. Hell, we kept an eye and ear out, we all wanted Cara to be all right. But she kept getting into trouble, fighting with other kids."

"Her cousins, you mean?"

"Naw, Joan's kids were just babies. It was other kids in school. Teachers, too. Then she started seeing things."

Roarke sat up sharply. "Seeing things like what?"

"Hallucinations. Schizophrenia, they thought. Joan took her to about a million doctors. Turned out it was all too much for Joan to handle, especially on her own, so Cara went into the system." Jeffries' face reddened under his tan. "Damn travesty is what it is."

And yet no one in the town volunteered to take the child in. Why was that, I wonder?

"It is," Roarke said. "A travesty. So no one in town stepped up to take Cara in?"

Jeffries flushed deeper. "I see what you're getting at," he said evenly. "Maybe that was wrong. But what happened to the Lindstroms was so — beyond imagining. People were afraid."

"Of a five-year-old?" Roarke asked as neutrally as he could.

Jeffries looked out over the golf course, his eyes following the arcing mist of the rain birds. "I know it makes no sense. But maybe they thought that whatever came for the Lindstroms would come back to finish the job."

Roarke sat for a moment with that, and realized he understood.

Jeffries was also silent. He looked as if he were debating something. Finally he spoke. "And then there was the thing with the counselor."

Roarke felt a warning chill of significance.

"What was that?" he asked, careful not to let his agitation into his voice.

"At the group home she was in. She was twelve or so? Got into a fight with another kid, older kid, and hurt him pretty bad, got sent up to Youth Authority for a couple of years. Though I want to ask you what you think was happening when a twelve-year-old girl attacks a fifteen-year-old boy."

The pressure in Roarke's chest increased. "Yes, I wondered about that. But you said there was a counselor..."

"A counselor who had been at the home when the fight happened. Two years later, a week after Cara got released back into state care, he turns up dead."

Roarke spoke through a dry mouth. "How?"

"Throat cut while he was in bed."

Roarke couldn't believe Singh hadn't turned this up. "A counselor at the home? I never saw any record of that."

"Oh, he'd moved on from the home. He wasn't even in town any more, had moved to Palm Desert. But when I saw his name turn up on the county homicide list, I wondered."

Roarke looked at him. "You didn't check it out?"

"Not my jurisdiction," Jeffries said.

"That's not what I meant," Roarke said.

Jeffries looked at him levelly. "No, I didn't check it out. If you want the truth — I didn't want to know."

Roarke held his gaze, and then nodded. "I understand." He tried to pull his mind back from the shock and focus back on anything else he might be able to uncover.

"Is there anyone else in town I could talk to? Anyone who would have known her?"

"As a child, you mean?" Jeffries frowned.

Roarke hesitated. "Any age."

He put his hands on his knees and stood. "I have something might be along the lines of what you want."

Chapter 60

What Jeffries had was a tape of Cara.

Not the TV tapes, the ones with reporters shamelessly shouting at the little girl: *"Cara, what happened? Who was in your house? Who killed your parents?"*

It was a copy Jeffries had made of the police interview tape, a child psychologist asking the questions fed to him by the case detectives. Very delicate questions, very gently asked, although Roarke could actually *feel* the tension of the detectives and the psychologist vibrating in the room; the one goal to make this kid cough up something, anything, that would nail the killer.

"It grabbed me and scratched me."

"It did, Cara?"

Roarke started to listen to it in the patrol car on the way back to the house in Blythe, but immediately turned it off. He couldn't bear to have the policeman who was his driver beside him with the tape playing; he needed to be alone with it.

So he had the driver take him back to the Lindstrom house.

Lam met him in the cavernous, empty living room. "No prints that match Cara Lindstrom's in the house. I've been all over it, and I don't think she's been here."

No, if she's coming, it's tomorrow. Or tonight.

"Okay, Lam," he told his agent. "They've got us in rooms in a motel in town. The driver's waiting to take you over." He paused and then added casually, "I'm going to stay here for a while."

"Not alone," Lam said instantly.

"No, not alone," Roarke agreed. "Blythe P.D. is staking out the house. Epps will be coming in, too. I'll be fine."

He made himself a nest in the bedroom that five-year old Cara had shared with her eight-year old sister; the pristine room that had once been painted with Cara's blood. There was a window ledge, as there were in all the rooms, and he had a bedroll one of the detectives had brought him from the car.

He spread the case files around him and he set up the tape recorder to play the tapes, and he laid the crime scene photos from the Lindstrom massacre out on the floor in order like a film of the night, and he started from the beginning, working through the entire case file again, in order, deliberately waiting to play the tape of Cara until its proper place in the chronology. When he finally turned it on, a shiver of anticipation and dread raced through him.

"This is Dr. Edward Martin, consulting psychologist with the Blythe Police Department. I am interviewing Cara Elizabeth Lindstrom, age five years, about the events of October seventeen, 1987."

On the tape, the psychologist put on a soothing voice, obviously meant for speaking with a child. *"Now, Cara, we're going to talk about what happened that night, is that all right?"*

There was silence on the tape, and Roarke felt a surge of anger. As if the child had had any choice in the proceedings.

And then there was a whisper, so slight Roarke couldn't make it out. Of course, Cara's throat had been cut, it was a miracle she could make any sounds at all.

"What was that, Cara?"

Roarke reached to the volume dial and jacked it up to maximum, just in time to hear the child speak again. Even at maximum, she was barely audible. *"Bad."*

The psychologist cleared his throat. *"Yes. We're going to talk through that night, Cara, and I'll be right here, no one can hurt you, do you understand?"*

Roarke stood. He couldn't stand to be seated. It was wrong on so many levels, what was happening. There was nothing worse than inexperienced shrinks doing forensic interviews. In this situation, it was unbearable.

"On the night, the bad night, what do you remember, Cara? What were you doing?"

"Sleeping," the child's voice responded.

"And did you wake up?"

There was a silence and then the interpretation of the psychologist, *sotto voce: "Subject nodded."*

"Why did you wake up?"

A barely substantial whisper. *"Screaming."*

"You heard screaming?"

There was a silence, then again the spoken notation, *"Subject nodded."*

"Who was screaming, Cara?"

A pause, and then the most heartbreaking sound Roarke had ever heard. *"Mommy,"* the little girl choked out.

"Your mommy was screaming?"

"Mommy. Donny. Amber. Screaming, screaming, screaming."

"What else?"

"Breathing. Scratching. Coming." The terror in the child's voice had all of Roarke's flesh raised. He stood at the window, looking at the door, and found he couldn't breathe.

"Did you open your eyes, then, Cara?"

Silence, and the notation, *"Subject nodded."*

"What did you see, Cara, when you opened your eyes?"

Silence, and Roarke could have sworn he felt a vibration, a pressure through his entire body.

"Open your eyes and tell me what you see."

Silence.

"Do you see the door, Cara?"

The faintest whisper. *"Yes."*

"Tell me what comes through the door."

The bleakest pause imaginable. *"It."*

"It, Cara?"

There was a silence and the whispered note, *"Subject nodded."* The psychologist's next words were forced. *"You mean a man, don't you?"*

Roarke felt another swell of rage. Leading the witness was the worst possible thing to do when interviewing a child. Useless.

"Look again, Cara. I want you to look. What is 'it'?"

The little girl's voice, in a broken, rasping whisper.

"It. It. It."

"I know this is hard, Cara. You're being a very brave girl—"

She said something so softly the psychologist had to ask her to repeat it, and she said, *"Beast."*

Roarke felt a chill, gooseflesh rising all over his body.

"Beast?"

"Monster. Beast. Monster," the child's rasping voice cried.

The psychologist was silent for a long time.

"What does the monster look like?"

"Big. Horrible."

"What is it doing?"

"Eating. Eating."

"Eating what?"

A broken voice. *"Eating Amber."*

Roarke swallowed, sickly. Amber was Cara's sister.

"Wet. Lots and lots of wet."

"And then what?"

An indecipherable sound.

"*Say it again, Cara.*"

"*It. Horrible. Grab me. Scratch me.*" The child broke into help-less sobs that Roarke could feel shaking his soul. "*Mommy. Mommy. Mommy. Mommy.*" Her voice faded to nothing... and after the longest hiss of nothingness, the psychologist's voice.

"*Interview terminated nine-forty-seven am.*"

There was a click, and silence.

Roarke had to walk through the entire house several times to regain any sense of self or equilibrium.

It was full dark outside, now, and he stepped outside the sliding glass doors of the patio to breathe.

The desert wind was warm on his skin; it whispered in the euca-lyptus grove, rattling the dry leaves like bones.

There were no outside lights on around the house, and so few neighboring houses, and Roarke was unnerved to see a sky full of actual stars, stars the way they only appeared in the desert or out on the ocean. Blackness, infinity, and a hundred million diamond lights. Even with the moon full and radiating a wash of brilliance across the sky, it was still low enough on the horizon that Roarke could pick out Orion and Cassiopeia, every star in the constellations clear and brilliant.

He stood in the wind and the whisper of leaves and looked up.

A million thoughts swirled through his head. Snyder reminding him that the adult Cara Lindstrom would be fixed at the age of her trauma. The fact that — to all appearances — she had abducted a five-year-old boy because she had sussed out an imminent and horrifying danger to him. And the child Cara's absolute conviction that her family had been attacked not by a man, but by a monster.

He could barely think through his own confusion.

There was a crunching step behind him and he spun, his hand already on his weapon, when a voice came through the dark.

"Everything all right, sir?"

Roarke focused in the dark and identified one of the officers on watch. The uniform's whole body was tense and on alert. Roarke relaxed his grip, withdrew his hand from his Glock.

"Fine. Just getting some air. Didn't mean to startle you."

The officer nodded and faded back into the bushes, resuming his post, and Roarke was left with the night and the wind and the stars.

Finally, he turned back toward the house and went inside, walking through the empty rooms, returning to his plan of going through all the case files again. They were spread out in the girls' former room, as he had left them.

Instead of turning on the light, he stood in the light of the moon, looking at the small tape recorder for a long time. Then he hit REWIND and started the tape again.

"What does the monster look like?"

"Big. Horrible."

"What is it doing?"

"Eating. Eating."

"Eating what?"

"Eating Amber."

Roarke jerked forward and turned it off.

He couldn't bear to hear any more, so he reached for another one, the tape of the police officers walking through the house.

He put it in, turned it on, and listened to the unbearable sounds of the officers' harsh breathing as they traversed the bloody house... the strangled, *"Oh shit,"* that marked their entrance into the girls' room. And then the stunned exclamation:

"Jesus Christ. This one's alive."

And then in real life, a shadow moved at the doorway of the bedroom. Someone stepping through.

Roarke had not turned on the lights, and there was only moonlight through the bedroom windows to light her face. But Roarke saw her as clearly as he had on the street.

She stood in the doorway, perfectly still.

"Cara," he said, his mouth dry.

She looked at him.

She was beautiful. Roarke felt his heart constrict. There was nothing harsh or hard about her. She was wary, she was wired, but she had the vulnerability of an animal, of a child... and that sheer sense of presence. And she held a gun trained calmly on him.

"I'm Roarke," he said, not moving.

"I know," she said, and her voice was low and husky, and thrilled him.

He was startled; it had never occurred to him that she might be following him. *Or hunting*, his mind told him.

"You've been tracking me," she said. "Since San Francisco."

And suddenly he was not surprised that she knew. There had been more, to her, to this, from the very beginning.

"I've been looking for you—" he stopped. "Since I was nine."

She looked at him with curiosity. Her face was as translucent as the moon.

"Since that night. Here." He looked around her former bedroom. Strangely, he had no thought that he would be shot. He wasn't about to try lunging across the entire room to take the gun from her; she was undoubtedly on a hair trigger and beyond capable of killing him instantly. But he wasn't in fear, either.

In the silence between them he became aware that the crime scene tape was still playing; there was a scuffling and then shouted voices and the very faint sound of a child's sobbing. Her own sobbing.

Without taking her eyes or her aim from him, she stepped to the tape recorder and shut it off. Her eyes stayed fixed on his.

"That was you," he said through a dry mouth. "I know everything, Cara. I am so terribly sorry for what happened to your family. To you."

She looked at him without speaking.

"And I know they never caught who did it. And I know..." his voice dropped. "That leaves an open wound."

"They were looking in the wrong place," she said, and Roarke almost stopped breathing.

"What do you mean?"

"They were looking for someone human."

He felt a chill start at the base of his spine. Could she really think that there was something supernatural at work? It was insane. But wasn't killing seven, eight, however many people, the definition of insane? How many *had* she killed, herself?

The girl is stone crazy, Epps voice whispered in his head.

"Who should they have been looking for, Cara?" he asked her softly, and looked into those luminous eyes.

"It," she said.

In his head he heard her on the psychiatric tape, the child's voice speaking of the thing. The Beast. *It.*

He took a shallow breath. "Tell me. I want to understand what happened."

Her voice was dry, and hollow. "I don't expect anyone to understand."

He spoke slowly, carefully. "I think I'm starting to. In San Luis Obispo. We found the mother's dealer. We saw the photos of the boy."

Her face froze, as clear and still as glass. "I couldn't... leave him with her."

Roarke found her eyes again, willed her to listen. "I know you couldn't. We know about her, now. Shared custody is over."

There was a flicker of something on her face; relief, he thought. He continued, never raising his voice.

"I know about Wann, and Preacherman, and the trucker. I know what they did. I know that you knew about them. I know that — you saw something in them."

"It," she said again.

"Tell me about *it.*"

She looked around the room and her voice was very small, like a child's. "It was here. It scratched me."

"You saw a monster?" he asked, using her word from the tape. "Not a man?"

She sighed, a terrible, weary sound. "It was a man with a monster inside. The monster was using him. He killed…" her voice trembled. "He killed everyone."

"He didn't kill you," Roarke said softly. "You were such a strong girl."

"It should have killed me," she said, and the loneliness in her voice wrenched at Roarke's heart.

"I don't want you to be dead. You're not a bad person," he said, and believed it. "You've been terribly wounded."

"Not wounded," she said, and again Roarke felt chills. "I was scratched."

"Scratched," he repeated, having no idea what she was trying to say.

"You know." She pulled open her shirt, a gesture so matter-of-fact and yet so sensual that Roarke gasped.

And then was looking at it, the scar: a faint white and jagged line across her throat.

"I was marked, and now It plays with me."

"It plays with you?" he repeated, feeling short of breath.

"It watches me. I see It in the shadows. It lets me see It when It wants."

"Where?"

She whispered, and Roarke felt the hairs stand up on his arms and the nape of his neck. "Everywhere. All the time."

Her words hung in the stillness of the house.

She looked away from him, around the room. "I come back here… If only I could find It here, I could kill It for good."

Roarke had a sudden adrenaline spike, thinking she might somehow mistake him for what she sought. Her aim on him had not wavered, though she did not seem inclined to fire.

"Is that what you're doing?" His throat was so dry he could barely speak. "You see the monster in these people and you're killing it?"

"There's never just one," she said wearily. Roarke's own words. "You cut off one head and seven more grow back."

"I know," he said, and meant it.

"You can kill It over and over but It never dies."

"I know." And then, even if it meant she would kill him, he had to ask. "What did you say to Greer?" he asked.

She tilted her head, puzzled. "Greer?"

"My agent. The man in the street."

Her face went flat. After a moment she spoke. "I said, 'I can smell the women you just raped.'"

Roarke breathed out. But what he was feeling was not surprise. "I'm sorry."

Her eyes were fixed on his, and he had never had a woman look at him like that.

There was silence between them, and an intimacy that Roarke had never known.

"I want to help you, Cara. Let me help you."

"It's too late," she said, breaking his heart. She looked around the room, and focused on the door.

He spoke quickly. "Where will you go?" he asked, even knowing it was an impossible question.

"Nowhere," she said almost absently. "It doesn't matter."

Then something changed in her face. "Turn around," she said, with a sudden hardness in her voice. "Sit down. On the ground."

This is it, then, Roarke thought. *She can kill me. I can try to jump her. I can refuse to do anything...*

He turned and sat slowly on the floor. "I want to help you," he said again. There was only silence behind him.

Then he heard the click of the door closing and another click that he realized was a lock turning.

He leaped up — to find he was alone in the room. He ran to the door, grabbing for the knob, twisting and pulling at it.

It was locked, she'd locked him in, she somehow had a key.

Because she lived here, his mind managed, even as he yanked at the door with all his strength. The wood was solid. He ran to the window and pulled at it. It took a moment to realize there were security locks engaged, and another moment to figure the device, then he had it open and was heaving himself up on the sill, bursting out through the frame, dropping to the ground, and running through the dark in the yard, running through wind and eucalyptus-spiced shadows, under vast sky and the moon and the millions of stars, his breath harsh gulps in his throat, running.

There was no one.

He did not call out to the officers, not until he'd circled the house himself. But she was gone.

As he was questioning the uniforms, he wondered if that had been deliberate, the holding off. Whether it was her life or their lives he had been concerned with was an open question he wasn't prepared to answer.

"You saw no one?" he demanded of the men. They were tense, humiliated.

"Only you, Agent Roarke, when we spoke," the younger one, Tyson, said.

It seemed a thousand years ago now.

"No cars, no sounds?"

The officers exchanged a glance. "Nothing.

In his adrenalized state, Roarke was almost ready to believe he had imagined the whole encounter; it was about as plausible as what really had happened. And yet there was a sense... she wanted something from him.

But that's crazy.

Officer Tyson called in an APB on the car, going by the description the boy had given Epps. Even as Roarke was listening to the officer describe it, he was certain that she would have dumped the car she'd driven the boy in long before she got to Blythe.

Officer Reynolds held up a hand. "Wait a minute, listen."

Both officers and Roarke tensed at the sound of a car, turning into the drive and approaching. They all reached for their weapons.

But the car was driving straight up the drive, without effort at concealment, and Roarke could recognize the boxy shape of a Crown Vic, a law enforcement wagon. As he stared at the windshield, he could see at least two shapes inside.

"It's Morales," Tyson said, relaxing. "Must be bringing your guy, Agent Roarke."

Chapter 61

E pps had Sebastian and the boy in tow. They had been flown in by the Los Angeles FBI from San Luis Obispo and met by Blythe PD at the airport.

Roarke pulled himself together, putting the dreamlike encounter with Cara aside in his mind to deal with later. He stepped to Officers Tyson and Reynolds and quietly told them to call for more surveillance on the house.

Then he moved to the car to meet Epps and Mark and Jason Sebastian. He led them into the house and spoke quietly with the father in the arched entry hall while Epps showed the boy the house.

"Mr. Sebastian, we're very grateful that you and Jason are willing to assist the investigation. It's a huge service you're doing."

"Anything. I'm just glad to have Jason back safely," Sebastian said. His voice was tight; Roarke hadn't exactly made a friend, here.

"We'd like to question him about his time with—" Roarke stopped. He'd almost said *Cara*. "—with Leila French," he finished. "You'll be in the room at all times and can terminate the interview if you feel it necessary."

Sebastian looked at Roarke, and his eyes were bleak. "We want to help," he said softly. His eyes drifted, to the house, the hallways.

"This is where it happened," he said, not really a question.

"Yes," Roarke answered.

Sebastian spasmed slightly, a shudder that Roarke guessed he wasn't even aware of. He knew the feeling. "God help us," Sebastian said, under his breath. And Roarke would be willing to bet he wasn't a religious man.

The boy was bouncing off the walls with excitement to have flown in an FBI helicopter. Roarke was at first afraid that they wouldn't be able to get a useful thing out of him. But his father said quiet things to him; Roarke could hear the words "important" and "police," and "help," and Jason settled down, wide-eyed but calmer.

They sat on the window seats in the empty family room, with the dark trees and brilliant stars outside the wide wall of glass. When he was still, the boy was tiny, and a very focused little person.

As Roarke took a seat, his jacket fell open, and the boy immediately zeroed in on Roarke's gun. He spoke to Epps, pointing. "Is that for the bad people?"

"That's right, little man," Epps said, and Roarke could see that Epps had worked his magic on the boy during the trip. It never failed; witnesses of all ages and sexes responded to the big man's earthy presence. Epps continued very seriously: "Jason, this is Agent Roarke. We work together; we're a team. And Agent Roarke has some important questions for you."

Roarke saw the tactic instantly; Epps was treating the boy as an adult, as an equal. He followed Epps' lead, and crossed to the boy to shake his hand gravely. "Jason, glad to meet you. Thank you for coming in to help us."

Jason straightened with pride, and Roarke could see his father being both impressed and touched with the way the agents were treating his son.

"Jason, we know you've had a long day."

"We went on the helicopter!" the boy said, with shining eyes.

"That's right. We only do that with our important witnesses," Roarke said. "And before that you were with Cara," he stopped himself. "Leila... in the morning, in the car, weren't you?"

"We drove for a long time," Jason said.

"Did you stop anywhere?"

The boy thought. "McDonald's. And the bathroom."

"So you mainly drove."

"We drove a lot. Then we went to someone's house."

Epps stepped forward with his camera phone, and showed the boy photos of Torres' house. Jason automatically reached for the phone and scrolled through the photos himself.

Kids and technology, Roarke marveled, startled. *The boy is five and he handles a Smartphone better than I do.*

"Yes," Jason said definitively, holding up the phone to show a photo of the house. "We were there."

"But you didn't go in?"

"We waited for a long time, and then she took me in and told me to stay with the policeman." The boy looked to Epps. "And I did."

The next question was tricky. Before they had flown down from San Luis Obispo, the boy had been examined by a doctor and he had found no signs of sexual or physical abuse. But touching didn't show up in a medical exam. Roarke proceeded carefully. "Jason, did Leila ever hurt you? Or touch you in some way that made you feel bad?"

The boy looked frankly appalled. "She *loves* me," he pointed out.

All three of the men shifted, perceptibly. There was silence for a moment. Then Roarke asked, "How do you know she loves you?"

"She said she does, she said she loves me. I know she does."

His certainty was unassailable; Roarke would have staked his own life on it at that point. He breathed out, and felt a deep relaxation at the center of his being.

"When she drove you, did she tell you where you were going?"

The boy frowned. "No..."

"Did she tell you why?"

At this the boy nodded firmly. "She drove me away because I was afraid."

Roarke felt a jolt. "Afraid of who?"

The boy's face darkened. He looked away, and kicked his heels against the window seat. "Bad people," he said finally. "Bad people."

Roarke looked at Epps. Epps scrolled with his phone, and stepped forward to show Jason a mug shot of Torres. "Do you know this man, Jason?"

The boy looked silently down at the photo, and this time didn't reach for the device.

"Yeah," he said, turning his face away. "He comes over and makes my mommy sick."

The drugs, Roarke thought.

"Does he ever take pictures of you?"

"No," the boy said, but his reaction was so revolted that Roarke had a strong suspicion the boy knew there was something wrong going on. Beside him Sebastian was so tense it looked like he might shatter. Roarke moved on smoothly.

"So Leila told you to stay with the policeman. But when she left, did she tell you about where she was going to go?"

The boy answered promptly, without having to think. "To take care of them."

Roarke felt himself tense; the blood was suddenly pounding in his head. "Take care of who?"

"The bad people." He looked at Roarke and Epps, that clear, level gaze. "The ones who were going to be bad."

Epps looked to Roarke. Roarke knew they were both thinking the same thing. *"Going to be bad." Future tense.*

Roarke focused back on the boy, and kept his voice neutral. "What did she say to you, exactly?"

"She said the monsters are going to leave me alone, now."

Sebastian had been increasingly agitated in his seat beside the boy. At this point he stood up. Roarke shot him a warning look, and returned his gaze to the boy.

"Jason, you've been a big help. We're going to talk to your dad for a minute, now, okay?"

He looked at Sebastian and nodded to the hall, and the two agents and the father congregated outside the living room, within sight but out of earshot of the boy.

"Did you know this man?" Epps showed Sebastian the mug shot of Torres he had on his cell phone.

Sebastian looked down at the screen, his face stormy. "No."

"You never saw him with your wife?"

"Ex-wife," Sebastian said pointedly. "No. I knew there was someone, but I never saw him."

"Do you have any idea who Jason is talking about when he says, "The bad people?" Roarke asked.

"No," Sebastian said tautly. "God, no."

"Did your ex-wife have any plans that you know of to take Jason anywhere? This weekend, or any other time?"

"She's required to inform me of exact locations of any outings. She didn't say they were going anywhere this week," Sebastian said. The fury in him was controlled, but just barely below the surface.

"And Jason never said anything about outings, field trips?"

"Nothing more than his grandparents' house or McDonalds."

"Okay—"

"But..." Sebastian said, and the agents looked at him. He swallowed. "I don't know," he said finally. "I don't know where she might have taken him."

Roarke nodded, and then motioned to Epps. But as they started to leave, Sebastian held up a hand, stopping them. "This is so — strange. She saved him, didn't she?"

Epps and Roarke looked at each other.

"The important thing is that Jason's safe," Epps said.

Roarke couldn't find the words. "We'll be with you in a minute," he said to Sebastian, who turned away from them and moved into the living room toward his son.

Epps stepped to Roarke, and Roarke spoke low. "Set them up in a motel and get one of Blythe PD to drive them over. We can't have them here in the middle of a stakeout — God only knows what might happen tonight. We can question them more tomorrow."

"You bet, boss."

As Epps started to turn away, Roarke spoke again. "Epps."

His agent turned back to him.

"That was great work, today," Roarke said.

Epps smiled slightly in acknowledgement. "The kid is terrific, isn't he?" he said, and stepped back into the big hollow cave of the living room.

Roarke moved to join them but his phone buzzed; he glanced at it irritably, and saw an unknown number. He clicked on and snapped. "Yes?"

"Agent Roarke?" Cara Lindstrom said.

It took every ounce of control Roarke had not to move.

"Agent Roarke?" she repeated. That husky voice.

"Yes," he said, his tone flat. Epps looked toward him inquiringly from inside the living room and Roarke waved a hand: *No, nothing important here.* When Epps turned away, Roarke said again, "Yes. I'm here," and he moved deep into the hall, toward the front door. Moonlight filtered through the beveled glass insets as he stopped in the dark.

Cara's voice spoke calmly into his ear. "You said you want to help."

His mouth went completely dry.

"Yes."

She spoke, and he listened.

Chapter 62

The moon was high and full and bright, a wash of light over sand and hills, as Roarke drove into the desert. The mountains loomed, purple-black shadows against an indigo backdrop, and there were stars at the edges of the moonlight, a spectacular, dreamlike setting.

Blue Moon, Roarke thought. *Huntress Moon.*

Cara Lindstom had given him an address, a location, no more than that. She said she would be there —*"If you want to help."* And then disconnected.

Help.

He was fixated on the idea as he drove through the night after her.

What she meant by *helping*, he had no clue. But what *he* meant was psychiatric institutionalization. The most compassionate caregiving he could find for her. He'd call in every chit he had. He'd get Snyder to testify on her behalf. He'd use the media if he had to, push the story of her background. He could make it happen. He was fairly sure he could. He had to. The things she'd said in the house, when they were alone together, haunted him.

"It scratched me. I still see It. Everywhere. All the time. You can kill It over and over but It never dies. It should have killed me."

But another voice whispered in his head.

The girl is stone crazy.

Epps.

Epps had been suspicious. Roarke had lied to him, there was no other way to say it. He'd told Epps he had to go into town briefly to meet Jeffries again, and he'd taken the fleet car the Blythe PD had left at their disposal. He knew that it looked wrong, a completely strange thing for him to be doing, when Epps knew very well that the plan had been to wait at the house, that Cara could show up at the house that night. He was fairly certain Epps hadn't believed him.

And Roarke was not sure how he was supposed to feel about the lie. It was not the best of signs.

He also didn't know what exactly the hell he was doing. He told himself that he didn't want Cara killed in a mass law enforcement take-down, which given her temperament and the child abduction was a distinct possibility. He had the best chance of bringing her in alive by himself, and since she was willing to meet him, that's what he intended to do.

He was aware that she could kill him. But he didn't think that was her purpose, even though it might happen, purpose or not.

But she could have killed him back in the house in Blythe, if she'd wanted to, and she hadn't. Instead she'd asked for his help.

Help for what?

He couldn't begin to imagine.

And so he drove.

The flat road ahead of him was headed for a break in a mountain range, and once Roarke got closer to the gap in the hills, he could see that the road wound its way upward.

When his car crested the hill, Roarke understood where he was going. The first thing he saw was the alluvial flood plain, a vast wash of earth and rock fanning out from the base of the mountain, winding like a dry riverbed with its layers of tumbled rock and fine sand. Under the blue moon it looked like a river of light, a spectacular, surreal sight.

And looming on one of the banks of that dry river was a concrete plant; a skeletal metal tower of silos, long diagonal conveyor belts, chutes and pulleys and ladders. Surrounding the tower were huge ant-hills of gravel and sand, a few pre-engineered outbuildings, a quarry, machinery pits.

It looked primitive in the night, medieval, even. There was one bright light glowing like a Cyclops eye on one of the water towers; otherwise the few lights were dim and orange, the minimum necessary. A closed plant, then, another victim of the housing collapse and recession. There was nothing else remotely like a habitation in sight. Beyond that, the setting seemed almost inevitable.

Off to Roarke's right there was a dirt road off the highway that wound under a railroad trestle and up toward the plant, and because of the isolation, there was no way not to signal his approach. Roarke turned off his headlights anyway. The wind would provide some cover for the engine sound, but not enough. He would have to leave the car and walk it.

The turnoff was between two sand ridges and he could park the car where it would be unseen by anyone up at the plant.

He calculated he could make it up to the plant in fifteen minutes by foot. So he checked his Glock and the smaller back-up weapon in his ankle holster, rooted in his bag for extra ammo and his Maglite, left the car and started up the road, over the hill.

The wind was dry and a strange mix of warm and cool. Roarke realized that the earth beneath him was still warm from the day, radiating heat, while the night air was cool and getting colder, the chill of the desert.

His footsteps in the packed sand were heavy; he'd been in the Kevlar vest all evening, and was glad to have it now, though it weighted him down.

The rising moon bathed the sand and hills and towers of the factory in radiance. But the shadows were long and ominous. It was like a lunar setting, unearthly, and in the dry wind and the stars and the moonlight, with that incredible surreal dry river below him, Roarke thought he might simply be dreaming. What could he be doing here in the middle of the night? And what had she brought him here for?

As he crunched on through the sand up the slope of the road, breathing air as cool and clear as ice, he wondered if she knew that he had come alone, and if she had, what that meant. For him, for her, for them.

If she wanted to kill him, then they both had an even chance, he thought. He'd never killed and had zero intention of starting now. She'd killed five — six — men that he knew of and many more that he could imagine; it was almost inconceivable that the ones he knew about were the only ones. He had a gun, but was beyond pretending to himself that he was going to use it. Even though he knew she had at least one now, she did not seem to operate with guns.

If her intention was to kill him this was a good enough place to do it, although only if she'd known that he wasn't going to bring backup. But he suspected she knew a great deal.

It had also occurred to him that she might have brought him here to kill *her*. Suicide by cop was a very real syndrome and she was unbalanced enough to be capable of it. If that was her intention, she was going to be disappointed; he'd already decided that.

He was almost up to the batch plant now: a tower-like collection of mixers, bins, long diagonals of conveyor belts, silos, radial stackers, heaters, chillers, and dust collectors, set among huge conical piles of sand, asphalt, aggregate, and chunks of rock.

It all looked like a huge erector set model deposited in the sand, abandoned by some giant child on the beach.

On one side of the site was the wide alluvial plain, on the other side an extensive labyrinth of quarry, with long even hills and piles of sand, gravel and stone.

On the far end of the site there were metal storage sheds; on the opposite side, a prefab office with barred windows. All was dark, and from the picked-over look of it, Roarke suspected it had not been legitimately used in years; an active plant would have housed a small fleet of concrete mixer trucks and heavy earth-moving equipment.

The wind whistled through the metal constructions as Roarke scanned the sandy grounds.

There was no sign of her. But there were myriad places to hide.

His mind was racing. She'd said she needed help. She had brought him here for a purpose.

Without a clear plan, he headed toward the storage shed, moving in the shadows at the base of the towering heaps of earth.

As he neared the rusty metal prefab structure, Roarke flinched at the sudden sound of a door squealing open. He ducked to the side of one of the sand pyramids, and crouched in the shadows, watching as a parallelogram of light fell on the sand and a man stepped out. All Roarke could see was silhouette, but he had long hair caught back in a ponytail and was wearing a plastic apron and rubber kitchen gloves, which he stripped off as he moved outside. He killed the light inside the room behind him, and stuffed the gloves into a back pocket of his jeans as he walked back in the direction of the main plant.

The gloves, of course, were a dead giveaway, even if Roarke hadn't suspected already.

He watched from beside the sand pile as the man moved a considerable distance away from the outbuilding. Then he stopped, and Roarke saw the flame of a cigarette lighter flare in the dark, and the glowing tip of a cigarette as he lit up. Roarke darted out from his place beside the pile of sand to hug the side of the shed, then eased around the wall to look inside the door.

It was the smell that confirmed where he was; there was no other reason for the nail polish bite of acetone in a place like this, and there was an underlying stench of cat piss he knew wasn't coming from the presence of actual cats. As his eyes adjusted to the dark space he could make out an assortment of camp stoves, stacks of kitty litter tubs, gas cans, propane tanks. Metal shelving held sloppy rows of canning jars and glass jugs with liquids and sediments inside, a clutter of glassware and jugs, pressure cookers, plastic tubing, funnels, coffee filters, aluminum foil.

Someone was using the abandoned plant as a meth lab.

It was a perfect place for it: isolated and relatively safe, with metal buildings and nothing but sand around them, endless pits to bury the toxic chemical waste. If one of the traffickers had some kind of in — a former worker, a contractor who knew the factory had been closed — it would be easy enough to take over.

Roarke moved out of the door before the cook could come back from his smoke break, and slipped back around the side of the shed. His mind was racing.

Only one man, here. Roarke could easily make an arrest. Apparently Cara had brought him here knowing illegal activity was going on. But attacking one meth cook was not her style, and nothing she would need Roarke's help for, anyway. He was virtually certain that there was more to what was going on in the location, he just hadn't found it yet.

He skirted around the shed and headed back toward the batch plant.

The metallic skeleton towered in the moonlight like some construction out of the *Road Warrior* films. The wind was light and the crunch of sand under his feet seemed deafening.

As he weaved between the piles of sand and crushed rock, he nearly stumbled over a human form on the ground. A man's body, with dark wet sand all around him, soaking underneath him. The stench of urine and feces mingled with the coppery stink of blood, the smells of death.

Stepping closer, Roarke saw that the dead man's pants were down, his ass cheeks pale and exposed in the moonlight. And for a sick moment Roarke thought the blood was from castration. But as his eyes swept the body, he saw dark trails leading off where arterial blood had sprayed from the man's cut throat, and bone and cartilage gleaming from the gaping smile of a wound.

A faint sound of scuffling came from behind him and he whipped around, aiming his weapon—

At the base of a rock hill, a shadow huddled, a girl, crouched on her heels.

Not Cara, Roarke registered immediately, his heart hammering.

She was slight and undeveloped, no more than eleven or twelve, and Roarke thought from her dark hair and eyes she was Mexican, though it was hard to say from the pale concrete dust covering her skin. Her shirt was ripped down the front, only the last two buttons intact and closed. She was swaying and whimpering, in shock.

Roarke put up a hand in what he hoped was a calming gesture and moved carefully closer. The girl crossed her arms tighter over her breasts, and it wasn't hard to understand what had happened, or almost happened.

"Police," Roarke said softly, because it was simpler than explaining the details of who he was. "*Policia. Soy ayuda. Calmate.*" *I am help. Be calm.*

She looked up at him, black eyes liquid with anguish. He could feel her terror and bewilderment pulsing in the air between them, and he felt a black fury rising up in him, ancient and overpowering.

He held up a hand between them, and forced his voice steady. "*Estancia aqui. Te escondes.*" *Stay here. Stay hidden.* He had no idea what would go down before he could get this girl to any kind of safety, but she didn't look like she was about to move anywhere anytime soon, and for the moment, that was a good thing.

And then, because he had to know, he asked, "*¿Qué pasó?*" *What happened?*

She looked out at the body of her attacker with huge, dark eyes. "*Santa Muerte*," she whispered.

Roarke stared down at her and repeated, "*Estancia aqui*," then he backed away into the sand corridors, hoping to God that she would stay until he could gain some control over the situation. How exactly he was going to do that, he had no idea, at least until he scoped out more of what the situation actually was. This was obviously not just an active meth lab. Christ only knew what other criminal activity was going on on the side.

Drugs, guns, and people, his years of Bureau experience whispered in his head. Where there was one girl, there were bound to be others. If Torres was selling photos of a little white boy, his associates certainly could be selling other children of any number of races in the flesh. And that kind of enterprise, he knew instinctively, was much more likely to draw Cara's attention and wrath than a meth lab.

"Where the bad people are," the boy had said, when asked where Cara was going.

She was here, Roarke had no doubt. The slashed throat of the would-be rapist was more than enough evidence for him. But the Mexican girl's words rang in his head: *Santa Muerte.* Meaning Saint Death, or Holy Death. It was a Latin American cult belief, the worship of an unconsecrated saint, adopted by criminals and the non-criminal downtrodden alike as a protector of the desperate and abandoned and damned.

The other loose translation, though, was "Lady Death," or the "Black Lady," or alternately, "White Lady," a skeletal figure of implacable doom, prayed to by her followers for help and protection. In the few seconds Roarke had to contemplate it, it seemed not only apropos but inevitable.

"Lady Death," he whispered. "Where are you?"

He turned and made his way through the narrow passageways between the dark and towering pyramids of crushed gravel and sand, toward the other side of the site. He could feel the heaviness of the earth and rock around him. He passed a conical hill of asphalt, black as tar, and smelling just as strongly.

He stopped as he reached the last pyramid of sand, staying hidden to the side of it to look out over the metal towers of the batch plant.

He was startled to see a concrete mixer truck parked in one of the truck bays under the platforms of the batch tower. The sight puzzled him; clearly the site was not actively producing and shipping cement.

But a mixer truck would be the perfect innocuous transport, for any number of things.

Drugs, guns and people.

Driven by the need to know, Roarke ran light-footed across the exposed strip of sand and slipped inside the dark bay beside the truck. Behind the lifting axle on the back of the truck there was a round hatch into the drum, standing slightly open. Roarke climbed up on the axle, grasped the handle and pulled it open. He was assailed by a stench of piss and sweat from inside the dark cylinder.

His heart dropped into the pit of his stomach. Though a quick flash with the Maglite showed him that aside from paper trash the mixer was empty, it was clear what had been transported in the truck. The cargo had been human.

Now he was sure what Cara was here for, what she had brought him here for.

You said you wanted to help.

He moved to the inner edge of the truck bay, staying inside the dark cavern to look out over the moon-drenched plant site.

To the far side of the plant structure, there was a row of room-sized concrete cubes, hollow blocks of cement intended for use for storing aggregate and sand.

There was a metal door on each cube. And as Roarke watched, a man walked around the side of the row. Across his shoulder was an automatic rifle, M-16, AK-47, something ugly and deadly.

He walked slowly down the cement row, and paused, taking a watching stance.

First time I've ever seen an armed guard posted to watch over sand, Roarke thought grimly, and his grip tightened on his own weapon.

He stayed at the side of the sand piles, watching the man with the assault rifle walk a slow sentry duty outside the row of cubes.

Then Roarke tensed... as a metal door opened in one of the cubes, and another man exited.

Roarke strained in the darkness, and was chilled to hear the faintest sound of human sobs coming from the dark cavern of the cube, before the door clanged shut and was bolted again by the man who exited.

The man nodded to the watching guard, and picked up another rifle resting at the side of the cube. He shouldered it casually and moved to the side of the cement wing.

Roarke eased slowly forward around his concealing pile of sand to keep watch on the man as he circled the block of cubes toward the back.

And suddenly the man with the rifle stumbled and fell hard onto the packed dust of the ground; Roarke could hear the muffled sound of breath being knocked out of him.

Then as fast as lightning, there was a rush of dark, and a slim human shadow crouched over the downed man, grabbing his head by his hair, and Roarke saw a silver flash and the dark spray of arterial blood.

Roarke instinctively lurched forward, but someone grabbed him from behind. As he twisted, ready to fire, he heard the single low word, *"Boss."*

The voice.

He focused on the dark figure in front of him. "Jesus Christ," Roarke whispered, as he faced Epps in the dark.

"Close enough," Epps whispered back, letting go of him and backing up into the shadows of the sand pile. Roarke instinctively moved with him, out of the sightline of the guard.

As Roarke stared at Epps, trying to silence his pounding pulse, Epps muttered, "You didn't think I was going to let you get out here alone." Then he glanced toward the storage cubes, tensely. "There's an armed patrol, there."

"I think they're holding people inside. I found a girl..."

"Yeah," Epps said, quietly, but with an unmistakable fury in his tone. "All kinds of bad news here. We've called it in to the local sheriffs. We're waiting for back up."

"*We* called it in," Roarke repeated.

"You and me," Epps said implacably. "We. We called it in as soon as we got here."

Roarke understood that his man was going out on a limb to cover for him.

Epps continued, and his eyes were squarely on Roarke's face. "We need to wait for back up. No one else needs to get hurt."

A fine plan, if there wasn't already a plan in motion, Roarke thought.

As if in answer, Epps spoke, and his voice was taut. "There's a lot of bad guys here, boss. I counted six on the other side of those storage cubes, unloading a couple of trucks. Cargo is boxes, some heavy, some really light. You?"

Roarke responded automatically. "One at the metal shed on that side, a cook. And two men down."

Epps stared at him through the dark. "Two *down*?"

"She's here."

"Cara Lindstrom..." Roarke could see Epps processing it. "And she's planning to take down..." Epps moved a few paces, shaking his head. His voice never rose above a whisper, but the intensity went up several dozen decibels. "Unfuckingbelievable."

"We need to get those people out of here," Roarke said, and looked toward the cement cubes.

"I disagree," Epps said, and his whisper was harsh. "Whatever they've been through, and my heart bleeds for them — but they can wait another fifteen fucking minutes for reinforcements. Ain't going to do no one no good to storm in there like Batman right this second. We are seriously outnumbered and those people can stay put. Safer all the way around. We are *not* going to do anything stupid."

Roarke stood silently, with the moon above them and the dry wind on his face. He knew Epps was dead right in a tactical sense, but something deep inside him told him they didn't have that kind of time. For one thing, whatever Cara was planning, she was going to do it with or without him, or them. He knew that she would wait for nothing and no one, and he knew that she needed to be out of there before any backup showed up.

That last thought was unconscionable, but he didn't have to consider it... because at that moment the meth lab exploded.

Chapter 63

The fireball blazed in the night, and there was running and shouting from all over the plant site. Even as Roarke stood mesmerized by the roaring orange rush of flames against the dark, he understood Cara's plan instantly; she was drawing the guards away from the storage cubes where the hostages, cargo, *product* were being kept.

And this time she was armed; from the right spot she could pick them off at will.

"Guard the people inside those storage bins," he hissed at Epps, who was already staring toward the line of cement bins. "We may have to get them out. But keep covered at all time, stay out of sightlines, do you hear me?"

"What about you, boss?" Epps started, tensely.

"I'll be there as soon as I can."

Epps started to protest and Roarke said, "*Go.*"

He shot a last glance toward the apocalyptic rush of fire against billowing black clouds, then started back toward the shed, running through the heaps of sand and gravel. Almost instantly he heard gunfire, a barrage of metallic hacking that could only be the death rattle of an assault rifle.

Roarke's adrenaline spiked higher. *The drug runners? Or Cara? She could have taken a rifle off either of the men she killed here, or gotten it from Torres.* He prayed she was armed with more than a knife and a handgun.

He sprinted through the narrow passage between rock heaps and stopped at the end of the corridor to look out.

The burning shed was painfully bright against the sky, and Roarke could feel the blistering heat from where he stood. Two bodies were on the ground already, dark sprawled shapes, and his pulse spiked until his eyes focused enough to see, and he could see moving silhouettes of men with automatic rifles; one crouched at the base of another heap of slag, another two approaching the flaming building... as if there was anything left to be saved.

As Roarke watched, there was another burst of weapon fire and one of the creeping men exploded, or rather leapt up in the air, as he was hit by bullets, a quick lift into the dark, spasming and contortion, and a heavy fall to the sand. A split second later the same happened with the second exposed man.

Roarke's hair was standing completely on end.

He twisted around to scan the darkness where the gunfire had come from. *She's there, she must be there.*

A voice called in the dark, thick and thickly accented. "*Santa Muerte. Muéstrate.*"

Roarke knew *Muéstrate* meant "Show yourself." But the thug had said the same thing that the traumatized girl had said: *Santa Muerte.* Saint Death, or — the thought was a chill — Lady Death.

A female voice responded, a voice that Roarke already knew by heart, even speaking in another tongue. *"Ahora usted muere."* Now you die.

Gunfire flashed from two places, and Roarke's heart plummeted as he heard a feminine cry.

"*No, se muere, puta,*" the man shouted, and after a moment of agonizing stillness, he emerged from the side of the rock pile, M-16 at his shoulder.

In a cold rage, Roarke aimed his Glock and fired. The man's body blew backward and hit the ground. And Roarke realized that he was nothing but glad.

He held very still, scanning the darkness as the flames from the shed crackled and popped, the heated metal frame glowing red.

There was no motion, no human sound.

Roarke ran for the slag heap where he'd heard Cara's voice. It had come from some distance above ground.

He scanned the pile of broken rock and saw a dark, sprawled form about fifteen feet up. With his heart in his throat, he scrambled up the jagged rocks, slipping and sliding and scraping skin on the uneven slope until he reached her.

She was collapsed on the rocks, still as death. Roarke dropped to his knees beside her and passed his hands over her, finding the wet wound instantly. She was bleeding from her side; he could feel her high-necked sweater was soaked through. But she was breathing.

Roarke tore off his FBI windbreaker and his shirt underneath, balling up the shirt to make a compress against the wound and tying the windbreaker around her hard, to create pressure. Then he gathered her into his arms and lifted her, stumbling down the rocks again, placing one foot at a time, struggling for balance until he hit the sand. He turned his back to the still raging fire and started fast for the batch tower, headed for the cement truck in the loading bay, feet sinking into the sand as he held her tight against him.

"Roarke," she said faintly. He could feel her struggling to breathe against his chest.

"I've got you," he said, and held her tighter as he strode through the sand.

She said something so softly he couldn't hear. "Don't talk," he said. "I'm getting you out of here."

"You can never kill them all," she whispered. "They keep coming back."

"Be still, Cara. Breathe."

He stumbled for the dark cavern of the truck bay. Inside he reached a hand to jerk open the passenger door of the mixer truck, and climbed up onto the runner to hoist Cara into the truck, where he laid her down across the seat inside. Bent over her, he checked the compress he'd made with his windbreaker, tightening it to keep the pressure on the wound, which seemed to be seeping blood less rapidly, but perhaps that was his own hopeful imagination. She was limp on the seat, eyes closed and breathing shallowly. Her face was so pale...

"I'm getting you out of here," he told her. "Just hold on." And in his head he added, *Please.*

He pulled out of the truck cab and shut the door. Then he circled the truck to get to the drivers' side. It was a long circle; the truck was sizeable, and Roarke had to step outside the bay to move around to the other side.

Moonlight hit him first, and then a shadow was looming up in front of him, a silhouette toting an M-16.

"Alto, policia," a voice snarled—

Roarke fired and lunged at the same time, and so did the shadow. Roarke's own gun went flying but so did his assailant's weapon, and they were grappling, hand-to-hand. He could smell sweat and gunpowder and ammonia and sex on the man: the smell of a criminal, the smell of wanton destruction of human life. And Roarke was angry, killing angry. He was glad to be locked in mortal combat with this scum, glad to need no compunction about fighting with deadly force. He grabbed for the man's throat and used the momentum of his spin and body weight to smash the thug against the truck, and then kept smashing, gripping his captive's throat and pounding his head against the thick shining metal of the cement mixer, pounding until he heard cracking, until his hands were wet with blood and the body in his hands was lifeless, dead weight in his grasp.

Roarke released the body and heard it slide against the slick side of the truck and thud on the ground. He was panting, his own blood pounding in his veins. But he was alive, and his assailant was dead, and he had work to do.

He staggered a bit as he tried to walk, and then pushed off from the truck and moved as fast as his body could manage around the other side, the seemingly endless distance to the driver's door.

He wiped blood from his hands on his pants, reached for the door handle to pull it open and boosted himself up inside...

To find he was alone in the dark cab.

"No," he rasped.

The passenger door was closed, the passenger seat was empty. Cara was gone.

"No!" Roarke shouted.

As he scrabbled for the handle of his own door, the passenger door was pulled open at his side.

Roarke twisted — and stared into Epps' face.

"Boss," Epps said, relief etched into his voice.

And as the two agents stared at each other, the sound of sirens layered upon sirens screamed through the dark stillness of the desert.

Roarke jumped down from the cab and ran past Epps, out of the truck bay into the moonlight, turning around himself, searching the landscape. The fire blazed on the periphery of the site, a white-hot core, surrounded by pulsing yellow and orange and plumes of charcoal smoke against the black sky. Bodies littered the sand.

The vast wash was empty, a river of light under the Huntress Moon.

Chapter 64

The arriving sheriffs rounded up four armed men. Epps had disarmed and locked up three, making those seven the only criminal survivors of the night's massacre.

The final tally of dead was thirteen. Ten of the gang who had been running the place: the cook, the guards, the smugglers. And three of the human cargo being held at the site: a twenty-five-year-old woman who appeared to have been beaten to death, a fifteen-year old girl who the other prisoners said had been shot while attempting escape, and a seven-year old boy with a heart condition who had simply died in transit in the barrel of the cement mixer; the sheriff's team found all three bodies buried in one of the gravel pits. All of the pits and quarries would have to be excavated; Roarke had no doubt other bodies would turn up. The gang had been using the site for some time now.

The Mexican hostages had thought they were paying a coyote to smuggle them across the border. Instead the coyote had dumped the men and delivered the women and children to be sold.

Nineteen hostages were saved, including the eleven-year-old girl Roarke had encountered in the sand heaps. Her name was Maribel. The doctors at the hospital where she and the other hostages were taken confirmed that she had not been raped.

Cara was gone.

Maybe she had taken one of the gangster's vehicles and vanished into the desert. Or maybe she had stumbled away in her weak and wounded state, and her body would soon be found somewhere on the flood plain, if animals didn't decimate it first.

Santa Muerte, Maribel said to Roarke, when he visited her in the hospital.

Santa Muerte, Roarke thought, each time he returned to the concrete batch site and looked out over the vast alluvial plain.

The moonlight on the dry riverbed was so beautiful.

Chapter 65

Roarke had been waiting for days to speak to the boy, unwilling to push the father, but passing every minute of the interim in an agony of impatience. It was in the middle of a briefing that his cell phone vibrated and he saw the Sebastian number.

The father said only, "You can come now."

The house was a ranch-sized spread outside San Luis Obispo that felt like it had been in operation for generations. From the massive porch, Roarke looked out over a red-gold sunset spilling light over gently rolling hills dotted on one side by oak trees, and orchards of gray-green olive trees on the other. Sebastian opened the door, and as Roarke stepped through the doorway and saw Sebastian take him in, a quick, hard glance, he felt the same awkwardness as before; the feeling of visiting a rival to whom he was uneasily connected by divorce or remarriage.

"How's his mother?" Roarke asked.

"She failed the drug test," Sebastian said shortly. "Only supervised visits from now on." The look on his face was like the sunset, light and dark.

Sebastian led Roarke into a large den, which had its own play area set up for the boy. He sat drawing at a small table in front of an enormous picture window overlooking the hills. Roarke was again impressed by the boy's calm stillness. He seated himself on an ottoman that would make him lower, closer to the boy's height.

"Hi Jason. I'd like to ask you some questions, if that's okay with you."

The boy looked up from the page, which seemed to be covered with a cloud of brightly colored butterflies. "Dad said I can see your gun."

"Of course." Roarke pulled his jacket open to show the shoulder holster. "When we've talked a little, I'll unload it and you can hold it, deal?"

The boy shrugged. "'Kay."

"I'm looking for Leila."

The boy looked down at his drawing. "She went away."

Roarke tried not to let his face tighten. "Yes, I'm going to try to find her. And I think you can help me."

The boy was silent, busy with his crayon.

"You talked to her a lot, didn't you?"

He nodded.

"And she talked to you."

He nodded more slightly.

"Did she ever tell you where she was going?"

The boy looked toward the wide picture window, where the sun was blood red now, sinking beneath the hills. "She said it was time for her to go. Like the Monarchs."

"What else did she tell you?"

The boy shrugged. "Lots of stuff."

Sebastian moved forward from the doorway, crouched beside his son. "Tell him what she told you about the powers."

Jason looked at Roarke. "She said we all have special powers, like the Pache."

Roarke frowned at Sebastian. "Pache?"

"Native Mericans," the boy told them. Again, the men looked at each other. They were thinking of that blond, blond hair.

"Like, I find lost people," the boy explained proudly. "And make them not lost."

His father put his arm around the boy, kissed the top of his head. "Yes you do."

Roarke leaned in closer. "So she has a power?"

"Uh huh." The boy concentrated on his drawing, filling in butterfly wings with a crayon the color of the setting sun. Roarke waited, and for a moment he thought he was going to have to prompt him.

The boy looked up at him. "She sees monsters."

Sebastian was silent as he walked Roarke out the door, into the blue twilight. When they stopped on the porch and Roarke turned to him, Sebastian looked out at the curving shadow of the road.

"Should I be worried? Do you think she'll come for him?"

Roarke looked at him. "Do you?"

"No," Sebastian said. Then he looked away. "So you're going after her."

It was Roarke's turn to look away. "I have to."

He stepped off the porch, and as he walked out to his car, he looked up into the night sky, and watched the clouds chasing the moon.

• • • • •

Keep reading for a preview of
BLOOD MOON
Book II of the Huntress/FBI Thrillers
by Alexandra Sokoloff

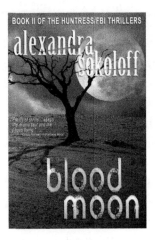

CHAPTER ONE

The dark concrete corridor stretched out before him, smelling of blood and semen and terror.

Roarke had been here before, these stinking hellholes, cellblock rooms barely big enough for a mattress and bed stand. Twenty-five girls to a block, locked in the rooms and drugged to the gills, servicing twenty-five to forty men a day, twelve hours a day, seven days a week. Not just ordinary johns tonight: it was a new shipment, private party for the traffickers themselves.

He could hear the shallow breathing of the agents surrounding him, feel the warmth of bodies: four men before him, three in back, encased in camouflage body armor and hoisting riot shields, brandishing an entire armory. Somewhere down the hall there was sobbing, a young girl's cries. "*Mátame. Por favor, mátame.*"

Kill me. Please kill me.

The number one man gestured the signal and the team shot forward in formation, then peeled off in a fluid dance, odd men to the right, even men to the left, kicking through doors, shouting: "FBI, drop your weapon! Face down on the floor!" Elsewhere in the corridor, shots blasting, more screaming, heavy thuds and the jangle of cuffs as men were wrestled to the floor.

Roarke covered the agent ahead of him until the tiny room was secure, bad guy kissing concrete. Roarke looked once at the terrified teenage girl cowering naked on the filthy mattress, and said "*Es terminado.*" *It's over.* Then he moved out the door, leading with his Glock, down the corridor, past doorways open to similar scenes of hell.

He kicked open the next closed door and burst in—

A man with his pants half off turned with an enormous, ugly AK 47. Roarke shot twice, straight into his center mass. The man's chest opened, blooming red, and his body went down, jerking as if Tasered.

Roarke stood, his heart booming crazily in his chest.

And then, though the trafficker was as dead as a person could get, Roarke followed procedure and turned the corpse over to cuff him.

As he straightened he saw the girl, tiny and frozen, huddled on the floor against the mattress, her back pressed into the wall, her eyes wide and glazed with fear. This one twelve or thirteen years old at most, dressed in nothing but a cheap, stained camisole. Roarke felt a wave of primal anger he was able to suppress only by telling himself he must not frighten this child any further.

"*Estás seguro,*" he told her in the softest voice he could muster through the adrenaline raging through his bloodstream. *You are safe.* Although he wondered if any of the girls who walked out of this place, this night, would ever feel safe again.

There was movement behind him and he twisted around... to see Special Agent Damien Epps in the doorway. Tall, dark, lithe, and righteously pissed.

"All clear," Epps reported. His whole body was tense. "Ten of the fucks in custody, three —"

He paused as he glanced down at the dead man at Roarke's feet. "Four dead." And his face and body were suddenly tense in a different way. "Nice shooting," he added.

Roarke felt the jab. He had twelve years of Bureau service and before two weeks ago, he had never killed in the line of duty. The man at his feet was his third since then.

He gave Epps a warning look, nodding at the girl huddled against the wall. He wanted to help her up, give her the shirt under his vest, but he figured she wouldn't be wanting any man near her for a very, very long time. "Social Services?" he asked Epps quietly. They had social workers waiting in vans outside to take the rescued girls to hospitals and on to a shelter that specialized in support for trafficking victims.

"On their way in," Epps said.

Roarke spoke directly to the girl. "*Mujeres vienen. Usted se va a la casa.*" *Women are coming. You are going home.*

The girl didn't move, didn't acknowledge him. He stood for a moment, helpless, knowing he was not the one to help her. He moved to follow Epps out. And then he stopped, his eyes coming to rest on the bed stand.

Just above the gouged surface of the table there was a small drawing on the wall. Roarke stepped closer... to look down at a figure scratched in the concrete, a crude skeleton wearing a flowery crown. Scraps of food and torn bits of lace were laid carefully in front of it.

Epps was staring, too, stopped in the doorway. "What is it?"

"An altar," Roarke said. "To *Santa Muerte*." Lady Death, Holy Death, protector of the lost.

He looked at the girl, still and silent on the floor, with her old and wary eyes, and wondered if somehow her prayer had been answered and the saint had intervened.

Social workers led the girls out of the former storage facility as dawn streaked the sky with orange over the desert. A good bust: thirteen traffickers arrested, twenty-five victims freed, hopefully before irreparable damage had been done.

They called these prisons residential brothels. Many of them were race-specific: this one was an LRB, Latino Residential Brothel. The location was a former storage facility, horrifically appropriate, since the girls were no more than objects to the men who stole and then sold them. Girls nineteen, sixteen, fourteen, thirteen, sometimes even younger, were kidnapped or tricked into leaving the poverty of their native towns and coming to the U.S. expecting legitimate work. It was a thirty-three billion dollar a year industry, a rising tide of evil that no agency under the sun had the resources to control, rivaling drugs and arms trafficking for the most profitable enterprise in the world, because after all, you could only sell a drug or a gun once, but you could sell a girl to the walking vermin known as johns twenty-five times a night.

As Roarke walked the empty corridors one last time, he felt more than emptiness surround him. It was more than the reeking, rancid smell. It felt like a darkness behind the doors, a concentration of malignance so outrageous it felt like a live thing.

How anything resembling a human being could do that to another human being, let alone a child...

He had to get out.

The sun was scorching the desert, searing his eyes, as he stepped out of the facility to see agents loading the last perps and victims into vehicles. The bust would be processed and prepared for prosecution by the Los Angeles Bureau. It was their jurisdiction, not San Francisco's. But since Roarke and Epps had made the initial bust leading into the trafficking ring, at a deserted concrete plant in the Mojave Desert, the two agents had come along for the takedown. Epps was coordinating with the Los Angeles Assistant SAC, meaning Roarke could leave, now. It was out of his hands. He ran his hands through his thick black hair, and rolled his neck to ease muscles still knotted with adrenaline. He felt relief, and emptiness.

He'd checked every inch of the facility, but his other quarry, the mass killer Cara Lindstrom, was nowhere on the premises. And yet he felt her presence.

Santa Muerte...

It had been Cara who'd led them to this trafficking ring.

She'd escaped from his custody at the concrete plant two weeks ago, and perhaps in some hidden part of his mind he had feared some trafficker had snatched her up. Her beauty would fetch any price in any number of countries. She would have killed others or herself before she'd let herself be taken, but she had been so badly wounded that night she may not have had the strength.

Roarke dreamed her almost every night, and he always awoke feeling the curves of her body molded to his, as if she had seared into his own flesh that night that he had lifted her and carried her, wounded, across the sand past the bodies of men she had slain.

Cara Lindstrom was in his dreams.

Otherwise, he had no idea where she was, or if she was alive or dead.

But she had killed thirteen men that he knew of, probably many, many more, including one of his own team. It was his job to arrest her, and he was very good at his job.

He would find her, and he would bring her in.

• • • • •

Acknowledgments

This book would not exist without:

The initial inspiration from Val McDermid, Denise Mina, and Lee Child, at the San Francisco Bouchercon.

My mega-talented and merciless critique partner, author Zoë Sharp.

My incomparable writing group, the Weymouth Seven: Margaret Maron, Mary Kay Andrews, Diane Chamberlain, Sarah Shaber, Brenda Witchger and Katy Munger.

Joe Konrath, Blake Crouch, Scott Nicholson, Elle Lothlorien, CJ Lyons, LJ Sellers, Ann Voss Peterson, Robert Gregory Browne, Brett Battles, and JD Rhoades, who showed me the indie publishing ropes.

Lee Lofland and his amazing Writers Police Academy trainers/instructors: Dave Pauly, Katherine Ramsland, Corporal Dee Jackson, Andy Russell, Marco Conelli, Lieutenant Randy Shepard and Robert Skiff. My forensics and procedural mistakes are entirely my own!

Siegrid Rickenbach and Captain John Rickenbach, who gave me the Rickenbach tour of Central California.

The best early readers on the planet: Diane Coates Peoples, Joan Tregarthen Huston, Ellen Margolis, Billie Hinton and Pat Verducci.

ABOUT THE AUTHOR

Thriller Award-winner Alexandra Sokoloff's debut ghost story, THE HARROWING, was also nominated for a Bram Stoker Award and an Anthony Award for Best First Novel. Her second supernatural thriller, THE PRICE, was called "Some of the most original and freshly unnerving work in the genre" by the *New York Times* Book Review. She is the daughter of scientists, which may explain the scientific undercurrents of THE UNSEEN, based on real-life experiments conducted at the Rhine parapsychology lab on the Duke University campus); and THE SPACE BETWEEN, her first young adult thriller, which explores school shootings, quantum physics, and lucid dreaming.

As a screenwriter, Alex has sold original horror and thriller scripts and written novel adaptations for numerous Hollywood studios; she is also the author of two writing workbooks based on her internationally acclaimed workshop and blog: SCREENWRITING TRICKS FOR AUTHORS. She writes erotic paranormal on the side, including THE SHIFTERS, Book 2 of THE KEEPERS trilogy, and KEEPER OF THE SHADOWS, from THE KEEPERS LA.

She is currently working on COLD MOON, the third book in her Thriller Award-nominated Huntress/FBI thriller series (HUNTRESS MOON, BLOOD MOON), which will be out in December 2013.

In her spare time (!) she is an avid dancer, and very active on Facebook. But not an addict. No, seriously, it's under control.

http://alexandrasokoloff.com
http://screenwritingtricks.com